THE SIGN OF THE PROPHET

A TALE OF TECUMSEH AND TIPPECANOE

BY
James Ball Naylor
Author of "RALPH MARLOWE"

Fredonia Books
Amsterdam, The Netherlands

The Sing of the Prophet:
A Tale of Tecumseh and Tippecanoe

by
James Ball Naylor

ISBN: 1-4101-0118-5

Copyright © 2002 by Fredonia Books

Reprinted from the 1901 edition

Fredonia Books
Amsterdam, The Netherlands
http://www.fredoniabooks.com

TO

SAMUEL G. MCCLURE

*of The Ohio State Journal,
who encouraged my early
literary endeavors, this book
is gratefully dedicated.*

Very Truly,

JAMES BALL NAYLOR

THE SIGN OF THE PROPHET

CHAPTER I.

IT WAS a hot, sultry morning in the latter part of August, 1811.

A dugout canoe containing two occupants was swiftly speeding down the Scioto, at a point near which the city of Columbus now stands.

The clear green water wimpled musically at the bow of the vessel, and a frothy wake bubbled and eddied at the stern. The surface of the stream lay cool and dark in the shadow of the overhanging trees ; but where the red rays of the rising sun shot through the dense foliage and fell upon the pulseless bosom of the sluggish tide, they gave it the metallic luster of burnished copper. Great trees ranged themselves as stalwart sentinels along the shores, a part of the grand army that stretched away to the far distance on either hand. Their leaves were dark-green and glossy. Yellow and purple wild flowers lifted their fair faces to the morning sun and nodded a welcome. Feathered songsters fluttered among the gray boughs and chirped and warbled merrily. A venturesome fish popped several feet out of the water — just ahead of the swiftly flying dugout — and flashed its silver scales in a tantalizing manner.

The occupants of the canoe gave little heed to the beauties of the scene. Seated in the bottom of their quivering, rocking craft, they rapidly and rhythmically dipped their light paddles. At each stroke the frail vessel lifted itself and sprang forward, like a thing of life. The forest receded from the western bank of the river, and low-lying fields of tall, rank corn took its place. Walled in by the growing maize, lay the straggling village of Franklinton — a cluster of rude log-huts. Cleared spaces appeared in the woods upon the eastern shore; and several cabins stood out against the background of encircling trees — the germ, the nucleus of the Capital City of to-day.

The two paddlers looked neither to the right, nor to the left, but laboriously bent to their work. Suddenly a man parted the bushes upon the western shore and, stepping down to the water's edge, called lustily :

" Hello! That you, Ross Douglas ? "

" Yes," answered the man in the stern of the dugout. " What do you want? "

Both paddlers ceased their efforts and allowed the craft to drift with the lazy current.

" W'y, y'r dog come to my cabin this mornin' — all wet an' draggled as though he'd swum the river," returned the voice from the shore. " He 'peared to be tuckered out an' hungry — an' went whinin' 'round as if he was huntin' fer you. I fed him, an' then tied him up in the cabin. Do you want him?"

The paddler in the bow of the canoe turned his head and looked at his companion, at the same time uttering a grunt of surprise and incredulity.

"You may keep him until I come back," called the man who had answered to the name of Ross Douglas, lifting his paddle and preparing to resume his journey.

"Hold on there, Ross!"—shouted the individual on shore. "What do you mean — where 're you goin'?"

"Going to join General Harrison's army at Vincennes."

And the suspended paddles dipped, and the dugout leaped forward.

"Stop, I say!" bellowed the man who had hailed the voyagers, running along the shelving sands and gesticulating wildly. "Ross Douglas, you ain't a goin' to run off like that an' leave an ol' friend, without shakin' his paw an' biddin' him good-by — I'm danged if you are! Stop, 'r I'll send a bullet spinnin' out there — I will, by Sally Matildy!"

"But I'm in a hurry," Douglas laughed good-humoredly.

"It don't make no differ'nce," persisted the other. "Come in here."

"Turn the prow toward shore, Bright Wing," Douglas said in a low tone to his companion.

"Ugh!" grunted the latter — and obeyed.

A few moments later the canoe beached itself and
the two paddlers sprang ashore. The one who had
occupied the bow of the craft was an Indian —
young, lithe, and strong. His forehead was high
and narrow; his nose, slightly aquiline. His eyes
were small, black, and piercing; his brawny chest and
muscular arms were bare. His straight, blue-black
hair — braided and ornamented with beads and per-
forated shells and coins — reached his waist.
Breeches, leggings, and moccasins of tanned buckskin constituted his dress. In his belt were tomahawk and scalping-knife; and he carried a heavy
rifle. He belonged to the Wyandot tribe, and was
an adopted son of the noble chief, Leatherlips.

The Indian's companion was an American — tall,
active, and sinewy. His complexion was swarthy;
his steel-gray eyes were bold and keen. But the stern
cast they gave to his countenance was relieved by a
pair of smiling lips, indicating gentleness and great
good-nature. A mass of soft brown hair clustered
in short ringlets about his temples and rippled down
upon his broad shoulders. The well-fitting suit of
buckskin that he wore revealed the rounded contour
of his shapely limbs; and the broad-brimmed soft
hat that surmounted his silky curls set off his dark
beauty to the best advantage. His weapons were
of the finest workmanship, and gave evidence of the
loving care their owner bestowed upon them. Apparently he was about twenty-eight years old.

The man who had hailed the two voyagers — and
whom they now stood facing — was a typical back-

woodsman of middle age. His face was oppressively ugly — prominent nose, wide mouth, and pale-blue, watery eyes. His hair was scant and straw-colored; his body and limbs, were long, lank, and ungainly. His garb was in keeping with his character — hunting shirt and breeches of coarse linsey-woolsey, heavy cowhide boots, and peaked fur-cap. He was a grotesque, incongruous bundle of bones and sinews — a whimsical, eccentric hunter and trapper. But a more valiant, loyal, and loving heart, than Joe Farley had, never beat in man's bosom.

Now he stood leaning upon his long rifle, a quizzical smile illuminating his rugged features.

"What do you want, Joe?" Douglas demanded briskly.

"Want to know where you're bound fer," came the drawling reply.

"I told you — to Vincennes, to join Harrison's army," Ross answered, a shade of annoyance in his tone.

"You don't mean it?"

"But I do."

"Is the Injin goin', too?"

"Ugh! Me go, too," said the redman, drawing himself up proudly.

"Seems to me it's goin' to be a strange sort o' war," Farley chuckled dryly. "Injins an' white men on one side — an' white men an' Injins on t'other. 'Cause that's what it's comin' to. The danged Britishers has got the'r fingers in the pie ag'in —

an' ther' ain't no tellin' where the thing 'll stop. So, Bright Wing, you're goin' out to fight ag'in your own people, are you?"

"*Not* my people," grunted the Indian, his black eyes flashing. "*Me* Wyandot — me fight Shawnees."

"It don't make no differ'nce — they've got red skins," Joe remarked.

"Ugh! You much big fool!"

And the impulsive young warrior's hand involuntarily sought the handle of his tomahawk.

Farley's face flushed, and he cried sharply:

"Keep y'r hand off y'r hatchet, redskin. That's a game two can play at."

Quickly Douglas stepped between the two and, turning upon Farley, said sternly:

"Joe, you may not *be* a fool, but you're acting the part of one, at any rate. You know as well as I that the Wyandots are the friends of the Americans, that the Shawnees are the allies of the British. Of course, there are traitors in both tribes; but what I have stated is true in the main. Bright Wing is my comrade — your friend. If you're a man, you'll beg his pardon."

"An' that's jest what I'm goin' to do," Farley shamefacedly muttered. "'Pears that I'll never git to understandin' Injins. They're so *danged* touchy."— This in an aggrieved tone.— "But I had no business to be tormentin' Bright Wing — he's a redskin with a white man's heart in his breast.

Injin, here's my hand. I didn't mean to hurt y'r feelin's.''

"All right — me know,'' murmured Bright Wing in guttural accents.

Then he moved aside and seated himself upon the prow of the canoe.

"Now, Joe, we must be off,'' Ross began hurriedly.

"You mean what you've said — you're goin' to jine the army?'' Farley interrupted.

Douglas nodded.

"Goin' to leave y'r land an' everything an' go off to fight Injins — an' Britishers, maybe?''

"The land will keep,'' Ross laughed. "Little good it does me, at any rate. I have never cut a stick of timber upon it.''

"That's what I mean,'' replied the other earnestly. "You ort to stay an' clear it up an' make a home of it. Quit y'r huntin' an' traipsin' 'round with such fellers as me an' Bright Wing, an' settle down. It don't make much differ'nce what *I* do. But you've got book learnin' an' good sense. You're wastin' y'r time.''

"I 'm well pleased with the life I lead, Joe.''

"That's jest the trouble — you're *too* well pleased with it.''

"I promise you I'll reform when I return.''

"An' you're goin' away an' leave that little sweetheart o' your'n?''

"You mean Amy Larkin?''

"Of course.''

"Yes, I must leave her. But I shall be back soon — in a few months, perhaps. Then I'll marry her and settle down — become a model husbandman."

"You're puttin' off till to-morrer what you ort to do to-day."

"What do you mean, Joe?"

"You know ol' man Larkin don't like you none too well — jest on account o' y'r shiftless ways, as he calls it?"

"I am aware that he doesn't look upon me as a promising son-in-law — yes."

"An' he *does* think a heap o' George Hilliard?"

"Y-e-s."

"Well, you won't be gone a month till George Hilliard 'll be standin' in y'r shoes."

"I have no fears on that score."

"All right! — but you'll see. Gals is gals — they're all false an' fickle. A bird in the hand's worth two in the bush, Ross. You'd better stay here an' be gittin' a cage ready fer y'r bird. Ol' Sam Larkin's got a heap o' good land — an' a heap more money. He's rich. An' Amy's a purty nice gal — an' the only child. You don't want to let all that slip through y'r fingers, my boy."

"You're talking nonsense, Joe. Amy loves me — she don't care a fig for George Hilliard. I'll marry her on my return, with or without her father's consent. Hilliard is a Canadian — an English sympathizer. Mr. Larkin will not forget that. Besides, if we have another war with Great

Britain — as appears likely — this neighborhood
will become too warm for the forehanded George.
I care nothing for Amy's prospective fortune, but I
love her. And I'm going to marry her, no matter
who may oppose."

The young man's chest heaved, and defiance to
the whole world shone in his gray eyes.

"It's a good thing to have plenty o' grit an' confidence," Farley chuckled; " but ther's a chance o'
havin' too much o' even a *good* thing — I swan
ther' is! An' lawzee! Hain't I had the 'xperience?
Many's the purty, rosy-cheeked gals I could 'ave
got in my younger days. W'y, they used to tag
after me an' pester me 'most to death. I've had
more 'n a dozen of 'em dead in love with me at one
time — fairly scratchin' each other's eyes out,
quar'lin' 'bout which one 'ld git me. All of 'em love-
sick over my beauty — my purty form an' features.
But I jest stuck my nose up in the air an' passed 'em
by. An' see me to-day! I'm an everlastin' warnin'
— a livin' monument to disap'inted love an' dangnation foolishness. Ther' ain't a piece o' linsey-
woolsey in the whole settlement that 'll even look —
Snakes an' garters! What's that?"

Both white men started. The Indian stolidly
maintained his position upon the prow of the canoe;
but his ready finger rested upon the trigger of his
gun. A heavy body came crashing through the
weeds and bushes upon the bank. Then the vines
and branches parted; and, with a hoarse yelp of joy,
a large dog sprang into the open and crouched at

Douglas's feet.   He was a magnificent black-and-
tan animal, lithe and strong as a panther — an im-
mense bloodhound.   He was wet and muddy; and
as he lay at his master's feet, he rolled his red-
rimmed eyes and panted and whined.   A piece of
thong was about his neck, to which was fastened
a short sharpened stake.

"Well, if that don't beat my reckonin'!" bawled
Farley, opening his wide mouth and hawhawing
heartily.   "How in the name o' Julius Cæsar did
that dog ever git loose?   That stake was druv in the
hard floor o' my shack, deep enough to hold a bull
— it was, by the Queen o' Sheba!   An' he's pulled
it up.   But how in the plague did he git out o' the
cabin?   Must 'ave crawled up the chimbly — by
cracky!   'Cause I latched the door as I come out —
I'm certain of it.   Dang-it-all-to-dingnation!   But
it does beat all!"

The dog now attempted to raise his head and lick
his master's hand.   Failing in this, he slowly arose
to his feet, tremulously wagged his tail, and beseechingly fastened his eyes upon Ross's face.   Then
he whined.

"Down, Duke!" Douglas commanded sternly.

The dog obeyed; but rolled his great eyes upward toward the being he loved and worshiped, as
though begging pardon for his misconduct.

"Joe, I want you to take him back to your cabin
and keep him until I return.   I tried to run away
from him this morning, but he has trailed me —
although I traveled by water.   I left him at the

Wyandot village above here. Take him away, Joe;
I can't bear to leave while he's looking at me like
that."

And there was a quaver in Ross Douglas's
voice.

"Duke him much good dog — him heap big
brave," volunteered Bright Wing, nodding vigorously.

"Quick, Joe — take him away," Ross said huskily.

"I ain't a-goin' to do it," replied Farley, with a
stubborn shake of the head.

"Why?" Ross inquired in surprise.

"'Cause the dog loves you an' ort to go with
you — that's why. He'll jest natur'ly pine away
an' die if you leave him behind you."

"But I can't take him with me," Douglas argued; "he would be in the way — he would get
himself and me into trouble."

"Ther's another reason why I won't take him
back to my cabin," Joe remarked, his pale eyes
twinkling.

"What is it?"

"Jest this: If you're goin' to war, I'm goin'
with you. I hain't got a chick n'r child to leave —
an' I'm goin'."

"You?"

"Yes."

"With Bright Wing and me?"

"Fer sure."

"I thought you were opposed to my going?"

2

"I was—an' I am yit. But if you go, I go, too."

"Perhaps we don't desire your company."

A smile fluttered about the corners of Ross's mouth.

"It don't make no differ'nce," was the dogged reply ; "I'm goin' anyhow. So move y'r things 'round in the dugout an' make room fer us. I'm all ready. Ding-it-all-to-dangnation ! I can't stay here an' see you go — an' I *won't*."

"Shall we take him, Bright Wing ? " Douglas mischievously inquired.

"Ugh! " exploded the Indian. "Joe him got heap long gun — him shoot much straight. Him go. Three braves kill sight more bad Shawnees than two. Joe go."

"Very well," Ross said slowly, with assumed reluctance in his tone, "you shall go, Joe. Is there anything you want to bring from your hut ? "

"Nothin'." — With a decided shake of the head.

"In you go, then — and let's be off."

A few minutes later there were " three men in the boat — not counting the dog,"— and they were moving rapidly down the stream, in the shade of the overhanging trees. When some two or three miles below the village of Franklinton, Douglas addressed a few words in the Wyandot tongue, to the Indian, who again occupied the bow of the canoe. Bright Wing nodded and immediately turned the prow toward a little cove upon the eastern shore. A moment later the boat grated upon the sandy beach, and Ross sprang ashore.

"Keep Duke with you," he cried as he ran lightly up the bank. "I'll not be gone long."

"Say! wher' you goin' now?" Farley called after him. But the young man did not deign to reply.

"I was a fool to ask the question," Joe muttered to himself. "Might 'ave knowed he was goin' to bid his sweetheart good-by. I jest fergot fer a minute we was opposite to ol' Sam Larkin's place. Down, Duke, an' behave y'rself. Y'r master don't need you in this affair. Oh, jeminy — no! Two's company an' three's a congregation, when it comes to love-makin'. Hain't I been through it, hey? Gol-fer-ginger! What a heart-breaker I was! S'pect I'll never git fergiveness fer the way I've used the women. Dang-it-all-to-dingnation! W'en a man begins to git old, his youthful sins an' follies all comes back to him. Mine ha'nts me o' nights till I can't sleep. An' I can't eat, neither. First thing I know I'll worry an' fret over the cruel way I've used the women folks, till my beauty 'll begin to fade — an' like as not peter out entirely. An' I wouldn't 'ave *that* happen fer nothin'. Gol-fer-socks *no*! Say, Injin, 'ave you got any tobacker?"

Without a word Bright Wing opened the pouch at his side and gave the lugubrious Farley a handful of tobacco. The latter filled his short-stemmed pipe, lighted it, and puffed away in silence for some time.

The bloodhound lay watching the place where his master had disappeared. Presently he half arose, shook his pendulous ears and growled ominously. Then, ere he could be restrained, he leaped from the canoe and dashed up the bank, into the woods. With an exclamation of surprise and anger, Joe stumbled ashore and set out in pursuit of the dog, closely followed by Bright Wing.

On leaving his friends, Ross Douglas entered the forest and hurried along a dim path, until he reached the edge of a clearing a few hundred yards from the river. In the center of this cleared space, and upon a slight elevation of ground, stood a double log-cabin with a hall or passage between the two rooms. The house stood facing the river; and the doors and windows were open. Back of the building was a field of corn surrounded by a fence of brush and poles, and in front of it lay a small patch of potatoes and garden vegetables.

Ross shaded his eyes with his hand and looked from his cool retreat, across the sun-baked clearing, toward the cabin. Presently a face appeared at one of the small windows. Douglas stepped forward and beckoned. Then he hastily sprang back among the trees. The face quickly disappeared from the window; and a few seconds later a young woman emerged from the door and tripped nimbly down the path leading to the fringe of woodland along the river-shore. She was neatly clad. Her frock was of linsey-woolsey; her shoes were of calfskin. A wide-brimmed straw hat set jauntily upon her brown hair added to the piquancy of her fair oval face. Her cheeks were rosy; her teeth, white, and even.

Entering the wood she called softly:

"Ross, where are you?"

"Here, Amy," he answered in a low joyful tone, stepping from his place of concealment and hurrying toward her.

With a glad cry she sprang into his outstretched arms, and hid her blushing face upon his shoulder. For a full minute he strained her to his breast, and neither spoke. When at last she raised her face it was wet with tears; and a catch was in her voice as she said:

"And you are going, Ross?"

"I must go, darling," he replied softly.

"Why must you go and leave me here alone?" she cried. "Why must you run into danger, Ross? Stay here with me — please do! You may never come back."

"There — there, little one!" he whispered soothingly. "Of course, I shall come back. Then we'll be married; and I'll settle down on my piece of land and never leave you again."

"But you may — may get — killed," she sobbed.

"I must take my chances along with others, Amy," he answered firmly. "I feel that it's my duty to go."

"I — I can't understand —— " she began.

"It's like this," he interrupted as he seated her upon a mossy log and placed his arm around her waist. "Seventeen years ago — when you were a baby — General Wayne made a treaty with the Indian tribes at Greenville. That treaty has protected the border-settlements until now. The savages have kept to themselves and left the white settlers unmolested. And the vanguard of civilization has moved rapidly and steadily toward the setting sun. But now all is changed. The British are again encouraging the Indians to take up arms against the Americans. Tecumseh and his brother, the Prophet, are doing all in their power to form an Indian confederacy that will be able to drive the Americans from the Ohio and Mississippi valleys. Tecumseh is brave and ambitious ; the Prophet, cruel and cunning. Already they have aroused the redmen to a pitch of frenzy that threatens the safety of every border-settlement — including this. General Harrison is forming an army at Vincennes, to march against the allied tribes. I know the woods — am acquainted with the Indian mode of warfare. I can render service to my country — my people. I must go, Amy."

She had dried her tears. Now she kissed him and said coaxingly :

"Please — *please* don't go ! Stay here and — and — marry me — *now*."

"You little siren — you little traitor !" he laughed, playfully patting her cheek. "With your enchantment you would win me from the path of duty. You tempt me sorely — but it may not be. Duty calls——"

"Oh, duty — duty !" she cried, impatiently stamping her small foot and pouting her red lips. "Do you care more for *duty* than you do for *me?*"

"That's not fair, Amy," he said gravely. "You know that I love you dearly — better than I love anyone else in the wide world. You should be a brave little woman and help me to do the right. Besides, if I should play the poltroon and stay here, you yourself would despise me for a miserable coward — a mean wretch unworthy of a good woman's love and respect."

He stopped to note the effect of his words. She hung her head and blushed deeply. But whether with shame or anger he could not tell. He waited for her to speak; but she said nothing. He continued:

"At any rate, your father wouldn't consent to our marriage, and you wouldn't be willing to wed me without his permission."

The young woman lifted her head. Her face brightened. Laying her hand caressingly upon his knee, she murmured faintly:

"Father wouldn't oppose our marriage, Ross, if you would quit your roving ways, give up your Indian friends and rough associates, and settle down to work. He thinks you shiftless — that you wouldn't provide well for me — would never accumulate anything."

Douglas's handsome face flushed hotly as he asked:

"Is that all the reason your father had for ordering me from his door and forbidding me to speak to you?"

She was silent for a moment. Then she replied hesitatingly:

"Y-e-s — the main reason."

"And the others?"

His voice was hard and cold. She dropped her lids, but did not answer.

"Amy, tell me," he cried almost fiercely, catching her wrist in his firm grasp.

"He says you — you don't — know who your father was," she faltered.

He sprang to his feet, his face aflame.

"It's a base lie!" he began. Then he set his teeth and paused a moment to regain control of himself. Presently he resumed in quiet, even tones:

"Amy, it's a mistake. I know who my father was — or is, if he be alive. I'm no illegitimate child. My mother's husband was John Douglas, an intelligent but dissipated and unprincipled man, who abused her — and finally deserted her, shortly after I was born. Her health rapidly failed; and she died when I was but a child, leaving me to the care of her brother, a roving and adventurous fur-trader. This uncle wandered from tribe to tribe, bartering arms, blankets, and trinkets, for peltries. On one of these trading trips he took me with him — when I was eight years old — and left me with the Wyandots, while he proceeded on his journey. For four years I remained with the savages. They were kind to me. I learned their ways; I played with the youth of the tribe. I absorbed their ideas, manners, and customs — I fell in love with the wild, free life of the redmen. Then my uncle again put in an appearance, and, taking me with him, returned to the East.

"There he placed me in school; and again disappeared. Eight years passed; and in all that time I saw nothing of my relative — my guardian. At last came word that he was dead — and that I was penniless. I left school. My soul hungered for love and sympathy. I was fatherless — motherless. Of acquaintances, I had many; of warm, helpful friends, I had none. I thought of my old friends, the Wyandots. I made my way westward, rejoined them — and was received with open arms. But a change had come over me. I had the instinct and tastes of a hunter — but I was no longer a young savage. For a time I lived with the Wyandots; but I spent my time in hunting and in trading among the red hunters of Ohio and the lakes. I made money. I learned three or four Indian tongues — I acquainted myself with all the arts and wiles of the different tribes. But at last the white blood in my veins asserted itself. I began to long for the companionship of my own people. So I established myself here at Franklinton and took up land. But I have continued to trade among the Indians — I have retained the friendship of the Wyandots. I have made more money in one month than your father and George Hilliard have made in twelve. A year ago I met and loved you. It's needless to say more — you know the rest."

She had been watching his face intently and drinking in every word he said. Now she clasped her hands and murmured pleadingly:

"Oh, Ross! If only you will tell father what

you have told me, all will be well. He'll give
his consent to our marriage — I know he will."

"As soon as I return, I'll do so, Amy."

"No — no!" she pouted prettily. "*Now* is the
time. Come to the house with me at once."

"I cannot, dear. Be patient a little while. As
you say — all will be well."

Quickly arising to her feet and catching him by
the arm, she cried playfully:

"You *shall* not go. See — I'll hold you."

He bent and kissed her. Then slipping his arm
around her yielding waist he remarked:

"Amy, there is another reason why I should go
to fight against the allied tribes. Leatherlips, the
foster-father of Bright Wing, was one of my steadfast friends. As you know, he was brutally murdered a year ago last June, at the instigation of the
Shawnee Prophet. His death should be avenged."

A startled look crept into her eyes, and involuntarily she shrunk from him as she whispered tremulously:

"Ross — Ross! Surely you don't mean to do
murder! You're not an Indian. I'm almost afraid
of you."

With a merry laugh he caught her to him and
answered:

"What a timid little body you are, Amy. Of
course I don't mean to do murder. But I *do*
mean that the Prophet shall be shorn of his power
to do further mischief, to commit further acts of
violence — and that I should help to do it.

And''— in a low, fierce tone—"if ever I meet him in open battle one of us will die. Bid me good-by now. I must be going—my comrades are waiting for me.''

But she burst into tears and clung to him, sobbing:

"Don't go—don't go, Ross! For some reason I feel—that you will not come back—to me, that I shall—shall be forced to—to marry George Hilliard.''

"There—there, child!'' he interrupted soothingly. "Now dry your eyes and kiss me farewell. Indeed I am tarrying too long.''

She drew herself erect and, dashing aside the tears that blinded her, said icily:

"In spite of all I have said and done, you're going, are you?''

"I 've told you over and over that I *must* go, Amy,'' he replied sadly.

"Then go!'' she cried angrily. "It shows how much you think of me—to leave me here in a hell upon earth—without a mother to sympathize with me or advise me. I will marry George Hilliard at once—and have done with it.''

"Amy! Amy!'' he whispered reprovingly. "You don't mean that; you're angry. Wait——''

The sentence was left unfinished. It was cut short with a suddenness that almost took away Douglas's breath. By an unseen and unexpected power, the lovers were caught and violently flung apart. Two armed men stood between them. One was a tall, rawboned man whose hatchet face was outlined by a mane of iron-gray hair. The other was younger — short, thickset, and red-faced.

The older man's countenance was livid with rage. His lips worked — but no words came forth. At last he managed to articulate:

"Git off my land instantly, Ross Douglas — you infernal sneak an' scoundrel! Tryin' to steal my daughter, was you? There's no man about you! Didn't I order you from the place an' forbid you speakin' to her? Go, I say! Go before I shoot you — you sneakin' dog!"

A dangerous light blazed in the settler's eyes. He gripped his gun and shook it menacingly at Douglas. The latter was unarmed — except the hunting-knife in his belt — having left his rifle in the canoe. However, he composedly folded his arms and casting a pitying glance at Amy, who had dropped to the ground and was weeping bitterly, said quietly:

"Mr. Larkin, I don't merit the harsh words and rude treatment you have accorded me. I have done nothing dishonorable — nothing beneath the dignity of a gentleman. I love your daughter; she loves me. When you ordered me from your house and forbid me to hold further intercourse with Amy, I told you that I wouldn't obey your mandate — that I would meet her clandestinely. I have done so. Just now I came to bid her good-by. I'm on my way to join Harrison's army at Vincennes. When I return I'll call upon you and ask you for her hand in marriage. If at that time you refuse my request, I'll carry her off before your eyes."

"You impudent hound!" snorted the irate Larkin. "I have a notion to shoot you where you stand."

"Have a care, Mr. Larkin," Douglas replied coolly. "I don't care to have a physical encounter with my future father-in-law. But if you offer me violence, your gray hairs will not save you, I warn you. I have no fear of you or your weapon. But I'm trespassing, and will leave your place and your presence."

Ross's cool assurance awed Larkin to silence. A moment he looked at the young man in utter amazement. Then he turned and bent over his daughter and, lifting her to her feet, cried roughly:

"Come, my young lady, an' go to the house with me. I'll see to it that you don't meet that scalawag ag'in."

"Good-by, Amy," Ross called as he turned to leave the spot.

"Good-by, Ross," she sobbed faintly. "I didn't mean what I said. I'll — I'll — be true——"

But her father clapped his hand over her mouth and shouted over his shoulder:

"George Hilliard, why don't you break every bone in that insolent scoundrel's body?"

Up to this time the thickset man had maintained a discreet silence. Now he felt called upon to defend himself against the imputation of cowardice, implied in Larkin's question. So he replied valiantly :

"That's just what I'm going to do if he don't make himself scarce around here in about ten seconds."

These words fell upon Ross Douglas's ears and roused him to instant fury. He had borne much — he could bear no more. Whirling in his tracks, he dealt Hilliard a blow that felled him to the earth.

For a few seconds the prostrate man glared confusedly around him. Then with cat-like quickness he sprang to his feet and threw his gun to his shoulder. He was insane with rage. The light of murder twinkled in his small pig-like eyes. His finger was upon the trigger of his weapon. But he encountered Ross's look of steadfast courage — and hesitated.

"Shoot him !" Larkin bellowed. "Shoot him in self-defense !"

Hilliard bent his head and squinted along the gleaming barrel of his rifle. Douglas whipped out his knife and sprang toward his adversary. But quick as were his movements, he would have been too late had not a trusty friend been at hand.

With a low, fierce growl Duke bounded from the underbrush, where he had been crouching, and landed full upon Hilliard's chest. The gun cracked, but the bullet sped harmlessly over Ross's head. Amy ran screaming toward the cabin. Her father, with a muttered oath, strode toward the scene of conflict. Duke sought to fasten his fangs in Hilliard's throat. Gun, man, and dog went to the ground together.

"Loose him, Duke! Loose him!" Douglas commanded.

The hound obeyed, and crept whining to his master's feet. Blood was streaming from Hilliard's shoulder, where the dog had set his teeth.

"Curse you! I'll finish you!" Larkin shrieked frantically, flinging his piece to his shoulder and taking deliberate aim at Ross.

"Go slow there, ol' man, 'r you'll never know what hurt you," said a drawling voice. "Drop that gun an' behave y'rself, 'r I'll put a chunk o' cold lead into you — I will, by Hanner Ann!"

And two shimmering gun-barrels protruded from the green foliage.

Larkin obeyed, and leaned against a sapling, panting. With some difficulty Hilliard got upon his feet. His flabby face was pale; his hairy hands were trembling.

Farley and Bright Wing stepped into the glade.

"Mr. Larkin," Douglas remarked calmly, "I'm very sorry this occurred. You'd better take your comrade to the house and dress his wounds. I'm off."

Followed by his two friends and his dog, the young man silently made his way back to the canoe. A few minutes later they were rapidly paddling down the stream.

The day was excessively hot. The three men maintained a moody silence, as with steady, sweeping strokes they shot the dugout forward. The sweat trickled in rivulets down Farley's furrowed face. Presently he muttered in an undertone :

"S'pect I'd 'ave done better, if I'd shot that cuss of a Hilliard — yes, an' ol' Sam Larkin, too. They deserved to die anyway — the dirty cowards ! An' they'll make no end o' bother fer Ross — 'r I'm badly mistaken. An' they'll torment that little gal to death, purty near. I can see it all. Ther's trouble ahead fer somebody — an' likely it's fer Ross Douglas. Well, it all comes o' fallin' in love with a few pounds o' the female gender. An' hain't I had the 'xperience? Lordy ! I should say so !"

CHAPTER II.

A WAGON-and-pack-train was slowly winding its way through the trackless wilds of the valley of the Wabash. Like some monstrous serpent, it dragged its sinuous body along the margin of the boundless prairie that stretched away to the north and west, and wormed itself in and out among the clumps of scrubby trees that marked the course of the stream. Ahead of it rode a compact body of mounted men; and on both sides and behind, marched a straggling mass of soldiers.

The wheels of the heavily laden vehicles half buried themselves in the soft loam of the valley. "Squeak! Creak!" were the tortured cries of the wooden axles. Whips cracked and drivers swore; horses neighed and oxen bellowed. William Henry Harrison, governor of Indiana Territory, was on his way to the Prophet's Town, to make peace or war with its inhabitants.

It was the fifth of November, 1811; and the sunless day was drawing to a close. The wind, biting and keen, swept across the prairie from the northwest, bringing with it driving clouds of mist-like rain and stinging snow-pellets. The officers and mounted men buttoned their coats closely about them and, dropping their chins upon their

(33)

breasts, rode forward in silence. The weary soldiers laboriously trudged onward — and grumbled.
The veiled sun sank lower and lower in the west.
The wind, increasing in force, grew colder. Dark
shadows stole out of the scrub and threw themselves across the prairie. Night was settling down.

All through the summer and fall, the heterogene-
ous band of Indians at the Prophet's Town upon
the Upper Wabash had increased in numbers. Bold
and savage warriors from various tribes — prompted
by the words and example of the eloquent and
sagacious Tecumseh, and inspired by the fanatical
zeal of the cunning and bloodthirsty Prophet —
had taken up the hatchet and expressed a readiness
to make war upon the Americans. Aided and
abetted by the British — who still manifested a
rancorous hostility toward the United States — they
had made petty incursions into the defenseless
settlements, bent on pillage and murder.

For several years the wily leader of the warlike
Shawnees, Tecumseh, had been visiting the tribes
of the north, west, and south, urging them to form
a confederacy that would be powerful enough to
eject the Americans from the Mississippi and Ohio
valleys. He was a brave, resolute, and ambitious
man ; and had faith in the feasibility and success of
his project.

Harrison, as governor of Indiana Territory, had
become aware of Tecumseh's scheme and had
realized the great danger that threatened the
growing but unprotected settlements, and had

taken prompt measures. Empowered by his commission, he had held a council with Tecumseh
and a number of his followers, at Vincennes, in
1810. But the haughty Shawnee had retired from
the governor's presence, angry and defiant. Then
Harrison had apprised the government at Philadel-
phia of the state of affairs and had asked for aid.
The Fourth regiment of regulars, under Colonel
Boyd, had been sent to him. And with these
troops and several companies of Kentucky and
Indiana militia — nine hundred men in all — he had
left Vincennes, on the twenty-eighth of September,
and taken up his march for the Prophet's Town,
resolved to make a lasting peace or strike a telling
blow, while Tecumseh was absent on a mission to
the southern tribes.

About seventy miles up the Wabash he had built
Fort Harrison. Then, on the twenty-ninth of
October, he had left the place garrisoned, and had
resumed his journey toward the Prophet's Town.

He was now moving along the northwestern
bank of the Wabash, a short distance from the
village he sought.

The long line of vehicles and troops came to a
sudden stop. Tired horses lowered their heads to
the cutting blast and shivered. Weary oxen leaned
heavily against the wagon-tongues. Footsore soldiers threw themselves upon the damp ground and
feelingly rubbed their aching limbs. Drivers
stamped their feet and slapped their palms together to restore the circulation to their benumbed

members.   Far down toward the rear of the line, a
militiaman was singing :

> "I left my home in ol' Kaintuck,
>   An' my wife an' babes behind me;
> An' if the Injins gits my scalp,
>   My folks 'll never find me."

"An' by the everlastin' Kinnikinnick, I don't
b'lieve his fam'ly 'ld grieve much 'bout him, if
he's in the habit o' singin' that tune 'round
home!'' growled a tall angular ox-driver, resting
his arm upon the yoke and whipping the water
from his fur-cap, with the butt of his gad.   "Did
anybody on earth ever hear such a dang cater-
waullin'?   Whew, but I'm cold an' hungry !

"Drivin' oxen ain't to my likin' — not, by a
dang sight !   But here I am doin' menial servitude
fer my country, when I never disgraced myself by
doin' anything o' the kind fer Joe Farley.   'Pears
that I've become the plaything o' fate — it does, by
Melindy !   Come out here to fight Injins an' help
save the gover'ment; an' they've set me to
whackin' bulls.   By my gran'mother's goggles, I
ain't a-goin' to stand it !   I'll desert an' go over to
the redskins, bag an' baggage !   'Tain't fair —
'tain't.   Jest 'cause a driver gits sick an' has to be
left at Fort Harrison, they take an' put me in his
place.   I ort to be out scoutin' with Ross
Douglas an' Bright Wing.   An' I would 'ave been
— dang it ! — but my limber tongue got the best o'
me an' let out that I'd druv oxen, w'en a boy.

"Well, ther's one consolation, anyhow. We're purty near to the end o' our journey; an' then I'll git to tote a rifle ag'in an' feel like a man. Whoa, there, you brindle-hided brute! What in the dangnation 're you tryin' to *do?* Think you can crawl through that bow? Whoa, I say! Bless my peepers, if I ever *did* see such a c'ntrary critter, anyhow! *Whoa*, now!"

And Farley applied the gad to the ribs of the lank ox, as though he were energetically beating a bass drum.

At the head of the long column, a little knot of mounted officers were holding a consultation in low tones. The central figure of the group was a tall, spare man of middle age. He sat his horse — a wiry chestnut sorrel of trim form and slender limbs — with the ease and grace of a practiced and fearless horseman. His nose was large; his smooth-shaven features were irregular. But his face was redeemed from plainness by a pair of dark, penetrating eyes and a mouth indicative of courage and resolution. Intelligence and benevolence beamed from his rugged countenance. He wore the uniform of the United States army; and his arms consisted of a brace of pistols and a sword.

Shaking the rain-drops from his military cocked hat, he replaced it atop his dark wavy hair and remarked:

"I'm loath to camp here — especially as none of the scouts have returned to inform us of the designs and movements of the enemy. We are nearing the hostile village, I'm certain. It can't be many miles away. Here we have the open plain on three sides of us. We should be unprotected from a surprise ; and as you well know, Colonel Boyd, a surprise is what we have to fear — a surprise in the early morning when the troops are soundly sleeping. I would prefer a more sheltered place. And it gives me some concern, that none of the scouts have yet returned. I can't understand it."

"May I offer a suggestion, governor?" asked the man addressed as Colonel Boyd, gracefully saluting his superior officer.

"Certainly." And Governor Harrison bowed low over the pommel of his saddle.

"Then, this is what I would suggest : That we form a semi-circular barricade of our wagons, and encamp under their cover. Also, that we double the usual number of our sentries. I like the site no better than you do, but men and teams are exhausted — and we can go no farther. We must make the best of it."

"Very well," Harrison answered decidedly. "I don't like the plan. But perhaps extra vigilance will save us from a night-attack ; that is, if the Indians be in the vicinity — which we do not know. Give the command, colonel. The men are impatient."

This order the governor addressed to Colonel Owen, one of his aids. The officer whirled his horse and dashed away. At that moment two men, followed by a large dog, emerged from the fringe of woodland, and with rapid strides approached the group of officers.

"Whom have we here?" muttered Harrison, straining his eyes through the semi-gloom. "Ah! scouts. Now we shall know something positive of the savages."

As the two shadowy figures drew near, the governor spurred forward to meet them. The other officers followed his example; and soon the two scouts were surrounded by a ring of jingling spurs and rattling scabbards. One of the newcomers stopped suddenly and looked hurriedly about him, as though seeking a chance to escape. The other advanced boldly until he stood at the commander's side. Then he lifted his hat and announced with quiet dignity:

"Governor, I have the honor to inform you that my companion and myself have performed our mission, and are ready to report."

"Who are you?" inquired the commander, bending forward and peering into the speaker's face.

"Ross Douglas — a scout in your service."

"Yes, to be sure," Harrison answered. "I should have known you from your manner. But the darkness bothered me. And your companion?"

"Bright Wing, the Wyandot."

"I am ready to receive your report."

"Here?"

"Yes — and at once."

"We went up the valley as you directed. We continued our course until we came in sight of the Prophet's Town ——"

"You are sure that you made no mistake — that you saw the Prophet's Town?" Harrison interrupted.

"We made no mistake," Douglas replied a little stiffly.

Without heeding the young scout's tone or manner, the governor continued:

"And how far are we from it?"

"About ten miles."

"Did you encounter any savages?"

"A few — when we were within a short distance of the place."

"You saw no large body of Indians — nothing like a war-party?"

"None."

"How did those you saw deport themselves?"

"They fled."

"In the direction of their village?"

"They did."

"In what language did you address them?"

"We tried several different Indian tongues."

"Judging from what you know of Indian character, and what you have seen to-day, Douglas, do you think the savages desire peace or war?"

"War," Ross answered promptly and emphatically.

"The reasons for your opinion, if you please," the commander said quietly.

"Had they desired peace," was the quick reply, "a deputation of their chiefs — headed by the Prophet himself — would have met you ere this. They have been aware of your coming. They mean to give you battle."

Several of the officers nodded their heads in acquiescence of the opinion expressed, but the governor murmured in a low, musing tone:

"You may be right, Douglas; but I can hardly believe that you are."

Then huskily, a shade of alarm in his voice:

"You don't think they will attack us here — under cover of the darkness?"

"I do not."

"Very well. I believe that's all. Call at my tent early in the morning. I want you and the Wyandot to act as interpreters, as we approach the town. But why doesn't he come forward — why does he stand off by himself?"

"He is an Indian," Ross answered simply.

Smiling at the reply he had received, the governor turned and rode away in the gathering darkness, accompanied by his staff.

"Bright Wing," Douglas called.

"Ugh! Me here," the Wyandot answered, gliding to his friend's side.

"Where is Duke?" Ross asked, glancing around.

"Duke him gone hunt meat — him big heap hungry dog," was the guttural reply.

"Well, I'm big heap hungry myself," Douglas laughed as he shifted his gun from one shoulder to the other. "Come; let's find Joe and have some supper."

By this time the wagons had been arranged in a semicircle inclosing several acres of prairie. Soldiers were busy erecting tents and lighting campfires. Teamsters were watering their jaded beasts at the river and feeding them in the inclosure. The two scouts threaded their way among the mass of men and animals, until they reached the farther end of the area.

There Farley had picketed his two yoke of oxen, and, assisted by a number of militiamen, was unloading his vehicle. Their camp-fire blazed and crackled cheerily; and about it a half-dozen soldiers were preparing to cook their evening meal. As Douglas and Bright Wing drew near they heard Joe saying whimsically:

"Go 'way, Duke, an' behave y'rself. Have some manners, an' wait till y'r victuals is cooked. Drat it all, I never *did* see such a hungry dog! I've give him 'bout two pound o' raw meat, an' he's lickin' his chops fer more. By cracky! If he gits much hungrier, he'll eat me an' the oxen. Git out o' the road, you rascal, 'r I'll fall over you. Wher've you been all day — an' wher's y'r master? No use to roll y'r eyes an' whine — I ain't a-goin' to feed you no more. I wish you could talk — I do, by Samanthy! It makes me feel sort o' creepy an' uneasy — you a-comin' in here, an' no sign o' y'r master 'r the Injin.

"Ding-it-all-to-dangnation! Why *can't* a dog

talk? They've got sense an' they've got souls, an' they *ort* to have the power o' speech. Do git out from under my feet, 'r you an' me'll have a fallin' out d'rectly. Hello! Here comes y'r pardners."

"Good evening, Joe," Douglas cried. "What's the prospect for a hot supper?"

"Fair to middlin'," Farley answered, a comical expression overspreading his ugly features. "One o' the fellers is mixin' up a corn pone, an' we've got plenty o' meat an' coffee. But you come jest in the nick o' time — you did, by ginger!"

"Why so?"

Seating himself by the fire, Ross smiled as he extended his hands toward the red blaze.

"Well, you see, it's this way, Ross Douglas," Farley replied, winking at the militiamen: "Y'r dog come in with such a pow'rful appetite that he was likely to eat us out o' house an' home. I had to choke him off 'r ther' wouldn't 'ave been anything left fer us *human* critters. An' I've been watchin' him keerful ever sence, fer fear he'd begin on me 'r the oxen. You ort to give him somethin' to improve his eatin' capacity, Ross — you re'ly ort. I'm 'feard he's goin' into a decline."

Douglas rubbed his hands and joined in the laugh that went around. Bright Wing sniffed the savory odors of the cooking food and grunted:

"Duke him much smart dog — him smell meat far off. Him find it soon — very quick. Him walk far — work hard. Then him eat."

Again the militiamen roared in glee. The prospect of a warm supper and a night's rest had put them in a good humor. The Wyandot's stern visage relaxed into a smile; but Joe cried in an injured tone :

"Well, if workin' hard gives anybody a right to eat, I ort to eat 'bout a ton to-night. A man that's tramped twenty miles in the cold an' wet — an' whacked bulls every step o' the way — ort to feed on the fat o' the land. Nothin's too good fer him. He's earned a right to go to glory — wher' ther' ain't no fightin' Injins n'r drivin' oxen, if I've been rightly informed.

"But still things ain't as bad as they might be. Mortals ortn't to complain, fer fear things might git worse. An' nobody ever hears *me* doin' it. The only time in my whole life that I ever give way to a fit o' complainin', was when a dozen women was wantin' to marry me at once — an' I had to leave the settlement to git red of 'em. Golfer-socks! I never *saw* the like — I never *did*. They was jest *crazy* over my beauty. But ther's no use in rakin' up the past an' makin' you fellers feel sorry. From the way that pone smells it's gittin' done. Le's have supper. Whew! But the steam o' that coffee tickles a feller's nose. Eat, drink, an' be merry, I say; fer to-morrer the redskins may have our scalps an' the buzzards be pickin' our bones."

The hungry scouts and militiamen needed no second invitation. Seating themselves about the camp-fire, they ate and drank with a relish born of exercise in the open air. After they had finished, and filled and lighted their pipes, they talked over the events of the day and speculated about what the morrow would bring forth.

The wind fell and the rain ceased, but the broken and ragged clouds continued to scud across the starlit heavens. The twinkling camp-fires burned low. Drowsy officers sought the shelter of their tents. Privates rolled themselves in their blankets and, with their feet to the fading embers, fell asleep. Silence rested upon the camp — broken only by the faint murmur of voices here and there, or the restless pawing of some tethered steed. Beyond the barricade of wagons a double line of sentries was on guard.

One by one Ross Douglas's companions sought slumber. At last he alone remained sitting by the dying fire, his hand caressing the head of the bloodhound that lay stretched beside him. He was thinking of Amy — the girl he had left behind him.

"Dear child!" he whispered to himself. "Perhaps I should not have left her as I did. Her lot will not be pleasant, I fear. But I couldn't help it — I felt that duty called me. And already I have been able to render some slight service to my country. When I return to her, I'll devote my life to her care and comfort —— "

He broke off suddenly and flung up his head, that had been resting upon his hand. The silence

was disturbed by the voice of a man lustily
singing :

> "I left my children in ol' Kaintuck,
>   In the cabin with the'r mother ;
> And if the Injins kills the'r pap,
>   They'll never git another."

The words were lamely strung together ; and
their meaning was somewhat ambiguous. But
Ross was in a sad mood ; and the homely sentiment of the improvised song touched him.

"Poor fellow !" the young scout muttered under
his breath, as he arose and sauntered in the direction whence the voice came. "His words may be
premonitory of the fate that awaits him."

After walking a few rods, he came upon the
singer seated with his toes in the ashes of an expiring fire.

"Hello, friend !" Ross cried cheerily. "You
seem to be suffering from an attack of homesick-
ness."

"Y-e-s, I am a little homesick," the fellow admitted reluctantly. "You see, I left the little
woman an' the babies 'way down in ol' Kaintuck.
An' sometimes I git to feelin' that somehow I'll
never see 'em ag'in." — And a sob was in his big,
coarse voice.— "I thought ev'rybody was asleep
an' I'd jest sing a bit. Some people cries when
they're sad — *I* sing. It always makes me feel
better, too. Hope I didn't wake you up with my
bellerin'."

"Oh, no!" Douglas hastened to say. "I was awake. But probably both of us had better try to sleep; it is late."

"I s'pect we had,"—admitted the Kentuckian — and lapsed into silence.

Ross retraced his steps to his own fire and lay down. But restlessness had possession of him. Again the voice of the singer fell· upon his ears. This time Bright Wing opened wide his black eyes and sat erect; and Farley rolled over, grumbling sleepily:

"Dodrot the critter! Can't he quit his cater-waulin' day n'r night? He ort to be off on a desert island by hisself."

Joe's voice ended in a long-drawn snore. Bright Wing nodded a few times and rolled over upon the damp ground, his head wrapped in his blanket. Douglas threw some dry wood upon the fire and continued his vigil. An hour passed. Utter silence reigned around him. Presently the bloodhound growled ominously and sprang to his feet. Ross laid a restraining hand upon him and commanded him to lie down. But Duke refused to obey. Instead he broke from his master's grasp and disappeared in the darkness.

"What does it mean?" Ross muttered as he hastily arose and set off in pursuit of the animal.

He caught a glimpse of the shadowy form of the bloodhound flitting past one of the dying camp-fires — going in the direction of the river. Silently but swiftly he followed. On reaching

the bank of the stream, he stopped in the black
shadows of the trees and strained his eyes and
ears, in a vain effort to catch sight or sound of
the dog. But all was silent blackness. He was
on the point of calling the animal, when a faint,
buzzing hum greeted his sense of hearing. The
sound was a series of whispered syllables. Dropping upon hands and knees, he crept toward the
river's edge. Suddenly he dropped flat upon his
face and lay motionless. The sharp snap of a
breaking twig, a few feet ahead of him, had warned
him that he was close upon the speakers. Then he
distinctly heard these words:

"Negro's all right — fix him in the morning —
no failure — be off."

Immediately following this came the sound of
rippling water. Some small object was stealthily
pushing away from the shore. Douglas hastily
arose and swiftly but silently retraced his steps to
the edge of the timber. There he met Bright Wing
and Farley.

"What's up — what're you nosin' 'round out here
fer?" inquired the latter in a strident whisper.

"Sh!" cautioned Ross, laying his hand upon Joe's
arm.

At that moment a man stepped from the edge
of the wood and started across the area, toward
the barricade of wagons. He had taken but a
few steps in the open, when a black body rose in
front of him; and Duke's low, threatening growl
broke the oppressive stillness.

"Good fellow, good fellow!" the man said wheedlingly.

But Duke refused to be moved from his path or his purpose. The man attempted to go around him, but the sagacious animal headed him off and growled more threateningly.

"Curse the brute!" the man muttered fiercely. "I don't dare to shoot him — the report of a pistol would bring a dozen soldiers to the spot. What am I to do?"

Douglas stepped forward, remarking placidly:

"I wouldn't think of shooting the dog, if I were you. His owner might raise objections. Perhaps I can help you out of your dilemma."— Then to the dog:— "Here, Duke! Come here and lie down."

Reluctantly the bloodhound obeyed, still growling. Farley and Bright Wing kept their distance. The man had recoiled a step. Now he recovered himself and mumbled surlily:

"What's you an' y'r infernal cur out here stoppin' honest people fer?"

"What were *you* doing at the river shore?" Ross returned boldly.

The man's hand flew to his belt. Dimly Douglas discerned the shadowy movement. Bright Wing's eagle eyes saw it, too; and the sharp click of his flintlock broke the stillness. The man peered in the direction whence the ominous sound came — and his hand dropped to his side, as he answered in a husky voice:

4

"I was jest wanderin' 'round the camp—I couldn't sleep. I was goin' back to my place when y'r dog stopped me. You'd better keep the cross brute tied up o' nights, 'r somebody 'll kill him. Git out o' my way."

And he made a move to leave the spot.

"Wait a moment," Douglas requested. "When you spoke to the dog, your language marked you as an educated gentleman. Explain."

"I don't have to give no explanations to you 'bout anything—you ain't no officer," was the defiant reply.

And the fellow stalked away in the darkness.

Farley could restrain himself no longer. Hurrying to Douglas's side, he asked excitedly :

"What's it all mean, Ross?"

"I don't know," was the truthful answer.

"Did you know the feller?"

"No—I couldn't see his face."

"He's one o' the soldiers, ain't he?"

"I don't know, Joe," Ross replied rather impatiently. "Let's go back to our places."

As the three friends moved across the inclosed space, toward the site of their camp-fire, they were met by an officer of the guard, who cried angrily :

"You men go back to your places and stay there. You know it is against the regulations to stray about the camp at this time of night. The next time you break the rules, I'll report you."

Farley was ready to fling back an angry retort, but Douglas headed him off with :

"We meant no harm, lieutenant. And we thank you for your consideration."

Much mollified, the officer resumed his rounds. In silence the three friends reached their place of bivouac, and, rolling themselves in their blankets, sought repose. But what Ross Douglas had seen and heard rendered him still more wakeful. He racked his brain for a solution of the mystery — but found none. Who was the man he had encountered — and what had he been doing at the riverside?

"Treachery of some kind is afoot," the young scout murmured to himself. "Perhaps I should have caught the mysterious personage and delivered him into the hands of the guard. But what could I have proven — what charge could I have brought against him? And now I've not the faintest idea who he was, whence he came, or what was his purpose. He tried to disguise his voice; he altered his language. He sought to conceal his identity — and he succeeded. There 's nothing to do but watch and wait. But black treachery of some kind is among us."

An hour passed. Ross Douglas's lids were closed, and his breathing was deep and regular.

CHAPTER III.

A^T FOUR o'clock the next morning the troops —
who had slept upon their arms — were roused
from slumber and ordered to fall into rank.
There they stood, guns in readiness, until the first
faint rays of the cold, gray dawn dispelled the en-
veloping darkness and revealed near-by objects with
clear-cut distinctness. Governor Harrison realized
that he was in the enemy's country. He was well
aware that the wily foe with which he had to deal
preferred to attack in the early morning. He had
not served under Mad Anthony Wayne in vain.
Nor had he forgotten the lesson of St. Clair's awful
surprise and defeat.

Immediately after the order to break ranks was
given, the soldiers began to prepare their break-
fasts, while the teamsters went to water and feed
their pack and draught animals. The camp-fires
were relighted, and soon the appetizing odors of
cooking food pervaded the place.

Douglas left his companions to the performance
of their various duties, and went to report at the
tent of the governor. He found a number of
scouts — who had returned to camp too late to report on the previous evening — in conversation

with the commander and his staff. Ross took up
a position near the door of the tent, to wait until
the others should finish their business and take
their departure.

The central figure of the group of scouts was a
tall, broad-shouldered man of fifty years. His long
black hair was plentifully sprinkled with silver, and
his countenance was a crisscross of fine care-lines.
His dark blue eyes were alert and beaming with
native intelligence. But a puckered red scar on the
right cheek drew up the corner of his mouth and
marred the symmetry of his face. He wore the
picturesque garb of a backwoodsman; but there
was an indefinable something about him that gave
the lie to his outward appearance.

Ross had seen the man almost daily since leaving
Vincennes, but had not formed his acquaintance.
Now, for some reason, the young man's attention
was closely drawn to the scar-faced scout. He
heard him saying in answer to a question from the
governor :

"Yes, I was clear inside of the Injin town;
that's why I didn't git back till late last evenin'."

Douglas started. The man's husky voice sounded
strangly familiar. Governor Harrison was remarking :

"And you found the savages friendly, Bradford?"

Ross strained his ears to catch the answer.

"Yes, governor, I did."

"Who went into the village with you?"

"Nobody—I was all alone. Price an' Hunter, there"— indicating two other scouts—"started out with me, but we got separated somehow."

"Did the Indians avoid you as you approached their town?"

"No, they was sociable. I talked with quite a number, an' they said the'r chiefs wanted peace an' was ready to hold a council with you."

There was the faintest hint of suspicion in Harrison's tone, as he said quickly:

"But other scouts bring me different reports, Bradford."

"I can't help that," the man replied doggedly. "I can only report what I've seen an' heard. Anyhow, none o' the others had the grit to go into the town."

This last he said with a toss of his head and a defiant look at the other scouts.

"I don't think your comrades lack courage," the governor replied coolly. "Their reception was different from yours. On the march to-day I want you to remain within call. As you speak several of the Indian tongues, I may want to use you as an interpreter. Your comrades have already received their orders. You may go."

Was Ross mistaken, or was there a look of malignant triumph on Bradford's scarred face, as with the others he left the tent?

The young scout now stepped forward and saluted the commander.

"Ah! You are here, Douglas," was Harrison's pleasant greeting. "You have come for your orders?"

"I have, governor."

"Very well. To-day you and the Wyandot are to remain near me. I'll use you as interpreters."

Ross bowed and withdrew. As he sauntered away from the tent, he felt that he ought to return and inform the commander of his experience of the night. Yet what had he to tell? Perhaps his imagination was magnifying a molehill into a mountain. He halted — half turned about — then proceeded upon his way.

Just as he was passing a point midway between the governor's quarters and his own mess-fire, he discovered Bradford in earnest conversation with a burly negro — an ox-driver, named Ben. The scar-faced scout and the black man were standing between two of the covered wagons. The darkey's brutal visage was alight with pleasure, as he jingled a number of silver coins that Bradford had just dropped into his outstretched palm. Ross heard the white man say:

"Now, Ben, if you don't do what you've promised — well, you'll hear from *me*. Git away from here now — we mustn't be seen together."

Douglas screened himself behind a wagon. Now he knew why Bradford's husky tones had sounded so familiar in the governor's tent. It was the same voice he had heard at the river-side. The scar-faced scout was the mysterious personage he had met the night before.

The negro slyly slipped away from the spot. A half minute passed. Then Bradford boldly stepped from his place of concealment. As he did so, he swept a hurried glance around him — and fastened his keen eyes upon Douglas.

"What the devil 're you doin' there?" was his expressive question.

His disfigured countenance was aflame with rage; and drawing his tall form to its full height he nervously fingered the trigger of his rifle.

"Attending to my own business," Ross answered with provoking coolness, as he strode forth and faced his questioner.

"Meddlin' with mine, more likely," was the growling rejoinder.

"No," Douglas replied laughingly, "but if the negro ever sues for his wages, I can be a witness to the fact that you've paid him."

"What do you mean?" blustered Bradford, his face purple.

"I was passing and saw you give the darkey the money. Are you the contractor that employs those black fellows?"

"You know very well I'm not. What 're you insinuatin'?"

"Nothing."

"What was you spyin' upon me fer?

"I wasn't spying upon you. Why should I?"

"You're a liar — you *was* spyin' upon me!"

Douglas's steel-gray eyes flashed and his nostrils dilated. For a few moments he glared hard at the other—his thin lips compressed. Then he said with icy calmness:

"Bradford—if that be your name—you have mistaken the mettle of the man to whom you applied that term. Let me warn you. Put a curb upon your hasty tongue—or stand ready to defend yourself. Your bluster didn't frighten me last night—nor does it now."

"What—what do you mean?" Bradford faltered, recoiling a step.

"You know well what I mean," Ross went on quietly. "You're not what you seem. You're masquerading. For what purpose I don't know."— Bradford's face brightened; he was recovering his equanimity.—"You're an educated man—you *may* be a gentleman and a patriot."

"I might return the compliment," the older man interrupted sneeringly. "You, too, are an educated man. Perhaps *you* are masquerading—you are so ready to accuse others. At any rate, I know less of you than you do of me. I don't know your name, even."

"I'm not *certain* that I know yours," Ross replied meaningly.

An expression of alarm flitted across Bradford's scarred face, but he answered promptly:

"Yes, you know my name. It's Bradford— Hiram Bradford."

"And my name's Ross Douglas."

Bradford dropped the butt of his gun to the ground with a thud.   An ashen hue overspread his face, and the red scar upon his cheek stood out with a vividness that was startling.

"Ross Douglas, you say?" he asked with livid, trembling lips.

The younger man was greatly surprised at the effect the announcement of his name had produced upon his companion. But he kept control of himself and simply nodded in answer to the question.

Bradford's hand shook as he fumbled with the buttons upon his rough coat.

"And your—your mother's name?" he inquired.

"Why should I answer your questions?"

"Tell me — tell me!" the other panted.

"Mary."

"Your father's?"

"John."

A wonderful change came over the scar-faced scout. He appeared to age ten years in as many seconds. With the words—"My God! My God! And I would have killed him!" He shouldered his rifle and hastened from the spot, leaving his companion staring after him.

Ross slowly made his way toward the place where his messmates were preparing the morning meal. His mind was in a tumult. What was the meaning of it all?   Who and what was the mysterious scout?

"Why did the announcement of my name so affect him — and why did he wish to know the name of my father and mother?" he asked himself over and over.

He forgot where he was and passed the spot he sought, without knowing it. He was aroused to a sense of his surroundings by hearing Farley bawl:

"What's the matter o' you, Ross Douglas? Have you gone daft an' blind, that you don't know y'r own comrades an' go right past 'em without speakin'? Say!"

Ross forced a laugh and joined the men at their morning meal. But he ate little and talked less; seeing which, one of the militiamen remarked mischievously:

"Douglas, you don't 'pear to be very peart this mornin'. You must be grievin' 'bout the gal you left behind you. You'd better pitch into the grub; it'll be gone purty soon. We may have a fracas with the redskins 'fore night. An' a man always fights best on a full stomach."

"Ugh!" Bright Wing grunted approvingly. "Eat heap much — fight heap hard. Kill many Shawnees. Ugh!"

"That's ph'losophy fer you," grinned Joe. "The Injin knows w'en his bread's buttered — he does. Ross, you ain't eatin' enough to keep a pigeon alive. You'll be lanker 'n a starved houn' 'fore night — you will, by Melissy! Peart up, man; don't let love-affairs git you down. Lordy!

I've had hundreds of 'em — an' I'm able fer three square meals a day yit. What 're you so down in the mouth bout?"

"I'm all right — nothing ails me," Douglas replied hastily, arising and walking away.

Duke followed him. The intelligent animal knew that something had gone amiss with the master he loved. Farley looked after them and lugubriously shaking his head muttered:

"Well, if that don't beat my reckonin', my name ain't Joseph Peregoy Farley!"

It was mid-forenoon ere the army was again upon the march. Very slowly the great serpent — that was intended to choke the life out of Tecumseh's infant confederacy — dragged its cumbersome body forward. Governor Harrison and his staff rode in the van. Ross Douglas and Bright Wing kept near him. When the army was four miles from camp, savages were seen skulking from one sheltered point to another. The commander halted his troops and sent forward a number of scouts and interpreters. The men returned and informed him that they could not come up with the redmen, who fled from them, with insulting words and threatening gestures.

Among the interpreters sent forward were Douglas and the Wyandot. On his return to Harrison's presence, Ross reported as follows:

"Governor, the Indians fled from us, as on yesterday. They mean mischief. You must be prepared for treachery, if you hold a council with them. You know now that Bradford attempted to deceive you this morning, when he told you the savages were anxious for peace."

"You heard his report?" Harrison asked quickly.

"I did."

"By the way"— and the governor glanced hurriedly around — "where *is* the man? I ordered him to remain within call."

"I haven't seen him since we left camp," Ross answered.

The commander bent forward in the saddle and motioned the young scout to come closer. Then drawing down his brows until his eyes were almost closed, he whispered:

"Do you believe Bradford entered the Indian town at all?"

"Yes, I do," was the positive reply.

"Ah!" The governor looked relieved.

"Yes," Ross continued in a low, cautious tone, "I think he entered the village. And no one but a friend of the allied tribes would dare to do that — in my opinion."

"You mean —— " Harrison began, but stopped suddenly, and, smiling, shook his head.

"I hardly know what I mean," Douglas said with an uneasy laugh. "However, I'll explain as best I can."

He told the commander of Bradford's suspicious words and actions, concluding:

"It's not for me to offer you advice, governor; but if you'll pardon my boldness, I would suggest that you keep an eye on Bradford and the negro ox-driver, Ben."

A worried look rested upon Harrison's rugged countenance, as he murmured slowly :

"I thank you for your information — for your watchful loyalty to your commander and your country. You did well to tell me. Appearances are against Bradford, but I can't believe him a traitor. As to keeping an eye on the two — it's easier said than done. I don't know the negro. And it seems impossible to get an eye on Bradford to-day — to say nothing of keeping it on him. However, I'll be watchful. If you learn anything more definite, come to me at once."

Then turning to an aide, he commanded :

"Find Bradford, the scout, and bring him to me."

In a few minutes the young officer returned to report that the man could not be found. The governor looked grave, but gave the order for the column to move forward.

By mid-afternoon the advance guard was within three miles of the Prophet's Town. Here the ground was broken by ravines and covered with scrub timber. It became necessary to exercise the utmost precaution, to avoid an ambuscade. Scouts and interpreters were pushed to the extreme front, and every pass was reconnoitered by mounted riflemen before the main column entered it. Harrison kept changing the relative positions of the various corps, as he advanced, that each might have the ground best suited to its maneuvers.

Within about two miles of the town, the trail descended a steep hill, at the bottom of which was a small creek running through a narrow strip of swampy prairie. Beyond this was a level plain covered with oak forest without underbrush. Near the ford, the woods were very thick — an admirable place for the Indians to practice their mode of warfare.

The governor apprehended that the savages would fall upon him at the crossing — if they meant to give him battle at all — and arranged his troops accordingly. Indians were seen hovering around the front and flanks of the army, but they made no move to attack. The long column crossed the creek unmolested and formed on the other side. The redmen retreated toward their village, a mile and a half away.

The afternoon was far advanced, so the commander decided to go into camp. But a number of his officers urged him to move quickly forward and attack the town at once. This he refused to do, saying:

"My orders are to avoid a conflict with the savages, if possible. However, I'll determine what their intentions are as soon as I can — and act promptly as soon as I have positive information. I can't imagine what has become of the friendly chiefs I sent out from Fort Harrison. They should have met us miles back. I hope they are in the village and will come out to us this evening. We'll fortify ourselves as we did last night—and await the issue.''

"But, governor," urged Major Daviess, "the Indians mean to give us battle—their actions indicate the fact. They are attempting to draw us into a trap. Our men are in high spirits and anxious to attack. We should take advantage of their ardor and——"

"And fall headlong into the trap of which you speak," Harrison interrupted. "No, it won't do to advance until we know more of the ground between here and the town. Already we are badly situated—these woods and ravines are favorable to the Indians. A small body of the enemy could harass us terribly. If I knew what lies between here and the village, I would consent to a cautious advance—but not otherwise."

"The rough ground soon ends," Major Daviess answered. "The town lies upon the low bottoms of the Wabash and is surrounded by level, cultivated fields."

"How do you know this, major?" the governor inquired.

"Adjutant Floyd and myself advanced to the precipitous bank that descends to the valley, and had a fair view of the place."

"Then," said the commander, reluctantly, " I'll advance slowly and in order of battle, provided I can get some one to enter the town ahead of the army with a flag of truce."

Captain Dubois of Vincennes stepped forward and volunteered his services. Harrison turned to Douglas, who was standing near, and said:

"Douglas, will you and the Wyandot accompany Captain Dubois, as interpreters?"

"Of course, governor," Ross replied cheerfully.

"Be off, then—and note carefully all you see and hear. Captain, obtain a positive answer from the Prophet, whether he will comply with the terms I have so often proposed. Have a care that you don't get cut off from the army."

Taking with him several soldiers and the two interpreters, Captain Dubois set out for the town. The army moved slowly after, in order of battle.

When the captain and his comrades were within a mile of the town, they encountered a large body of Indians. The interpreters tried to open communication with them, but the treacherous savages gave no heed to repeated hails. All the while they circled around the little band of whites, attempting to separate them from their friends in the rear.

"It's useless and dangerous to proceed further," the captain exclaimed angrily. "Brown," addressing a soldier, "go back to the governor and inform him of our want of success, and of the perilous position we occupy."

On receiving the word from his peace messenger, Harrison set his teeth and said firmly:

"I've done with the Prophet's dillydallying; I'll treat him as an enemy. Recall Captain Dubois and his men, and order the entire army to

5

advance at a brisk pace. If the Indians don't come out to treat with me, I'll attack their town at once.''

In a few minutes Dubois and his comrades had rejoined the command. An animated scene presented itself to their gaze. Orderlies were galloping hither and thither; officers were giving hurried commands; and regulars and militiamen were exchanging oaths and jokes, as they stood in line, awaiting the order to advance. Every man thought an engagement imminent — and was depressed or elated at the prospect, according to his temperament.

''Forward !''

The compact lines moved. But scarcely were they in motion ere they were met by a deputation of three chiefs — including the Prophet's chief councilor — who had come from the village to meet the commander and confer with him.

Again the army halted. Officers swore and privates grumbled. Why should they listen to such tardy envoys? Why not make prisoners of them — and proceed to the attack? But Harrison gave no heed to the stormy protests of his staff, nor to the sullen mutterings of the rank and file. He had resolved to give the chiefs an audience. He did so; and received from them the information that the Prophet was desirous for peace — that he wished to know why so large a force of armed men was approaching his town. Also, they said the Prophet had sent back the Potawatomie and Miami chiefs —

whom the governor had dispatched from Fort Harrison — with a pacific message, but the friendly emissaries had made their return journey on the south side of the Wabash, and for that reason had missed the army.

All this seemed so fair and candid that the commander agreed to an armistice and told the chiefs to inform the Prophet, that he — Harrison — would hold a council with him the next day.

Once more the columns moved forward. The commander intended to camp on the low ground near the village, which occupied a slight eminence overlooking the wet bottoms. But not finding the place to his liking, he sent Major Waller and Taylor to select a more suitable location. The site the officers chose was an elevated piece of dry ground, a short distance northeast of the Indian town and directly facing it.

Toward this spot the army proceeded. As the lines of soldiers filed past the village, numbers of armed warriors sallied forth, and appeared ill-humored and threatening.

When the troops were nearing the chosen site of the encampment, an incident occurred that created a momentary ripple of excitement. Ben, the negro ox-driver, suddenly threw down his whip and, leaving his companions, ran off at full speed toward the Indian town. A number of braves — as though expecting him — met him and conducted him within the walls. The other drivers hooted in derision, and flung curses at the woolly head disappearing within the gate of the palisade surrounding the village.

"Dang-it-all-to-dingnation!" shouted Joe Farley. "Let the black deserter go. I wish I had my ol' rifle out o' the wagon, fer jest a minute! I jest hope the redskins 'll roast an' eat him. It'll do two good things—be the end o' the nigger-traitor, an' kill the Injins. *Dang* a nigger, anyhow!"

Governor Harrison's attention was attracted by the hubbub and he inquired the cause of it.

"One of the negro ox-drivers employed by the contractor has left his team and entered the Indian village," explained an aide at the governor's elbow.

"What's the fellow's name?" Harrison asked quickly.

"I don't know, governor."

"Send Ross Douglas to me at once," was the sharp command.

The aide obeyed. And soon the young scout was at the commander's side.

"What's the black's name, who just went over to the Indians?" Harrison asked, bending down until his face was on a level with Douglas's.

"Ben," was the curt reply.

"The same of whom you told me?"

"The same, governor."

"Lieutenant"—addressing an officer of his staff—"go and bring the negro back. Take with you a squad of men—and yonder Wyandot, as interpreter."

Then again turning to Ross:

" Have you seen that man Bradford, to-day?"

"I have not, governor."

" Do you know what has become of him?"

Douglas silently shook his head.

A fierce scowl darkened the commander's face as he said in a low tone:

"Nor do I—but I have an opinion. He's an infernal traitor—and has deserted. I have no doubt that at this moment he's in the Prophet's Town. Dark and devilish treachery is afoot. But thanks to you, my young friend, I shall not be taken by surprise. When I again have that man before me, I shall know how to deal with him. The black is a mere tool—an ignorant dupe. Keep your knowledge to yourself. I'll defeat Bradford's purpose—whatever it may be."

The army reached the elevated piece of ground three-quarters of a mile from the village, and went into camp. It was late in the evening. The sun was sinking in a bank of dun-colored clouds—an indication of a dark and rainy night.

The teamsters disposed of their wagons, as on the previous evening. Wood and water in abundance were near at hand, for a clear creek, bordered by trees and bushes, flowed at the rear of the camp. Night shut down and a drizzling rain began to fall. But supper was under way, and the appetizing odors of broiling meat and boiling coffee cheered the hearts and loosened the tongues of the tired men. The merry snap and crackle of dancing flames drowned the doleful voice of the wind sweeping across the open prairie and soughing among the scrubby trees.

While the men were unloading the vehicles and pack-horses and preparing supper, several Indians from the town ventured within the lines. Having in mind the mysterious disappearance of Bradford and the open desertion of Ben, Governor Harrison promptly ordered the red warriors to betake themselves to their own camp. At the same time he requested them to send back the negro — whom the staff officer had failed to find, and who was still in hiding at their village. This they promised to do.

Ross Douglas listened silently to the idle tales of his companions, but his thoughts were far away. He was thinking of Amy Larkin — as he had thought of her a hundred times that day. He wished that he might see her, if only for a few seconds. He felt lonely and depressed. Then the disfigured countenance of Hiram Bradford arose before his mind's eye and shut out the fair face of his sweetheart.

Ross rubbed his eyes and tried to rid himself of the unwelcome mental vision. But it would not depart at his bidding. His thoughts refused to revert to Amy, but persisted in dwelling upon the scar-faced scout. It made him angry ; and he arose and sauntered about in the darkness.

On returning to the fire he heard a militiaman remarking :

"Well, I reckon this ends the whole matter. We've come on a reg'lar fool's errand — a wild goose chase. To-morrer the gov'ner 'll hold a powwow with the Injins—make another treaty with 'em that they'll break 'fore we're back to Fort Harrison. Then what? W'y, we'll march back to Vincennes an' be discharged. Cuss it! We ort to whip the red devils while we've got 'em cornered. It puts me in mind o' the ol' story 'bout the king o' Spain; how he marched up the hill—an' then marched down ag'in. The idee of a man totin' a gun every day fer six weeks, to git a shot at a red-skin, an' then when he's got the critters holed, somebody sayin' he can't do it!"

"I don't know 'bout y'r not gittin' a chance to shoot," Joe Farley answered reflectively. "Wouldn't be s'rprised you'd git the chance when you was least expectin' it. Injins is dang cunnin' varmints, sure's you're born. From all I've seen an' heerd o' this Prophet an' his band, I'm o' the 'pinion we'll have a scrimmage with 'em 'fore we git out o' this clearin'. An' if we *do*, it'll come mighty sudden—an' in the night, most likely—an' you'll have a chance to shoot y'r gun off more times 'n you're hankerin' fer.

"The idee o' you complainin' 'bout totin' a rifle! You ort to be ashamed—you had by Jerushy! If you'd had to whack bulls from Fort Harrison— wear y'r back out a-lickin' 'em an' y'r breath out a-cussin' 'em—you might complain. But I'm through with it at last—thank the Lord! I've resigned my commission. Somebody else 'll drive 'em back 'r they won't be druv — that's all. The idee o' puttin' a free-born American along with a lot o' niggers to drive oxen! It's a disgrace — a shame — a blot on the Constertution! Laugh, dang y'r skins!" — His companions were haw-hawing boisterously. — "Laugh at the agony of an abused man! But you chaps 'll be laughin' out o' the other corner o' y'r mouths, 'fore mornin' — 'r I miss *my* guess."

The laughter suddenly ceased. And one of the militiamen inquired gravely:

"What do you mean, Farley?"

"Jest this," Joe replied impressively. "I'll bet any man a pound o' powder we have a rumpus with the Injins 'fore sun-up to-morrer mornin'. What do you say, Bright Wing?"

The Wyandot deliberately removed his pipe from his lips, with the stem of it waved aside the cloud of smoke he blew from his lungs, and answered in guttural but not unmusical tones:

"Bad Shawnees much sly, like fox. Make believe all time want peace — all time want war. Paleface camp here. Shawnee town there — two, three rifle shots away. Bad Shawnees — bad Winnebagoes — bad Senecas — all bad. But much brave — heap cunning. Big Prophet talk, talk. Night dark — palefaces sleep — Indians come and kill, Ugh!"

The Wyandot resumed his pipe; the militiamen sat speechless.

"There it is, as plain as the nose on a man's face!" Joe shouted, exultingly. "Ross Douglas, you hain't said a word. What do *you* think?"

Douglas answered quietly:

"I think the savages mean to try to surprise and massacre us. But whether they'll make the attempt to-night, I don't know—I have no idea."

"Hark!" cried a militiaman, nervously springing to his feet. "What's that hullabaloo 'bout?"

His companions hastily arose and stood listening intently. A chorus of shouts, mingled with curses, came from the direction of the governor's tent.

"I'll soon see what's up," muttered Farley, bounding away toward the spot whence the sounds came.

The others seated themselves and anxiously awaited his return. The uproar suddenly ceased. A few minutes later, Joe again stood within the circle of light. A broad grin irradiated his homely features.

"What was it?" bawled half a dozen voices at once.

"W'y, ding-it-all-to-dangnation!" Farley exclaimed excitedly. "The *nigger's* come back. An' Cap'n Wilson's captured him an' got him in charge."

"Where did he capture him?" Douglas asked quickly.

"Right behind the gov'nor's tent—the dang sneak was a-hidin' in the shadder of it."

"And he returned to murder the commander," Ross muttered under his breath. "So that, at least, was a part of Bradford's plan; and it has miscarried. Who *is* that man—an agent of the British? He's foiled for the present, at any rate. But what does he know of me? Why was he so agitated when he learned my name? And no doubt he's at the Prophet's Town, impatiently awaiting the news that the governor is assassinated. Thank God, he's doomed to disappointment!"

Gradually the noises of the camp died out. Wrapped in their blankets and with their guns at their sides, the soldiers stretched themselves around the fires and fell asleep. The wind moaned dismally; the flames cast grotesque shadows over the sleeping forms. In the outer darkness the sentries paced their lonely beats. The murmur of shouting savages and barking dogs came in on the wings of the fitful gale, telling that the inhabitants of the Prophet's Town were still astir. Then the fickle wind veered to another point of the compass—and all was still. Suddenly the silence was broken by the voice of a lusty singer. The sleepers stirred uneasily as they heard in their dreams:

> "The Injins hankers fer my scalp,
>   To sell to the highest bidder;
> An' when I'm dead an' in my grave,
>   My wife 'll be a widder!"

"Drat the critter, anyhow!" grumbled Farley, flopping over upon his stomach and raising his head. "He's at it ag'in. Seems he can't sleep, n'r let anybody else. I wish to gosh he'd stayed in ol' Kaintuck with his wife an' babies — I do, by Tabithy!"

Then in a startled voice:

"Say, Ross, wake up! Y'r Injin's took his departure. Ther' ain't hide n'r hair of him to be seen."

Douglas rubbed his eyes and sat erect. Bright Wing had disappeared.

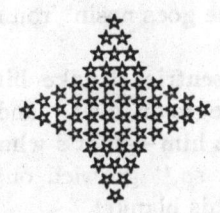

CHAPTER IV.

"WHEN did you discover his absence, Joe?" was Douglas's first question.

"Jest this minute," Farley replied promptly. "That dang Kaintuckian waked me up with his caterwaulin'—an' I found the Injin gone. Then I called you. Listen to that critter squallin'—an' he calls it singin'!"

"What can have become of the Wyandot?" Ross asked, unheeding Joe's complaining tone— as he arose and peered into the shadows.

"Don't know," Joe answered, with an expressive shake of the head. "But I know what *will* become o' him, if he goes nosin' 'round the camp."

"What?"

"Some o' the sentries 'll take him fer a prowlin' redskin from the town over yander, an' put an ounce o' lead into him—that's what."

"That's 'bout so," growled one of the militia-men from under his blanket.

"You are right," Ross admitted. "I'll make a circuit of the camp and try to find him."

"An' while you're gone, kill that Kaintuckian 'r have the officer o' the guard buck an' gag him," Farley snarled as he again threw himself upon the ground.

(76)

Douglas failed to find his red comrade and returned to his place by the fire.

"See anything o' the Injin?" Joe sleepily inquired.

"No," was the monosyllabic reply.

"Well turn in an' go to sleep. He's able to take keer of hisself. Injins is Injins — the best you can make of 'em. They're jest like other wild varmints — always prowlin' 'round o' nights. He'll turn up in the mornin'. Go to sleep."

Douglas was worn out with the day's toil and excitement ; so, rolling himself in his blanket, he lay down. While he slumbers, let us follow Bright Wing.

The Wyandot had left the others sleeping, and had stolen to the outskirts of the camp. While Ross was searching for him, he was in hiding behind one of the wagons, awaiting a chance to slip through the line of sentries. At last his patience was rewarded; and with consummate skill and cunning, he wormed through the tall grass and bushes growing along the slope upon which the camp was situated. When he found himself safely beyond the lines, he nimbly arose to his feet and sped across the strip of wet prairie lying between the camp and the town of the Prophet.

On nearing the latter place, he halted and carefully reconnoitered. Apparently convinced the way was clear, he boldly ascended the grade leading to the village, and found himself under the walls of the fortified town.

The Prophet's Town was a sacred place—the Mecca of his fanatical followers. Here he muttered incantations and performed miracles; here he blessed the faithful and condemned to perdition all unbelievers. Many pilgrims came and went each day. And on this night the place was full of fierce warriors—mad with fanaticism and thirsting for blood.

The town itself consisted of a large number of flimsily constructed log-cabins and lodges of poles and skins. These rude habitations were scattered irregularly over several acres of ground. The council lodge—or cabin—was centrally located. Surrounding the whole was a palisade of poles and logs. Two or three narrow openings in the wall served as gateways. To-night they were closely guarded; for the enemy lay without—and within important business was engaging the attention of chiefs and braves.

Bright Wing crouched in the shadow of the palisade and listened intently. The din of many voices came to his ears. Above the sullen, monotonous roar, occasionally arose the exultant whoop of some excited brave. Through a crack between two of the upright timbers, the Wyandot caught a glimpse of flaring torches and flaming bonfires. For a brief moment he glued his eyes to the opening. Then he arose and ran along the outer side of the wall, until he came to a point where a log-cabin occupied an angle—filling the space between two wings of the palisade. Near it was a guarded gateway. Like a squirrel the Indian clambered up the projecting ends of the logs of the hut—and boldly dropped to the ground within the inclosure.

"Ugh!" was the startled grunt of one of the guards at the gateway.

"What is it?" inquired his companion in the Shawnee tongue.

"A noise at the cabin," was the answer.

"It was the wind rattling the bark upon the roof."

"It may have been a paleface."

"No!"—Contemptuously.—"The palefaces are cowards. They fear the wonderful power of Tenskwatawa—The Open Door."

The two guards lapsed into silence. Bright Wing cautiously arose to his feet and, dodging from cabin to cabin, made his way toward the center of the village. At last he reached a spot where he could look out upon the square in which stood the council lodge—the Prophet's temple.

The space was ablaze with fires and torches. A dense mass of savages, talking, whooping, and gesticulating, surged around the entrance to the lodge. Many different tribes were represented. The young Wyandot saw several members of his own tribe among the half-nude fanatics. Thinking, therefore, that his presence would not arouse suspicion, he resolved to mingle with the excited braves and learn what plans were afoot.

Slowly he edged forward until he reached the outskirts of the crowd. Apparently no one took

notice of him — all eyes were fixed upon the door of
the council lodge. He elbowed his way into the
surging mass and stood still — his finger upon the
trigger of his rifle.

The braves were in war-paint and feathers. All
were fully armed. Shoulder to shoulder, stood
Winnebago and Wyandot; cheek by jowl, were
Shawnees and Pottawatomies.

Suddenly a mighty shout went up from the
savage horde. It was prolonged for several minutes. A thousand bronzed warriors bellowed themselves hoarse. They danced, and swayed, and
gyrated. Squaws and children added their piercing treble to the thunderous bass of the men.
"Tenskwatawa!" was the cry. Then, as suddenly
as it had arisen, the tumult subsided. Naught but
the heavy breathing of the multitude could be
heard.

Bright Wing riveted his gaze upon the front of
the council lodge. A procession was issuing from
the doorway. First came a number of torchbearers,
walking two abreast. They stepped apart on reaching the open air, to form an avenue through which
passed a dozen forms fantastically clad and painted,
making a hideous din by beating shallow drums
and rattling strings of dried deer-hoofs. These
were followed by a group of dignified chiefs in
full war-dress. Last of all appeared a solitary figure, awful in its grotesqueness — the horrible vision
of a nightmare.

"Tenskwatawa!" was the whisper that arose.

It began in the front rank of the crowd and ran
toward the rear, until every pair of lips in the sea
of faces was moving. "Tenskwatawa! The
Open Door!" Then a deathlike hush fell upon
them.

The grotesque figure was that of the Prophet.
He ascended a small platform to the right of the
door of the council lodge, and stood looking out
over the heads of torchbearers, musicians, and
chiefs. The glare of blazing torches fell upon him.
A buffalo-robe enveloped his body. The horns surmounted his head and gave him a demoniac aspect.
The tail of the animal, whose skin he had assumed, trailed upon the ground behind him. His
hideous, repellent face — in which shrewdness, ava-
rice, and cruelty were reflected — was striped and
smeared with black and yellow paints. From nose
and ears depended large silver crescents; and
around his neck was a string of bears'-claws. His
one eye twinkled balefully.

For a full minute he stood with folded arms.
Then he slowly raised his right hand toward the
black heavens. As he did so, a ring upon his index
finger caught the rays of the red and smoking
torches and emitted a fitful stream of sparkles.

"The Sign of the Prophet! The Sign of the
Prophet!" wailed and sobbed the throng of savages.

Many of them prostrated themselves to the
earth, some in convulsions — frothing at the mouth
and gibbering incoherently; others in a state of

6

cataleptic rigidity — their eyes wide open and staring, their limbs immovably fixed.

The Prophet's lips moved ; but no words came forth. He was praying. At last he dropped his arm to a horizontal position, and, slowly and impressively moving his hand from side to side, began in low-pitched, resonant tones :

"Arise, children. I come to you with a message from the Great Spirit."

The groveling braves got upon their feet, and, leaning forward, listened eagerly to every word that fell from his lips.

He continued :

"The forests and streams belong to the redmen. The Great Spirit gave them to his wild children. The palefaces have stolen our lands. The Great Spirit is displeased with his children that they have tamely submitted. All this you have heard before. The time has come for action. You must strike a blow to recover your own. The palefaces are without the gates. They come to take from us the little we have left. This is holy ground — the feet of our enemies shall not defile it. They come at a time when your great leader — the noble Tecumseh — is absent. They think to force you to submit to their propositions. They demand a council. We have promised to meet them. But we shall meet them to-night — not to-morrow. We shall take with us the *tomahawk* — not the *peace-pipe*. Our guns shall speak for us. My children, the Great Spirit sends you this message."

Tenskwatawa paused to note the effect of his words. The warriors silently gripped their weapons and, with blazing eyes, waited for him to proceed. Pitching his voice in a higher key, he resumed :

"The black man has returned to the palefaces. I have put a spell upon him — he will perform his mission. Ere the turn of the night the great paleface chief will be in the spirit land, with his fathers. Then will fear seize upon his warriors. In the early morning, my children, you will fall upon them and destroy them. The Great Spirit has promised me the victory. Darkness will shelter the redmen — while a great light will reveal the palefaces. I have brewed a drink of which each of you shall sip — and shall not taste death. Bullets shall pass him by — and long knives shall refuse to harm him. The Great Spirit has promised — and I have told you. I have put a spell upon the palefaces. Already one-half of them are dead or crazy. The victory shall be yours — the Great Spirit has promised."

Again he paused, his one eye fixed upon the sea of dusky faces before him. The braves stood spellbound — awed to silence by his words and manner. Raising his voice to the highest pitch, he cried :

"If there be a coward among you, let him eat dirt and stay with the squaws. I would lead you myself, but the Great Spirit forbids. But my power shall be with you — my sign shall accompany you. See !"

Again he raised his right hand ; and again the ring upon his finger scintillated dazzlingly.

"The Sign of the Prophet ! The Sign of the Prophet !" was the awe-stricken whisper of the multitude.

"Listen !" shouted Tenskwatawa. "Three brave chiefs shall lead you — Winnemac, White Loon, and Stone-Eater. I have said that my sign shall go with you. So it shall. See ! I place it upon the noble Winnemac's finger. It shall bring you victory over our enemies. My children, I have spoken."

Wrapping the buffalo-skin closely around him, he descended the platform and re-entered the council lodge. The chiefs, musicians, and torchbearers followed him, in order. Then the pent enthusiasm of the warriors broke loose. They whooped, howled, and danced ; they embraced each other and rolled over and over upon the ground. In a fanatical frenzy, they caught up burning firebrands and ran hither and thither. For several minutes pandemonium reigned.

Bright Wing had learned all he desired. He turned to slip away unmolested, and had reached the edge of the crowd and was rapidly making his way toward the palisade, when he came face to face with a white man. The Wyandot uttered a grunt of surprise, as he recognized the form and features of Hiram Bradford.

"Hello !" cried the latter. "Where are you running so fast, my red friend — and what are you doing here?"

The young Indian haughtily drew himself erect and retorted:

"Bright Wing among his people. What paleface scout do here."

"Good — very good!" Bradford chuckled huskily. "Well, I'll answer your question, Wyandot, and then you shall answer mine. I'm here as an agent of the British, and I'm doing what I can to help your people to recover what belongs to them. Now, what are *you* doing here?"

"Bright Wing come help, too," was the quick reply.

"Y-e-s," the scar-faced scout answered doubtingly, "but you've been among the palefaces — I saw you there, you know. You've been scouting for them."

"Ugh!" Bright Wing grunted. " *You* scout for palefaces, too. Me see *you* there."

Bradford was disconcerted by the Wyandot's shrewd replies. Now he cried irritably:

"Let's understand each other, my red friend. I was among the Americans as a spy. What were you doing in their service?"

"Bright Wing him spy, too," was the unmoved rejoinder.

"And you have left them and come to fight with your people?"

"Ugh! me fight with friends. Paleface fight with redmen?"

"No," Bradford reluctantly admitted; "I shan't fight with them. I can better help them in another way. Where are you going?"

"Bright Wing him go find friends. Good-night."

The Wyandot stalked away, leaving Bradford staring after him.

"It may be all right," muttered the latter, "but I greatly doubt it. I suspect that cunning fellow's here as a spy. But how did he pass the guards at the gate? Ah! here comes Gray Wolf!"

Gray Wolf was a gigantic, vicious-looking Shawnee. Evidently he and Bradford were old acquaintances. They held a hurried conversation. Then Gray Wolf hastened away in pursuit of Bright Wing. He came upon the Wyandot in an obscure corner of the inclosure, just as the latter was preparing to scale the palisade.

"Why is my brother here by himself?" the Shawnee suavely asked in his own tongue.

"Perhaps it pleases him to be alone," Bright Wing answered haughtily, in the same language.

"And perhaps he means to leave the village?"

"And if he does, has he not the same right to go and come as the birds of the air or the beasts of the forest?"

"But Tenskwatawa has given orders that none shall leave the village until the appointed time. I know my brother. He is Bright Wing, a Wyandot."

"And *I* know my brother. *He* is Gray Wolf, a Shawnee."

The two warriors stood glaring at each other in the darkness. Gray Wolf was the first to speak again. He said in a low, intense tone of voice:

"My brother is the friend of the palefaces — the enemy of his race."

Bright Wing replied proudly:

"The words that fall from my brother's lips are not the words of truth. Bright Wing is the true friend of his race."

"Does he stand ready to prove it?" Gray Wolf asked sneeringly.

"He does," was the frigid reply.

"Has he the Sign of the Prophet?"

"He has."

"Bright Wing has a forked tongue — it refuses to speak the truth," Gray Wolf cried triumphantly. "Many have *seen* the Sign of the Prophet, and felt its power — but Tenskwatawa alone *has* it."

"Gray Wolf knows that he lies!" Bright Wing answered fiercely. "For at this moment Winnemac bears the Sign of the Prophet."

The Shawnee was taken aback. The answer was unexpected. He growled savagely:

"Bright Wing is the dog of the palefaces. What does he here?"

The Wyandot leaned forward and hissed in the other's ear:

"He comes to tear the throat of the wolf that helped to murder the great and kind chief, Leatherlips. Die, whelp of a Shawnee!"

Gray Wolf tried to spring out of reach of his Nemesis, shaping his lips for a war-whoop, as he did so. But the Wyandot's tomahawk descended and buried itself in the Shawnee's brain. The whoop ended as a death-rattle in his throat. His great bulk sank to earth, an inert mass. One bubbling expiration of the breath — and Gray Wolf was a corpse.

Bright Wing wiped the blood from his tomahawk and replaced it in his belt. Then he whipped out his scalping-knife, muttering in his own tongue :

" He helped to murder my father. His footprints will blight the flowers and grass no more. The Great Spirit willed that Gray Wolf should die by the hand of Bright Wing —— "

He closed the sentence abruptly, and jerking off the reeking scalp of the Shawnee, caught up his rifle and darted away in the darkness. The sound of approaching footsteps had come to his quick ears.

A minute later a prolonged war-whoop reverberated from one end of the village to the other. In answer to it came a hundred others. All was excitement and confusion. Torches bobbed and flared here and there. An enemy was in the camp.

Bright Wing flattened his form against the sloping roof of a cabin — where he had taken refuge — and breathlessly awaited the outcome. The hut upon which he was perched stood near the edge of the inclosure, and the roof sloped toward the palisade. He was far from the blazing bonfires, and darkness sheltered him. His enemies searched

high and low, but failed to discover him. Three or
four times groups of them stood under the low
eaves and jabbered in guttural accents. Gradually
the excitement subsided and darkness and silence
reigned.

Hours slipped by, but Bright Wing did not dare
to leave his hiding-place. He realized fully the
dangers that beset him, and he shuddered, thinking
of his white friends. He must give them warning.
But how? He thought of many reckless plans, but
abandoned each in turn.

Midnight passed — and morning was drawing
nigh. Again the town was astir. The Wyandot
heard the buzz of myriad voices, and knew what it
meant. The allied tribes were preparing for the
attack. He stretched his cramped limbs and cautiously descended to the ground. If he was to give
warning, he must be off at once. He would make
an attempt — no matter how reckless. For several
minutes he stood in the shadow of the low building,
vainly striving to map out a plan of procedure.
The steady tramp of hundreds of moccasined feet
greeted his ears. The Prophet's braves were
marching forth to battle.

Bright Wing ran to the palisade and sought to
scale it. Failing at one point he tried another.
Frantically he dug his fingers and toes into the
crevices between the upright timbers. His efforts
were fruitless. He did not dare to approach the
spot where he had entered the inclosure; the guards
near at hand were alert. The tramp-tramp of the

marching warriors drew nearer. They were approaching the northeastern gate. The Wyandot
made a final effort to climb the wall — and fell back.
His heart sickened. Was he doomed to failure?
The thought made him desperate. Recklessly he
strode to the northeastern gateway and assayed to
pass out. The click of a gun-lock brought him to a
standstill. A guard stepped from the shadow and
said :

"Has my brother the Sign of the Prophet?"

"He has *seen* it," Bright Wing mumbled, "but
Tenskwatawa alone *has* it."

"Why does my brother seek to go out alone?"

"At the order of the great Winnemac he goes to
scout," was the quick-witted reply.

"Ugh!" ejaculated the sentry, taking a step
backward.

The nimble-footed Wyandot darted through the
gateway and disappeared — just as the head of the
column of braves came in sight.

Down the incline, across the swampy prairie, and
up the slope leading to the camp of the whites,
Bright Wing sped like the wind — never pausing
until he drew near the line of sentries. The sky
was thickly clouded ; a gentle drizzle was falling.
Dropping upon the ground, he watched and waited
for a chance to elude the vigilance of the pickets.
A white man would have given the alarm, by stepping forward and permitting himself to be chal-
lenged ; but the proud Wyandot scorned to do
anything of the kind. Minutes passed. Suddenly,

a light footfall attracted his attention ; and the next moment Duke's cold muzzle touched his hand.

"Go 'way — go to master!" Bright Wing commanded in a stern whisper.

In answer the dog threw up his nose and sniffed the damp air. Then with a low growl, he bounded away toward camp.

"Duke him smell redmen," the Wyandot muttered to himself. "Me must go in quick — right away."

Little by little he wriggled forward — the sentry pacing his beat within a few feet of him. The next instant the intrepid young brave was upon his feet. Like a scudding cloud he glided to the barricade of wagons, and disappeared among them. A moment later he bent over the sleeping form of Ross Douglas and, shaking him roughly, cried:

"Wake, Fleet Foot!"—The Indian name of his white friend.—"Up! Up! Winnemac and heap many braves come — come soon."

Douglas threw off his blanket, and, leaping to his feet, cried excitedly:

"Did you say the Indians are coming, Bright Wing?"

"Ugh!" grunted the imperturbable Wyandot. "Come quick soon — sight many."

"You mean they're almost upon us?"

"Ugh!"

"How did you learn the fact?"

"Bright Wing go to Prophet's Town — learn big heap."

Duke now dashed into the circle of light and out again, barking furiously. His hoarse voice wakened Farley and his messmates. They stumbled to their feet, sleepily rubbing their eyes.

"What in dingnation's all this hullabaloo 'bout, anyhow?" Joe demanded irritably.

"The Indians are upon us!" cried Ross. "Secure your arms—and make yourselves ready for battle. I'm off to warn the officers."

And striking the breech of his rifle, to prime it, Douglas bounded away toward the governor's tent.

"Jest as I pr'dicted," Farley growled. "Dang-it-all-to-dingnation! Hang-it-up-an'-take-it-down-an'-cook-it! Did anybody ever hear o' such dang fools as Injins is? Git up in the *night* to fight! Dodrot that Kaintuckian! He's the cause o' all this—he is, by the Queen o' Sheby! He might 'ave knowed his caterwaulin' 'ld bring on a rumpus —even Injins can't stand no such unearthly noise as he makes. Great snakes—it's darker 'n a squaw's pocket!"

It was about four o'clock in the morning—the darkest hour in the twenty-four. The moon had risen, but was veiled by heavy clouds. The rain still fell. The smoldering camp-fires shed a faint, uncertain light over the scene. Governor Harrison had already arisen and was sitting by the fire in front of his tent. He had just pulled on his boots and was conversing with the members of his staff, who sprawled upon blankets, in a circle around the red embers. They were waiting for the signal to turn out. In a few minutes the drum would have beaten reveille. Of a sudden the report of a rifle, followed by an Indian yell, broke the stillness of the camp, and brought the officers to their feet.

"What's the meaning of that?" Harrison asked sharply.

At that moment Ross Douglas leaped into the circle of light, shouting:

"An attack! An attack, governor! The savages are upon us! A sentry has just fired upon one and ——"

His words were drowned in a torrent of Indian war-whoops. Then followed the crash and roar of discharging firearms. A streak of flame ran along the western picket line. The sentries came flying into camp. The Indians were making an onslaught on the left wing.

In a moment all was bustle and excitement. The suddenness of the attack almost caused a panic. But the commander was the firm rock upon which the wave of consternation broke. Hastily mounting his horse, he dashed toward the point of conflict, shouting his orders right and left as he went. Drum and bugle called to arms. The soldiers tumbled out, formed in line, and rushed to meet the foe. The battle was on in earnest.

The fires were stamped out, leaving the camp in darkness. Pandemonium broke loose. The rattle of discharging rifles grew to a roar. The redmen's war-whoops were answered by yells. The castanet-like click of rattling strings of deer-hoofs

mingled with the muttering roll of drums and the
piercing peals of bugles. Terrified oxen lowed and
bellowed; frightened pack and draught horses
neighed shrilly as they broke their tethers, and ran
madly about the camp. Officers — pistol in hand —
rode along the lines, encouraging their men to stand
firm.

The impetuosity of the savages — born of igno-
rance and fanaticism — was a fair match for the cool
valor of the whites. Neither party would give
ground. The battle spread until it raged fiercely
upon three sides of the camp. The Indians forgot
their ancient tactics and boldly fought in the open.
They met the soldiers face to face — and madly
charged the lines of bayonets. Again and again
the opposing forces came together with a reeling
shock. Blood drenched the dead grass. Curses
and groans commingled; and over all rose the weird
voice of Tenskwatawa — upon an eminence a short
distance away — chanting his war-song.

Major Daviess and Colonel White fell mortally
wounded. Captain Spencer and his lieutenants
were all dead; and Captain Warwick was dying.
Colonel Owen dropped at the governor's side. He
was mounted upon a white horse at the time; and
as Harrison had ridden a white horse on the previous day, undoubtedly the Indians mistook the
aide for the commander. Dead and dying braves
and soldiers lay thick upon the hotly contested field.

During the battle Harrison spurred from one part
of the camp to another, disposing his troops to the

best advantage. His officers begged him not to expose himself, but he persisted in being where the fire was hottest. His courage and coolness did much to hold the men steady under the deadly fusillade in the darkness. One ball pierced his hat rim and another cut a lock of hair from his temple — but still he rode unharmed through the scathing fire. Seeing an ensign — a Frenchman — sheltering himself behind a tree, the governor cried, angrily :

" Out from behind that tree, you cowardly rascal ! "

" Me not behind ze tree," explained the ensign ; "ze tree in front of me. Zere, ze tree — here, my position. What can I *do*, governor ? "

With a laugh Harrison rode on and left the fellow.

A Winnebago broke through the lines of militia and dropped dead within the camp. A tall militiaman sprang forward to scalp the prostrate savage — but received a death-wound.

" Served him right ! " snarled Joe Farley, who was loading and firing with the rapidity and precision of a piece of machinery. " Tryin' to make an Injin of hisself — the heathen ! "

The left flank began to give way before the desperate and persistent foe. Ross Douglas and Bright Wing were fighting side by side, in that quarter. A half-dozen warriors sprang through the broken lines, brandishing their arms and yelling fiendishly. Four of them fell dead in their tracks. Douglas and his comrade engaged in a hand-to-hand combat with the other two. The Wyandot quickly dispatched his opponent, but Ross was not so fortunate. His foot slipped upon the blood-soaked sod, and he fell prostrate. His savage foe, with raised tomahawk, was upon him. The young scout closed his eyes, expecting death. But the next moment the Indian lay gasping for breath, with Duke's keen fangs buried in his throat.

"Ugh! Duke him here at right time!" grunted Bright Wing, as he rammed home another charge.

The ends of the broken line swung into place — and still the battle raged.

The rain ceased to fall; the sky began to clear. Darkness gave place to dawn. The commander ordered a charge all along the lines. Inch by inch the savages gave way — in spite of the bravery of their chiefs, and the inspiration of Tenskwatawa's war-song. At last they could stand the cold steel of the bayonets no longer. They broke and fled. Down the slope and across the boggy prairie, toward their town, they hastened, carrying many of their dead and wounded with them. Victory had perched upon Harrison's banner; and the palefaces had won the battle of Tippecanoe.

The victorious troops pursued the fleeing savages, until the yielding surface of the wet prairie compelled the mounted riflemen to halt. Then the whole force returned to camp. The whites had lost one hundred and eighty in killed and wounded; the Indians, probably, had lost an equal number.

At sunrise squads of soldiers were engaged in burying the dead and carrying the wounded to the surgeon's quarters. Joe Farley was on the detail. At the southwestern angle of the camp, he came upon the body of a tall and lank militiaman. The man lay upon his side — a contorted, blood-stained heap. His head rested upon his arm, and his face was partially concealed. Supposing that the poor fellow was dead, Farley caught him by the shoulder, to turn him over. The dying man moaned feebly. Bending over him, Joe said tenderly:

"I didn't mean to be rough, friend, I thought you was — was — are you hurt bad?"

The blue lips moved — and these words were breathed into Farley's face:

> "I left my children in ol' Kaintuck,
> In the cabin with the'r mother;
> And now the'r pap has got his death —
> An' they'll — never git — an-oth-er!"

The faint voice ended in a whispering quaver. Joe sprang erect, his limbs trembling, his face as white as chalk.

"Poor critter!" he murmured, pityingly. "He's dyin'; but he's still thinkin' of his wife an' children. Poor little woman — an' poor little boys an' gals — down in ol' Kaintuck! You'll never git another husband an' father, that's a fact; not one that 'll think as much of you, anyhow. His words has come true. He must 'ave had a prem'nition o' what was in store fer him. Ding-it-all-to-dangna-

7

tion! I'm sorry fer him — poor feller! An' I wish I hadn't growled so much 'bout his caterwaulin'— I do, by Katherine! But I thought he was jest foolin'— I didn't know he was pourin' out his soul in singin'.''

Joe broke off suddenly and dashed the tears from his eyes. The dying Kentuckian gave one expiring groan — and passed over the dark river. The woodman stood silently looking down at the lump of senseless clay for several minutes. Then he turned and strode away, muttering:

"I don't like this buryin' business, nohow. It makes me down in the mouth. It's worse 'n drivin' oxen, by a long shot. Poor little boys an' gals down in ol' Kaintuck! They ain't got no pap now — they'll never be rocked to sleep in his arms no more.''

He stopped and shook his head sadly, reflectively.

"Where Fleet Foot and Duke?''

Farley glanced up and beheld Bright Wing at his side.

"Ross an' the bloodhoun'?'' he inquired.

"Ugh!''

"I don't know. But where you find one of 'em you'll find t'other, most likely. I hain't set eyes on the dog sence last night, but I saw his master this mornin'— jest after the Injins broke an' run. You'll find 'em both 'round the camp somewheres.''

"Me look — no find,'' answered the Wyandot with a positive shake of the head.

"Well," Joe returned dryly, "I wouldn't lose no sleep 'bout 'em, Injin, if I was you. They're able to take keer o' the'rselves."

"Me look much long time — no find dog — no find master," the Indian persisted.

"That so?" Joe replied — a shade of uneasiness in his tone. "Well, you've got nothin' else to do — so go *on* huntin'. When I git through with this bloody business o' helpin' to take keer o' the dead an' wounded, I'll take a look 'round with you. By the way, I'm gittin' most pow'rful hungry. But a feller told me a little bit ago the beef an' meal was all gone, an' some of us 'ld have to eat hoss flesh fer our breakfast. Fer my part, I ain't a *hankerin'*. I can go purty nigh anything, but I draw the line at hoss-steaks. It's a sight worse 'n havin' a lot o' women in love with you. W'y, Injin, one time so many female genders got in love with me, I——"

The voluble fellow stopped speaking and looked around. The Wyandot had disappeared.

"By my gran'mother's ear-trumpet!" muttered Joe. "That redskin comes an' goes like a shadder. S'pose he didn't like my talk 'bout women-folks. He must 'ave some ol' love affair ranklin' in his gizzard. I'm mighty awful hungry, I swan. Well, if I can't eat, I can smoke."

And filling and lighting his pipe, he hurried away to procure help in removing the body of the Kentuckian to the place of burial.

After a scant breakfast. the soldiers busied themselves about the camp, righting overturned vehicles, securing stampeded animals, interring the dead, and throwing up a ring of fortifications. Governor Harrison deemed the latter proceeding a necessary precaution. He thought the savages might renew the battle as soon as darkness came again.

The day passed. Night came — a night of feverish expectancy and unrest to the exhausted soldiers. Joe Farley and Bright Wing did not sleep, but sat by the fire all night long, starting at every unusual sound and longing for morning. All the afternoon they had searched for Ross Douglas and his dog, but had found no trace of either. It was the opinion of all to whom they spoke, that the rash young scout had ventured too far in pursuit of the savages and had been killed or captured.

Dawn came at last. After breakfast, General Wells took the dragoons and mounted riflemen and went to reconnoiter the Prophet's Town. Farley and Bright Wing obtained permission to accompany the detachment.

The general found the place deserted. But one inhabitant remained within its walls — a chief with a broken leg. The whites dressed his wound and made other provision for him, and told him to say to his people that if they would desert the standard of the Prophet and return to their own tribes, they would be forgiven.

The troops found a large quantity of corn, which was very acceptable; also some hogs and domestic fowls. These they removed to their camp.

The savages had fled precipitately, leaving many of their arms and household utensils behind them. A large number of the guns were yet wrapped in the coverings in which the British had imported them.

Farley and Bright Wing found no trace of their friend, until they were slowly and sadly returning to camp. Then, a hundred yards from the northeastern gate of the palisade, Joe picked up a silver button belonging to Douglas's hunting-shirt. He showed it to the Wyandot, who simply nodded meaningly and pointed in the direction in which the Prophet's followers had fled. On reaching camp, Farley carried the memento to Governor Harrison and remarked :

"Gov'nor, Ross Douglas has been missin' sence the battle. I picked up this button close to the Prophet's Town. Ross is a pris'ner 'mong the Injins, as sure's shootin'— him an' his dog, too."

"How did it happen?" cried Harrison.

"I don't know. But me and Bright Wing wants to foller the dang redskins an' try to rescue him ——"

"It's madness to think of such a thing," the governor interrupted. "You'll throw away your lives to no purpose."

"It don't make no differ'nce," Joe said doggedly. "Life ain't worth *much* to such poor scamps as me, at best — an' it won't be worth *nothin'* if Ross Douglas is tortured an' killed by the Injins. No, gov'nor, me an' Bright Wing's goin'

after him.   You'll give us leave to go — an' not
have us desert, won't you, gov'nor?"

Joe asked the question pleadingly, tears standing
in his pale, watery eyes.

"Yes, *go!*" Harrison said, grasping the woodman's calloused hand.   "I discharge you here and
now.   And may the Almighty's protecting power
accompany you!"

"Amen!   Thank you, gov'nor — an' good-by,"
Farley answered.

That afternoon Farley and Bright Wing shouldered their rifles and set out on the trail of the Indians.   The next day the army started upon the
return journey to Fort Harrison and Vincennes —
the wagons loaded with wounded soldiers.   The
campaign had been short, sharp, and effective.

CHAPTER V.

ON THAT fateful morning of the battle of Tippecanoe, Ross Douglas fought in the front ranks until the savages broke and fled. Then he joined in the hot pursuit. Duke kept close at his master's side, growling and baying viciously. In the charge Bright Wing got separated from his white comrade, and returned to camp. Ross impetuously pressed onward, keeping his eyes upon the flying foe and glancing neither to the right nor the left, until he found himself at the foot of the slope leading up to the Indian village. He looked around in surprise — he and the dog were alone. He beheld the troops — a dense, dusky mass — a half mile away.

"Cowards!" the young man muttered scornfully. "Why have they given up the pursuit? Now's the time to win a glorious victory and make a lasting peace. Fools! To come hundreds of miles to indulge in a mere skirmish. They should follow up their success, and annihilate the Prophet and his bloodthirsty band. If they stop at this, nothing will have been accomplished. But I may as well go back with the others. Ah! who's that? Bradford!"

It was indeed the scar-faced scout. At full speed he came running down the slope, gesticulating wildly. What could it mean? Ross had just reloaded his rifle. Now he rested his finger upon the sensitive trigger and wonderingly awaited the deserter's approach.

"Flee — flee for your life, Douglas!" Bradford shouted excitedly.

Duke, who had been trying to warn his preoccupied master of approaching danger, by a series of low hoarse growls, now began to bark furiously. Ross hastily glanced around him. He was almost surrounded by a party of Indians. They had been in hiding behind a clump of bushes near the foot of the incline, awaiting the chance to cut off the retreat of some venturesome white. The gray fog rising from the marshy prairie had helped to conceal them. While the unsuspecting Douglas had stood gazing at the walls of the town, his cunning enemies had risen from their hiding-place, and like silent specters glided out upon the soft prairie and thrown themselves in a semicircle around him. Now they yelled exultingly and began to close in.

Ross did not wait to see or hear more. Instantly he resolved to make a dash for liberty. "Come, Duke!" he cried; and with the fleetness of a deer sprang away, attempting to break through the line of his foes.

Bradford was at the bottom of the slope. "Hold!" he shouted frantically. "It's too late — you'll throw away your life!"

But Douglas did not heed the warning. He eluded the grasp of one of the Indians who barred

his way ; discharged his rifle full in the face of another ; struck down a third — and leaping over his
prostrate body, sped on. A half-score of guns
cracked simultaneously. But the bullets failed to
reach the moving mark ; and master and dog were
beyond the line of their enemies. They would
have distanced their pursuers and escaped, had not
an unforeseen accident occurred. Ross's foot became
entangled in a bunch of coarse, wet grass, and he
tripped and fell heavily. Ere he could rise his enemies were upon him.

Duke sprang at the throat of the foremost assail-
ant, and dog and brave fell to the ground. Over
and over they rolled — the hound striving to bury
his fangs in the Indian's throat, the savage attempting to sheath his knife in the animal's heart.

Douglas got upon his feet, clubbed his rifle, and
laid about him vigorously. But his foes overpowered him and pressed him to the earth. Seeing
which, Duke relinquished his hold upon the throat
of his prostrate adversary and flew to the aid of his
master. The dying warrior gasped, and attempted
to arise — blood spurting in crimson jets from his
lacerated arteries.

At the critical moment, Bradford rushed among
the braves, and flinging them right and left, thundered in the Indian tongue :

"Hold, you mad devils ! Would you overpower
and murder a man who has fought bravely for his
life ? Harm not a hair of his head, or your lives
shall pay the penalty. He is *my* prisoner."

Bending down, he assisted Douglas to arise. As soon as he could speak, the young man called to the bloodhound :

"Here, Duke !   Down — down, I say !"

The obedient animal left the savage with whom he was struggling, and crouched at his master's feet — panting, whining, and rolling his blood-rimmed eyes. The Indians drew apart a short distance, grunting and grumbling in a surly and threatening manner. For a full minute the two white men stood looking at each other. Douglas's chest was still heaving from his recent exertions; and his words came brokenly :

"You saved my life. I thank you for it ! But I'd rather you had left me to my fate."

"Why ?" Bradford asked coolly.

"Because I don't like to be under obligations to a traitor," Ross replied boldly.

The younger man expected to see the older's face pale with anger. But a smile actually rested upon Bradford's scarred visage, as he returned calmly :

"You're mistaken, my young friend. I'm no traitor. *You* are loyal to the Americans — *I* am loyal to the English."

"Then you are a spy in the employ of the British."

"Y-e-s. Or an agent to look after their interests among the Indians, rather."

"I despise you none the less," Ross cried.

Bradford continued to smile as he said :

"You are young — therefore you are indiscreet.

I have saved your life ; I would be your friend. But if you don't desire my friendship, I can turn you over to the tender mercies of those red fiends, who are hungering to tear you limb from limb. Even now they are grumbling about my interference. I may lose my life for my temerity. You're ungrateful.''

"If you regret your act of mercy and fear for your own safety," Douglas sneered. "call your savage hounds and tell them to do their worst. I can die fighting.''

"I don't regret what I have done," Bradford returned huskily, a shade of sadness in his voice, "nor do I fear for my own safety. I don't value life — I don't fear death. And I'll save you or perish with you. But you must listen to reason ; you must do my bidding. Just at present I have great influence with the Indians. I'll exert it to the utmost in your behalf. But you and your vicious dog have sorely punished your assailants. Two warriors are dead and several others are wounded. Their comrades thirst for revenge. Hist ! Here they come. Say not a word — leave it all to me.''

A stalwart Indian came forward and grunted surlily :

"The paleface's arm is strong — his aim is sure ; the fangs of his dog are long and sharp. Two braves are sleeping with their fathers ; and three others are binding up their wounds. The paleface and his dog must die.''

" No, he shall *not* die, chief," Bradford cried angrily. " He fought for life and liberty. You assailed him twenty to one. I rescued him — he is my prisoner. I shall take him to the village with me."

" He is *not* Scar Face's prisoner," the chief returned fiercely, laying his hand upon his tomahawk — while his warriors crowded around him, muttering threateningly.

" Tenskwatawa shall decide," Bradford answered coolly.

" Tenskwatawa is a squaw ! He promised us victory ; we met defeat."

"Say that to Tenskwatawa, and he will cast a spell upon you."

A grayish pallor overspread the chief's dusky visage. His eyes dilated and his jaw dropped. Bradford quickly followed up the advantage he had gained. Leaning forward, he whispered in the Indian's ear :

" Shall I repeat your words to the Prophet ? "

Abject terror took possession of the chief. He trembled, and gasped for breath. His warriors uttered startled grunts and drew away. Bradford continued sternly :

" Then, take your braves and be off to the village. I will follow with the prisoner."

Without a word in reply, the savages obeyed the order. Bradford waited until they had disappeared within the walls. Then turning to Douglas, he said :

"Come—you must accompany me."

"We're alone," Ross answered quietly; "you can't compel me to go with you."

"*My* gun is loaded—*your's* is empty," was the significant reply.

"True—but you wouldn't shoot me."

Bradford started.

"What makes you think that?" he asked quickly.

"I don't know. But you wouldn't."

"No, I wouldn't injure you—even if you left me to my fate."

"Your fate? I don't understand you."

"If you leave me to return to the village alone, I shall meet death at the hands of the savages. They'll kill me for breaking faith with them."

"Then go with me to the camp of the whites——"

"And be shot as a *spy!*" Bradford completed.

"True!" Douglas said slowly and impressively. "Bradford, you *are* a British spy—an enemy of my country. I hate you—I despise you!"—The older man turned pale to the lips, but did not interrupt his companion.—"But you have befriended me; and I'll not be guilty of the sin of ingratitude. You shan't sacrifice your life for my liberty. Take my arms. I'm your prisoner."

"Keep your arms," Bradford returned hoarsely, his chest heaving, his white lips twitching. "Reload your gun. We may have to fight shoulder to shoulder. Let's be prepared to sell our lives dearly."

Silently Ross reloaded and primed his rifle. Then he said simply :

" I'm ready."

" Come," was the gruff response.

Side by side, the two men ascended the slope and entered the unguarded gateway of the palisade. Duke accompanied them. An extraordinary spectacle met their gaze. Hundreds of armed warriors — Shawnees, Winnebagoes, Miamis, Wyandots, and others — were swarming promiscuously about. Squaws and children bearing bags and bundles hurried hither and thither. All was bustle and confusion. The whole resembled a hive of angry bees into which some venturesome youngster had thrust a stick.

" What's the meaning of all this ? " Ross inquired of his companion.

" They are preparing to abandon the town," was the reply.

" Shall we go with them ? "

" If we're alive at the time — yes."

They elbowed their way through the throng, attracting no little attention.

" Scar Face," muttered a Winnebago, as they passed.

" Fleet Foot," grunted a Wyandot.

" Does he mean you ? " asked Bradford turning to his companion.

" Yes."

" You merit the name. Does the Wyandot warrior know you ? "

"Undoubtedly. I've traded among the members of the tribe, for years."

"Do you speak their language?"

"I speak several Indian tongues."

"So much the better. Our mutual knowledge may be of value to us."

They were conversing in low tones, all the while proceeding in the direction of the council-lodge.

"And they call you Scar Face," Douglas carelessly remarked.

"Yes," answered his companion, in a tone of intense bitterness — the red scar upon his cheek blazing like a beacon light of danger.

Ross instantly realized his mistake, and hastened to say :

"I didn't mean to hurt your feelings. I wouldn't do that needlessly, though I look upon you as an enemy."

"I fully understand your feeling toward me," Bradford replied, his features working. "It's unnecessary for you to explain."

Douglas was surprised. Who was this strange man, to whom he owed his life and for whom he felt such antipathy — and who appeared determined to be his friend? To relieve his embarrassment, the younger man asked :

"Have you spent much of your life among the Indians?"

"Half of it," was the curt reply.

By this time they were nearing the entrance of the council lodge ; and Bradford continued :

"There—we have safely run the gauntlet of scowling looks and threatening gestures. I feared we should not get through so easily. Now we'll have an interview with Tenskwatawa. Oh! there he is."

In front of the council lodge stood the Prophet. He was alone. His head was bowed; his chin, buried in the folds of his buffalo-robe. He was a bronze statue of gloom — the personification of utter dejection.

"Come," whispered Bradford to Douglas. "Let's hurry to him while he's alone. Our safety depends upon our winning him to our side."

Ross hesitated and drew back.

"Don't be a fool!" Bradford hissed. "This is no time for squeamish notions of independence."

"But I hate him!" Douglas panted. "I would *kill* him!"

"Nevertheless," was the unmoved reply, "he holds the winning cards, at present. Our lives are in his hands. No doubt the chief and his warriors have been to him. Come — and leave everything to me."

At that moment Tenskwatawa lifted his head and fixed his one eye upon them. A malicious smile flickered about the corners of his sensual mouth — and was gone. Again he was a graven image.

Bradford was about to speak, when a gigantic Indian accompanied by a score of warriors unceremoniously elbowed him aside and stopped before the Prophet. The newcomer was Winnemac, the great

Pottawatomie chief. His hands were clenched; his features, black with rage. The Prophet kept his gaze fixed upon the ground and gave no heed to the angry chief's presence.

"Tenskwatawa is a Shawnee squaw!" Winnemac thundered.

"He promised us success; we received defeat. He said the palefaces were crazy; but they were in their senses, and fought like devils. He told us that we should rejoice over the destruction of the White Chief's army; we mourn for our young men slain. He assured us that we should not taste death; we feasted upon it. Tecumseh is a brave warrior; Tenskwatawa is a squaw! See, braves! I spit upon him and slap his face!"

And suiting the action to the words, the enraged chief spat upon the Prophet and dealt him a resounding slap upon the cheek.

The assembled warriors yelled in derision. Scores of others, attracted by the uproar, came running to the spot. Bradford and Douglas found themselves in the center of a mob of hooting, gesticulating demons, ready to wreak their rage upon any object that offered. The two white men looked anxiously about them, but saw no way of escape.

Tenskwatawa did not resent Winnemac's insult. Instead, he lifted his hand to command silence; and, as soon as he could make himself heard, began meekly:

"Tenskwatawa is no warrior — he is the Prophet of the Great Spirit. Tenskwatawa is no squaw,

8

though he has borne the burdens of his people for many moons. The Great Spirit promised Tenskwatawa the victory, and he gave the message to his children. The Great Spirit did not lie——''

''Tenskwatawa lied!'' Winnemac shouted fiercely.

Unheeding the interruption, the Prophet continued :

''The Great Spirit made no mistake ; but Tenskwatawa blundered. He parted with his sign—his power. He gave it to the noble Winnemac, that he might lead his warriors to victory. Tenskwatawa robbed himself of his power—he was helpless. The noble Winnemac could make no use of the sign—he knew not the secret of its power. The battle was lost. Tenskwatawa blundered.''

Grunts of approval followed this apparently frank confession. Seeing which, Winnemac cried sneeringly :

''Tenskwatawa lost his power—and it is gone forever. He is a babbling papoose !''

''Return to him his sign, and he will show the noble Winnemac that he is mistaken,'' the Prophet returned quietly.

''Take it !'' sneered Winnemac, drawing the ring from his finger and contemptuously flinging it at the feet of its owner.

Tenskwatawa secured the talisman and restored it to its accustomed place upon his right hand. Instantly a remarkable change took place in his aspect and demeanor. No longer was he a humble suppliant begging pardon for past mistakes. He proudly drew himself erect, his lips curling scornfully. The pupil of his eye contracted. The ring upon his finger scintillated in the rays of the morning sun. With a sinuous, snakelike movement, he glided to Winnemac's side ; and suddenly pushing the sparkling jewel before the startled chief's eyes, hissed :

"The sign — the power ! Look — look ! you cannot take your eyes from it !"

Winnemac's features froze — became rigid, expressionless. His eyeballs bulged from their sockets and remained fixed. The Prophet slowly waved his hand to and fro. The Pottawatomie's head turned from side to side — his gaze followed the movements of the talisman. Faster and faster the Prophet's hand flew. Then, of a sudden, he leaned forward and whispered in the chief's ear :

"You are drowsy. Sleep — sleep ! Your limbs are heavy — feeble. Sleep — sleep !"

Winnemac's eyelids dropped ; his frozen features thawed. He trembled, swayed — and sank upon the ground, a senseless clod. Tenskwatawa pointed his finger at the sleeping warrior and shouted triumphantly :

"Look, children ! Look upon the valiant Winnemac. He doubted my power, he spat upon me and defied me. See ! he lies helpless at my feet. The Great Spirit willed it — and he sleeps. Awaken him, if you can. You cannot. The loudest thunder would not rouse him ; the keenest torture would not cause him to stir. Thus will he sleep forever, unless the Great Spirit, through me, wills that he awake."

The assembled braves pressed forward and craned their necks, to gaze upon their vanquished chieftain. One look was sufficient. To their untutored minds, a miracle had been wrought. They surged backward — silent, awestruck.

"Listen!" screamed the Prophet, his countenance purple with rage and excitement. "My children, you have scoffed at my power. Shall I do with you as I have done with the great Winnemac? Shall I cast a spell upon you — shall I cause you to sleep forever?"

Again he lifted his hand and flashed the glittering gem before their eyes, his head swaying from side to side in a serpentine manner. Shrieks and groans of terror arose from the assembled warriors. Some prostrated themselves to the earth and pled for mercy; others fled from the scene — craven fear depicted upon their faces.

"What's the meaning of it all?" Douglas inquired in a low tone, of his companion. "Is it a clever play — for our benefit?"

"No," answered Bradford with a positive shake of the head. "Tenskwatawa possesses some wonderful power. I don't know what it is — but I've felt it."

"And couldn't you resist it?"

"*I* could — yes. But *many* can't — as you have witnessed. Hush — he is speaking."

The Prophet was saying :

"Arise, my children. The Great Spirit forgives you — *I* pardon you. Have no fear ; no harm shall befall you. Go and prepare for your journey. We must leave this sacred spot ; the white man's presence has defiled it. But the Great Spirit will go with us. He has promised. At another time, He will give us the victory over our enemies. The noble Winnemac shall sleep no longer. See !"

Tenskwatawa, clapping his hands thrice in quick succession, cried sharply :

"Winnemac, awake — arise !"

The Pottawatomie suddenly opened his eyes ; and, springing to his feet, gazed wildly around him, a bewildered expression upon his face. Little by little he recovered his scattered faculties and remembered where he was and what had happened. A horrified look settled on his countenance, as his eyes rested upon the Prophet. He shivered like one with an ague ; and his teeth chattered.

"The bold and warlike Winnemac has been asleep in the early morning," Tenskwatawa remarked sneeringly.

"Ugh !" was the guttural reply.

Drawing his blanket over his head to hide his face, the Pottawatomie turned and staggered from the spot. The assembled warriors quickly followed him, leaving the two white men alone with the Prophet.

"Again I have witnessed the power of Tenskwatawa," Bradford said, smiling and extending his hand toward the red hypnotist. "Surely he speaks with the Great Spirit."

Evidently the Prophet understood the flatterer's purpose; for, ignoring the extended hand, he answered sternly:

"Yes; Tenskwatawa speaks with the Great Spirit. And the Great Spirit informs him that the young man at Scar Face's side must die."

Bradford was not disconcerted. He returned coolly:

"Is Tenskwatawa sure he heard the Great Spirit's words aright?"

"Tenskwatawa heard aright," was the haughty reply. "The young paleface is of the Seventeen Fires. He is an enemy of the redmen. To-day he fought against them, slaying two and wounding three. The Great Spirit says he shall suffer death by torture."

" Did the Great Spirit inform Tenskwatawa that this young man — Fleet Foot — is my friend?"

"No. But is not Scar Face the friend of the redmen?"

"He is."

"Then how can an enemy of the redmen be the friend of Scar Face?"

"Fleet Foot fought only to save his life. He was attacked by twenty braves. I ran to his rescue. I saved his life and brought him here. He is my prisoner. Let Tenskwatawa enter the council lodge and again talk with the Great Spirit."

"Tenskwatawa has no need to talk further with the Great Spirit nor with Scar Face," the Prophet muttered in a decided tone. "The young paleface is of the Seventeen Fires; he fought with the great White Chief — he must die."

"If Fleet Foot meets death at the hands of the redmen, I meet death with him," Bradford said firmly.

An evil smile flickered around the corners of Tenskwatawa's wide mouth, as he replied menacingly :

"If Scar Face be so anxious to meet death, he has not far to go. I will call my children and give him and Fleet Foot as toys, into their hands."

The Prophet opened his lips, to carry his threat into execution. As though understanding the import of what had been said, Duke raised his bristles and growled hoarsely. Startled by the sound, the Prophet recoiled a step. Taking advantage of his unguarded attitude, Bradford dropped his gun, and leaping forward, caught the Shawnee around the body and carried him into the council lodge. Douglas and Duke quickly followed.

Setting the red hypnotist in the center of the bare floor, Bradford panted fiercely :

"You infernal impostor and scoundrel! Your uncanny power has no influence over me. I am no superstitious Winnemac. You would give Fleet Foot and me into the hands of your red fiends, eh? Well, you shall die first!"

Bradford spoke in the Shawnee tongue ; and the

Prophet understood every word. The boastful braggart cowered and trembled. Cowardice was written in every lineament of his features. A sickly pallor overspread his face. He could not articulate a sound. He fearfully rolled his eyes from side to side. But no chance of escape offered —no attendants were at hand.

Turning to his companion, Bradford asked hurriedly :

" You brought my gun in with you?"

Ross nodded.

"Well, see that both pieces are in order. I'll kill this miscreant — then we'll make a running fight for it. It's all that is left us."

Tenskwatawa was shaking like one with senile palsy. Bradford drew his knife and swiftly advanced upon him. The base wretch dropped upon his knees and supplicatingly raised his hands. He tried to speak ; but naught save the chatter of his teeth broke the stillness of the big, dark room.

" Die, treacherous devil !" Bradford hissed as he raised his arm to strike.

" Mercy !" Tenskwatawa managed to gasp.

" Mercy !" sneered Scar Face, still holding the knife aloft. " Dare you beg for mercy? What mercy have *you* ever shown? You condemn my friend and me to death — yet ask me to show mercy to *you!*"

" Mercy !" the craven lips whispered. " Scar Face and his friend shall go free ; my children shall not harm them."

A husky laugh gurgled in Bradford's throat, as he answered :

"You are a fool — you think to deceive me. As soon as we are out of your presence, you will call your red hounds and set them upon us. No! I cannot trust you — your hour has come. Prepare to meet the Great Spirit whose name you have defamed. You are a treacherous cur — and you shall die!"

"Have I ever deceived you, Scar Face?" the Prophet asked tremulously, in his terror dropping the figurative form of speech to which he was addicted, and speaking in the first person.

"N-o," Bradford admitted.

"Nor am I deceiving you now," the kneeling savage hastened to say. "You and your friend shall go free — none shall molest you. You shall come and go at your pleasure. I was mad to threaten you ——"

"Indeed, you were!" Bradford interrupted, dropping his arm, but still retaining a firm hold upon his knife. "Now, Tenskwatawa, if you have come to your senses, arise and give heed to what I say. This is the second time you have pitted yourself against me — and both times you have been worsted. The next time I shall not bandy words with you. Do you understand my meaning?"

The Prophet, who had arisen to his feet, nodded meekly.

"Very well," Scar Face continued, "you are desirous of wresting your lands from the grasping

Americans. The British are your allies. They have furnished your children with arms, ammunition, and clothing. I am their agent. Do you wish me to return to my people and tell them you sought to take my life?''

Tenskwatawa sullenly but emphatically shook his head.

Bradford proceeded : '' Had you caused my death, my people would have learned the fact. They would have withdrawn their help, and avenged my murder. You know I speak the truth. You were mad to harbor the thought of opposing my will. Your brother — the great and warlike Tecumseh — is my friend. What would he have said to you?''

The Prophet shivered and was silent. Bradford hastened to conclude :

''Let us have a final understanding, then. This young man is my friend ——''

'' Hold !'' testily interrupted Douglas, who had been chafing under the oft-repeated assertion. ''I'll not admit that I'm your friend, to save my life, even.''

Tenskwatawa uttered a grunt of surprise. But Scar Face resumed placidly :

''He *is* my friend, although he denies it. But he is an American ; and as an American, is the enemy of the redmen and their allies, the English. This morning he fought against us ; he would fight against us again. Therefore we shall keep him prisoner. But he must receive neither insult nor injury at our hands. Tenskwatawa, you have made two mistakes within the last twenty-four hours. You must not forget your promise to me — and thereby make another."

"Tenskwatawa will not forget his promise," the Prophet answered humbly.

Bradford approached the Indian and whispered a few words in his ear. The latter nodded and glanced toward Douglas. Then the two white men and the dog withdrew from the lodge. When they were out of sight and hearing, the Prophet stamped the earth and tore his hair, in a frenzy of impotent rage.

On reaching the open air, Bradford turned to his companion and said briskly :

"Wait for me here. I'll be gone but a few minutes."

And without tarrying for an answer, he disappeared around the corner of the building. On his return he remarked :

"Well, we have escaped from our difficulty. It was a bold plan that I followed — but the only one ; and it succeeded admirably. But Tenskwatawa is a weak and treacherous villain, and will bear close watching. His success in overpowering Winnemac made him reckless — mad."

"Do you think he'll keep his promise?" Ross asked.

"Yes."

"Then you are safe ; and I'll return to the army."

"But you can't," Bradford answered smilingly.

"Why?"

"Because you are my prisoner."

Douglas's anger arose; and he answered hotly:

"Your prisoner! Hiram Bradford, you saved my life. Then I accompanied you here, that the vengeance of the savages might not fall upon you — that you might not suffer for my escape. You have cowed the Prophet — you are safe. I'm going back to my friends."

"Again I say — you *cannot.*"

"And again *I* say — why?"

"Because you are my prisoner and must accompany me whither I'm going. I have just given the order that you be closely watched. Escape is impossible. Give me your promise that you'll not attempt it."

"I'll do nothing of the kind," Douglas cried angrily. "Do you imagine for a moment I'll submit to your high-handed proceeding? Do you think I'll remain a captive when the way of escape lies open?"

"There *is* no way of escape, my boy," was the cool reply. "You'll gracefully submit to the inevitable."

"Why have you done this thing?" demanded Douglas, almost choking with fury.

"I?" returned Bradford with lifted brows. "I have done nothing but save your life and look after your safety. Your temerity led you into the lion's jaws. They snapped shut — and you are a pris-

oner. And a prisoner you must remain for the
present. If I permit you to return to your people,
I endanger myself. Besides, you heard me promise
Tenskwatawa that I would hold you captive, to
keep you from fighting against the British and Indians, in the war that is surely coming. Then, I
have other reasons for desiring to keep you with
me — reasons I don't care to divulge at present.
Come, be reasonable! We shall be the best of
friends yet. I — I have learned to like you, although you persist in saying that you hate me
—— "

"Hate you!" Ross broke forth. "Hiram Bradford, I despise you — I *loathe* you! You shall pay
for this. Here, you are surrounded by hundreds of
murderous savages ready to do your bidding — and
I'm helpless. But I have friends who will follow
and rescue me. Some day I shall meet you alone.
Then I'll plunge my knife into your black heart
— and rid the world of a villain!"

"No — no! You don't mean what you say —
you cannot!" gasped Bradford, his disfigured face
as pale as death and his lips quivering.

But Ross made no reply. Tossed by a tempest
of rage, he whirled and strode away to a distant
part of the inclosure. Bradford silently watched
the young man until he disappeared among the
groups of savages. Then the older man sunk his
chin upon his breast and groaned bitterly:

"He hates me — despises me! God! How
great is my punishment! I love him; I would

gladly shed my last drop of blood for him.   And
he loathes me — would murder me !''

A few minutes later, he was his cool, collected
self ; and was moving from place to place, searching for Douglas.

CHAPTER VI.

IT WAS the middle of the forenoon. Ross Douglas stood at one of the openings in the palisade, moodily watching the stream of savages filing through the gateway and setting out upon their journey toward Wildcat Creek, twenty miles away. The sun was bright; the air was light and warm. But Ross's heart was cold and heavy. His emotions were at war. He condemned the impetuosity that had led him into such a trap, and pronounced himself a fool. He cursed the cowardice of the soldiers who had neglected to follow up their advantage, and had left him to fall into the hands of the Indians. And he gritted his teeth when he thought of Bradford, who — as he thought — had meanly deceived and tricked him. Then his thoughts reverted to Franklinton and Amy Larkin — and he groaned aloud.

"Let's be moving; we have a long tramp before us."

He glanced up and encountered the gaze of Bradford.

"What's our destination?" Ross inquired stiffly.

"We are going to camp on Wildcat Creek, twenty miles from here," Bradford returned pleasantly.

"Shall we cover the whole distance to-day?"

"Certainly."

"It's a long jaunt."

"Do you consider it so?" in evident surprise.

"Yes; it's a longer walk than I feel inclined to undertake."

"Aren't you used to long journeys afoot?"

"Yes; but I'm not accustomed to making them against my will."

"Oh" — and the older man smiled. "Perhaps you'd prefer to ride."

"I'm no horseman."

"I can easily overcome that difficulty."

"How?"

"I can have you tied on the animal's back," was the frigid reply.

Douglas remained silent; he was too angry to speak.

"Come, now," Bradford said coaxingly. "There's no use in kicking against fate. You're going with me — willingly or unwillingly. I would be your friend. Don't force me to deal harshly with you. You hate me, I know. But I have your good at heart, and I'm your friend, in spite of appearances — in spite of all you may say or think."

Tears were in the speaker's eyes, and his voice was trembling. Ross looked at him wonderingly. For a half minute both were silent. Then the younger man said quietly:

"I'm ready."

Side by side, the two dropped into the moving line and passed through the gateway.

For an hour they walked onward over the uneven ground, neither speaking. Squads of savages were on all sides of them, all bearing in a southeasterly direction. Some were mounted, some were afoot. All were in a panic to escape from the vicinity of Harrison's army. Squaws and children bent and groaned under their burdens, as they stumbled along; but the haughty warriors, bearing their arms only, scorned to offer them assistance.

Another hour passed. The sun had almost reached the zenith. The way was growing rougher, but with dogged persistence the rabble pressed forward.

All this time the silence between Douglas and his companion remained unbroken. Now the latter laid his hand upon the former's arm and said:

"You have had nothing to eat to-day?"

"Nothing."

"I have some dried-beef. Will you share it with me?"

"Gladly."

They drew out of the line, and seated themselves by the side of a small stream. Bradford produced a quantity of dried-beef and a horn drinking-cup from the pouch that hung at his side. Silently they ate of the food and drank of the water from the brook. Duke seated himself upon his haunches and begged for his share. Ross patted the hound's

9

head and tossed him several strips of the cured flesh.   Seeing which Bradford remarked :

"You'd better eat that meat yourself or save it for another meal.   The Indians, in their haste, have left behind nearly all their supplies.   There's not food enough among them to last twenty-four hours ; and the chance of procuring more isn't good.   Don't you see how the braves are scowling at you as they pass?   When there's scarcity of food, the Indian eats sparingly ; his dog fasts."

"Yes, I know," Douglas returned as he dropped another piece of beef into Duke's capacious mouth. "I'm not unacquainted with their customs."

"And when famine threatens," Bradford pursued, "they kill and eat their dogs."

"I'm aware of the fact."

"Do you catch my meaning?"

"I do."

Neither again spoke for some moments.   Ross noted that some of the Indians that passed were munching parched corn and nibbling pieces of dried-beef.   Others had no food at all, apparently. They looked gaunt and haggard, but stoically plodded onward, without a murmur.

"Well, what do you think about it?" Bradford asked suddenly.

"About what?" was the quiet rejoinder.

"You know what I mean.   Shall I shoot the dog?"

"Of course not," Ross answered unmoved.

"You can step aside and ———"

"You're considerate of my feelings."

"Believe me, it's better so," Bradford went on earnestly.

"It takes a large quantity of food to appease the hunger of fifteen hundred human beings. The supply is meager. Scarcity is already here; absolute want will soon arrive."

"A flattering prospect you hold out to your guest," Ross remarked dryly.

"I'm telling you the truth, at any rate. By the way, how much better off would you be with Governor Harrison? I know that the supplies of the army were almost exhausted two days ago. By this time, the soldiers are feasting on horse-flesh."

"I should be a free man, at least," Douglas interrupted in a tone ot deep dejection.

Bradford sighed as he resumed :

"At this season of the year, game is scarce in this locality. If the worst comes, the savages will kill and eat all the horses and dogs in camp — your own surly brute included."

"Not until they have disposed of me," Ross answered, his eyes flashing, his nostrils dilated.

"That's just what I fear. The dog will get you into trouble. Let me put a bullet through his brain."

"The moment you do, I'll put one through yours," was the fierce reply. "Let me hear no more on the subject. That dog is one of the true and disinterested friends I'm fortunate enough to have. He'd give his life for me — I'd shed my blood for him."

Again Bradford sighed deeply; but he said no more. They arose, shouldered their guns, and resumed their toilsome march. Just as they dropped into the moving line of savages, Tenskwatawa, mounted upon a magnificent black horse,— a gift of the English government,— rode past them. At the side of the clean-limbed steed, trotted a nimble, sure-footed gray pony ; and seated upon its back was a young woman. The robe of rich furs that enveloped her person neatly concealed the fact that she rode astride. The hood of her cloak was thrown back, and a cataract of fine red-gold hair rippled down her shoulders. Her face was beautiful, her skin milk-white and satiny; and her eyes were the violet-blue of the midsummer skies. The rein she held in her small shapely hand was of braided horsehair, ornamented with shells and jingling coins ; and the housings of her plump palfrey were of crimson cloth, trimmed with a fringe of gold.

The Prophet sat stiffly erect in the saddle, looking neither to the right nor to the left ; but not so, his fair companion. Douglas and Bradford stepped aside to let the riders pass. As they did so, the prisoner glanced up and encountered the young woman's gaze fixed upon him. He could not remove his eyes from her face ; he did not try to do so. Boldly he stared at her until her lids dropped, her cheeks flamed, and the faintest hint of a smile parted her red lips, revealing a row of even, white teeth. Then she shyly peeped at him from under her long lashes ; and turning aside her face, rode on.

Ross was surprised ; excited. He stood staring after the lovely apparition — his lips apart, his chest heaving — until Bradford, touching him on the arm, said :

"What's the matter — have you seen a ghost ?"

"An angel, rather," Douglas replied so solemnly that his companion burst out laughing.

But the younger man did not join in the older's merriment. Instead, he asked impatiently :

"Who is she ?"

"An Indian squaw."

And Bradford continued to laugh as though greatly amused.

"Squaw !" Ross answered in a tone of deep disgust. "She's no squaw — not a half-breed, even. She's a vision of loveliness. If she be mortal, she's a pure Caucasian. Who is she ?"

"Tenskwatawa's daughter," replied Bradford, his bright eyes twinkling mischievously.

"The Prophet's daughter — bah !" was the scornful rejoinder. "Do you expect me to believe so transparent a falsehood ? Do you think me blind ? She's a Caucasian, I tell you. Her eyes, her complexion, her hair — all indicate the fact."

"You forget there are red-headed Indians," Bradford suggested.

"I forget nothing. I have seen red-haired savages. But their complexions were swarthy, their eyes black."

"And I've seen them fair, with blue eyes and auburn hair."

"They were of mixed blood, then," Douglas said positively.

"Possibly."

"Possibly! You know they were. No Indian, male or female, pure blood or cross-breed, could be as fair as this young woman. Her features, her manner, her every characteristic bespeaks the white blood in her veins and stamps her as a white woman. You're trying to deceive me. Now tell me. Who is she?"

"I have told you what Tenskwatawa says and what his tribe believes. Like you, he calls her an angel, and tells how the Great Spirit sent her to him."

Again Bradford was smiling, a peculiar, unfathomable smile.

"The lying impostor stole her somewhere," Ross answered earnestly.

His companion continued to smile, but said nothing.

"How long has she been among the savages?" the younger man pursued.

"Since her birth, perhaps. How should I know."

"But you *do* know."

Again the older man was silent.

"Why do you refuse to answer my questions?" Ross cried irritably.

Once more that peculiar, fleeting smile elevated

the corners of Bradford's mouth and accentuated
the puckered scar upon his cheek.

Swiftly the two strode forward, overtaking and
passing groups of stragglers, as they went. De-
scending into the river valley, they overhauled the
main body of savages ; and with them crossed the
stream. As they were toiling up the opposite slope,
Douglas turned to his companion and asked suddenly :

"What's her name?"

"The Indians call her La Violette," Bradford
answered, as he gave a hitch to the pouch at his
side and shifted his gun from one shoulder to the
other.

"Ah!" Ross ejaculated.

"What do you mean by that knowing exclamation?" the older man inquired sharply.

"Nothing ; only —— "

"Only what?"

"That's not an Indian name."

"No?"

"No, it's not. It's French."

"Indeed?"

"Yes."

"And it signifies?"

"You know its significance as well as I. La Violette means the violet."

"Well?"

"Her name confirms my belief. She's a white
woman."

"Ah!"

" Yes. The appellation refers to the color of her eyes."

" Do you think she's French ? "

" I don't know — but *you* do, Hiram Bradford. Some person familiar with the French language gave her the name. She's a prisoner — was kidnapped when a child, probably."

" What a keen observer and logician you are," Bradford chuckled dryly.

" I'm no blind fool, at any rate," Douglas retorted angrily.

Then in an injured, half-pleading tone :

" Why don't you tell me all you know of her ? "

" Why should I ? " laughed the other, huskily. " You're making your own observations and drawing your own conclusions. And no doubt your preconceived opinions would remain unshaken, no matter what I might say."

" I have formed my opinions from what you've told me and what I've seen."

" Is it possible you give credence to my words ? "

" Of course "— in a surprised tone. " Why not ? "

" I know of no reason except this : You hate me — consider me an enemy — and doubt my integrity."

Bradford said this in a voice thick with emotion. Ross stopped and stared hard at the speaker. He felt himself imperceptibly drawn toward the man. His heart was gradually softening — as wax in a warm hand. To relieve his embarrassment and conceal his feelings, he returned gruffly :

"But you have told me the truth in this instance?"

"So far as I've told you anything — yes. But why are you so interested in the Prophet's daughter? Are you so susceptible — are you already smitten — that you insist on throwing such a glamor of romance around her?"

"Nonsense!" Douglas exclaimed.

But his cheeks flushed; and he did not meet his companion's steady gaze.

"Have a care!" Bradford cried.— And Ross could not tell from his countenance, whether he meant his words in jest or in earnest.—"You must not set your affections there. The Prophet's angelic daughter cannot be for such as you—a despised paleface, a member of the Seventeen Fires. Tenskwatawa has placed her above all things earthly. His followers idolize her — worship her. She has as much influence with them, almost, as the Prophet or Tecumseh. Stern chiefs have sighed for her; young braves have died for her. Her smile is considered a benediction; her frown, a calamity. Her word is law. It is said she twists Tenskwatawa around her finger and holds Tecumseh under her thumb——"

"And you accuse me of throwing a glamor of romance around her," Ross smilingly interrupted.

Bradford laughed heartily and continued:

"At any rate, you'll do well to heed my warning. I don't want to see you cut into giblets, for daring to aspire to her heart and hand. Shun her

presence as you would shun a pestilence. Tenskwatawa's daughter is not for you."

Douglas, looking at the speaker, again encountered that inscrutable smile.

Both remained thoughtful and silent for some time
— all the while steadily plodding onward. The sun
declined toward the western horizon. The surface
of the country through which they were passing
was seamed with gullies and ravines. The trail
sprang from one, only to tumble headlong into another. Precipitous hills succeeded sloping eleva-
tions. The forest grew denser. Just as the sun
dropped into the brown billows of the prairie beyond
the Wabash and disappeared, the long line of weary
and hungry savages began to descend into the valley
of Wildcat Creek.

Here the trail was narrow and difficult. Douglas
and his companion were marching with the main
body of Indians — immediately behind Tenskwatawa and his daughter. The shadows gathered
around them ; the air grew chill. The sharp click
of a hoof upon a loose stone, or the guttural exclamation of a stumbling brave alone broke the silence.
Into Ross Douglas's mind came the thought to dart
into the bushes, that bordered the winding path, and
attempt to escape. Hurriedly he glanced around
him — impatiently he awaited a favorable opportunity.

"Don't think of such a thing," said Bradford's
husky voice in his ear.

Douglas started. Was it possible his companion

read his thoughts?   He returned in a tone of well-assumed surprise :

"Don't think of what?"

"You have it in mind to try to escape," was the quiet reply.   "Banish the thought — the attempt means death.   Don't you see the braves have drawn close around us and are watching your every movement?"

"Y-e-s," Ross hesitatingly admitted.   "At whose order has it been done?"

"Mine."

"I didn't hear you speak."

"It wasn't necessary — a sign was sufficient. No, you'd be taking a foolhardy risk to ——"

The sentence was cut short by a storm of shouts and exclamations coming from the head of the column, farther down the trail.   A pack-horse, stumbling, had fallen from the narrow path into a deep ravine.   The tumult raised by the savages frightened several others of the beasts of burden ; and they whirled and came flying back up the trail. These in turn stampeded others still — and the whole swept the narrow way like an avalanche.

Ross Douglas heard and understood all.   In the panic that was sure to ensue he saw a chance to escape.   To right and to left sprang the warriors.   Ross loosened the knife in his belt, firmly gripped his rifle, and was ready to dart away in the darkness.

"Quick !" shouted Bradford.   "Let's scramble up this bank.   Quick — or we shall be trampled to death !"

Grabbing Douglas by the arm, he sought to drag him in that direction. But the younger man held back. The thunderous roar of the galloping horses drew nearer. They turned a sharp bend in the road and loomed into view. In the gloom they resembled a rapidly approaching thundercloud. Tenskwatawa's black steed neighed wildly and, taking the bit in his teeth, whirled and dashed away. The gray pony crouched in its tracks and trembled. Douglas jerked loose from his companion's restraining grasp and leaped toward the brink of the ravine on the right, intending to drop into the depths. But at that moment La Violette's shrill scream of affright smote upon his ear. Abandoning all idea of escape, forgetting his own danger—everything, he threw down his gun and sprang to her assistance.

"My God!" groaned Bradford, staggering toward a place of safety. "Both will be killed! In my excitement I didn't think of *her*. Too late — too late!"

Reaching the bank on the left, he sank upon the ground and covered his face with his hands.

A bound brought Douglas to the young woman's side. It was the work of a moment, to snatch her from the saddle and bear her limp form up the slope. Relieved of its fair burden, the terrorized pony turned and fled up the trail, with the stampeding pack-horses snorting and panting behind it. As they labored up the steep grade, with their heavy packs still clinging tenaciously to them, their terror gradually subsided ; and near the top of the hill, the Indians surrounded and caught them.

When the stampede had thundered by, Bradford got upon his feet and stared wildly around. In the deep gloom he caught a dim outline of Douglas supporting the trembling form of La Violette. Running to them, he exclaimed in a voice faltering with emotion :

"Both of you are alive. But are you unharmed?"

"Unharmed and untouched," Ross replied calmly.

"Thank God!" was the fervent response.

The young woman lifted her head from Douglas's shoulder and, gently withdrawing from his embrace, said tremulously :

"I sincerely thank you for rescuing me from death. But I do not know you. Will you tell me to whom I owe my life?"

She spoke in excellent English, but with a slightly foreign accent. After a moment's silence, Ross answered :

"My name is Ross Douglas."

"You are an American?"

"I am."

"And a prisoner?"

"Yes."

Extending a small, warm hand — which Douglas quickly imprisoned in his broad palm — she remarked naïvely :

"You risked your life to rescue me from danger, although you are an enemy of my people. I will

not forget your valor.   I will do what I can to procure your release ——"

"Perhaps, La Violette, you are not aware that
your rescuer is *my* prisoner," Bradford interjected,
laughing.

Petulantly stamping her moccasined foot, she replied proudly:

"I neither know nor care *whose* prisoner he is.
He has saved me from a horrible death; I will befriend him."

Then hastily withdrawing her hand from Ross's
detaining clasp:

"But my father!   Where is he?"

"Have no fear for Tenskwatawa's safety," Bradford said in reassuring tones.   "His horse carried
him out of danger.   Ah! I hear the sound of hoofs.
He's returning."

The panic-stricken savages were resuming the
march.   Down the trail came a body of braves with
the runaway pack-horses.   At their head rode the
Prophet, leading his daughter's pony.

"La Violette!   La Violette!" he called wailingly.

"Here, father — here I am," she answered in a
clear, bird-like voice, as she descended to the trail.

Tenskwatawa sprang to the ground and, enfold-
ing her in his strong arms, murmured gutturally:

"The Great Spirit is very kind.   He spared your
life, my daughter."

"Yes, father," La Violette assented; "but the
young paleface carried me out of the way of danger."

"Who?" in a low, fierce tone.

"Fleet Foot," Bradford answered from the darkness.

"Ugh!" the Prophet grunted ungraciously.

Then he quickly lifted the young woman to her saddle; and, remounting his own steed, again set forward. Bradford and Douglas closely followed the two. The young scout had recovered his rifle, and was again watching for a chance to dart away in the darkness. But the Indians were close about — the risk was too great. He felt that in saving La Violette's life he had thrown away his one opportunity of regaining his freedom; and he tried to condemn himself for a sentimental fool. But when he essayed to shape the thought in his mind, the girl's fair face arose before him and rebuked him.

An hour after darkness had fallen, the Indians encamped upon the site of an old village. Several ramshackle huts were still standing. Two of these Tenskwatawa appropriated to his own and his daughter's use. Bradford seized upon a third for himself and his prisoner.

Soon huge fires were blazing along the banks of the stream, effectually dispelling the cold and darkness. The savages cooked a liberal part of the food they had; and — like true children of the forest — feasted upon it, nor asked how or whence more was to be obtained.

In the middle of the dirt floor of one of the cabins standing near the creek bank a fire burned brightly. The smoke escaped through a hole in the dilapidated bark roof.   On opposite sides of the pile of blazing faggots sat Bradford and Douglas.

" Are you sorry you didn't escape at the time of the stampede?" the former asked suddenly.

"Of course," returned the other, without looking up.   "Why do you ask?"

"Oh!" Bradford chuckled, " I thought perhaps the fact that you had formed the acquaintance of the charming La Violette — and had received her promise of aid — had reconciled you to captivity."

" It's unnecessary to make answer to such a nonsensical supposition," Ross replied pettishly.

Then after a moment's silence :

"How long do you mean to keep me prisoner?"

" Truly, I don't know."

" A few weeks? "

" Yes ; or months — or years."

" Humph!   Do you take me for a child?" Ross cried scornfully.

"Oh, no !" was the suave reply.

"Do you expect me to make no further effort to escape? "

"I trust you won't."

"Why?"

" Because it would be useless — dangerous."

"Useless !   What's to hinder me from stabbing you to the heart, at this very moment, and making my escape in the darkness? "

" Peep out at the door," Bradford returned coolly. "There's a better answer to your question than I can give you."

Ross acted upon his companion's suggestion, and beheld two stalwart braves standing guard, one on each side of the doorway. Returning to the fire, the young man flung himself upon the ground and maintained a moody silence.

"There — there!" the older man murmured kindly. "Don't take it to heart. I must be cruel to be kind. To-day I've allowed you to keep your arms, thinking you might need them to defend yourself against the defeated and maddened Indians. But that danger is past. And now I must ask you to give them up. Will you hand them over quietly or must I force you to give them up?"

"Why should I make useless resistance?" Douglas cried passionately. "You have me in your power — your red fiends stand ready to do your bidding. Take my arms. But, remember — you shall pay dearly for the indignities you are heaping upon me!"

Hiram Bradford sighed deeply as he arose and passed Ross's gun and knife through the door, to one of the guards outside. Then, rolling himself in his blanket and hugging his own rifle to his breast, he remarked:

"I'm going to try to sleep. You'd better follow my example."

Douglas made no reply. Duke curled up at his master's side, and lay blinking at the red coals. The fires gradually burned down; and slumber and silence fell upon the camp.

10

CHAPTER VII.

SEVERAL days passed. Ross Douglas's arms
were not restored to him. He was permitted
to wander about the camp at will; but he
noted that whenever he approached the confines of
the place, two or more armed and watchful warriors were always near him. Each night he was
closely guarded; each day he was constantly
watched. He evolved one plan of escape after another—only to cast them aside as impracticable.
He fumed and fretted—it did no good, however.
He was still a prisoner—and doomed to remain
such, so far as he could foresee.

Bradford remained cool, suave—but inflexible as
steel. He procured for his prisoner the best the
camp afforded; he granted him many privileges.
But all the while he maintained a rigid surveillance
over his every movement. Ross could not understand the man or his motives; nor could he ana-
lyze his own feelings toward him. One moment the
younger man enjoyed the older's company, and
chatted pleasantly with him; the next he hated
the sight of the scarred face, and was ready to leap
upon its possessor and tear him limb from limb.

La Violette kept to herself. When she left her
cabin she did not mingle with the savages. An

aged squaw was her attendant. More than once Ross saw her straying up and down the bank of the stream. But she took no notice of his presence; and he did not approach her. Yet at night he met her in the land of dreams, and held converse with her.

Soon the small quantity of food the Indians had brought with them from the Prophet's Town was exhausted. Absolute want prevailed. Hunting parties went out in all directions, but returned scantily laden with game. The Miamis left for more favorable hunting-grounds; the Winnebagoes departed for their northern homes. But the Shawnees, Pottawatomies, Delawares, and others remained. The gaunt wolf of famine was staring them in the face. Bradford's prediction came true. The savages began to kill and eat their dogs and horses. But Duke and his master still had cornbread and venison three times a day.

One morning Douglas, accompanied by the bloodhound, was walking about the camp. In front of Tenskwatawa's cabin he was met by a concourse of braves, in the midst of which stalked a tall and commanding figure.

"Tecumseh!" was the cry that rose on all sides. It was the redoubtable chieftain. Unheralded he had returned from his southern tour, to find his people defeated, discouraged, and in want. The work of years had been undone in an hour. Cohesion was lost, and the tribes were scattering. To the great warrior's mind, his brother's egotism and precipitancy were to blame for it all. He had just arrived. His handsome features were set and stern ; his black eyes, ablaze with anger.

Unheeding the joyful shouts that greeted him, he strode up to the Prophet's hut and unceremoniously kicked open the rickety door.

"Tenskwatawa, come forth !" he thundered.

A guttural exclamation, followed by the sound of shuffling footsteps, came from within. Then the Prophet, bowing and smiling, stood in the doorway.

"Welcome, my brother !" were his words of greeting.

Dashing aside the extended hand, Tecumseh cried angrily :

"How dare you bid me welcome to this poor place — you who have disobeyed my orders and defeated my purpose !"

Tenskwatawa scornfully curled his lip, as he replied :

"My brother, after a long absence, returns to his people. I bid him welcome and extend to him my hand. He rejects it — and, in answer to my greeting drops angry words. I fail to understand his meaning."

Tecumseh drew his magnificent figure to its full height and keenly eyed the speaker. His deep chest heaved spasmodically. The assembled warriors maintained a breathless silence. Instinctively they knew that a struggle for the mastery was on between the two Titans of the Shawnee tribe.

"You know well what I mean!" Tecumseh at last managed to articulate. "For years I have labored to bring about a union of the tribes. I have traveled far — I have sat by many council-fires. You offered me your advice and aid. I accepted both. I loved and trusted you. Together we accomplished much. A few months ago I went to visit our brothers of the land of flowers and sunshine. They have promised to join us in a war to recover our own. When I started on my journey, I cautioned you to do nothing that would excite the suspicions or arouse the animosities of the Seventeen Fires. You promised to follow my advice — to obey my orders. But scarcely were my footprints cold, ere you allowed our young men to go forth to pillage and murder. You had certain knowledge of this — yet you winked at it. The inevitable happened. I return to find my people defeated — humiliated. You, Tenskwatawa — you alone are to blame for all! Wag your deceitful tongue, and let our people know what excuse you can fashion!"

The Prophet's repulsive countenance was contorted with rage, as he burst forth:

"I have nothing to say to my children. I have explained all to them; and they are satisfied. But to you, Tecumseh, my brother, I have this to say: I have aided you; I have furthered your plans. You went away and left me to hold in check our restless young men. They refused to listen to my words. I could not control them. The palefaces

sent an army against us. I talked with the Great
Spirit. He promised me the victory. My children
went into the battle. They fought valiantly; but they
were overcome. Smarting with defeat, they heaped
reproaches upon me. They buffeted me and spit
upon me. I bore it all. I showed them my power
— I acknowledged my mistake. And all was well.
Now you come to abuse me. I have borne much —
I will bear no more!''

Scarcely had the Prophet concluded, when Tecumseh, beside himself with boiling fury, shouted:

''Yes, you *will* bear more — you will bear *this* at
my hands!''

Springing forward, he caught his brother by the
throat and choked him until his brutal face was
purple. The savages looked on in utter amazement; but no one offered to interfere. Tenskwatawa's tongue protruded. He gurgled and gasped
for breath. Douglas turned his back upon the sickening spectacle. As he did so, his eyes met those
of Bradford. In answer to the younger man's mute
appeal, the older sadly shook his head. Ross understood. Not a soul in the assemblage dared to brave
Tecumseh's mad rage.

Nevertheless, there was one in the camp who did
not stand in awe of the great chief. That person
was La Violette. From her cabin door she had
noted Tecumseh's arrival, had observed the meeting
of the two brothers, and had witnessed their wordy
encounter and its result. Now she appeared upon the
scene. The warriors saw her coming and respect-

fully stepped aside to let her pass. With the speed and grace of a fawn, she ran toward the spot where the Prophet was struggling in the iron grasp of his enraged brother. Her light feet appeared scarcely to touch the ground; her unconfined tresses streamed behind her; her violet eyes sparkled with excitement.

A small white hand was laid upon Tecumseh's arm, and an imperious young voice commanded:

"Hold, noble chief! Would you kill Tenskwatawa — the prophet of his people — my father!"

Like one suddenly recalled from a delirium, Tecumseh loosened his hold upon his brother's throat and staggered back a step. Slowly he lifted his eyes. They met those of La Violette — and he stood abashed before her.

The Prophet, released from the other's cruel grasp, sank upon the ground, shivering and moaning. The purplish hue forsook his face; a deathly pallor succeeded it. He attempted to arise, but his limbs refused to do his bidding. His lips trembled. He was overcome with fear.

La Violette looked upon the cowering wretch, and her face flushed scarlet. Her violet eyes snapped angrily. Shame — not pity — was in her voice, as she cried:

"Arise, father! You are not badly hurt. Here — let me help you."

Stooping, she assisted the craven to his feet. He stared helplessly around him — and could hardly stand. With the whispered words, — "Go and hide

your weakness!"—La Violette pushed him into the
cabin. Then boldly walking up to Tecumseh and
taking him by the arm, she said in a low tone:

"Is it thus that wise men settle their differences?
For shame! Follow Tenskwatawa — and come not
forth until you have a message of good cheer for
your disheartened people."

Tecumseh haughtily straightened his lithe form
and folded his arms upon his chest, as though about
to resent her cutting words. But again their eyes
met — and, bowing differentially, he stalked into
the hut, closing the door after him.

La Violette — like Tecumseh and Tenskwatawa
— had spoken in the Shawnee tongue; but Bradford and Douglas, standing near, had heard and
understood every word. Now she stepped in front
of the two white men and, addressing the older, demanded in English:

"Scar Face, why did you not interfere in Tenskwatawa's behalf?"

"I didn't dare," Bradford replied truthfully.

"Dare!"—tossing her head contemptuously—
"Are you not a man?"

"Yes; but——"

"But a coward?"

Bradford's face colored a dull red as he answered:

"La Violette, you know I'm no coward — whatever else I may be. But it would have been worse
than useless for me to interfere. I should have
incurred Tecumseh's lasting displeasure — and
accomplished nothing."

"Did *I* not accomplish something?" she cried
disdainfully. "And are you not stronger than I?"

"Stronger, yes," Bradford replied calmly. "In
your weakness lies your strength. Tecumseh and
Tenskwatawa grant you privileges they would
accord to no other. You can safely do and say
things for which another would be sentenced to
death!"

"Bah! You lack courage—you fear death!"
she retorted scornfully. "You are afraid of the
great Shawnee chief and his brother, the Prophet.
Yet you are the agent of the English—sent among
the tribes to counsel and guide them. Do you think
Tecumseh and Tenskwatawa have strengthened
their influence over their people, by quarreling before them—by making a spectacle of themselves?"

Bradford silently shook his head. Douglas
looked with wonder and awe upon the frail, beaut-
eous being before him. Her face was alight with
animation; her form quivering with restrained feeling. Ross had seen the influence she exerted
over the two crafty Shawnees. A sudden realiza-
tion of wherein lay the real strength of the Indian
confederacy flashed upon his mind; and he started
and changed color.

La Violette proceeded:

"Hiram Bradford, you are the agent of the British. You are here to look after their interests. Are
you fulfilling your mission when you allow the two
great organizers of the confederacy madly to tear
down all they have built? Look! Look at the braves

of the different tribes talking among themselves. Do you not know what it means? Winnemac is jealous of Tenskwatawa; Stone Eater covets Tecumseh's power and place; White Loon is ripe for revolt. The warriors are defeated, dispirited. They stand ready to join in open rebellion and follow a new leader — a new prophet. The edifice that Tecumseh and Tenskwatawa have built is tottering to its fall. The open quarrel between the two has further weakened its crumbling foundation. When Tecumseh arrived — but a few minutes ago — the braves greeted him with shouts of joy. Now all are sullen and silent. Listen! Some are whispering that Tecumseh is in the right; others are saying that Tenskwatawa cannot be in the wrong. But by far the greater number are declaring for a new leader — and a new prophet. Are you blind and deaf, Scar Face? Have not the English made common cause with the Indians? Tecumseh's overthrow — Tenskwatawa's downfall — mean ruin to the plans and projects of your people. Rouse yourself! There is work for you to do. All may yet be well; but the breach between Tecumseh and the Prophet must be closed. Will you come with me and help to do it?"

"Yes," Bradford answered meekly, an expression of great perplexity upon his scarred visage. "But what can I do?'

"Come. I will show you."

Taking him by the hand, she led him into the Prophet's hut.

Like one in a trance, Douglas stood staring at the closed door. He was dazed — thunderstruck.

"Am I mad or dreaming?" he muttered to himself. "Who is she — *what* is she? So young — so beautiful! I thought her a helpless captive; I find her the power behind the throne. All is mystery — chaos. Bradford's an impenetrable sphinx, but she — she's an inexplicable riddle. She's no ignorant savage; she's an intelligent, educated white woman. What then? She's not Tenskwatawa's daughter — that's plain. But who *is* she? What does she among the Indians? Bradford, even, bends to her will. She regards the savages as her people; she's hand and glove with the English. Evidently she hates all Americans. And she didn't deign to notice me" — with a sigh — "who saved her life. So graceful — so charming; but mystery of mysteries! She has forgotten her promise to me — ah!"

He cut short his whispered soliloquy and quickly glanced around him. In little groups and knots, the braves were talking and gesticulating. Down by the creek, half-naked children were paddling in the icy water and shouting and laughing. Three squaws, bearing bundles of fagots with which to replenish the camp-fires, passed the spot where the young man was standing. One of the trio — a bent and wrinkled hag — revealed her toothless gums, in a sardonic grin, and, pointing to Duke, cackled hoarsely, in the Delaware language:

"See! See the dog. He is big and fat. The sight of him makes my mouth water. What a stew he would make! Why has he not been killed?"

"Come on," chuckled one of her younger companions. "The dog belongs to Fleet Foot. Do you not see him standing there? I know him — he used to buy furs of my father. But he is Scar Face's prisoner now. Come on! To-night the dog will disappear from his master's side; and to-morrow we shall pick his bones. My husband told me. To-morrow we shall feast."

"And the paleface — Fleet Foot — should die, too," grumbled the third squaw. "He has a great appetite — he eats much. And there is no food to spare —— "

Then the three passed out of Ross's hearing. He smiled grimly as he whispered to himself:

"So they would kill Duke to *eat* — and kill me to keep me from *eating*. And that comely Delaware squaw remembers me. I wonder how many others in the camp know me — and how many would befriend me, if I should appeal to them. And I used to live among such beings; they were my associates, my friends. Bright Wing and a few others alone remain true to me. By the way, I wonder where that Wyandot and Joe Farley are. Are they grieving over my strange disappearance? How excited the savages are. I will act upon the idea that occurred to me a little while ago. Oh! to regain my liberty — to see Amy once again —— "

His soliloquy ended in a long-drawn sigh. Softly whistling to the hound, he set off toward the upper end of the camp. Apparently the Indians gave no heed to him, as he made his way among them. Soon he had left them behind and was at the eastern limit of the camp — and alone.

At this point a shallow ravine sloped into the creek from the south. Its bed was half-filled with logs and brush, and its sides were covered with a dense growth of tall bushes.

On reaching this natural barrier to his further progress, Douglas stopped and hurriedly cast a glance behind him. He was several hundred yards from the nearest group of savages. What was to hinder him from wriggling through the tangled growth that lined both sides of the ravine, gaining the open forest on the other side, and making his escape? The Indians, busy with their own affairs, would not notice his absence for some time — hours, perhaps. True, he had no arms with which to protect himself from wild men and wild beasts, or with which to procure game; but he could hide during the daytime, travel at night, and live upon bark and roots until he reached a settlement. He resolved to make the venture. Hope rose high in his breast. He whirled to take a final look at the camp. As he did so, his heart sank into his moccasins. Unperceived by him, three warriors had crept along under the shelter of the creek bank, and now stood a few yards from him, closely eyeing his movements and grinning broadly.

Mentally cursing his ill-luck, Ross turned to retrace his steps toward camp. At that moment Duke rubbed against his leg and whined softly.

"What is it, old fellow?" the master asked, stooping and patting the dog's head.

Again the hound whined plaintively, and rolled his great eyes toward the ravine a feet away.

"Something in there, eh?"

Duke wagged his tail and capered about. Ross's heart beat tumultuously.

"It must be a friend, then," he murmured tremulously. "If it were an enemy — man or beast — he'd growl. Can it be possible that Bright Wing or Joe ——"

"Hist!" was the faint whisper that came to the young man's ears and interrupted his cogitations.

Duke gave a short, sharp yelp of joy.

"Hist!" said the voice again in the softest whispered tone. "I see you, Ross Douglas — an' I see the redskins watchin' you. Me an' Bright Wing's hid in the brush here. Don't look 'round, fer God's sake! Do you hear an' understand me?"

Douglas slyly nodded.

"Well," continued Farley's voice, "listen to what I'm goin' to say. We've been hidin' 'round the camp fer three 'r four days. We've come to rescue you — but we can't do it this time; you're too close watched. Go back to camp an' never let on you've heerd anything. We hain't had a bite to eat fer twenty-four hours. We've got to move

away from here an' hunt somethin'. To-morrer
evenin' at dusk, stray out here ag'in. Bring a gun
an' ammynition with you, if you can. Come anyhow. We'll git you out o' y'r scrape 'r die a-tryin'
— we will, by Kizziar! Now go — an' tie up the
dog. He might come nosin' 'round an' spile everything. You hear all I say?"

Again Ross almost imperceptibly nodded.

"All right. Be off — the Injins is watchin' you
mighty close an' suspicious-like."

Dropping his chin upon his breast, the young
man walked toward camp, the bloodhound trotting
at his heels. The intelligent animal did not so
much as cast a look behind him. Shouldering their
guns, the three warriors brought up the rear.

On reaching the center of the camp, Douglas perceived the savages flocking toward the Prophet's
cabin. He followed them; and in front of the door
saw Tecumseh and his companions. The great
chief was addressing the multitude:

"My warriors and people, I returned from the
land of sunshine and flowers, to find you defeated
and scattered. In my anger, I heaped censure and
abuse upon one who was not to blame. I lost control of myself — I bow my head in shame as I
acknowledge it. Tenskwatawa has done well; no
one could have done better. *I* could not have done
better. He is your prophet. You know his power
— you trust him wisely. We have met with temporary defeat, but final success shall be ours."—
Lusty whoops and cheers.—"The tribes of the

north and west are steadfast; the tribes of the
south have promised to join us. The Seventeen
Fires shall feel our might. Our white brothers
across the big water will still aid us. We shall regain the land that is ours; we shall repossess the
graves of our fathers. In a few days we shall remove to the villages of the Miamis, upon the Mississinewa. There we will bide our time — await our
opportunity. It will not be long in coming. Hundreds of braves will join us. Their number will be
greater than the leaves of the forest. The Seventeen Fires will tremble at the tread of the brave
redmen and their English friends. Scar Face — "
and he laid his hand upon Bradford's shoulder
— "is your friend. He has advised and helped us
in the past; he will continue to do so. He will see
that our brothers across the big water send us
plenty of arms, ammunition, blankets, and food."—
Prolonged cheering and yells of delight.—"I have
done. Tenskwatawa, my brother, whom I love and
honor" — he affectionately placed his arm around
the Prophet's neck — "has something to tell you
that you will be glad to hear. Let him speak."

The grave and dignified chief waved his hand
and, drawing his blanket around him, re-entered
the hut. The assemblage went wild. Warriors
shouted, danced, and yelled; squaws shrieked and
children screamed. Those who had been foremost
in the contemplated revolt lent their voices to the
mad uproar. Such was the magnetic power of the
great Tecumseh!

Now the Prophet stepped forward and raised his
right hand, to command silence. As he did so, the
magic circlet upon his finger caught the rays of the
sun. A hush fell upon his audience, broken only
by the breezy whisper, — '' The Sign of the Prophet !
The Sign of the Prophet !''— Then all was pro-
found silence. Tenskwatawa swayed gracefully —
rhythmically — to and fro, as he began :

'' The past is gone ; the present is before us ; the
future is in the hands of the Great Spirit. My
children, we have made mistakes. Now let us bury
them forever ; and with them our sorrows, our disappointments, and our regrets. If ever again I
transfer my power — my sign — to another, it will
be to one who can use it. And you will obey the
orders of that one, as you would obey my words.
Hold fast to what I say. Listen ! Again I have
talked with the Great Spirit. He has sent me to
you with a message of good cheer. He allowed
you to suffer defeat to try your courage — to test
your loyalty. You have suffered much — you shall
rejoice more. You have groaned at your failure —
you shall shout in triumph. You hunger to-day —
you shall feast to-morrow. Hear what the Great
Spirit says through me, his prophet. All that
Tecumseh, my brother, has told you is true. All
that you desire shall be yours. You have been
scorched by the fire of death — you shall be healed
by the water of life. I am your father — you are
my children. The Great Spirit has told me all
these things.''

He stopped speaking. A faint murmur of approbation started with those immediately in front. It grew and swelled into a thunderous roar of applause. "The Open Door! The Open Door!" they yelled until their faces were purple and their lips dripped foam. Many of them fell to the ground and raised their arms supplicatingly. Silencing them with a wave of his hand, Tenskwatawa proceeded:

"Listen, my children — and heed what I say! Your acts, your words, your thoughts, are known to the Great Spirit — and through him are known to me. You have cursed your prophet; you have planned to depose Tecumseh and Tenskwatawa — to choose others to lead and advise you. The Great Spirit understood all. But all is forgiven; for you were mad with defeat and shame."

Again he paused. Closely he scanned their faces for the effect of his words. The stillness of death reigned on all sides. The ringleaders in the revolt bowed their heads and glanced furtively at the dread being before them. Suddenly the Prophet's whole attitude and manner changed. Every sinuosity of his graceful body became a hard, straight line. Rigidly erect, his brows lowering, his face contorted, his one sinister eye flashing — he was an avenging demon.

"Listen!" he shouted in thunder tones. "My children, you have displeased the Great Spirit. Another word — another thought — of the kind, and he will desert your cause and ally himself with

the Seventeen Fires.   If there be one among you
that doubts my words, let him stand forth ; and
through the power the Great Spirit has bestowed
upon me, I will slay him with a look.   With a
motion of my hand I can smite you blind.   Do you
still doubt?   You have seen what I did with the
noble Winnemac.   Is not White Loon as brave and
strong?   Is not Stone Eater as valiant and bold?
Look then ! ''

Again he was the bending, swaying, sinuous
hypnotist.   The glittering talisman upon his finger
shot its light into the eyes of the two chiefs.   Like
charmed birds they fluttered and tried to free themselves from its spell.   Their frantic efforts were
vain.   Then they became stiff — motionless, seeing
nothing but the magic ring, hearing nothing but
the Prophet's voice.

"Come ! '' he cried.

In straight lines the two chiefs advanced.

Bradford paled slightly.   La Violette turned aside
her face.   Ross Douglas had his eyes fastened upon
the glittering jewel.   Slowly he began to move forward.   Many others were coming under the hyp-
notic influence — were approaching Tenskwatawa.
The young American shook himself, dropped his
eyes to earth — and retreated to a safe distance.

"Stop ! ''

Like automatons the chiefs obeyed.

"You see nothing — you are blind ! ''

Tenskwatawa's voice rang out clear and cold.
Scores of the savages clapped their hands to their

eyes and groaned aloud. Stone Eater and White Loon uttered piercing wails.

"You are helpless — you drop to the ground — you sleep!"

Down they fell like tenpins — the two chiefs at the Prophet's feet.

"Behold the work of the Great Spirit!" he shouted triumphantly. "Now who doubts Tenskwatawa's power?"

A full minute he waited for a reply. Awe — consternation — were written upon the faces of those who had not come under his influence. At last he clapped his hands and cried shrilly:

"Awake — arise! Live and see!"

Those upon the ground tumbled over one another, in their efforts to get upon their feet. Rubbing their eyes, they stared stupidly around. Then, in a shame-faced manner, they silently slunk away from the presence of the red hypnotist, who, dropping his voice to a sing-song monotone, continued:

"Yes, my children, all will be well. Your chief, the great and powerful Tecumseh, has spoken words of truth and wisdom. Do not despair; be steadfast to our cause. The Great Spirit is with us — and all will be well. He has promised. In a few days, at most, we will go to the Mississinewa. Our white brothers across the lakes and beyond the big water will send us supplies. Also, we will make our enemy — the Seventeen Fires — furnish us with salt and ammunition. All will be well. The Great Spirit, through his prophet, has spoken."

Tenskwatawa rejoined Tecumseh within the hut; La Violette returned to her own cabin. The Indians cheered and capered about in an ecstasy of delight. This lasted for several minutes. Then they quietly dispersed and commenced the preparation of their dinners. All thought of rebelling against the rule of the self-elected chief and self-appointed prophet was at an end. The kingly presence and sturdy eloquence of the one, coupled with the serpentine grace and mesmeric power of the other, had the desired effect upon the minds of the ignorant and superstitious redmen. The threatened revolt was at an end.

"Well, what do you think of Tecumseh?" remarked Bradford, as he approached the spot where Douglas was standing.

"He's every inch a warrior," Ross replied quietly.

"And every inch a man," was the quick rejoinder.

"But a savage, still."

"Yes. But a savage whose valor is equaled by his honor, whose thirst for fame and power is tempered by his sense of right and justice. He has the good of his people at heart; he believes their cause is just——"

"Can you say as much for the English, who are urging the Indians to take up the hatchet against the Americans?" Douglas interrupted. "Have they the good of the savages at heart?"

Bradford laughed a forced, uneasy laugh as he answered:

"Please don't interrupt me with ill-timed questions. That's a matter of national ethics—a problem that you and I cannot grasp or solve. It would be useless for us to discuss it. We look at it from different standpoints. You're an American; I'm an——"

"American, also," Ross interjected.

The older man sharply eyed his companion for a half minute. Then he said slowly:

"You're a keen and intuitive observer. By birth I *am* an American; but I'm in the service of the British, and bound to do their will. To return to Tecumseh, he's the noblest Indian I've ever met. He is the soul of honor—the personification of manly courage. His word is as good as his bond. His people trust him, love him. Had he been at the Prophet's Town there would have been no battle. He wished to avoid a conflict until he was ready for it. But a general Indian war is coming—inevitably. The Americans will be arrayed on one side; the Indians and British on the other. The Americans will fight to hold what they have gained; the savages, to regain what they have lost; the English, to add to their territory. You have learned much since you've been a prisoner. It wouldn't do to have you escape and return to your people. A captive you must remain."

Bradford ceased speaking, but Douglas offered no word in reply. The former resumed:

"Tenskwatawa, also, is a wonderful man. He's eloquent, cunning, forceful."

"He's a cowardly scoundrel!" Ross said savagely.

"Yes," Bradford admitted, "he's a coward. I don't admire him. He's a hypocritical knave. But he's devoted to La Violette, and you can't deny that he's shrewd and eloquent."

"No."

"Nor can you explain the power he exercises over his people."

Ross shook his head.

"It's something wonderful, startling, uncanny. The more I see of it, the more I'm puzzled. I have felt it——"

"And I."

"You?"

"Yes."

"When?"

"To-day."

"Ah! And yet you cannot understand it?"

"No."

"It *is* strange — very," Bradford remarked musingly. "He says he receives his power from the Great Spirit. I'm not a believer in miracles; yet, for all I know, he tells the truth. But he has the power — there's no gainsaying that. You didn't come completely under his influence?"

"No; but I should have done so if I hadn't exerted all my will-power and removed my eyes from the talisman — his sign."

"I understand. Well, I'm hungry. Let's hunt something to eat."

"Where did he obtain the ring?"

"I don't know. He has had it for years. Come on."

Together the two sauntered away from the vicinity of the Prophet's cabin.

The day passed quietly. Several hunting-parties returned to camp, laden with game. The savages had an abundance of meat for supper and retired to rest at an early hour. Bradford and Douglas stretched upon the earthen floor of their hut and fell asleep. Duke occupied his usual place. At the door, stood the two copper-colored guards. About midnight Bradford was aroused by the sound of voices outside. He arose, softly opened the door, and stepped out into the darkness. It was raining steadily. The two guards were parleying with a company of braves who demanded that the hound be brought out and given to them.

"What are you doing here?" Bradford asked sharply.

The leader advanced and answered shortly:

"The big dog."

"Who sent you?"

"Lone Jack, the Delaware chief."

"Well, go back to Lone Jack and tell him I said to come himself — that I will give him a taste of powder-and-ball instead of dog-meat. Be off!"

Grumbling and snarling, the braves disappeared in the darkness; and Scar Face re-entered the cabin.

At that moment Douglas stirred uneasily and murmured :

"Joe and Bright Wing — come — rescue ——"

Bradford raised his head and listened attentively. Ross's lips were moving, but the words were so softly spoken that the listener could not catch them.

"Poor fellow !" the older man whispered pityingly. "He's dreaming of rescue. How sweet is freedom. Well — well, the whole of life is but a dream — a miserable nightmare ——"

"At the ravine — to-morrow evening," Ross mumbled.

Then he sighed deeply, changed his position — breathing heavily — and again slept soundly.

Bradford started and sat erect.

"Ah !" he muttered, shaking his head. "There *may* be something in that dream — more than I thought. At the ravine — to-morrow evening. What can *that* mean ? I must investigate. Perhaps his friends are near — and he has met them at the ravine above here. What more likely ? Forewarned is forearmed."

And, smiling grimly, he replenished the fire, rolled himself in his blanket — and was soon sound asleep.

CHAPTER VIII.

STEADILY, monotonously, the rain poured down all night long. The morning dawned cheerless and murky. The earth was sodden; every rivulet was swollen; and the creek was bank full. A dense fog rose from the water-courses and spread itself over the land. The feeble rays of the winter sun could not penetrate it; and at midday the depths of the forest were gloomy and oppressive.

The savages huddled together in their mean hovels and silently watched the dreary downpour. Nothing broke the stillness, save the steady drip of the rain and the rumbling roar of the fast hurrying streams. All the fuel was wet, and the fires burned dismally. It was a wearying, soul-trying day.

Douglas and Bradford sat by the fire that smoldered in the middle of the floor of the miserable hut they occupied. Occasionally, one or the other arose and peeped out at the pouring rain. But the scene was too depressing; and, shivering, he returned to the fire. The pungent smoke refused to find its way out at the hole in the bark roof, but swirled and eddied about the interior and added to the general discomfort.

Neither man was in a talkative mood. Hour after hour, they sat staring into the ash-masked embers, each busy with his own thoughts.

(170)

As the day advanced, Ross's apathy left him. He grew strangely restless, and like a caged animal paced from one end of the cabin to the other. Bradford noted his companion's changed mood, but said nothing. By four o'clock it was growing dusk. Douglas suddenly picked up his hat and started for the door.

"Where are you going?" Bradford inquired.

"For a walk," was the non-committal reply.

Duke arose, stretched himself, yawned, and rubbed against his master's legs.

"Surely you're not going out in such a rain," Bradford remarked. "You'll get wet to the skin."

"What's a little rain to a man who has spent his days in the open air," Douglas returned quickly, still moving toward the doorway.

"Wait!"

And Bradford sprang to his feet and placed himself in front of the other, his broad back against the closed door.

"What do you mean?" Ross cried, drawing himself up stiffly.

It was a strange scene. The flickering firelight alone lighted the black interior and outlined the forms and faces of the two men. The bloodhound stood looking from one to the other. Outside, the rain fell and the wind soughed fitfully.

"I mean that you're not going out to-night," Bradford answered firmly.

Douglas's temper was rising.

"You dare to say that I shan't go out to-night, if I choose?" he asked.

"Yes; that's what I mean."

"And you think I'll submit?"

"You must — you can't help yourself."

"That remains to be seen."

"Oh!"

"Yes."

They stood glaring at each other, like brutes at bay. The older man was cool and collected; the younger, angry and excited. Each was striving to stare the other out of countenance; but neither shrank from the ordeal.

"Stand aside!" Ross cried chokingly.

"I will not."

"The consequences be upon your own head, then!"

Scarcely were the words out of his mouth, ere Douglas leaped forward and grappled with his antagonist. Around and around the small, dark room they whirled, each striving to trip and throw the other. Douglas was the stronger, the more active; Scar Face, the cooler, the more skillful. They were evenly matched.

Duke snarled viciously, and ran around the two combatants, seeking an opportunity to leap at Bradford's throat. Both men were breathing heavily. The terrific exercise and excessive strain were telling upon them. But the younger man's wind was the better — was in his favor. Besides, each moment he was growing cooler, more deter-

mined, while his antagonist, seeing defeat staring him in the face, was losing his presence of
mind.

Of a sudden, Douglas swung Bradford clear of
the ground, and with stunning force dashed him
against the log wall. Scar Face's hold relaxed,
and he dropped to the floor, senseless. In a moment
the dog was upon the helpless man, and would
have buried his fangs in the throbbing throat, had
not Ross panted:

"Down, Duke; out of the way !"

The hound sullenly obeyed, growling fiercely.
Douglas leaned against the wall and breathed hard
for some seconds. Then he stooped and carefully
examined his fallen foe.

"He's only stunned; thank God I didn't have
to kill him !" he ejaculated.

Then, taking a bundle of thongs from a peg upon
the wall, he proceeded to bind the prostrate man,
hand and foot. When he had finished, he secured
the other's gun, ammunition, and knife, and calling
to the dog left the hut, noiselessly closing the door
behind him.

By this time it was quite dark. Along the creek
bank, the camp-fires twinkled like watchful eyes.
With long, sturdy strides, Douglas set off toward
the ravine up the stream. The smell of the heavy
fog was in his nostrils; the booming roar of the
turbulent creek in his ears. He met or saw no
one. He left the camp behind, and neared the spot
where he expected to meet his friends.

Suddenly he stopped and whistled softly. No reply. He drew nearer to the ravine, and again he whistled. Still no reply. The bloodhound whined and impatiently scratched the soft, wet earth.

"Find them, Duke," Ross commanded.

The dog ran forward and disappeared in the bushes.

Douglas awaited the outcome of his experiment. Presently he heard an eerie-like whisper:

"Come right straight ahead, Ross Douglas. Crawl into the bushes, an' be mighty still while you're doin' it."

It was Farley's voice. Douglas obeyed the words. Dropping upon hands and knees, he wormed his way through the thick copse of wet bushes, for some yards. Suddenly a hand was clapped upon his shoulder, and these whispered words fell upon his ear:

"Drop down an' keep still. The Injins is all 'round us. They've got onto our game, some way, an' have been huntin' fer our hidin'-place ever sence the middle o' the afternoon. Me an' Bright Wing's laid here fer twelve mortal hours, without a bite to eat. How the redskins got onto our scheme is more 'n I can tell; but they've done it. Have you got a gun with you, Ross?"

"Yes," was the cautious reply.

"All right. We didn't dare to answer y'r whistle, fer fear the Injins might hear us. They was mighty close right then. That dog o' yours's got a heap o' sense — he has, by ginger! He jest nosed 'round us an' never barked n'r nothin'. Wher' are you, Bright Wing?"

"Me here," came from the depths of the Wyandot's chest.

"Well, lead off, an' we'll foller you. This is a ticklish business, 'r my name ain't Joe Farley! Ross, y'r dog was goin' back to you, but I c'ncluded I'd best risk callin' you. Go ahead, Injin, we're right at y'r heels."

"Ugh!" was the guttural response from the blackness.

To the bottom of the ravine they stealthily descended; crept through the water and mud of its bed; and ascended the opposite bank. Bright Wing led the way; Duke brought up the rear. Reaching the open wood, they arose to their feet and silently threaded their way through the intricate mazes of the black forest.

They had proceeded but a short distance, however, when Bright Wing dropped to the ground and lay motionless. The others followed his example. Duke growled menacingly, and ere his master could lay a restraining hand upon him, darted into the wall of blackness ahead. To the ears of the three comrades came a sharp exclamation, followed by the sounds of a tussle. Then all was silent.

"What's the meaning of those sounds?" Ross inquired softly of Farley.

"Don't know," was the reply in the same cautious undertone.

"S'pect the purp got hold of a redskin's guzzle, an' shut his wind off so quick he couldn't——"

"Ugh! Duke him bite bad Shawnee much hard," the Wyandot volunteered. "Here Duke him is now. Come."

The dog trotted back to his place and, panting, threw himself upon the ground. Again they moved onward, creeping along inch by inch and pausing frequently to listen. In this manner they covered quite a distance. They had arisen to their feet, and were congratulating themselves that they had eluded the vigilance of their watchful foes, when the patter of moccasined feet sounded on all sides of them. They were surrounded.

A short and sharp conflict in the intense darkness ensued. Rifles were discharged and blows were struck at random. Then the three comrades found themselves beyond the line of their enemies, and blindly dashed away in the impenetrable blackness.

For some time they continued their mad flight, through thickets and over fallen logs, stumbling, falling, scrambling to their feet and running on. At last they paused momentarily to listen. All sounds of pursuit had died out. Naught was to be heard but the patter of the raindrops upon the dead leaves and the boom of the creek near at hand.

"We have distanced them," Douglas panted.

"Yes," Farley gasped in reply. "But it was a mighty close shave. Is either o' you fellers hurt?"

"I'm not," Ross replied.

"Me no hurt," Bright Wing grunted. "Where dog Duke?"

"Here at my side," Douglas answered.

"I guess I'm the only critter that got a scratch," Joe grumbled. "I alluz was an unlucky mortal. One o' them red devils has raised a strawberry on my cheek, as big's a walnut. He must 'ave struck me with the butt of his hatchet. I'm much obleeged to him that he didn't use the blade. I'd 'ave needed a surgeon, I would, by Polly Ann! Seemin'ly the cusses didn't want to kill us; they didn't fire a gun. Wanted to take us alive, I reckon. But our charge was too much fer 'em. But we want to reload our rifles, an' git out o' here. They'll git torches an' be hot on our trail 'fore a half hour, 'r I miss *my* guess. Gol-fer-socks! But I'm hungry. I could eat hoss-meat now an' relish it. Say, fellers, which way do we want to steer?"

"It makes little difference," Ross answered impatiently. "Any direction that will carry us from this vicinity is good enough for me."

"That won't do," Joe said firmly. "We've got to do one o' two 'r three things: steer fer Fort Harrison on the Wabash, Fort Defiance on the Maumee, 'r make a break 'cross the country fer Franklinton on the Scioto. The question is which way 'll we go. What do you say, Injin?"

"Me say go toward rising sun; go toward home," Bright Wing answered promptly.

12

"What do you say, Ross?"

"I'm willing to abide by Bright Wing's deci-
sion. But let's be off."

"All right," returned Joe. "We've got to ford
the creek then, an' keep bearin' east. We want to
strike through by Greenville an' Fort Recovery.
Come on. Le's git out o' here, an' find a place
where we can cook some meat. The Injin's got
some in his pouch. I'm jest 'bout starved, I am,
by cracky! Injin, take the lead."

All night they pressed forward, bearing toward
the northeast. At daylight they went into camp
upon a rocky elevation, and, after kindling a fire
and cooking and eating a quantity of venison,
stretched themselves upon the damp ground and
fell asleep.

While they are snatching a few hours of repose,
let us go back to the Indian camp upon Wildcat
Creek.

Fifteen minutes after Douglas's departure, Bradford regained consciousness. At first he lay and
stared vacantly around him. Then a keen remembrance of all that had occurred came to him, and
he attempted to arise. He tugged at his bonds;
half arose to a sitting posture; and fell back helpless.

"Overpowered, but not outwitted!" he muttered,
rolling his aching head. "The Indians are on the
qui vive, and will recapture him. Also, they will
take his venturesome comrades prisoners. I hope
thev'll not hurt either of the three.

"How long have I lain here? I must have received a severe blow; I'm dizzy, and my head aches. It's a wonder he didn't kill me while he had the chance. Perhaps he doesn't hate me as he did. God grant that it may be so! Of course he has taken my arms with him. Well, I can't blame him; I robbed him of his own. I was a fool to send away the two guards. I should have kept them at hand day and night. Why don't the redskins come; what can be the cause of their delay?"

Again he essayed to arise, and again fell back with a groan. The fire had burned down; the room was in darkness. No sound came to his ears, but the patter of the rain upon the bark roof, the fitful sough of the wind, and the sullen boom of the rushing stream. A half hour passed. He strained at the thongs that bound his limbs, but accomplished nothing.

"Curse the luck!" he cried angrily. "Why don't the red hounds put in an appearance? Can it be possible he has escaped them? How strong and active he is. He was too much for me, with all my skill as a wrestler. Mercy, how my head aches! And how manly and brave he is; a young man of whom any father might be proud! But he hates me—hates me! In the name of all the fiends, must I lie here helpless while he makes his escape? I shall go mad. Hark! Footsteps and voices."

A moment later the door flew open, and a number of braves strode into the room.

"Is that you, Long Gun?" Bradford asked excitedly.

"Ugh!" grunted the leader of the party.

"And the palefaces—where are they?"

"Gone."

"Gone!" shouted the prostrate man, writhing like one undergoing torture. "Gone! You shall pay dearly for allowing him to escape!"

Long Gun kicked the half-burned faggots into a blazing pile. Then folding his arms upon his brawny chest, he answered composedly:

"Scar Face should not talk big and loud. See! He lies helpless, like a tethered dog. He can bark, but he cannot bite. He snaps and snarls, and finds fault with Long Gun and his warriors, because they did not capture the armed palefaces, in the black forest. But Scar Face could not overpower *one unarmed paleface, in his own cabin.* The young man joined his friends. They fought in the darkness and made their escape. My warriors bear the marks of the fight."

"Fool!" Bradford bellowed chokingly. "Don't stand their gloating over my predicament! Sever my bonds at once."

The chief silently obeyed. Bradford struggled to his feet, shook himself, and rubbed his stiffened limbs. Then he inquired briskly:

"All three escaped?"

"Ugh!"

"And the dog?"

"Ugh!"

"Which way did they go?"

"Long Gun and his warriors tried to follow them, but could not. The black night swallowed them."

"Bah!" sneered the white man. "And you call yourself a Shawnee warrior! Do not palefaces leave tracks in the dark, as well as in the light? You must find their trail; you must follow and overtake them. Do you hear me? Rouse yourselves! Get torches! I will accompany you. Five pounds to the brave who first strikes their trail; ten pounds to him who first gains sight of them! Let's be off! Hurry! Hurry!"

Stimulated by the prospect of reward, the braves hurriedly prepared for the pursuit. Out of the cabin they trooped, Long Gun in the lead. Bradford accompanied them. The camp was enveloped in darkness; the rain still fell steadily — persistently. Up the creek they proceeded, their flaming torches lighting the surface of the muddy stream. They reached the ravine, crossed it, and disappeared in the thick woods. And still the rain fell, and still the camp was wrapped in darkness and slumber.

The next day, the allied tribes at Wildcat Creek packed their scanty effects and set out for the village of the Miamis, upon the Mississinewa.

Now let us return to the escaped captive and his friends.

The sun was several hours high when Ross awoke. The sky was clear; the morning air crisp and biting. The young man stretched his limbs and drank deeply of the sweet, invigorating atmosphere. The grateful odor of cooking meat greeted him. A brisk camp-fire blazed at his feet; and suspended over it, by means of a tripod of green sticks, was a hunk of venison, roasting. Douglas took in all this at a glance. Then he looked around for his companions. They were nowhere in sight.

"Strange," he muttered, picking up Bradford's rifle and carefully examining it. "Are mysteries never to end? Where can Farley and Bright Wing be? Of course they have not deserted me. But where are they? Why didn't they wake me? They have gone to investigate something, probably, for they have left the meat cooking. How soundly I must have slept! Their absence makes me uneasy."

Dropping upon the ground, he continued his critical examination of the gun he held in his hands, all the while communing with himself:

"An excellent piece of English manufacture, and richly carved and ornamented. It must have cost a pretty sum of money. Bradford will hardly thank me for relieving him of it. He must have set great store by it."—And the speaker smiled.—"I wonder what he thought and did when he regained consciousness and found me gone, and himself unarmed and tied. A mysterious personage! He kept me a prisoner; yet he was kind to me and protected me. And La Violette, how beautiful! A form and face to drive a man mad with love. But all her witcheries could not efface from my heart the image of little Amy Larkin. Pshaw! what nonsense I'm talking. Am I a love-sick schoolboy, doomed to fall in love with every pretty face I see? Divorce La Violette from her romantic environment, and she would be commonplace, perhaps. At any rate, she is naught to me; nor I to her. Why should I bestow a thought upon her? She forgot her promise to me, as soon as she had made it. I'll think of Amy — gentle, loving, faithful little girl!"

A moment he hung his head and was silent. The blazing camp-fire crackled; the roasting meat steamed and sputtered. Presently Ross shook himself, and again looking about him, murmured impatiertly:

"Confound the luck! Where can those two runaways be? We should be upon our journey. We are still within reach of the Indians and Bradford. At this moment a party may be hot upon our trail. We're wasting precious time. The campaign is over; and I'm anxious to return to Amy, to fulfill my promise. But Bradford! How my mind reverts to that man. The threads of our lives have crossed. Will they remain entangled? Ah! What are these letters engraved upon the stock of his gun? J. D.—eh? Those are not *his* initials. Evidently he stole the piece — as *I* did. Bradford! I hate the treacherous villain —but I could not kill him. Duke hated him, too. Ah!"

Hastily he scrambled to his feet and once more swept his eyes around the place, grumbling in an irritable undertone:

"Where *is* the hound? I hadn't thought of him. He wouldn't go far from my side, unless he were forced to do so. I'll call him."

As has been stated, the site of the three friends' bivouac was the summit of a small, rock-strewn elevation. It was bare at the top, but surrounded at its base by a fringe of stunted bushes. On all sides of it stretched the forest.

Douglas threw his rifle upon his shoulder and swiftly descended the slope, softly calling the dog's name as he went. Just as he reached the bottom of the gentle declivity, there was a stir in the underbrush, and Duke bounded forth to meet his master. A moment later, the limbs parted and the smiling face of Joe Farley peeped out. The hound fawned at Ross's feet and whined gleefully.

"He seems mighty glad to see you," Joe remarked as he stepped into the open.

"Yes," Douglas answered dryly, keenly eyeing his friend.

"What's the matter?" Farley laughed. "Did you sleep so long you let the meat burn up? A purty cook you'd make."

"The meat's cooking nicely," Ross interrupted. "But why did you leave it? What are you doing down here?"

"Jest stepped down here to take a squint 'round an' see if I could find anything o' the Injin."

"Bright Wing?"

"Yes."

"Where is he?"

"I don't know no more'n the man in the moon. When I woke up an hour ago he was gone. You was sleepin' so good I didn't want to wake you. So I hung up the chunk o' venison, started a fire under it, an' come down here to see what I could see. After a little while the dog follered me."

"And what discovery have you made?"

"None. I hain't seen hide n'r hair o' the Injin, n'r nobody else. I don't see what's become o' him. I can't make it out."

Douglas was silent; and Joe asked:

"What do you make of it?"

"I don't know what to think," Ross replied meditatively. "One thing is certain, however. We're tarrying too long."

"Of course," assented Joe.

"But we can't proceed until Bright Wing returns."

"No, of course not."

"What do you suggest?"

"That we go an' have somethin' to eat while we're waitin'. I'm as holler as a gun bar'l. I've fasted fer three 'r four days, an' it seems I can't git filled up, somehow. I'm jest like a feller in love—I am, by Caroline! Can't git enough of it. I remember one time when a score o' purty women was hankerin' after me. They was perfectly distracted over my good looks. But I wasn't in love with one of 'em; an' it didn't take me long to git enough o' their billin' an' cooin'. Then I remember another time w'en a small piece o' linsey-woolsey got in my mind, an' I couldn't git 'er out. She was purty as a pictur', an' sharper eyed 'n a blackbird. But she didn't keer a continental fer me; an' I nearly starved to death fer the want o' her love. I pined away to skin an' bone, an' become a reg'lar shadder. Served me right, fer the way I'd used them other women, I reckon. I ain't much on religion, but I b'lieve a man gits his punishment fer his evil deeds right here on earth — I do, by Samanthy! But what 're you thinkin' 'bout, Ross Douglas?"

Ross stood absent-mindedly gazing into the somber depths of the surrounding forest. Evidently he had heard little that his loquacious friend had been saying. But at the question he started, and replied serio-comically :

"I was thinking I had heard you speak of your numerous conquests before, Joe."

"So you have."— And the other nodded solemnly and vigorously.—"The Good Book says that from the fullness o' the gizzard the tongue wags—'r words to that effect. I never *was* good at quotin' Scriptur'. Anyhow, a man's liable to talk 'bout what's on his conscience. It's a consumin' fire that won't let him rest. As fer *me*, toyin' with women folks's affections has been my besettin' sin. Now I'm gittin' up in years, I'd like to find a purty woman, an' marry an' settle

down. But I've burned out the candle o' the
Lord's mercy an' blowed the ashes in his face, an'
he won't hear my prayers."—Here Joe sighed
deeply, lugubriously.—"Be keerful you don't do
the same thing, Ross Douglas. Let my horrible
example be a warnin' to you. Don't toy with
women's hearts. As I was goin' to say——"

"Did I understand you to say you're hungry,
Joe?" Douglas interrupted.

"Of course, I'm hungry," Farley answered in an
injured tone. "I'm alluz hungry. When I was a
boy I foolishly took a drink o' water out of a frog
pond, an' swallered 'bout a dozen tadpoles. Well,
sir, them tadpoles growed to frogs; an' they're in
my stomach yit. They take all the victuals I put
into my mouth; an' w'en they git *re'l* hungry, they
set up such a croakin' I can't sleep fer the noise
they make. Once I got to foolin' 'round a log
bear-trap in the woods, an' the door fell down an'
shut me in. I was a pris'ner fer 'bout a week; an'
was nearly starved to death an' crazier 'n a loon,
w'en some fellers found me an' let me out. Well,
sir, first them frogs went to croakin' fer somethin'
to eat, an' they kep' it up fer four days, never
lettin' up a minute. Then they got dry fer
water, an' they commenced hoppin' 'round in my
inside an' tryin' to git out. Talk 'bout sufferin'!
The ol' martyrs never had to stand what I stood
out there in that bear-trap. The 'xperience left
lines o' sufferin' on my comely visage, that I hain't
never got red of. It come purty near spilin' my

beauty ferever—it did, by Melindy Jane! W'y, dang-it-all-to-dingnation ! I tell you ——"

"Joe."

"Well?"

"If you don't mean to feed your colony of frogs on charred meat, you'd better look after that roasting venison. It's scorching ; I smell it."

"By my great uncle's snuffbox, but that's a fact! An' me a-standin' here, a-blowin' my bugle, like a shaller-pated fool ! "

Farley loped up the slope, to the camp-fire, and rescued the hunk of venison from the coals where it had fallen. Douglas followed leisurely, a preoccupied look upon his dark, handsome face. Duke trotted at his heels.

"It's done now—an' *good an' done!*" Joe grumbled. "But it's all we've got, an' we'll make the best of it. Dang a long an' limber tongue, anyhow ! Mine's alluz gittin' me into some dangnation trouble. Well, we can cut off the burnt parts an' feed 'em to the dog. Jest see the hungry purp ! Looks like he'd like to take a slice out o' me, this very minute. Ther', Duke, clap y'r jaws on that. Gone a'ready, an' wantin' more ? Ross Douglas, I may have a colony o' frogs in me, but this houn' o' yours is infested with a tapeworm bigger 'n a blacksnake—he is, by King Solermen's harem ! Git y'r knife out, an' le's fall to an' eat ; no use to wait on the Injin—no tellin' where *he* is."

Ross's preoccupied air had not deserted him ; and he ate sparingly of the tempting food. The eccen-

tric woodman ravenously devoured great slices of
the meat, grudgingly tossing the dog the burnt
portions. At last he paused in his masticatory pro-
cess and exclaimed:

"Ross, somethin's botherin' you the worst kind;
an' whatever it is, it's takin' y'r appetite."

"I'm thinking," Douglas replied.

"Well, what 're you thinkin' of?"

"Of what has become of Bright Wing."

"An' what's yer c'nclusion?"

"That he has gone back over our trail, to discover if we are followed."

"It's more'n likely," Joe assented. "But we
can't do nothin' but wait fer him, can we?"

"No."

"Well, that's settled then. Say!"

"Well?"

"Why didn't you kill that Bradford — the low-
lived skunk — when you had a chance? 'Twould
'ave saved us no end o' trouble, p'r'aps. Maybe
he's on our trail this minute, with a band o' murderin' red devils at his back."

"It's probable."

"Well, why didn't you kill him?"

"I had reasons for not doing so."

"What was they?"

"I don't care to say."

"Huh! You're gittin' closer 'n a clam," Joe muttered irritably.

Then he continued:

"An' you didn't kill that ol' cuss of a Prophet?"

Ross remained silent.

" N'r Tecumseh, n'r none of 'em ? "

" I was hardly in a position to make a wholesale slaughter of my enemies," Ross replied laughingly. " I was a captive, and surrounded by hundreds of bloodthirsty savages. I consider myself fortunate to have escaped with my life."

" Yes, that's so," Farley assented in a dissatisfied tone. " But it seems to me this campaign hain't amounted to much. Tecumseh's back among his warriors ; an' Bradford an' the Prophet's still alive. They'll be hatchin' more devilment, 'fore the next new moon. Howsoever, I've done *my* part an' hain't got nothin' to regret. But I don't want to be a soldier no more ; I'd ruther fight on my own hook. This thing o' drivin' oxen from one end o' the Indiany Territory to the other ain't what it's cracked up to be."— And he sighed feelingly.—" All I want's to git back to my cabin on the ol' Scioto — W'y, ding-it-all-to-dangnation! There's the Injin this blessed minute ! "

Both white men hastily arose and ran to meet their red comrade, who came bounding up the slope, with the speed and grace of an antelope. Ere they reached his side, they saw him place his finger upon his lips, in token of silence.

" What is it ? " Douglas asked in an anxious whisper.

Bright Wing drew a full breath and replied:

" Scar Face and many braves."

" Where ? How far away ?

" Three — four gunshots."

" And upon our trail ? "

" Ugh ! "

" Are they moving rapidly ? "

" Ugh ! Soon be here. Scar Face, bad Shawnees and Pottawatomies. Come fast ; soon be here."

" Let's be off, then," Ross said calmly. " We have no time to lose."

" Grab up that piece o' meat, Injin, an' put it in y'r pouch," Joe cried, excitedly. " You can eat it on the run. We've had our sheer. Dang the varmints, anyhow! They mean to give us a long an' hot chase."

Quickly they descended the eastern slope, worked their way through the fringe of bushes surrounding its base, and set off at a rapid pace through the forest. Bright Wing led the way. They bore toward the southeast. With the foresight and cunning of trained woodmen, they exercised all the arts of their craft to throw their pursuers off their trail. Here they followed the bed of a stream, soaking their moccasins in the icy water to hide their faint footprints ; there they doubled on their track and took a new direction. At intervals, they separated and made wide detours from the main course, only to meet again further on. Occasionally they paused momentarily, to drink from some running stream or to strain their senses for sight or sound of their enemies. Then on again—swiftly, tirelessly.

The noon hour came and went. The sun — now veiled by scudding clouds, now shining brightly —

began a descent of the western arc of the heavens.
The wind rose raw and disagreeable. Black cloud
banks began to pile up on the horizon, indicating
an approaching snowstorm. The short winter day
advanced rapidly.

The topography of the country again changed.
The surface of the land grew flatter ; open glades
appeared here and there in the thick woods. At
last Joe stopped and remarked complainingly :

" I've gone 'bout as far's I'm goin' in one day —
I have, by Molly ! My feet's wet an' cold, an' I've
got a crick o' the rheumatiz in my back, that's pes-
terin' me like the nation. Feels like a swarm o'
hornets had took a roost there. We hain't got
nothin' to eat, which is purty sad ; but we can build
a fire an' rest an' roast our shins, which 'll be some
sort o' comfort, anyhow. I'm o' the 'pinion we've
throwed the redskins off our track ; we hain't heerd
n'r seen nothin' of 'em sence we broke camp. I've
purty nigh come to the c'nclusion that you was mistaken, Injin—that you didn't *see* no one follerin' us."
Bright Wing's beady eyes flashed.

" Joe heap big fool some more ! " he grunted contemptuously. " Bright Wing see Scar Face and
many braves. Bad Shawnees and Pottawatomies
still on trail. Like hound ; no give up and go back.
Want scalps bad. Bright Wing go on. Joe stay ;
build fire ; loose scalp. Ugh ! "

" An' a heap you'll keer, if I *git* my hair raised,"
Farley retorted crossly. " You're jest like the rest
o' y'r people."

"Joe!" Douglas interrupted sternly.

"Well, what is it?" was the surly response.

"Once more you are talking idle nonsense. Your tongue will again get you into trouble. You know, as well as I, that Bright Wing has told us the truth. We can't stop here; we *musn't.* Such an act would be the sheerest folly."

"Yes, I s'pose you're right," Joe admitted in a mollified tone. "We've got to keep on. Dang the redskins, anyway! The doctors says exercise is a good thing; but I ain't hankerin' fer any more of it, jest now. They say it's a mighty powerful thing to give a feller an appetite; an' I can believe that statement without half tryin', fer them frogs in me has gone to croakin' like sixty. That's what made me so flustered an' cantankerous. Well, Injin, lead on. I'll foller you, if I wear my legs off up to my shoulders — I will, 'r my name ain't Joseph Peregoy Farley!"

Once more they set forward. But they had gone only a hundred yards, when the Wyandot, with a startled grunt, came to an abrupt stop.

"What 'ave you diskivered now?" Farley inquired, stepping forward.

"A fresh trail!" Ross exclaimed, stooping and examining the moist earth and damp leaves.

The three comrades bent down and closely scrutinized the numerous tracks. The light in the forest was dim; and they painfully strained their eyes over the alarming discovery, as they attempted to read its meaning aright. After a minute's exami-

13

nation, they arose and silently looked at one another. Presently Douglas said in an undertone :

" What do you make of it, Bright Wing ? "

" Redmen," was the emphatic reply.

" And quite a number of them."

" Ugh ! "

" Of course that trail was made by redskins," Joe volunteered in a stage whisper. " 'Cause ther's nobody else in these parts to make it. An' more 'n that, there's a score 'r more of 'em, an' they're movin' in the direction we're goin'. That trail ain't more 'n a few hours old, at most. I'll tell you my explanation o' the affair."

" What is it ? " Ross asked.

" W'y, dang-it-all-to-dingnation ! that Scar Face an' his murderin', scalpin' gang o' red devils has sarcumvented us an' got ahead of us, that's what. Though how in the name o' Dan'l Boone they ever done it, I can't imagine ! They must 'ave found some short cut."

Bright Wing decidedly shook his head and grunted:

" No believe."

" You don't believe Joe's theory that the trail was made by Scar Face and his band ? " Douglas said quickly.

" No believe."

" By whom, then ? "

" Winnebagoes."

" But," Ross objected, " the Winnebagoes have returned to their northern village."

" Not all go," the Wyandot asserted positively.

" Why do you say that ? "

" Winnebagoes make tracks. "

And the Indian pointed to the fresh trail.

Stooping and passing his finger over a moist spot of bare earth, Bright Wing replied triumphantly :

" See, moccasin track. No Shawnee moccasin, no Pottawatomie moccasin ; Winnebago moccasin. "

In silent wonder the two white men stood staring at their red friend. At last Farley burst forth :

" Well, if that don't beat *me !* The idee o' tellin' one moccasin track from another ! I'd as soon think o' tellin' one bear's track from another — I would, by Hanner Ann ! It's easy to tell a *wolf's* track from a *fox's*, but to tell *one* redskin's track from *another's* is a thing I never learnt ; an' I never could, if I lived a thousan' years. But no doubt the Injin's right, Ross Douglas. It's prob'ly a huntin' band o' the Winnebagoes that's loiterin' 'round in this neck o' woods. An' we've got redskins behind us, an' redskins before us. Now what 're we goin' to do? That's what I'd like to know. "

" It will soon be dark ; we must push forward, " Ross replied.

" An' tumble plump into the clutches o' the Winnebagoes, " Joe answered. " They're devils to fight; an' as cruel an' bloodthirsty as the Shawnees. "

" To remain here means to fall into the hands of the band upon our trail, " Douglas returned hastily. " The Winnebagoes know nothing of us ; perhaps we can avoid them. What have you to say,. Bright Wing ? "

"Scar Face and braves back there; Winnebagoes out there," the Wyandot answered, indicating each direction with his finger. "Go that way."

"You mean we should leave the Winnebago trail to the south, until we have passed them?"

"Ugh!"— With a vigorous nod.

"Very well. Let's be moving."

"But," cried Joe, "that's goin' to' take us 'way out of our course."

"It's better to leave our course than to lose our lives," was Douglas's answer, as he shouldered his rifle and followed the Indian.

Farley offered no reply, but silently brought up the rear. Duke trotted softly at his master's side. The shadows of night gathered noiselessly —swiftly. The four dusky figures moved forward. The sky was thickly obscured by clouds; the darkness was intense. Snow began to fall in fine, downy flakes. Still the four black forms — now a part of the general blackness — glided onward, slowly and cautiously.

"I say we've got far enough," Farley ventured at last, in a soft whisper.

Douglas was about to turn and make reply, when Bright Wing suddenly gave a grunt of warning and dropped to the ground. His companions followed his example. A hoarse growl rumbled up from Duke's deep chest, as he crouched like a tiger preparing for a spring. The next moment the sound of light footfalls came to the ears of all.

"Surrounded!" gasped Douglas.

"Fell into a trap, jest as I expected!" muttered Farley. "We're out o' the fryin'-pan into the fire!"

Duke uttered a vicious bay and sprang to his feet. Then the forest rang with a chorus of fiendish yells, as though all the imps of hell had broken loose at once.

In a moment the three men were upon their feet. The belching rifles of their enemies surrounded them with a ring of flame. Ross Douglas felt a stinging, burning sensation in his right breast. He discharged his gun, and staggered against a neighboring tree. Sparks of red and green light flashed before his eyes; a cataract roared in his ears. Dimly he discerned the savage forms swarming around him; faintly he heard the whoops of the Indians and the lusty cheers of his two comrades. Then he grew faint and dizzy. His limbs trembled; his brain swam. He coughed; and a stream of hot blood welled up in his throat. His legs failed him, and he sank upon the ground. As one in a dream, he heard Farley saying:

"The poor boy's done fer, Bright Wing! He's bleedin' from the mouth, an' senseless. 'Taint no use to stand by him no longer; he's past all help. Le's try to cut our way out o' this muss. We can't more 'n die! An' maybe it 'll draw the cusses away from the spot, an' save his scalp!"

The Wyandot's war-whoop and Farley's stentorian bellow again sounded above the yells of their enemies. Fainter and fainter grew the indescribable sounds of conflict in the darkness; and Ross was alone. No, not alone; for a dark body sprang to his side and, whimpering pitifully, crouched and licked his face. It was Duke.

Then the wounded man became blind, deaf, unconscious. And the soft snow fell and covered him, as a winding-sheet.

CHAPTER IX.

WHEN Ross Douglas regained consciousness, it was still night ; but the heavens were clear and starlit. The snow had ceased to fall ; the air was still and cold. A thin mantle of spotless white covered the earth. In the uncertain light, the bare tree trunks looked like files and squads of ghostly soldiers.

The wounded man attempted to change his position, but the pain in his right breast warned him to lie still. His attempted movement attracted the attention of his faithful, four-footed friend, who was sitting by his side. The hound whined plaintively, and licked his master's face. Ross put out his hand and patted the dog's head. This so pleased Duke, that he frisked about and barked joyfully, doing his best to entice his beloved master from his icy bed upon the frozen ground.

Douglas instantly remembered what had occurred, and fully realized his forlorn and helpless condition. But he was not one to yield to despair. Lying there desperately wounded — in a wilderness full of savage enemies, and far from any settlement — he resolved to outwit death or die gamely. He began an examination of himself and his surroundings. He found that he still lay at the foot of the tree where he had fallen. His wound had ceased to

bleed, but his hunting-shirt was stiff with frozen
blood ; and the saline taste of the crimson life-tide
was yet in his throat.   Every breath caused him a
pang ; and a deep inspiration gave him excruciating
torture.   But he could move his arms and legs
without much pain or difficulty.   Again he essayed
to arise, but fell back with a groan ; he was too
weak from fasting and loss of blood.

"If only I could get upon my feet !" he murmured.   "I shall freeze here."

Seeing that his master could not arise, Duke had
returned to his former position.   Now he tilted his
muzzle aloft and bayed mournfully.

"There — there, old fellow !" Ross said soothingly.   "Keep up your courage.   Things are not
entirely hopeless so long as we two are together.
Ah !   Perhaps you can help me to get up.   Here,
let me get my arms around your neck.   That's it.
Now, Duke, pull — pull !"

The bloodhound was accustomed to obeying his
master's every command.   Digging his claws into
the flinty earth, he stretched his lithe, muscular
body, in an attempt to do the bidding of the being
he loved.   Ross clung tenaciously to the noble
animal's neck.   The result was he was dragged to
a sitting posture.   The effort cost him much pain,
but he gained his object.   Duke was delighted ; he
ran about in a circle and barked vociferously.

Leaning his back against the tree-trunk, Douglas
panted :

"This is better !   I'm off the flat of my back —

half-way upon my feet. After a short rest I'll make a further effort. What should I have done without my faithful dog ? "

In attempting to shift himself to an easier position, he placed his hand upon his gun, which was lying where he had dropped it. With a joyful exclamation, he caught it up and feebly dragged it across his lap. Then, taking the skirt of his hunting-shirt, he carefully wiped and dried the weapon, remarking to himself as he did so :

"I have a gun — I have ammunition — I have flint and steel. If I can manage to light a fire, I shall be in no danger of freezing. Then, perhaps, I may be able to shoot some animal for food — provided it comes near my camp. I must have something to eat."

He sighed breathlessly. Then drawing his legs well under him and using his gun as an aid, he commenced slowly to arise to a standing posture, all the time keeping his back firmly pressed against the tree-trunk. The task was a herculean one ; but after several failures he succeeded. Duke simply went wild with delight, rolling over and over in the snow and barking frantically.

After resting a few minutes, Douglas, leaning heavily upon his rifle, tried to take a few steps. His legs trembled and threatened to give way under him, and every fiber in his body ached and quivered ; but he resolutely put out one foot after the other. His head swam, and he reeled and tottered like an infant. But he succeeded in making his way to another tree, against which he leaned, gasping for breath. Standing there, he tremblingly reloaded his rifle.

"Better than I expected!" he whispered with bloodless lips. "Much better! Now I shall seek a sheltered spot and build a fire."

Putting his resolution into action, he slowly and painfully worked his way to a small depression, a short distance from the scene of conflict. It was half-filled with drifted leaves and snow, and almost surrounded by bushes and briers. Near it were the dead and dry limbs of a fallen tree.

Staggering into this natural shelter, Ross dropped upon the ground. Duke accompanied him. The wounded man laboriously cleared the cave of the accumulated mass of snow and leaves. When he had finished his hard task, he took out his flint and steel, and, after several discouraging failures, succeeded in starting a fire. Upon the tiny flame he piled sticks from the fallen tree-tops, which soon were ablaze. With a sigh of relief and comfort, he fell back and closed his eyes.

After a time, however, the genial warmth penetrated his chilled and stiffened frame and aroused him from the partial swoon into which he had fallen. Sitting erect, he held out his hands to the welcome blaze and murmured tremulously:

"What a man *can do!* Oh, this cough! It almost strangles me; and the pain is awful. Still I'm better off than I was—much better. I shall not freeze, at any rate. But I must have food. I am *so* weak. Let me see,"—rolling his eyes heavenward,—"the stars indicate that it's after midnight. I'll rest by the fire until morning; then I'll do what I can to procure something to eat."

Again he coughed spasmodically — hackingly. When the paroxysm had passed, he continued his whispered, broken monologue:

"I wonder what became of Bright Wing and Joe. I'm glad they thought me dead. They'd have sacrificed their lives by staying; and done me no good. They may be dead; they may be prisoners among the Winnebagoes; or they may have escaped. If they got away unharmed, they'll return to Franklinton and report my death. My God! My God! Amy—dear girl! The news will break her heart. And—great heavens! She may be persuaded to marry George Hilliard!"

Bowing his head upon his hands, he groaned. He was suffering mentally and physically. His temples were throbbing; his skin was hot and dry. The demon of fever was dancing through his arteries.

For some time, he sat silently staring into the depths of the fire. Above him the stars winked pitilessly; around him the lean shadows glided among the trees and eerily mocked him. No eye but God's was upon him; no hand was stretched forth to save him.

He mused mumblingly — half deliriously:

"Even God will not help me. He would not,
if he could. He has laid down inflexible laws for
the government of the universe; he will not alter
them to accommodate the individual. But I'll
not despair — I *will* not! I will overcome all
obstacles; I will cheat fate. The snow has concealed all signs of our encounter with the Winnebagoes; has covered our trail. Bradford and his
braves will never find me. On the morrow I'll
procure food; then I shall be stronger. I'll
work my way eastward, by easy stages. Now
I'll lie down and try to snatch a few hours of
natural sleep. Oh! This terrific cough and pain!
And my head!"

He piled more dry wood upon the fire, and
stretched himself upon the ground. Duke nestled
at his back and helped to keep him warm. The
red blaze crackled cheerily; the smoke and sparks
ascended in gyrating columns. The wounded man
lay and watched them until his eyelids closed.

When he awoke it was broad daylight. The
fire had burned down; only a few gray embers and
charred bits of wood marked its place. Duke, with
bristles erect, was sitting by his master's side,
growling mutteringly — warningly. It was this
sound that had awakened the sleeper.

Ross rubbed his eyes and sought to arise. But
his limbs were as lead; his blood was as ice. He
stirred; and a thousand needles pricked his flesh.
By great effort he sat erect. His head gave him
keenest torture; his eyes threatened to drop from

their sockets. His sight was dim. Strange noises rang in his ears. He tried to take a deep breath; but the pain in his chest caused him to moan aloud. His heart was thumping tumultuously. Thor's hammer was beating in his brain.

Again the bloodhound uttered a hoarse, rumbling growl; and this time, sprang to his feet and advanced a step or two from his master's side.

"Someone or something is approaching," was Douglas's mental comment. Then aloud: "Watch them, Duke—but do not leave me!"

But the dog had no intention of deserting his charge. Rigidly erect, menace and defiance in his attitude, he stood his ground. Ross listened intently, and thought he heard stealthy footsteps beyond the fringe of bushes that shut him in. But, through the interstices in the brush and brambles, he could see no one. Once more the hound growled, and more sharply than before. Then Douglas caught the patter of moccasined feet upon the snow-covered leaves, and the buzz of whispered words. A moment later the bushes parted and a painted Shawnee peeped into the glade.

Duke's bristles quivered; his wicked eyes blazed. Revealing a double row of ivory fangs, he snarled savagely and crouched for a spring. Excitement lent strength to Douglas's limbs. In some way — he never knew how — he got upon his feet and flung his heavy gun to his shoulder. With a grunt of surprise and terror, the Indian instantly withdrew his painted visage.

Ross sank in a heap upon the ground, whispering brokenly:

"Too weak — too weak! I'm at their mercy. Ah! Duke, old fellow, our time has come — for you will die fighting for me!"

And closing his aching eyes, he lay gasping.

Then came a thunderous rush among the bushes; and a half dozen savages stood within the cove, and as many rifles were pointed at the form of the prostrate and helpless man. Duke leaped at the throat of the nearest brave, and with him rolled upon the ground. At that moment a husky voice bellowed:

"Stop, you cowardly curs! Would you murder a wounded and helpless man? Harm a hair of his head, and I'll have the life of the last one of you! Didn't I tell you he was to be taken alive? Out of my way!"

It was the voice of Hiram Bradford. Douglas had just enough consciousness left to realize what was occurring, just enough strength remaining to call off his dog. Then he swooned.

Bradford shoved the savages right and left, and bent over the form of the unconscious man. He placed his hand over Douglas's heart and listened to the faint, irregular respiration. He gazed earnestly, sadly, upon the pain-contorted features of the young man. His own face was pale; his brown, sinewy hand trembled. Arising, he said to the savage band he commanded:

"Start a fire; and be quick about it!"

Then to the Pottawatomie, whom Duke had attacked and who was now threatening to kill the dog, as the animal lay whining at the feet of his senseless idol:

"You shall not touch the dog. If you do, I'll shoot you dead in your tracks. The brute did his duty — that's all. He was protecting the life of his defenseless master. He is a noble specimen of his race. I command you to let him alone."

The Pottawatomie sullenly obeyed. Bradford again turned his attention to Douglas.

"Poor boy!" he murmured softly to himself, his lips quivering. "Although you hate me, and would kill me now, perhaps, had you the opportunity — I love you. God knows I've wronged you enough in the past. Yet, when you had the chance, you did not kill me. Would you do it now? Heaven knows! Oh! Why didn't you stay with me? Then this would not have occurred. Now you are wounded unto death — dying, I fear, before my eyes. No! you shall *not* die. I'll save you — I *will!* And who has done this monstrous deed? Is it the work of white men or red? Whichever it be, they shall pay for it, if I have to follow them to the ends of the earth. I vow it before God! Shot through the breast, there you lay in the ice and snow, until you regained consciousness. Then you pluckily made your way here and built a fire, bravely fighting against all odds. Somebody left you for dead — somebody deserted you. But your faithful dog stayed by you. I have hated the brute;

now I could kiss his surly face.   Yes, my boy, I
can read it all ; you have left in the snow a record
of your desperate fight for life ! "

The strong man bowed his head.   The savages,
engaged in building a fire and preparing to cook
some meat, did not notice the agitation of their
leader.   His features worked spasmodically, and
the scar upon his cheek twitched painfully, as he
continued to whisper to himself :

" God of heaven, tell me who has done this awful thing !   The snow has hidden all signs of the
conflict — if conflict there was.   It, also, covered
your trail, my boy, and I stumbled upon you by
chance.   But, my God !   Of what am I thinking ?
Do I mean to let you die without an effort to save
you ? "

Like one electrified, he leaped to his feet.   All his
emotion had vanished.   Once more he was himself — the cool, firm, diplomatic leader of savage
men.   His ordinarily husky voice rang out sharp
and clear as he cried :

"Listen, braves !   This man is not dead — he
must *not* die.   You have done well — you shall
have the gold I promised you.   In addition, each
one of you shall have five pounds, if you do all in
your power to help me to get him to camp alive.
Stir yourselves !   Cook your meat quickly.   Then
cut boughs and prepare a litter on which to carry
him.   Here, Long Gun, assist me."

By this time a huge fire was roaring, that rendered the cave warm and comfortable.   A part of

the company raked red coals from their bed, and
upon them commenced to broil slices of meat ; while
others began to cut limbs and withes, and weave
and bind together a strong and elastic litter.

Bradford seated himself and took Douglas's head
upon his lap. Then he produced a flask of brandy,
and with Long Gun's help succeeded in pouring a
small quantity down the unconscious man's throat.
A second and third time he repeated this, ere there
were any signs of returning life. At last the feeble
heart began to beat more regularly and forcibly.
The pulse at the wrist became perceptible ; color
commenced to creep into the marble face. A long-
drawn respiration heaved the wounded chest, and a
low moan escaped from the blue lips. The white
lids lifted ; but there was no intelligence in the
fever-bright eyes. The wan demon of death had
yielded his throne to the riotous imp of delirium.

Bradford shrunk back and shuddered as these
words fell upon his ear :

"Ah, Hiram Bradford, we've met at last, in a
death-struggle ! Now I have you at my mercy.
You kept me a prisoner against my will — you kept
me from the woman I love. You have wounded
me — starved me — frozen me. Now you shall
die — *die !* "

Douglas's hands were clenched as though he held
an enemy by the throat.

"Ugh !" ejaculated Long Gun. "The Great
Spirit has robbed the young paleface of his senses.

14

Like a dog dreaming of the chase, he fights in his sleep."

The Shawnee understood but little Ross said, but read aright the meaning of the wounded man's tone of voice and expression of countenance.

"Silence!" Bradford commanded sharply.

Then, caressingly smoothing the flushed face of the delirious man, he murmured soothingly:

"Don't fret yourself. Your enemies are gone; you are with friends now. I'll take care of you."

"Who are you?"

The bright eyes opened very wide.

"Don't you know me?" Bradford asked, anxiety in his tone and manner.

"Yes—yes, I know you, Joe Farley. Of course I know my old friend. I was sure you would come back. But where is Bright Wing?"

"He'll be here soon," answered Bradford, sighing deeply.

"And Duke—surely *he* hasn't deserted me—where is Duke?"

At mention of his name, the hound crept forward and licked his master's hand. The dumb caress appeared to soothe and assure the sick man more than anything else could have done. For, with a sigh of contentment, he closed his eyes and whispered feebly:

"Oh, yes! Duke, old fellow, you are still with me. You'll not let the Winnebagoes return and scalp me. Watch over me, good dog, for I'm sleepy—sleepy—"

Then he lay quiet. But his breathing was hurried; his pulse, bounding; and he continued to moan occasionally, and mumble and babble words that could not be understood.

"The Winnebagoes!" Bradford muttered, scowling darkly.

Arising, he began to hasten the preparations for departure. He partook of the parched corn and broiled venison the savages had prepared. Afterward he took a small portion of the tender meat, pressed its savory juices into a drinking cup, and poured the liquid down his patient's throat. Ordering the litter brought to him, he stripped off his own hunting-shirt — unmindful of the chill atmosphere — and rolled it into a pillow for Douglas's head. Carefully and tenderly placing his charge upon the springy bed, he covered him with a ragged, scarlet blanket which one of the Pottawatomies had worn around his shoulders; and selecting four of the most stalwart warriors and giving them minute instructions how to carry the litter, he ordered the band to start upon the return journey.

"Do we go back to Wildcat Creek?" Long Gun inquired.

"No," Bradford answered, "we go to the villages of the Miamis, upon the Mississinewa."

"But are our people there?"

"Yes, by this time."

"Ugh!" was the satisfied rejoinder.

And Long Gun relapsed into his wonted silence. All day long, the band trudged through the

sheeted woodland, stopping only at noon.   The Indians occasionally conversed in guttural under-
tones, but Scar Face maintained a moody silence.
A stillness as of death reigned in the forest, unbroken save for the sharp rattling rap of a wood-
pecker now and then, or the startling whir of a
partridge's wings.

Bradford walked beside the litter and looked after
the welfare of his patient.   He gave him frequent
doses of brandy, and at noon succeeded in getting
him to swallow a little shredded meat.   Douglas
coughed almost continuously, and groaned at every
sudden jolt of his swinging bed.   A circular bright-
red spot appeared upon each cheek, and the arteries
of his temples and neck pulsated visibly.   The
wound he had received and the consequent exposure
had done their work but too well.   He was suffering from pneumonia.

At one time during the afternoon, he became violently excited and made repeated attempts to arise
from his couch.   In vain Bradford sought to soothe
and quiet him.   Apparently understanding the
need of his presence, Duke trotted to the litter and
fondly licked the hot hand that was frantically
threshing the air. With a smile upon his face, Ross
lay back and wearily closed his wild, staring eyes.

"Wonderful!" Bradford muttered aloud, sadly
shaking his head.

"Wonderful—wonderful," repeated the delirious man, in a monotonous, parrot-like voice.   Then
with animation:

"Oh, Amy! you here? No, it's La Violette — or *is* it Amy? La Violette — Amy; La Violette — Amy. I don't know."

His words became an unintelligible jargon; but his fit of violence had passed.

At nightfall the Indians went into camp. Bradford placed the litter near the fire, and had a screen of boughs erected to shelter its occupant from the night wind. Again he got his patient to take a small portion of shredded meat and a little of the expressed juice. The supply of brandy was almost exhausted; and he wisely resolved to save what was left for an emergency. All night he sat by Ross's side, giving him water, for which the poor fellow begged piteously at frequent intervals, and protecting him as best he could from the cold.

Duke fared well. Seeing his unparalleled devotion to his master, the Indians took a fancy to the intelligent animal, and fed him all he would eat.

At daylight the wearisome march was resumed; and at noon the party was drawing near the Miami village upon the Mississinewa. As they entered the town, hundreds of savages swarmed around them, and gazed in stupefaction upon the unusual spectacle of four grave and dignified warriors bearing the litter of a wounded paleface.

Pushing his way to the center of the village, a large collection of well-built lodges and cabins upon the eastern bank of the stream, Bradford asked for the Prophet. Tenskwatawa's domicile was pointed out to him. Unceremoniously pushing aside the curtain of skins, he entered the dark hut. The Prophet lay stretched upon a fur rug near the center of the floor, his feet to the fire that alone lighted the dismal interior. He did not offer to arise at Bradford's entrance ; but greeted him with a grunt of recognition. The intruder went straight to the point, by saying :

"My prisoner escaped. I have recaptured him and brought him here. But he is badly wounded ; and I want the largest and most comfortable cabin in the village, in which I may place him and nurse him back to life."

The Prophet arose to a sitting position, before replying. Then he made the heartless rejoinder :

"Let the young paleface die ! He is a member of the Seventeen Fires — he is an enemy. His death will subtract one more from the number that ere long will appear against us, to do battle."

"He shall *not* die," Bradford returned firmly.

"Why ?"

"Because I will not have it so."

"Why does Scar Face so much desire to save the young man's life ?" the Prophet inquired, with a cunning leer.

"Why I wish to save his life — why I *will* save his life — concerns no one but myself," was the bold reply.

"Tenskwatawa, there is no use in our re-threshing old straw. I have told you that this young man is my friend. I repeat it. You know me well enough to realize that I will have my way — that I

will not be balked in whatever I undertake. Let's
have an end of all parleying. I want the largest
and best cabin in the place. Can I have it?"

"Scar Face asks for what is not mine to bestow."

"What do you mean? Be quick. I have no
time to waste in idle diplomacy."

"This is the village of the Miamis," was the
shrewd answer. "The lodges are theirs. They
have granted my people the privilege of staying
here, but we must erect lodges for ourselves. When
that is done, Scar Face shall have one placed at his
disposal."

Bradford's anger was rising. His face flushed,
then paled; the red scar upon his cheek quivered
tremulously and twitched the corner of his mouth.
He nervously fingered the trigger of his rifle —
which he again had in his possession — as he said
huskily:

"An end to your lies, Tenskwatawa! You cannot
deceive *me*. The Miamis are a part of your family.
You are here in one of their cabins. Tecumseh
has another; and your braves are busily engaged in
erecting others. I want the best one in the village;
and I am going to have it. Do you understand?"

The Prophet's repulsive face became more repulsive. He was angry — afraid. He bent his head in
reply, but did not open his lips.

"Well, go and give the order!" Bradford roared
impatiently. "Hurry! — before I lose control of
myself and stamp the life out of your miserable
carcass!"

Tenskwatawa slowly arose. His limbs were shaking; his lips, trembling. The arrant coward was desperately afraid his companion would carry his threat into execution. And no help was at hand. When he could command his voice, he said :

"But the best lodge has been given to La Violette and the woman who attends her."

"What of the council lodge?"

"I have made it a temple of the Great Spirit. You cannot have it."

And the Prophet flung up his head, with a gesture of weak defiance.

Bradford was furious. He was on the point of giving full sway to his seething passion, and beating the brains out of the miserable wretch before him; but he thought of the wounded man upon the litter outside, and checked himself.

"Where is La Violette?" he hissed fiercely.

As if in answer to the question, the curtain of skin was pushed aside, and the young woman stepped into the room. Bradford turned at her entrance. By the dim light of the flickering fire, he saw that she was pale and excited.

"Hiram Bradford, what is the meaning of this?" she cried sharply.

He thought she referred to his presence in the Prophet's hut, and was attempting to frame a suitable reply, when she imperiously stamped her little foot and demanded :

"Answer me! Why have you killed that young man? And you claimed to be his friend!"

"Do you mean Ross Douglas?" Bradford returned wonderingly.

"I mean Fleet Foot — Ross Douglas — yes."

"He's not dead," Bradford hastened to explain, "but he's —— "

"Desperately wounded," she completed in icy tones.

"Yes."

"Why did you do it?"

"You wrong me. I didn't harm him —— "

"No," she interrupted angrily, "but you permitted the warriors you had with you to shoot him, when he was trying to regain his liberty. It was murder! For shame! You are worse than a wild beast!"

As she finished speaking, her breast was heaving and tears were in her violet eyes.

In a few words Bradford explained to her what had happened, and asked her for the use of the cabin she occupied. The cloud partially lifted from her face, and she answered quickly:

"I am glad that neither you, nor the warriors under your command, committed this awful deed. For I have learned to look upon you as a brave man, and merciful even to your bitterest enemies." — Bradford winced slightly. — "You can have the cabin I have occupied, on one condition."

"Name it," he said promptly.

"That I be permitted to nurse your — your friend, shall I say? — back to health."

For a moment she keenly eyed him, to note the

effect of her words. Then, seeming to realize that she had made an unusual proposition, she continued confusedly :

"I — I promised when he saved my life, to do all in my power to set him free. I meant to keep my word. But his friends came to his rescue, and he regained his freedom without my assistance ; only to lose it again. Now he is in great need of tender care ; and I want to repay him for risking his life in my behalf. I feel that I am indebted to him. Do you accept my proposal ? "

"Gladly," Bradford answered quickly, a strange light flashing in his blue eyes. "Nothing would please me more than to have your assistance."

"Then it is settled," she returned quietly. "Carry him to the cabin at once. I will come soon."

The Prophet witnessed all that passed ; but he offered no opposition to the arrangement. Perhaps he felt it would be useless to do so.

After thanking the young woman, Bradford withdrew and had the wounded man carried to the place agreed upon. As he placed his charge upon a couch of soft furs and strove to make him as comfortable as possible, the older man whispered to himself :

"Oh, if I can save his life! If I can save his life! Fate is playing into my hands. All will yet be well. I shall realize my desire. But he might *die!* Oh, God! He *must* not, he *shall* not ! "

CHAPTER X.

FOR days Ross Douglas lay unconscious, fighting all the powers of fever and delirium — battling for his life. Hiram Bradford was his constant companion and nurse. La Violette was an able and devoted assistant.

On the day following his arrival in the village of the Miamis, Bradford procured from a French trader — who had just come across from Canada — a quantity of brandy, and a few drugs, the uses of which he knew. Armed with these, he assumed the province of physician and strove manfully to save the young man's life.

La Violette was unremitting in her tender care. She prepared hot poultices of cornmeal and dried herbs, which relieved the patient's distressing cough, and gave him rest, when all other means failed. Several times a day she brought him nourishing broths, and coaxed him to drink them. Her deft fingers rearranged his bed of furs; and her caressing touch soothed him to slumber. When Bradford was snatching a few hours' sleep or taking exercise in the open air, the young woman sat by the patient's couch — all her soul in her beautiful face. At such times her countenance was transfigured. Caressingly stroking Douglas's raven locks, damp with the dews of suffering, she fixed her violet eyes upon his dark, handsome features and listened eagerly to the words that fell from his lips. He was delirious — there was little sense to his babble. It mattered not to La Violette; she loved to hear his voice.

When he tossed restively and coughed and moaned, she patted his great brown hand and spoke soothingly to him. And with a smile flitting about his mouth, he fell asleep. Then with swift, timorous glances around her, she bent and tenderly pressed her ripe lips to his white brow. She was drinking deeply of the rosy, intoxicating cup of love, unmindful of the lees at the bottom.

Duke had a place in one corner of the cabin. At times he would leave his bed and, trotting to his master's couch, would fondly lick his hand. Then he would throw himself upon the ground and intently watch all that was going on. The hound barely tolerated Bradford's presence, and would growl warningly whenever the latter attempted any playful familiarity. But La Violette could take the surly animal's head upon her lap, and pull his pendulous ears, with impunity.

One day Bradford lay asleep upon a pile of furs, in one corner of the hut. La Violette was watching at Douglas's side. A violent fit of coughing assailed the patient, and he groaned aloud. His hands — growing thinner and whiter day by day — clutched frantically at his throat. His wan, emaciated countenance was contorted by a spasm of pain.

Duke softly trotted to the young woman's side and, dropping at her feet, beseechingly looked up into her face.

"Yes — yes, noble fellow," La Violette murmured tearfully, "I will do all I can for him. For" — in the faintest whisper — "we love him — you and I!"

At that moment Bradford awoke, and, through his half-closed lids, dreamily watched the play before him. He saw La Violette pat the dog's head and whisper to him. Then she turned her attention to the restless sufferer — renewing the poultice upon his chest, changing the position of his head and gently soothing him to rest, as a mother would quiet a fretful child. It was a pretty picture; and Bradford smiled a self-satisfied smile, as he gazed upon it. He was about to close his eyes, in an attempt to sleep again, when he observed La Violette bend down and passionately kiss the unconscious man's lips.

"Amy, Amy!" Douglas mumbled, his dry tongue hardly able to shape the words. "Is it you, Amy — and have you come to me at last? I've wanted you so long — so long! And you are still true to me? Say that you are, Amy. For I dreamed — or did someone tell me? — that you were false — false!"

La Violette started back as if someone had dealt her a sharp blow. She glanced apprehensively toward Bradford's couch; but he appeared to be sleeping. Her beautiful face was colorless; her violet eyes were swimming with tears. Bending over her charge, she whispered faintly:

"Who is Amy?"

"Amy, Amy," Douglas repeated, parrot-like.

"It is not Amy," she murmured tenderly — lovingly. "It is I — La Violette; and I love you!"

"Ah!" the delirious man ejaculated, and opened his eyes very wide.

She started back. She feared — yet hoped — he had recognized her, understood her meaning. His next words undeceived her, however.

"You — you cannot fool me," he mumbled huskily. "You are Amy. I — I love you, Amy ——"

And then he closed his eyes and lay quiet, the movement of his parched lips alone telling that he was communing with the phantoms that beset his feverish brain.

La Violette bowed her golden head and wept convulsively. Duke thrust his cold muzzle against her hand, in token of sympathy. Impulsively the girl threw her arms around the animal's neck, and hugged him. Then she again hid her face and gave way to her acute grief. Already she was beginning to taste the bitter dregs in the bottom of the cup of love.

Bradford arose, and, lightly moving to her side, laid his hand upon her shoulder. She sprang to her feet, an exclamation of alarm upon her lips. When she saw who it was that confronted her, she proudly threw back her head — her eyes alight with anger. Tossing aside her disheveled hair, she cried scornfully :

"Hiram Bradford, you have been spying upon me."

"I was awake," he returned quietly. "I saw all. You love him."

Her face grew crimson — then paled.

"And if I *do*?" she said defiantly.

"Nothing," he answered, his husky voice huskier than usual. "I'm glad you *do* love him. And — if he live — he shall be yours. You were made for each other."

"Do — do you think he is — is going to die?" she asked falteringly.

"No ; we two will save him. He'll learn to love you — the lesson will not be a hard one."

"But ——" and she hesitated.

"Well?"

"He loves another."

"How do you know that?"

"I had it from his own lips."

Bradford playfully patted her cheek — which caused Duke to growl menacingly — as he replied :

"Pshaw, little one! You must give no heed to the vaporings of a delirious brain. Wait until he's himself. You'll see how easily you can win his love. He babbled of you when I was bringing him here."

"Did he?" And a glad light sprang into her eyes.

"Yes. Leave everything to me. I've been your friend in the past; I'm your friend now.

And both of us are *his* friends. Now go for a walk
in the open air — and get some color into your
cheeks.''

The days and weeks dragged drearily. Ross
Douglas did not arise from the depths of fever and
delirium, into which his wound had plunged him.
Daily he grew weaker and thinner. In spite of the
unremitting care of his nurses, he seemed slowly
but surely drifting toward the shores of the unknown. November passed ; December came — and
Christmas was drawing near. And still the hosts
of death laid siege to the citadel of his life.

In the meantime, disaffection again arose in the
ranks of the Prophet's followers. The winter was
severe ; and food was scarce. Many of the Indians
drifted away from the Mississinewa, in search of
game, or returned to their old homes. Tecumseh sat
in his cabin, moodily pondering over the condition of
affairs. Yet had it not been for his presence, his
and his brother's followers would have deserted, to
a man. As it was, only the Miamis and a faithful
few of the various tribes remained. In the latter
part of November, Tenskwatawa sent messengers to
Fort Harrison, to ask for a share of the annuities
that were being distributed to the peaceable savages. These messengers succeeded in deceiving the
agent at the post, and returned to Mississinewa with
a large amount of provisions and other stores.

About this time, also, the English — learning of
the Prophet's defeat and misfortunes — sent him a
supply of arms, ammunition, blankets, and cooking

utensils. Bradford distributed these goods impartially.

Toward the last of December, the weather suddenly grew warmer and game again appeared in the vicinity of the village. Despondency and gloom gave way to feasting and rejoicing.

One morning, a few days before Christmas, La Violette sat by Douglas's couch. Bradford had been up all night. Now he lay sleeping the sleep of utter nervous exhaustion. The fire in the middle of the room burned dimly — casting angular shadows upon the rough log walls. Outside the rain fell drearily. The earth was water-soaked; the air, fog-laden and chilly.

Nothing broke the stillness of the room, but the muffled, sullen rush of the distant stream and the low, incoherent mutterings of the restless patient. Uneasily he moved his head from side to side, and aimlessly picked at imaginary objects in the air. He was the shadow of his magnificent self. His hollow, burning eyes were wide open and staring; his parched lips, drawn apart. No color was in his face, except the hectic spots upon his sunken cheeks.

La Violette was pale and worn. As she looked upon the wreck of virile manhood before her, she sighed deeply, and despondently shook her head.

Even as she looked upon the sick man, an abrupt change came over him. His lips ceased to move — and gradually turned blue; his teeth set themselves with a sharp click. The hectic spots upon his

15

cheeks faded, leaving his face of marble whiteness; and an icy sweat bathed his brow and temples. A rigor shook his emaciated form from head to foot; his breathing became irregular.

La Violette caught his hand in hers, and found it cold and clammy. Springing to her feet, she ran to Bradford and aroused him. He was wide awake in an instant.

"What's the matter?" he inquired anxiously.

"*He — is — dying !*"

The words fell like leaden balls. Bradford felt each of them strike his heart. The girl's face wore a horrified expression. Without waiting to hear more, Bradford ran to his patient's bedside. After a hurried examination he announced :

"The crisis has arrived! He's not dying — we can yet save him. Don't get excited — don't lose your head. Roll that hot stone in a blanket, and place it to his feet. That's right — you're as steady as a clock. Heat another blanket to wrap around him. Have no fear — we shall save him. Now get me the flask of brandy and the small white powders that are in the pocket of my hunting-shirt. What a brave little woman you are !"

Her hands were shaking like aspen leaves ; but she obeyed his orders. When the medicines were in his possession, Bradford poured out a quantity of the fiery liquid and dropped into it the white powder. Then quickly mixing the two, he forcibly poured the whole down the dying man's throat.

Silently he watched for the effects of the power-

ful draught. They were not long in showing
themselves. The rigor passed; and a warm glow
suffused the patient's neck and face, and rose to his
temples. Pulse and respiration gradually grew
steadier — stronger; and feet and hands regained
their accustomed warmth. A natural moisture
overspread the body. And the sick man sank into
a deep, dreamless sleep.

For an hour the two nurses sat by Ross's side —
neither speaking a word. At last Bradford yawned
and remarked:

"He's all right now, little girl. The worst is
over. I'm going to finish my nap. Don't dis-
turb him — let him sleep as long as he will. When
he awakes he'll be conscious. Call me, if he
rouses before I do. Be brave a little longer; and all
will be well."

For hours the two men slept. La Violette
scarcely dared to breathe, for fear of waking her
charge. Noon came. Bradford arose, and, approaching the couch, closely inspected the sleeper.

"He's doing nicely," he said. Then noting La
Violette's pallid face:

"Come — you must get out of here. I don't
care to take charge of another patient just now. I
never did like the practice of the profession. Take
a turn in the open air — and get something to eat
while you're gone."

But she resolutely shook her head, as she replied:

"I will stay by him until he awakes. You go —
you need air and exercise more than I."

"You'll go when I return?" he asked.

"If he be awake — yes."

Bradford smiled to himself, as he passed through the door, murmuring:

"I know your desire, my sweet maid. You want your face to be the first he shall see when he regains consciousness — your voice to be the first he shall hear. Ah! Love may make cowards of men; but it makes angels of women."

After Bradford left the cabin, La Violette kneeled upon the bare ground at the sleeping man's side and gazed long and earnestly into his face, moving her lips as though in prayer. Then she timidly took his thin hand between her soft palms and kissed it gently — reverently, again and again. At last he stirred and opened his eyes. The blank stare of delirium was gone; there was intelligence in the look he fastened upon her. Embarrassed, she dropped his hand and drew herself erect, her face aflame. His lips moved; and she caught the faint whisper:

"La Violette."

She nodded, but placed her finger upon her lips, in token of silence.

"Where am I?" he persisted.

"With friends," she answered feelingly. "But you are very weak; you must not talk."

Unheeding her words, he went on in a feeble, whispering tone:

"I'm so helpless. Have I been very ill?"

"Yes; you have been very ill. Please do not try to talk; the effort will hurt you."

Leaving his side, she brought a cup of gruel from the fire — where it had been warming upon the coals — and insisted that he drink it. Like a fretful child, he pushed it aside and whimpered :

" Answer my questions — answer my questions ! "

Seeing that he was growing excited, she said soothingly :

" Drink this for me, and I will answer your questions. Take it all — that's right. Now, what do you want to know ? "

" Where am I — at Wildcat Creek ? "

" No ; you are at the village of the Miamis, upon the Mississinewa."

" Who brought me here ? "

" Hiram Bradford."

" Bradford ? Ah, yes ! I remember now. I was wounded by the Winnebagoes. My companions left me, thinking I was dead. How long have I been here — several days ? "

" Several weeks."

" So long ! Who has taken care of — of — me ? "

He was panting for breath. Noting which, she answered kindly but firmly :

" Bradford has taken care of you. But you must talk no more — you are too weak. Close your eyes and try to sleep."

" And you have — helped to nurse — me," he went on brokenly. " I know — you have. I was dimly — dimly conscious of your presence. But I thought you were — were —— "

" You must talk no more," she sternly interrupted. "If you do not obey me, I will leave you here alone."

A feeble, flickering smile for one brief moment illuminated his ghastly features. Then it was gone, and he murmured faintly :

"No, don't leave me. I'll obey you."

And obediently he closed his eyes, and was soon fast asleep.

A few minutes later Bradford returned.

"Still sleeping?" he inquired softly, gazing into the upturned face.

"He has been awake," La Violette answered quietly.

"Ah! And he recognized you?"

She nodded.

"Did he ask you any questions?"

"He wanted to know where he was, who had brought him here, and who nursed him."

"You answered his questions?"

"Yes."

"And then?"

"I gave him some gruel and commanded him to go to sleep."

"And he obeyed you. I couldn't have done better myself. Now you must keep the promise you made me. Take a short walk; then eat something and seek the rest you so much need. I don't want to see you back here until tomorrow morning. Come — you must do as I say."

Listlessly, pathetically, La Violette left the cabin ; and Bradford took her place by Douglas's couch.

Ross improved very slowly. It was the first of February before he could totter across the room and take a peep at the outer world. He was greatly reduced in flesh and strength ; he was nervous and irritable. His muscles were soft, his buoyant disposition was gone, and his mind seemed feeble and apathetic. Bradford and La Violette did all they could to cheer and encourage him — but in vain. Like a water-logged vessel, he drifted this way and that in the eddy of conflicting emotions — and made little progress toward the haven of health.

Out of patience, at last, Bradford said to him :

"Look here, young man ! Do you want to get well ? If you do, you've got to rouse yourself. Shake off your lethargy and be a man. You're acting the baby. I'm ashamed of you."

Ross proudly straightened his thin form. His nostrils dilated and quivered. Something like his old self-reliance flashed in his hollow eyes, as he cried in piping tones :

"Hiram Bradford, you're very brave now ; you insult a man who is too weak to give you the drubbing your words merit. You've forgotten that I defeated you in a fair contest of strength and skill — when I was myself. Yes, I *will* rouse myself ; I will try to recover my health — if for no other purpose than to make you eat your words !"

A spasm of pain contorted Bradford's scarred face. But quickly recovering his equanimity, he chuckled huskily :

"That's it — get angry at me. I thought I could stir you. You feel better already, don't you?"

Douglas earnestly scanned the speaker's face for a full minute. Bradford burst out laughing. With a sheepish grin, the younger man said :

"I understand you now. Your words and actions are a part of your plan of treatment, eh? Well, I'll shake off my lethargy — if I can. I'll be a man, and strive to recover my health and strength. I *am* ashamed of myself. Please forgive my childish petulance. Here is my hand."

The two shook hands, silently — solemnly. Then Douglas continued :

"Twice you have saved my life, Bradford. I am grateful — I don't hate you as I did. I may as well confess that I rather like you — that I feel you are my friend. I want to thank you for your unremitting and tender care. Yet I cannot understand why you keep me a prisoner. And here I give you fair warning: As soon as I'm able, I'll again try to escape."

A smile almost beatific lighted the elder man's marred visage, as he replied feelingly :

"I *am* your friend ; and I am delighted to know you begin to realize it. Please say again that you don't hate me."

"I don't hate you," Ross said quietly.

"And you wouldn't harm me, if you could?"

"No — unless ——"

"Unless what?"

"Unless you should offer injury to me or some one dear to me."

"Which I'll never do," Bradford answered earnestly. "Now we understand each other. You're to try to get well; I'm to help you. You're going to try to escape; I'm going to try to prevent you from succeeding. Have I stated the case correctly?"

"Yes," Douglas returned smilingly.

"Very well. Now you'd better lie down and take a nap. You're tired."

From that day, Ross began to improve more rapidly. His cough gradually subsided; his appetite grew better. He commenced to regain strength and flesh. But the lancinating pain was still in his chest; and it took but little exercise or excitement to exhaust him. Then, too, his mind was perturbed. The stronger he grew, the more he chafed under the yoke of captivity. He worried about Amy. He thought of her by day, and dreamed of her by night. Was she alive — was she well? Was she grieving over his supposed death, or was she wholly unaware of the misfortunes that had befallen him?

"If I only knew!" he would groan in his anguish. "Did Bright Wing and Joe escape and return to Franklinton? If they did, have they told all they knew? And, thinking me dead, she may have married George Hilliard!"

Then, in his excitement, he would stride up and down the room, until he was in a state of nervous collapse and compelled to seek his bed, to lie fretting and planning until sleep came to his relief.

Bradford noticed that his patient was always worse after being left to himself for a short time, and shrewdly suspected the cause. He spoke to La Violette about the matter; and they decided that one or the other of them would be with Ross constantly.

As spring approached, the weather grew milder. On fine, warm days, Douglas and Duke — always accompanied by Bradford or La Violette — took short strolls through the village. But on wet, cold days, he was compelled to crouch by the fire in his miserable cabin, a prey to his own gloomy thoughts. It was on such occasions that La Violette came as a ministering angel to cheer and comfort him. She talked to him, sang to him, read to him — her heart upon her sleeve, her soul in her beautiful eyes. But he was blind — he saw nothing. To him she was a fair, lovable child — unused to the ways of the world. She talked to him; he heard only her words, and gave no heed to the tender inflection of her voice. She sang quaint little love ballads to him; he closed his eyes and listened dreamily to her bird-like notes — scarcely noticing the sentiment of the song. She read to him from two or three old French books, tales of love and chivalry; but he took the stories for what they were worth — and lost sight of the reader. He noticed her marked preference for his society; but thought only that she desired to amuse him — to be amused herself. He looked upon her and pronounced her very beautiful ; he thoroughly enjoyed her society. He was interested in her, and wondered who and what she was. He respected her, pitied her, felt grateful for what she had done for him. He would have fought for her — died for her. But did he love her — did she love him? He never asked himself the questions. Perhaps he did not dare to do so — perhaps he was willfully blind. At any rate, he was true as steel to Amy Larkin.

One day when La Violette had been reading to him for some time, she stopped suddenly and, closing her book, remarked naïvely :

"You are not interested in what I have been reading. Do you want me to sing to you, or talk to you?"

"Talk to me, please."

"Of what or whom?"

"Of yourself."

"Of myself?" — in pleased surprise. It was the first time he had manifested so great an interest in her.

"Yes, of yourself," he repeated.

"But there is so little to tell," she objected.

"There is much I'd like to know," he said earnestly. "May I ask you some pointed questions?"

He lay upon a fur rug at her feet. As he turned to look at her, their eyes met. He unflinchingly met her ardent gaze; she dropped her white lids and blushed. Then recovering herself she answered composedly :

"You may ask me any questions you choose."

"And will you answer them?"

"I will."

For the moment he was disconcerted. He had expected her to refuse his request. However, he said:

"How long have you been among the Indians?"

"Among the Indians?"—in well-feigned surprise.—"I *am* an Indian."

Her eyes were dancing mischievously.

"You are not a savage," he replied coldly. "You can't deceive me."

"I am not a *savage*—but I am an Indian, surely. Tenskwatawa is my father."

And she laughed merrily.

"Why do you tell me that? Do you expect me to believe so palpable a falsehood?"

Instantly her mood changed. Her lips trembled and unshed tears stood in her eyes, as she answered sadly:

"Because it is all I know to tell. My earliest recollection is of playing among the children of the Shawnees. Tenskwatawa was pointed out to me as my father. From that day until I was ten years old—as nearly as I know my age—I was under his charge. During all that time the aged Indian woman, who is my attendant now, ministered to my childish needs and wants—was all the mother I ever knew. At the age of ten I was an uncouth little savage. I went with the tribe from one camp to another. I knew no other life—I cared for naught but the companionship of my savage friends——"

"How similar to my own experience!" he muttered.

"What did you say?" she asked quickly.

"Pardon my interruption," he replied. "Please go on with your story."

"When I was ten years old, we were encamped upon the Maumee. There it was that I first saw Hiram Bradford — so far as I know. It was in the autumn when he came among us. He appeared to have great influence with my father, Tenskwatawa. One day I overheard the two talking — or quarreling, rather. Both were very angry. I heard my name mentioned; and with childish intuition I knew that some calamity threatened me. I ran and hid; but shortly my father found me, and told me I was to leave the tribe and accompany Scar Face — that is the name Bradford bears among the Indians. I remember I cried bitterly and clung to Crane Bill, my nurse. But Bradford took me in his arms and bore me away. He took me to Quebec and placed me in charge of some French women, who taught a mission school. There I remained six years — and there I received the little education I possess. Two years ago he took me from my good friends — whom I had learned to love dearly — and brought me back to the tribe."

She stopped abruptly, her breast heaving.

"Go on," Ross said gently.

"There is no more to tell," was the half-whispered reply.

"That's all you know of yourself?"

"It is "— nodding.

"Do you know anything of Bradford's history?"

"Nothing."

"You are eighteen years old?"

"As nearly as I know."

"And you know nothing of your people?"

"You are among them."

"You mean these dirty, idle savages?"

"Yes. They are all the friends I have ever known, except Bradford, the teachers and pupils at the mission school — and yourself."

"You haven't the faintest recollection of your parents — your childhood home?" he persisted.

"Sometimes," she answered chokingly, "I dream of lying as a babe in the arms of a fair-haired, blue-eyed woman, and seeing her smile down at me. But that is all — it is but a dream."

"Has Tenskwatawa always been kind to you?"

"Kind and deferential."

"But you know — you feel — that he isn't your father?"

For a few seconds she was silent. Then she said:

"The tribe believes he is my father — that I am a gift from the Great Spirit. Crane Bill, my old nurse, told me one time that Tenskwatawa found me in the forest, where the Great Spirit had placed me. That is all I know."

"Have you never questioned Tenskwatawa?"

"I have."

"What did he say?"

"He said that what the tribe believes is true — and would say no more."

"And Bradford?"

"He patted my cheek and told me to be patient — that one day I should know all."

"Nothing more?"

She shook her head.

"He has always treated you kindly — respectfully?"

"Always."

"And you like him?"

"I do."

"Better than you like me?"

He asked the question innocently — playfully, as he would have put it to a child, expecting her to answer in the same spirit. But she did nothing of the kind. Instead, she placed her hand upon his and began passionately:

"Fleet Foot, you will never know ——"

Then she suddenly checked herself, and, hiding her face, burst into tears.

Douglas was surprised — horrified. For the first time, he had an inkling of the truth. He did not know what to do — what to say. Her disheveled, red-gold hair, her beaded dress of bright-colored cloth, her slender form shaking with sobs — all gave her the appearance of a grieved child. The temptation assailed him to take her in his arms, kiss away

her tears, and tell her he loved her. But Amy
Larkin's face arose before him; and condemning
himself for a weakling, he set his teeth and regained
control of himself. When he felt equal to the task,
he gently but firmly removed her hands from her
face and said :

"There — you mustn't cry any more. I don't
doubt your friendship."— He accented the word.—
"You've been very kind to me; and I appreciate
all you have done. Now, if you'll listen, I'll
tell you the story of my life, in return for what you
have told me of yours. Are you ready to hear
me?"

"Yes," she answered in an almost inaudible tone,
as she dried her eyes and sought to compose her
features.

Unheeding her evident embarrassment, and the
dry sobs that at intervals shook her willowy form,
he proceeded to tell her of himself. She listened
with rapt attention. When he had finished his
narrative, he said :

"You see, La Violette, there is great similarity
in our experiences."

"Yes," she murmured softly.

"The knowledge should make us closer friends."
He laid stress upon the word friends.

"I cannot be a better friend to you than I have
been— than I have tried to be, at least," she replied
tremulously.

Then she arose and darted from the room.

When he had recovered from the surprise her

sudden departure had caused him, he muttered gloomily :

"Am I an egotistical fool, or has she — untutored in the ways of the world — shown me her woman's heart? I pity her — her lot is a sad one. Who is she? No matter ; I mustn't wrong her. She's innocence itself. A child — a mere child ! Yet a woman with a woman's heart ! She is beautiful — lovable. A wild flower — a violet. A face and form to charm an artist ! If it were not for — Bah ! Of what am I thinking? Oh, that I were my old self — that I might escape from this hateful place and return to the little woman who is grieving over my prolonged absence ! "

Contracting his brows, he strode to the door and looked out at the falling rain.

16

CHAPTER XI.

THE sprightly month of April brought sunny days and warm showers, opening buds and singing birds.

Ross Douglas had almost recovered his wonted health and strength. A slight twinge of pain in his chest, at times, and a little shortness of breath, on exercise, alone remained to remind him of his tedious illness.

He wandered about the village at will; but he was unarmed, and dozens of watchful eyes were upon him. He saw no chance of escape. At night Bradford occupied the cabin with him, never leaving him alone.

Frequently he met La Violette and tried to talk with her; but she was shy and reserved, and had little to say. He fancied that she avoided him — and it piqued him. Man-like he could not understand that she was trying to conquer her love for him; and he sought to re-establish their familiar companionship. His influence over her was such — she loved him so — that he succeeded. She could not resist his magnetic power. And with the true abandon of a simple, passionate child of the forest, she again drank of the intoxicating cup of love — and for the time was happy — in paradise.

Ross, also, became more cheerful. Perhaps he

had missed her companionship more than he would own — more than he knew. At any rate he was happier when she was at his side — when her violet eyes looked trustingly into his own gray ones, and her artless prattle fell upon his ear.

One day in the early part of the month, Bradford entered the hut and remarked:

"Douglas, I have your gun here — the one I took from you at Wildcat Creek. Do you want it?"

"Certainly," Ross replied with animation.

"You can have it — and this pouch of ammunition — on one condition."

"Name it."

"That you don't try to escape again."

"I won't try to escape — for the present."

"That's rather indefinite," laughed the older man. "Explain."

"When I have determined to make another attempt, I'll apprise you of the fact. Is that satisfactory?"

"Perfectly. Here's your gun. I think a little tramping about the woods will do you good. At least, it will help you to pass the time. You may go out with the Indians or by yourself, as you please. You have given me your word — I can trust you."

Having his trusty rifle again in his possession, Douglas felt more like a man — less like a prisoner. Every day, almost, he took a long jaunt through the woods adjacent to the village, his weapon upon his shoulder. His object was twofold. He desired to toughen his muscles and regain his old powers of endurance, and to become acquainted with the topography of the surrounding country. For he meant to make another desperate effort to escape, as soon as he felt equal to the task.

April gave place to May. The trees were in full leaf; the wild flowers, in full bloom. The air was warm and fragrant; and the birds sang all day long, in the dark, cool woodland.

Ross was now completely recovered from the effects of his wound, and ready for the project upon which his heart was set. But he was in a quandary. He could not make up his mind to break his promise to Bradford; yet he feared the result of making known his intentions. Would not his rifle again be taken from him and himself be confined and guarded as at Wildcat Creek? While he debated the question, the sunshiny days sped swiftly by.

About the middle of the month, a council of twelve tribes was held at the Miami village. Ringing speeches were made by various chiefs. Each tribe sought to lay the blame of the battle of Tippecanoe and its results upon the other. Much bad feeling existed. Tecumseh made an effort to reconcile and reunite the tribes of his confederacy, but failed. The council was a *fiasco* — so far as the great chief's desires and intentions were concerned. After indulging in mutual recriminations, and expressing themselves as being desirous of living at peace with the Americans, the members of the council took their departure — and the farce was at an end.

A number of white men were present, as specta-
tors, at the council. But Bradford kept a close
watch upon his prisoner; and the latter got no
opportunity to communicate with the visitors.
Whether they were Americans, or British subjects
from across the lakes, Douglas could not ascertain.

About the first of June, Tecumseh, accompanied
by a number of warriors, went to Fort Wayne and
demanded ammunition. He was very haughty, and
firm in his old opinions and intentions. The agent
sought to induce him to remain at peace with the
United States, but refused to give him ammunition.

Tecumseh made answer:

"My British father will not refuse my request.
To him I will go."

And giving a defiant war-whoop, he disappeared
in the adjacent woods.

He went immediately to Malden, where he joined
the English.

A short time after Tecumseh's departure for Canada, an Indian runner arrived in the Mississinewa
village. He brought the news that what had been
expected long, had happened at last — that war had
been declared between the United States and Great
Britain, and that both nations were making preparations for a final struggle for supremacy upon the
border. This intelligence greatly pleased Tenskwatawa and his braves. They saw a chance for
scalps and plunder — and promptly resolved to join
the British. The night of the messenger's arrival
was spent in feasting and rejoicing. Speeches were

made, and war-songs were chanted. When morning dawned, numbers of the warriors at once set out for the scenes of expected conflict.

If Hiram Bradford was elated over the news received, he succeeded in concealing the fact from Douglas. The latter was depressed and sorrowful. Well he knew what would be the fate of many exposed posts and settlements upon the border, as the result of such a war.

La Violette listened attentively to the impassioned speeches of the chiefs — speeches counseling murder and pillage — and sighed heavily. Yet when Ross questioned her as to what she thought, she replied firmly :

"The redmen have been wronged — deeply wronged. Their cause is a just one. They seek to recover what is their own; and they mean to take advantage of this opportunity. They should not be blamed ; for in vain have they pleaded for justice. They will join the English, hoping to recover the land of their fathers. If the Seventeen Fires be successful in the struggle, the condition of the redmen will be no worse ; if the English gain the victory, the condition of the redmen will be bettered — I hope, though I cannot fully trust the promises of the British. That the Indians will commit excesses is to be expected. No one deplores their mode of warfare more than I. But they are ignorant, superstitious, revengeful savages. God made them such."

"La Violette, you talk as though these same ig-

norant savages were your people, your relatives —
as though their cause was your own," Ross said
sadly.

Her eyes flashed and her chest heaved, as she said
angrily :

"What is it to you, Ross Douglas, how I talk —
what I think? These miserable beings are all the
friends I have — all I expect to have. You do not
care who I am, what I am, or what may become of
me ! Why do you concern yourself about what I
say or *think?* Your only desire is to escape and return to your — your home, to forget that you ever
saw me !"

Bursting into tears, she turned and left him staring after her.

For the next few days Douglas was in a fever of
unrest. Now he had an additional incentive to escape. His country again needed his services. He
could not delay much longer — he must make the
attempt, though he should court death in so doing.
He said to himself :

"I'll go to Bradford and give him warning of
my intentions. I cannot break my word — I cannot
act a dishonorable part, even to gain my liberty.
No doubt he'll disarm me and place me under
close surveillance. No matter; I'll elude the
vigilance of his red hounds in some way. Perhaps
I can make my way to Fort Wayne. The Indians
are inflamed by the declaration of war; it will not
be safe for me to remain here much longer — especially, if Bradford should be called away. Why does

that man hold me captive? Idle question! I can't answer it. Great heaven! Almost a year has passed since I left Amy. I'll delay no longer. I'll risk all upon one cast of the die!"

That evening another Indian runner arrived in the village. He came from Malden, and brought a message from Tecumseh to Tenskwatawa, to enlist all the warriors he could, and send them to Canada at once. The great chief promised that all who would come should be paid for their services and share in the plunder.

Tenskwatawa at once set about the work. His persuasive powers were great; the Indians feared his baleful influence; and scarcely a brave dared to disobey his orders. Within a surprisingly short time, he had a large number enlisted and ready to set out. Tecumseh had sent word that the women and children of the warriors enlisting should be sent, under escort, beyond the Mississippi; and that the Prophet should then raise another force to attack Vincennes. The great Shawnee promised to return and lead the attack upon that place. Tenskwatawa carried out his brother's orders to the letter.

La Violette did not accompany the women and children on their long and lonely journey. The Prophet desired that she should do so; but she appealed to Bradford, with the result that she was permitted to stay with the few Indians remaining at the village—most of whom were Miamis that stubbornly refused to cast their lots in with the British.

All this occurred within a few days after the arrival of the runner from Canada.

This messenger also brought a sealed message from the English commander, to Bradford. Immediately upon its receipt, the latter went to Douglas and said:

"As you know, I'm in the employ of the British. I've just received instructions to go among the various tribes still remaining neutral, and try to enlist their services in behalf of the English government. I must start at once. Probably I shall be gone some weeks. You will remain here until I come back. You'll not be lonely. La Violette will be your companion." — He smiled a meaning smile. — "On my return we three will go to Canada. I'm sorry to part from you — for so short a time, even; but it can't be helped. I don't mind telling you that if my mission proves successful — as it will — it means thousands of pounds to me. And you shall share in my good-fortune. You will do as I wish?"

"I will not," was the positive answer. "Why should I?"

"Because I desire you to do so," Bradford returned coolly.

"Then I should play the part of a passive traitor, simply to please you who have wronged ——" Ross began hotly, but came to an abrupt stop.

"Well?" And Bradford smiled broadly.

"I was going to say," Douglas resumed calmly, "that according to your admissions, I should play the traitor, to please you who have kept me a prisoner for months and still have me in your power."

"You'll not be playing the traitor; you'll remain neutral — that's all."

"A passive traitor is as bad as an active one. I cannot consent to your proposal. I've been here too long already, much against my will. I wish to revisit my home for a few days — then again offer my services to my country. You say you are my friend. In some ways you have proven your assertion. Let me depart in peace."

"You put my friendship to a severe test," Bradford laughed.

"You will not grant my request?"

"No — I cannot."

"Why?" — impatiently.

"Because to allow you to leave here would upset my plans."

"Your plans?"

"Yes; the plans I have laid for your future."

"Please explain," Ross said, a sneer curling his lip.

"I wish I *might* explain to you — tell you everything," Bradford answered very earnestly. "But I don't dare to do so at present. I fear it might prove disastrous. Be patient just a little longer. You shall know all ere long. Then you'll bless me for having kept you here."

"Never!" Douglas cried angrily. "I'm no child — and I'll not stay."

"You mean to try to escape again?"

"Yes."

For a half minute Bradford dropped his head in thought. Evidently he was greatly moved. At last he said sadly but decidedly — his husky voice hardly audible:

"You're an honorable, upright gentleman, Ross Douglas; you keep your word, even when the breaking of it would give you the liberty you covet. I would set you free — but no! You *must* not — you *shall* not leave the place, until I am ready for you to do so. I'm off now. Good-by."

Silently the two men shook hands and parted. Both were strangely moved.

A few minutes later Bradford was saying to a stalwart Shawnee brave — one of the few remaining at the Mississinewa village:

"Long Gun, you are not to join any of the expeditions against the Americans. Select a score of your most trusty warriors, and remain here to protect La Violette and guard Fleet Foot. This evening when the young paleface retires to rest, slip into the hut and disarm him. Do not lose sight of him at any time — and guard him well each night. Remember that he is fleet of foot, brave, and strong. Under no circumstances is he to be ill-treated or injured. Keep him safe until my return, and you shall have fifty pounds in gold. Here is ten pounds to bind the bargain. Can I depend on you?"

"Ugh!" ejaculated the imperturbable Long Gun, as one by one he dropped the jingling coins into his pouch.

Bradford hurried away toward Tenskwatawa's cabin. Arriving there, he found the Prophet alone; and, striding up to him, said brusquely:

"I am leaving upon a mission to the neutral tribes. During my absence, La Violette is to remain here. Do you understand?"

Tenskwatawa nodded stiffly.

"Heed my words, then," Bradford continued savagely. "If you drag her away from here in my absence — and thus defeat my plans — I will choke the life out of you, the first time I meet you. Beware!"

The cowering Prophet looked the impotent rage he felt, but did not open his lips. As he left the cabin Bradford chuckled huskily:

"I have cowed him. The miserable coward — he is afraid to say his life is his own!"

Then gravely:

"But he's cunning — treacherous. What a wonderful, uncanny power he exerts over his ignorant people! I must not be long absent. What a sweet revenge it would be to him, to frustrate my designs. The only thing that will restrain him is his abject cowardice. How he hates me! And for what? Because I have made him bow the knee to me — the craven! Because my wishes have run counter to his selfish purpose — because I have done as I please concerning the welfare of that dear girl."

Just outside of the door he met La Violette.

"I'm going away for a few weeks, La Violette,"

he remarked. "In my absence improve your opportunity to the utmost."

"What do you mean?" she asked softly, dropping her long lashes over her tell-tale eyes.

"You know what I mean, my little coquette," he laughed lightly. "You have ensnared Ross Douglas's heart. Throw a few more cords of love around it, to hold it secure."

"Snared his heart!" she cried, petulantly stamping her moccasined foot. "He *has* no heart — it is in another's keeping."

"Not so, little one," he answered positively. "He's *betrothed* to another — he muttered her name in his delirium — but he's learning to love *you*. Already he loves you better than you know — than he suspects. Yours is the name that falls from his lips during sleep. Be patient — but persistent. Devote yourself to his comfort — make yourself necessary to his very existence. Above all, see to it that he doesn't escape during my absence. Good-by."

Ere she could make reply, Bradford had turned the corner of the cabin and disappeared. A half hour later he had set out upon his journey, accompanied by a half score of picked warriors.

CHAPTER XII.

THE night of Bradford's departure was quite warm for the time of year. Ross Douglas sat in front of the cabin he had occupied since coming to the village. The balmy air was laden with the scent of wild flowers — sweet with the breath of the damp woodland. La Violette timidly stole to his side and whispered :

"You are lonely. May I talk to you ?"

"Certainly — I'm always glad to have your company," he replied, —sincerity in his voice and manner.

In low tones they conversed for some time, aimlessly rambling from one subject to another. Each put forth an effort to entertain the other; but in spite of their endeavors the conversation flagged. Silence fell upon them. The stars peeped out ; the moon rose above the tree-tops. At last the girl sprang from her seat, and with a soft "goodnight" slipped away among the shadows.

Douglas promptly got upon his feet, and calling to Duke — who lay dozing near the door — entered the hut. The place was in absolute darkness. Without removing any of his apparel, the young man threw himself upon his couch, murmuring :

"At last the opportunity has come; and I'm ready to take advantage of it. I'll snatch a few

(254)

hours of sleep. Then when the camp is wrapped in slumber, I'll steal into the black forest, and leave this hated place far behind me. No guards have been placed over me. I can hardly understand it. But I ought not to complain, if fortune sees fit to favor me for once. Ah, Amy! God favoring, I shall soon meet you and clasp you to my heart!"

A short time he lay, open-eyed and thoughtful. Then sighing deeply, he whispered:

"But I hate to part from La Violette. She's a sweet, lovable, trusting child. I have learned to like her very much. And — poor little girl! — she likes me only too well, I fear. But I'm in nowise to blame. I haven't sought to win her heart. I have tried to hold her at arm's length. But, simple child of nature that she is, she can't disguise her feelings. I pity her. I hate to leave her here — to such a fate. But I can't take her with me — it's out of the question. How lonely she will be! May God keep and comfort my little wild violet, when I am gone!"

With this fervent utterance, he resolutely closed his eyes and fell asleep.

An hour passed. Ross was awakened by the voice of the bloodhound. The animal stood by his master's bedside, growling fiercely. His bristles were erect; his eyes, fixed upon the open door, through which the mellow moonlight was streaming. Douglas raised himself upon his elbow and looked toward the opening in the wall. A dusky form for one brief moment darkened the doorway. Then, outlined in the bright moonlight, a stalwart Indian stepped into the room. Instantly Ross was upon his feet.

"What do you want here?" he demanded angrily, in the Shawnee tongue.

The brave made no reply; but, gliding forward, secured Douglas's gun that stood in the corner of the room near the bed. Then he nimbly leaped through the doorway — and was gone.

Beside himself with rage and disappointment, the young man shouted:

"Take him, Duke!"

Impatiently the bloodhound had been awaiting the word of command. With a bound he cleared the doorway. Another leap, and he fell upon the retreating savage, like an avalanche. The warrior dropped the rifle and drew his knife to defend himself, uttering a blood-curdling yell as he did so.

Ross hastened to the dog's assistance. Dark forms slipped from the shadow of the building, and silently surrounded the combatants. The hound seized the hand that held the glittering knife, and gave it a wrench that caused the weapon to fall to the ground. Douglas caught up his rifle, and watched for a chance to deal the savage a stunning blow. But, at the favorable moment, a number of warriors threw themselves upon him and bore him to the earth. Realizing that further resistance would be suicidal, he ceased to struggle and called off the bloodhound.

A few minutes afterward, he again lay upon his couch of furs in the cabin, bound hand and foot; while Duke, stretched full length upon the floor, lolled his red tongue and whined dolefully. Just within the door stood a guard — silent and motionless as a bronze statue.

The news of the attempted escape and consequent struggle quickly spread throughout the village, and occasioned no little excitement. Duke had seriously injured the Indian he had attacked; and the warrior's comrades and friends threatened dire vengeance upon the dog and his master. Long Gun sought to pacify the angry braves — but failed. They openly rebelled against the chief's authority, and swore they would kill the hound and his owner. In his extremity Long Gun went to La Violette and laid the case before her.

She answered him:

"Have no fear. Your prisoner shall not be harmed. Select those who *will* obey you, and closely guard him to-night. To-morrow I will interfere in his behalf."

Well pleased, Long Gun returned to his post of duty and carried out La Violette's instructions. But had he known what was her real intention, he would not have felt so complacent.

When the Shawnee chief had left her presence, La Violette threw herself upon her couch and sobbed bitterly:

"Yes, I must save him — save him by giving him his liberty, by parting from him forever! Oh,

17

it is hard — cruel!   For I love him — I love him!
But he must not die — and die he will, if he remains here longer.   The warriors are determined
to take his life; they cannot be restrained.   He
must leave to-morrow night, at the latest.   Oh,
Ross — Ross!   My love — my love!   You will
never know how I worship you — *never!* "

All night long, the village was in a buzz of excitement.   Ross Douglas lay upon his bed, a prey
to despairing thoughts and gloomy forebodings.
With wide-open eyes, he peered into the darkness
that surrounded him; with alert ears, he listened to
every sound.   The hum of many voices came to
him at intervals.   Occasionally, the soft breeze that
swept through the door brought a threat or an ob-
jurgation.   He realized the great mistake he had
made.

"All is over — I am lost!" he muttered chokingly, a black wave of despair engulfing his soul.
"I may as well resign myself to my fate.   Ill-luck
has followed me persistently.   Joe and Bright
Wing are dead, or helpless captives like myself;
Bradford is absent.   I've not a friend in the
place — except La Violette.   And what can *she* do?
Nothing!   What *would* she do, if she could?   I
don't know.   She wouldn't give me my liberty, I'm
sure.   And I would as lief die as remain longer
a prisoner!   She loves me?   Yes.   But she will
not aid me to escape — of course not.   She would
rather see me die before her eyes, than resign me to
another.   What a fool I was to try to recover my

gun! But I was crazy with disappointment. Ah! Duke, old fellow, you seem to realize the gravity of the situation. Three times we have contended against these red demons. They'll not spare us this time. Well, at least I can die like a man ; you can die like a hero. I wouldn't care so much — though life is sweet — were it not for Amy and La Violette. Yes, La Violette! I pity her ; I — I ——"

Slowly, endlessly, the night dragged itself away. The morning dawned warm and clear. At sunrise La Violette made her way to the cabin in which the prisoner was confined. The guard at the door did not oppose her entrance ; but he maintained his position just within the door.

Douglas looked up as the girl's light footsteps fell upon his ear. He saw that she was pale and haggard, that her eyelids were swollen with weeping.

"You heard of my ill-fortune and came to me," he remarked simply.

"Yes," she replied in a tone scarcely audible. "Do you not want something to eat ?"

"I want nothing."

"Nothing ?" And she eyed him sharply.

"Nothing but my liberty."

"It is impossible for me to give you that," she answered hastily, giving him a look that he could not interpret. "But you must eat something. You will need all your strength for the ordeal."

"What do you mean ?" he inquired in an unmoved voice.

Unheeding his question, she turned and left the hut. She was gone but a few minutes. When she returned, she bore a quantity of corn bread and meat.

"You must eat this — all of it," she said decidedly. "Here, Duke — here is your share."

After she had unbound his hands, Ross sat up and silently devoured the food to the last crumb.

"I thought you were hungry," she said as she took the platter from his hands. "Do you want anything more?"

"I'd like some water."

She brought it to him.

"That's all," he said, as he returned her the cup. "I thank you for your kindness."

"And you would like to have your liberty?" she queried in a half-mocking tone.

"Of course," he answered gravely.

"To join in a war against my people?"

"Against England," he corrected.

"My people are allies of the English."

"Still you can't blame me for wishing to fight for my country."

"And you cannot blame me for refusing to liberate you."

He remained silent. Again she gave him that meaning glance; but he could not fathom it. At that moment, the sound of voices in angry altercation came to their ears.

"Secure his hands!" La Violette cried to the guard, as she sprang past him and planted her slender form in the doorway.

The sight that met her gaze was one calculated
to unnerve the bravest man. Fifty armed warriors
had overpowered Long Gun and his faithful few,
and were rushing toward the spot where she stood.

Only too well she knew what it meant. The in-
furiated mob were bent upon murdering Ross
Douglas.

On they came, brandishing their weapons and
yelling like demons. Their painted faces were contorted with rage; their eyes gleamed with the fire
of their hellish purpose.

The hot blood forsook La Violette's face, and
surged in a sickening flood to her heart and brain.
Her vision grew misty; her limbs trembled. But
she set her white teeth and firmly stood her ground.

The leaders of the mob reached the hut. With
angry exclamations, they came to a sudden halt, as
they beheld the daughter of the Prophet barring
the entrance.

"La Violette must stand aside!" shouted a burly
warrior. "We want the young paleface. We
mean to kill him — to tear him limb from limb!"

The girl neither spoke nor moved; but she
sternly fastened her eyes upon the speaker — and
he recoiled a step.

"Out of the way! Out of the way!" bellowed
the mob.

"Never!" she answered in clear, ringing tones.

They surged forward, threatening to crush her
under foot. She did not flinch, but raising her
voice to the highest pitch, cried imperiously:

"Hold! I — La Violette — command you!"

They wavered — faltered — paused.

Taking advantage of their temporary indecision, she continued breathlessly :

"You shall not kill this helpless prisoner ! I — the daughter of the Prophet — command you to disperse. You shall not harm the paleface, unless you first kill me ! Do you dare to kill Tenskwatawa's daughter — the gift of the Great Spirit? Make but a move to touch me, and the Great Spirit will strike you dead in your tracks ! "

Her eyes were blazing ; her breast heaving. To the superstitious warriors who faced her, she was the living, breathing embodiment of supernatural power. Awed into silence, they forgot their purpose and began to draw away from her dread presence.

"Go — and quickly ! " she commanded sternly. "Ere I lose my patience and call down upon you the curse of the Great Spirit ! "

They waited to hear no more ; but silently, sullenly shrunk away and disappeared among the neighboring huts.

"Saved — saved for the present ! " La Violette panted, as she staggered into the cabin and sank in a quivering heap upon the floor.

"La Violette," Ross called gently.

In answer, she burst into tears and sobbed softly. After a time she regained control of her feelings, and, arising, went to his side.

"You have saved my life, at the risk of your own," he said with feeling.

"I have repaid the debt I owed you," she answered very quietly. "You will be safe for a time, at least. I must leave you now."

And ere he could make reply, she had withdrawn from the hut.

Just outside she met Long Gun. The chief's face wore a crestfallen and worried expression.

Addressing him in the Shawnee language, she commanded:

"Long Gun will take his men and occupy the cabin. If the mob return to take the paleface's life, Long Gun and his warriors will defend him to the last."

"Ugh!" replied the Shawnee, with animation unusual to him.

She continued:

"Long Gun will not hesitate to shoot down any that seek to harm the prisoner — or his dog. La Violette has spoken — Long Gun will obey."

"Long Gun's ears are open; he hears and understands," was the grim reply.

La Violette passed on to the Prophet's quarters. The latter was preparing to journey to Fort Wayne, with a hundred warriors, to demand ammunition of the American commandant of the post.

"Father," the girl said, as she stood in his presence.

"What does my daughter wish?" he asked kindly.

"You are preparing to leave the village?"

"Yes."

"To-day?"

" Ugh ! "

" You must not go."

He stared at her in open-mouthed surprise. She hastily explained :

" An attack has just been made upon Fleet Foot's life. I overawed the mad warriors ; for the present he is safe. But the attempt will be renewed. I may need your help. You must not leave the village to-day or to-night."

" Why does my daughter try to save the pale-face's life ? " he demanded angrily.

" Because Fleet Foot saved the life of La Violette," she answered promptly.

" Ugh ! " he ejaculated — and was silent.

" You will do as I desire ? " she inquired anxiously.

He nodded sullenly.

" Listen, then," she went on rapidly. " Fleet Foot must be protected to-day ; to-night he must leave the village."

" But Scar Face —— " Tenskwatawa began, a look of terror creeping over his repellant features.

" I know what my father would say," she interrupted. " But I will assume all responsibility. Fleet Foot shall not remain here to be killed. You have nothing to fear from Scar Face. I will shield you from his wrath."

The Prophet hung his head and made no reply ; and the girl left the cabin. As she passed through the doorway and dropped the curtain of skins behind her, the cowardly wretch muttered shiveringly:

" Scar Face will be very angry. But La Violette will have her way — I am helpless."

Then hiding his face in the folds of his blanket, he groaned aloud.

The day passed quietly. Evening came — and the shades of night began to gather. As soon as it was quite dark, La Violette went to Long Gun and, drawing him aside, said :

"The enemies of Fleet Foot are gathering in front of the council-lodge. Soon they will make another attempt to kill him. When they come, he must not be here. La Violette will take him to her lodge — will hide him where they dare not enter, where they cannot find him. As soon as Long Gun hears the mob coming, he and his braves will slip away in the darkness. Does Long Gun understand?"

Greatly relieved — for he had been apprehensive of the result of the attack that was sure to come — Long Gun replied :

"La Violette is wise and good. Long Gun will do her bidding."

" It is well," she answered simply, and entered the cabin.

Douglas lay upon his couch, dreading what the night might have in store for him. His guards had given him food and drink, at noon and early in the evening. Duke sat beside the bed, lovingly licking his master's manacled hands and whining softly. Ross first became aware of La Violette's presence, when she bent over him, severed his bonds, and whispered in his ear :

"Come with me — and do not speak or make a noise."

Without a murmur he arose and meekly accompanied her from the cabin.   Duke silently followed. La Violette's hut was but a few rods from the one Douglas had occupied ; but she took a circuitous route, to avoid observation, and approached the building from the rear.

On reaching its interior — which was in absolute darkness — she said in an agitated undertone:

"Remain here until I return.   I will be gone but a few minutes."

Left alone, Ross threw himself upon the floor, and rubbed and kneaded his stiffened and swollen limbs. He wondered what La Violette's intentions were. While he was still ransacking his brain for an answer, the young woman returned.

"Fleet Foot," she called softly, musically, as she stepped within the room and let fall the curtain of skins.

"Here," he replied, as he arose to his feet.

Guided by his voice, she found her way to his side, and murmured :

"Here is gun, knife, and ammunition.   In the pouch you will find food."

With the words, she placed the things in his outstretched hands.   Now he understood her intentions.   But he said nothing — his heart was too full.

"Have you flint and steel?" she inquired.

"Yes," he managed to articulate.

"But one thing more — then you must be off. Hold out your right hand."

He did so; and felt her placing something upon his finger.

"What are you doing?" he asked in a whisper.

"Giving you a ring."

"A ring?" in surprise.

"Yes; Tenskwatawa's talisman — the Sign of the Prophet."

"Why do you do that?" he inquired in wonder and amazement.

"You may be pursued and recaptured — or may fall into the hands of some roving band of redmen. In either case, the talisman will save your life. Boldly show it and say that Tenskwatawa gave it to you — that you are under his protection, that you have his magic power. The warriors — whoever they may be — will not ask you to prove your assertions. They have been led to believe that the power lies in the ring. And they heard the Prophet say at Wildcat Creek, that he would not again give the trinket into the hands of one who could not use it. It will protect you, Fleet Foot."

"But how did you obtain it?" he asked in an agitated undertone.

She answered naively:

"I went to Tenskwatawa's lodge, to get the gun and ammunition I have given you. He was sleeping. I slipped the ring from his finger and came away."

"But in so doing haven't you shorn him of his power?"

"No. There is no virtue in the talisman, except in the Prophet's hands. He is cunning. He will tell a miraculous story of its loss — and straightway procure another. I have robbed him of nothing but the bauble itself. But you are tarrying too long — you must go at once. Crane Bill, my aged attendant, may return at any time. She hates all pale-faces; she would raise an alarm. Hark!"

Both listened intently, holding their breaths in their excitement. Fierce yells came to their ears — yells of fiendish rage and disappointment. Both knew what the uproar meant; Douglas's enemies had discovered his escape.

Grasping her companion's arm with both her trembling hands, La Violette cried breathlessly:

"Go — go at once! They are searching for you. Soon they will be here. The cabin will be surrounded and your escape cut off. For my sake — go!"

Slipping his arm around her supple waist, he panted in reply:

"Come with me! This is no place for you. You are not safe here — they'll wreak their revenge upon you ——"

"No — no!" she answered brokenly. "It is impossible. You could not escape with me. I am safe here — they will not dare to harm me. Bid me good-by — and go — go!"

"Come with me, La Violette!" he insisted — tenderest pity, intensest love in his voice. "To-

gether we will return to the blessings of civilization.
I'll be your protector — your brother ——''

"No!" she interrupted sadly, but firmly — a sob
in her throat. "It cannot be. To-day I have been
instrumental in saving you — I may be able to save
others. At least, I can risk my life in trying. I
cannot go with you, Ross. Good-by — good-by forever!"

"Kiss me!" he whispered in her ear.

She lifted her face to his. In the darkness their
lips met. Each felt the tumultuous beating of the
other's heart. For a half minute he strained her to
his breast, ere he released her and softly murmured:

"Good-by, La Violette — and God bless you!"

Then he and his dog were gone — and she was
alone. She dropped upon the bare floor and hid her
face. But she did not weep. Her grief over her
loss, her anxiety for his safety, were too great. A
blood-curdling whoop and the patter of moccasined
feet, from time to time, came to her ears; but no one
entered the cabin. A prey to suspense, she arose at
last and went out of doors. Douglas's enemies
were continuing their search. She dimly discerned
their dark forms flitting here and there. Aimlessly
she sauntered toward the Prophet's hut. Just as
she reached it, a number of warriors were entering
the door. She followed them; and heard the leader
say to Tenskwatawa, who stood at one end of the
room, directly under a flaring torch stuck into the
wall:

"Fleet Foot has escaped. He is in hiding about

the village. Does Tenskwatawa know aught of him?''

The Prophet expanded his chest, and, raising his right hand, said severely:

'' Tenskwatawa is the father of his red children. He does not befriend the palefaces. Begone!''

At that moment, the speaker chanced to glance at his own hand. He saw that his ring was gone. An expression of unspeakable surprise overspread his horrid features. With the whimpering cry of a whipped child, he dropped upon his knees and began to search for the talisman. Not finding it, he silently arose to his feet, an expression of absolute imbecility upon his face. Then appearing to realize the magnitude of the misfortune that had befallen him, he dropped to the floor in a writhing heap, moaning and beating his chest.

'' Ugh!'' ejaculated the leader of the band. ''Tenskwatawa has lost his sign — his power. See! He is weak — he whines like a sick squaw! Ugh!''

And with a parting volley of contemptuous exclamations, the braves hastily left the room.

La Violette leaned against the wall and calmly looked upon the whining, moaning wretch at her feet. Now she fully realized what she had done; but she had no regret. She had done it for the sake of the man she loved!

The Prophet was indeed shorn of his power. From that day forth, his influence over his people rapidly declined.

CHAPTER XIII.

IT WAS the close of a hot July day. The surface of the placid Scioto glinted in the red rays of the setting sun. The dark-green forests surrounding the little village of Franklinton grew darker, as the tremulous twilight faded into dewy dusk. Blue smoke curled gracefully from the mud-daubed chimneys of the villagers' cabins. A tinkling cow-bell broke the stillness — a twinkling star peeped from the dusky vault above. Swallows skimmed low along the shores of the gently-flowing river. Insect voices joined in a monotonous threnody. Lights began to gleam from cottage windows and doors.

Upon the western bank of the stream — a few miles below the village — stood a solitary pedestrian, leaning against a rough-barked elm and looking toward the opposite shore. He carried a long rifle ; and at his side hung ammunition-pouch and powder-horn. His buckskin suit gave evidence of hard usage, being soiled, frayed, and ragged. The soft hat that surmounted his dark curls was battered and torn. His moccasins were ready to drop piecemeal from his feet.

Stooping and patting the head of a large blood-hound that sat panting beside him, the man sighed wearily and began :

"Well, Duke—old fellow, we're here at last. We've had a lonely and hazardous journey. But we're here—free, alive, and well."

The hound yawned and wagged his tail, as though he understood the words.

Ross Douglas continued:

"Yes, my faithful friend, together we have braved the numerous perils of the trackless forest. But we're free—free at last! True, you are footsore and weary; so am I. And both of us are hungry. But our journey's over. Soon we'll eat and sleep—sleep as we haven't slept in days."

The dog whined plaintively. Then he stiffly arose and looked beseechingly into his master's face.

"You're telling me it's time to be moving," Douglas remarked, a smile lighting his handsome features. "You're a knowing animal, Duke."

Then to himself:

"I must find some way to cross the river—I must see Amy to-night. But I don't want anyone to know of my return, until I know how affairs have gone in my absence. Therefore, I can't go to the village for a canoe. But I know where one of the settlers used to keep one hidden in the bushes."

Shouldering his rifle, he set out along the bank, Duke following him. He was not long in finding the canoe and launching it.

"Jump in and lie down, Duke," he commanded.

The intelligent brute obeyed. Ross seized the light paddle and pushed off. A few rapid and vigorous strokes carried the boat to the opposite side of the stream. Man and dog leaped ashore. Douglas beached the dugout, and set off along the path leading to the Larkin homestead—the path he knew so well.

By this time it was quite dark. The warm air was sweet with woodsy odors. Fireflies were flitting here and there among the trees. No sound broke the stillness but his own footfalls. As he hurried forward, his heart palpitating wildly, he murmured under his breath:

"At last—at last, Amy ! Soon I shall press you to my breast, and kiss away your tears. Perhaps I shall stand before you as one from the grave—but you will be glad to see me—will understand all instantly. With the devotion of a lifetime, I'll repay you for whatever you may have endured in my absence. And I've been true to you, my darling ! I could have loved La Violette, had I not loved you. When I leave you again, I'll leave you my wife. Then temptation will not dare to assail me. I'll brook no opposition now—no delay. You shall be mine—mine at once. Ah, the old love wells up in my heart ! "

Then, sighing, he shook his head and whispered very softly :

"But poor little La Violette—dear, sweet, little wild violet ! How my heart bleeds for her ! But I mustn't think of her now. No—no ! I must have but one thought in my mind—Amy ! "

He had reached the farther margin of the strip of woodland that skirted the river. The clearing was

18

before him. The stars were shining brightly. By
their faint radiance, he dimly discerned the house
standing in the middle of the cleared space. But no
welcoming light streamed from window or door.
All was darkness — silence. His heart almost stood
still ; a sense of suffocation came over him. A
thousand mad thoughts and fancies ran riot in his
brain. He leaned heavily upon his rifle and shivered — though the evening air was warm.

The red rim of the moon rose above the tree-tops
beyond the clearing. Then, big and round, it
floated upward and shed its gentle light upon the
scene.

But still Ross did not stir. He stood with his
eyes riveted upon the cabin — now clearly outlined
in the moonlight. To his sensitive ears, came the
faint, faraway echo of laughter from the village
above. It seemed to mock him, like the eerie voice
of a departed spirit. Of a sudden, Duke tilted his
nose aloft and howled mournfully. The sound
startled Douglas and recalled him from his reverie.
He glanced apprehensively into the surrounding
shadows, as if expecting to see a ghost. A sense
of utter loneliness such as he had never known took
possession of him. The hound crept to his side and
whimpered ; and, in the woods beyond, a screech
owl thrice repeated its petulant, mournful cry.

Impatiently shaking himself, Ross muttered
angrily :

"Bah ! I'm a nervous fool. I'll know the
worst — and at once."

Resolutely he strode toward the cabin door, a few rods away. On reaching it, he did not hesitate, but thundered loudly upon it, with his bare knuckles. The only answer he received was the hollow echo of his raps. He felt for the latchstring ; and, finding it, gave it a vigorous pull. The door swung inward so suddenly that he recoiled a step, expecting some person to face him. But no one put in an appearance. The interior was in absolute darkness. A musty, disagreeable smell — the odor of a room long closed to air and sunlight — greeted his nostrils. Boldly he stepped over the sill and stood upon the puncheon floor. It creaked to his tread ; his heavy footfalls rang out with startling distinctness. The house was empty — deserted !

Like a lost soul pursued by a legion of demons, Ross Douglas fled from the cabin, leaving the door ajar. With bowed head and drawn features, he sped into the forest back of the house, and hurried on and on, taking no heed of his course. The hound wonderingly followed him. Ross had forgotten his hunger, his fatigue — everything but the fact that Amy was gone. Wild fancies beset his brain. Mocking voices gibbered in his ears ; evil faces peeped at him from the surrounding gloom. At last, from sheer exhaustion, he dropped upon the earth and pillowed his aching head upon his folded arms. Duke crouched at his master's side and anxiously observed his every movement.

"Gone — gone !" the young man moaned in agony of spirit. "And whether true or false I

don't know. Gone — What can it mean? Amy!
Amy! Night after night during my dreary captivity, I dreamed of you. And now you're not
here. But I'm wronging you, dear girl — of
course I am. You've been forced to leave — you
wouldn't have gone otherwise. Then I have lost
you forever! God help me to bear my bitter disappointment!"

Far into the night, he lay moaning — striving to
reconcile himself to the inevitable, to regain control
of himself. Worn out at last, he fell into a deep
sleep — the sleep of mental and physical exhaustion.

At daylight he awoke, and stiffly arose to his feet.
His face was pale and haggard; his lips were set and
determined. Shouldering his rifle and calling to his
dog, he retraced his steps toward the river. Again
he reached the clearing surrounding the deserted
cabin. In the gray light of the morning, the scene
was more barren, more oppressive, than when softened by the shades of night. He shuddered and
involuntarily turned his head, as he passed the
desolate habitation. With quick, firm steps, he
hurried along the path leading down to the shore.
A half hour later, he had recrossed the stream and
was approaching the village.

The sun was just rising. He saw the blue smoke
ascending heavenward and heard the prattle of
children. Emerging from the forest, he stood for a
moment drinking in the beauties of the homely,
animated scene. Oddly-garbed figures, bearing
axes, hoes, and other implements of husbandry‘

were hurrying toward the woods and fields; buxom matrons and comely maids were bustling hither and thither. Another day had dawned; and the industrious hive was astir.

A tall, robust settler approached the border of the woodland, where Ross was standing. The young man stepped from the shadow of the overhanging boughs—and he and the villager were face to face. With a glad cry of recognition, the latter sprang forward, exclaiming:

"Ross Douglas, as I'm alive! Give us y'r hand, my lad!"

The two warmly clasped hands, and Ross replied:

"Yes, Amos Pritchard, it's I—Ross Douglas. Are you glad to see me?"

"Glad to see you?" yelled the other, dancing around in delight. "What a question! Of course I'm glad to see you. *Everybody'll* be glad to see you. But where in the world have you been so long—what 'ave you been doin' with y'rself? We'd all give you up fer dead. We knowed you went to fight with Gener'l Harrison; an' as you didn't come back an' we didn't hear nothin' of you, we c'ncluded you was dead. You was at the battle o' Tippecanoe?"

"Yes," Douglas answered briefly.

"Well, where've you been sence?"

"A prisoner among the Indians."

Pritchard opened his eyes very wide and ejaculated:

"You don't say!"

Ross nodded and smiled — a wan, sad smile.

"Ever sence the battle, last November?" the man inquired.

Again Douglas nodded.

"An' where's y'r comrades, Joe Farley an' that young Wyandot?"

"Haven't they returned?" Ross asked quickly.

"Not a bit of it. We hain't seen n'r heard nothin' of any of you, till this minute."

"Then I fear they're dead, or prisoners among the Winnebagoes."

And Douglas gave his companion a brief account of the battle and subsequent events. However, he said nothing of his own wonderful experience while a prisoner, made no mention of Bradford or of La Violette. When he had finished his short recital, he asked in as careless a tone as he could assume:

"How have things gone in my absence, Pritchard?"

"Much better'n they have with you," was the rejoinder, "judgin' from y'r looks. You're ragged and hungry-lookin'— an' that surly bloodhound o' yours looks all fagged out, too. I take it you've had a purty rough-an'-tumble time of it. Campaignin' 'g'inst Injins ain't no holiday, I guess. You'd better go right down to my shack, an' git somethin' to eat; an' then take a sleep fer a week 'r so. Go on — you know where I live. The ol' woman 'll fill you up on the fat o' the land. She alluz did have a soft place in her heart, fer you an' y'r dog.

"But you haven't told me the news of the settlement," Ross objected.

"The news 'll keep," Pritchard returned. "Anyhow, ther' ain't much to tell. Some new settlers has come in; an' some o' the old ones has left. Ol' Sam Larkin was the biggest s'rprise to us." — Ross pricked up his ears. — "*He* sold out an' left — le's see. It was in October after you left in August. Took everybody by s'rprise — that's a fact. He had one o' the best an' biggest pieces o' land 'long the valley — as you know — an' plenty o' money; but somehow he wasn't satisfied. Some folks says his title to the land wasn't clear. I don't know. Anyhow he jest sold off everything fer what it would bring, an' skipped out. Some feller from down 'bout the Ohio bought the land — but he hain't moved onto it yit. Well, I must be moseyin' to work. You go on down to the cabin."

"Where did he go?" Douglas inquired, moistening his lips with his tongue.

"I don't know," Pritchard answered as he changed his axe from one shoulder to the other. "Some says he went back to his ol' home in western Pennsylvany. Nobody 'pears to know. But wherever he went, that sneakin' Canadian, George Hilliard, went along."

"And — and his daughter, Amy?"

"Of course. But what 're you so concerned 'bout 'em fer, Ross Douglas? Oh! I see." — And the settler smiled knowingly. — "I remember now you was sprucin' up to that little gal o' ol' Sam's,

Well, I'm 'feared you've lost her, my boy. Hilliard was keepin' the trail hot the same time you was, an' you leavin' when you did give him the short cut 'cross the clearin'. I 'spect he's married her long 'fore this. The fact is, some folks says the couple was married on the sly, 'fore they left these parts. Of course, *I* don't know. But I must be gittin' to work, 'r I won't earn my dinner. I'll see you at noon. You're goin' to stay 'round fer a few weeks, anyhow, ain't you?"

"I don't know yet," Douglas truthfully replied.

The young man walked toward the collection of cabins not far away, leaving his companion staring after him.

"If I ain't bad fooled," Pritchard muttered as he entered the woods, "that young feller is purty much in love with ol' Sam Larkin's gal; an' her goin' off the way she did is worryin' him like all possessed."

For several days Douglas lingered about the village. He visited the Wyandot camp up the river; but found it abandoned. His red friends had left for parts unknown. Undoubtedly some of them had cast in their lots with Tecumseh, and were aiding in harassing the posts and settlements upon the extreme frontier.

During his brief stay at Franklinton, Ross made many cautious inquiries concerning the whereabouts of Amy Larkin and her father; but he learned nothing more definite than what Pritchard had told him. Many times he had heard his sweetheart speak

of her birthplace in western Pennsylvania ; and now
he resolved to visit that section of the country. He
discarded his well-worn suit of buckskin, for garments of homespun cloth ; and, with his rifle upon
his shoulder and his bloodhound at his heels, set
out upon his quest.

After an absence of four months, he again returned
to the settlement upon the Scioto, having learned
nothing of the persons he sought.

General Harrison was now commander-in-chief of
the Western armies. He had established temporary
headquarters at Franklinton, and was busily engaged in collecting and forwarding supplies toward
the lakes. Douglas was greatly pleased to learn of
his beloved commander's presence in the village,
and immediately repaired to his quarters. The general was surprised and delighted to see him, and
said :

"Ross Douglas, I can't express how glad I am
to meet you again — to see you alive and well.
When you fell into the hands of the Indians at Tippecanoe, I gave you up for lost. You appear as
one from the grave. Where have you been, how
did you escape, and what of your faithful comrades?"

Briefly Ross told of his capture and escape, carefully avoiding all mention of La Violette and Bradford. General Harrison listened attentively to
the narrative, uttering frequent exclamations of
surprise and incredulity. When the younger man
had concluded, the older remarked :

" And your comrades — Farley and the Wyandot — you don't know their fate?"

"I do not," Ross answered sadly. "But they are dead, or prisoners among the Winnebagoes."

"Too bad — too bad!" the general murmured feelingly. "They were noble fellows and devoted to you ——"

Then with animation :

" But your dog — the bloodhound that was your constant companion?"

" He's in the village with me."

While Douglas was speaking, he unconsciously toyed with the ring upon his finger. At last Harrison fixed his eyes upon the glittering jewel, and remarked :

" That's a beautiful and valuable ring you wear, my young friend. May I ask you to let me see it?"

Silently Douglas drew it off and placed it in his companion's outstretched hand. Scarcely had it dropped into Harrison's palm, ere he started and cried :

" Douglas, where did you get this?"

Ross was disconcerted. His face flushed as he stammered :

" A — a friend gave it to me, General."

" And where did your friend get it?" the commander demanded excitedly.

" I — I —— " Ross began ; but Harrison interrupted.

" There — you needn't tell me. However, I know the ring. I can't be mistaken. Several years ago I saw it upon the finger of Tenskwatawa, the Shawnee Prophet, when he came to visit me at Vincennes. At that time I took note of its beauty and value. He told me it was a gift from an English officer, who had obtained it in the far East, and hinted to me that it was possessed of some magic power. That stone " — tapping the gem with his finger, — "is a diamond of the first water. It's quite large, as you see, and worth a considerable sum of money. You are fortunate to possess so valuable and beautiful an ornament."

With the words, he returned the ring to Douglas. The latter sat looking at the jewel for some moments. Then raising his eyes to the commander's face, he said earnestly :

" General, I haven't told you all concerning my captivity among the Prophet's warriors. Would you like to hear the story in full ? "

" If you don't mind telling me, Douglas — yes," was the smiling reply.

For an hour they sat in the commander's quarters — the younger man calmly talking, the older gravely listening. At last Douglas finished and arose to go.

" Wonderful ! " Harrison exclaimed as he got upon his feet. " Your story sounds like a mythical tale of the long ago. And yet if I desired proof of its truthfulness — which I do not — you have it with you. Keep the ring, my boy, in remembrance of the perils and adventures through which you have

passed.   I trust that in your possession — whatever
its magic power — it may not work the evil to our
country, it has done in the hands of the Prophet.
Tenskwatawa — a wizard, a sorcerer, a cowardly
cur.   Hiram Bradford — an English agent among
the Indians, a spy among the Americans, your foe
— your friend.   La Violette — an untutored savage, a refined and intelligent white woman.   What
characters for a romance — a drama!   And yet
they are actual inhabitants of these Western
wilds.''

Then suddenly riveting his keen gaze upon
Douglas's handsome face :

"What is your purpose now — what are you
going to do?''

"I came to offer my services to you, General,"
was the answer.

The commander meditatively rubbed his chin for
some seconds.   At last he said :

"There will be but little active campaigning
until spring opens.   Then the war will begin in
earnest — and I shall need you.   However, there
will be expeditions sent out against the troublesome
savages, all through the winter.   By the way, I'm
going to send Colonel Campbell against the villages upon the Mississinewa, this month.   Would
you care to go as guide and scout?''

"I should be greatly pleased to go," Ross answered simply.

But his heart was beating wildly.   The thought

was in his mind, that he might again meet La
Violette — and, perhaps, persuade her to return
with him to Franklinton.

He heard the commander saying :

"The place is yours, then. The companies of
the expedition will assemble at Greenville. You
can join them there. Here's your commission.
Shall I bid you good-by ?"

"Yes," Ross answered decidedly.

They shook hands and parted.

Douglas accompanied Colonel Campbell's detachment. He took part in the several skirmishes of
the winter campaign, and saw much hard service.
In the various petty engagements, quite a number
of Indians were killed and captured. From the red
prisoners, Ross learned that Tenskwatawa, La
Violette, and Bradford had left the Miami villages,
shortly after his departure, and had gone to join
Tecumseh at Malden.

Colonel Campbell destroyed the towns upon the
Mississinewa, and in the latter part of December
returned to Greenville.

From this place, Ross Douglas went to Cincinnati.
He could not bear the thought of returning to
Franklinton. He was disheartened, moody, and
restless. So far as he knew, Amy Larkin was lost
to him forever. Had she been false to her vows?
He did not know ; and the maze of uncertainty
maddened him.

He spent the winter at Cincinnati. When spring
opened, he and Duke — wanderers upon the face of

the planet — drifted into Kentucky, where General Green Clay was raising a regiment of militia to reenforce the garrison of Fort Meigs, upon the Maumee. Douglas joined the command in his old capacity of scout and guide, and with it marched toward the seat of war.

CHAPTER XIV.

IN THE latter part of April, 1813, General Harrison, commander-in-chief of the Western troops, was at Fort Meigs, upon the Maumee.

War between the United States and Great Britain had been declared in June, 1812. In July, Fort Mackinaw had fallen into the hands of the English; in August, Hull had basely surrendered at Detroit, and the Americans had met defeat at the River Raisin. In the early autumn — September — the Prophet's braves had laid siege to Forts Wayne and Harrison, but had been unsuccessful at both places. Thus had closed the year.

In the early part of 1813, the Western campaign had opened in earnest. In January, General Winchester had been defeated and captured at Frenchtown. Immediately following this battle — or massacre, rather — General Harrison had moved forward to the rapids of the Maumee, and begun the construction of Fort Meigs. Here he had assembled all the troops at his disposal, intending to recover the ground lost through Hull's cowardice and Winchester's incapacity. But the weather had continued unfavorable; and the commander had returned to the interior of the state, with the view of raising re-enforcements. Hardly had he set to work, however, when he received word that a large force of the enemy was marching to attack the garrison upon the Maumee. The general had returned with all possible expedition, arriving at the fort on the twentieth of April.

Fort Meigs — so named in honor of the illustrious governor of Ohio — was situated upon the south bank of the Maumee, at the foot of the rapids. It stood upon high ground, about sixty feet above the surface of the river; and its walls of earth and heavy timbers inclosed nearly ten acres. In outline it resembled an irregular "D" — the curved portion of the letter facing the stream. At each of the angles of the outer wall, was a strong blockhouse; and traverses of earth were thrown up inside of the inclosure, to protect the occupants from the shells of an attacking army. The fort was a depot of stores of all kinds, for the approaching campaign; and at the time of General Harrison's return from the interior was garrisoned by about five hundred men — regulars and volunteers.

After his arrival, on the twentieth of April, the commander kept patrols out, watching for the enemy. On the twenty-sixth, he was apprised that the advance guard was approaching. A few hours later, a number of white men and Indians appeared on the opposite shore, and coolly and critically inspected the fortification. On the twenty-seventh, a party of savages crossed to the south side of the stream, and annoyed the garrison with a desultory rifle-fire. But little damage was done; and the

general and his men feverishly awaited the appearance of the main body of the enemy — which they
knew was not far away.

The morning of the twenty-eighth was clear, and
gave promise of a beautiful day. But the wind
sweeping up from the lake was raw and chill. The
soldiers within the fort were astir at an early hour.
To their unbounded surprise, they could discover
nothing of their enemies of the day before. Some
of the officers and men were of the opinion that the
Indians, discouraged by their ill-success, had gone
to meet their brethren and allies and inform them
the place could not be taken. But General Harrison did not harbor such belief. On the contrary, he felt that the withdrawal of the small band
of savages portended a systematic attack by a large
force — an attack he was not well able to withstand.
So he sent Captain Hamilton and a squad of men
down the river, on a reconnoitering expedition.
Then drawing his cloak around his shoulders, and
restlessly pacing up and down the inclosure, he in-
wardly condemned the niggardly and dilatory policy
of the government, and prayed that re-enforcements
might arrive in time to save him from an ignominious surrender.

His face wore an anxious and worried expression ;
but his thin lips were firmly set, his keen eyes
shone with the fire of an indomitable purpose. The
soldiers — every one of whom loved him and had unbounded confidence in him — looking upon him,
knew that no white flag would float over Fort

19

Meigs, as long as there was a man left to load and
fire a gun. And each one of them — from the
highest officer to the meanest subaltern — resolved
to die like a hero.

Near one of the blockhouses at the eastern extremity of the fort, stood a white man and an Indian. The former was slightly past middle age,
tall, stooped, and ungainly. The latter was much
younger, lithe, strong, and straight as an arrow.
For some time they stood silently watching the
commander, as he paced to and fro. At last the
white man blew his long nose vigorously, wiped the
tears from his eyes with the back of his horny hand,
and, screwing his homely features into a comical
grimace, said in a drawling tone :

"Injin, the sight o' the ol' Gener'l makes me sad
— makes me think o' him that's dead an' gone."

"Ugh !" his red companion grunted stolidly.
But the copper-colored face twitched ; the bare and
brawny chest heaved.

"Yes," the speaker continued, "the sight o'
Gener'l Harrison calls up things I wish I could
fergit — it does, by cracky ! Gol-fer-socks ! I
can't fergit 'em — not if I lived to be as old as
Methusaler, — 'r was it Nebbycaneezer? I'm a little
rusty on Scriptur', an' liable to git mixed, somehow. But, pshaw ! The past is gone — an' gone
forever. The comrade we both loved is dead.
Didn't we see him shot through the heart ? No —
come to think of it — he wasn't shot through the
heart ; 'cause he was shot in the right side — an'

the heart's on the *left* side, in *most* human critters. But he was dead, anyhow — killed by the danged Winnebagoes!''

Again the speaker paused long enough to blow his nose and wipe his watery eyes. Then he resumed in the same mournful, sing-song voice:

''Though I seen him dyin' with my own eyes, Injin, sometimes I find myself thinkin' he's still alive — I do, by Matildy Jane! I've dream'd o' him nights so much, it 'pears to me he *can't* be dead. But, of course, he *is*. 'Cause why? We left him dyin'. Well, it don't do no good to grieve. But ther's one thing I'd like to know right smart — an' that's what become o' the dog.''

''Ugh!'' ejaculated the Indian, nodding. ''Me heap like know where hound. Much good dog — sight big brave.''

The white man went on:

''An' dang-it-all-to-dingnation! Here we are — jest got back from eighteen months o' traipsin' from one Winnebago town to another, all over God's creation, all over the Northwest — an' we're right plump into another hornets' nest. Talk 'bout jumpin' out o' the fryin' pan into the fire! We've jumped out o' ice water into b'ilin' oil. Here we've been drug 'round fer a year an' a half, beat and starved an' cuffed every day in the week — an' give a double dose on Sundays. My heart's been in my mouth so much, I've chawed off one end of it an' spit it out with my tobacker — I have, by my gran'father's barn-door britches! An' now

we've made our escape at last — got halfway back
from p'rdition to glory — we're in another peck o'
trouble.

"As near as I can learn from the talk that's
goin' on 'mong the soldiers, Gener'l Proctor an'
Tecumseh's comin' to attack this place — with not
less'n three thousan' white an' red devils. Three
thousan' to five hundred! A purty pickle —
I swear! W'y, hang-it-up-an'-take-it-down-an'-
cook-it! They'll eat us up without salt 'r pepper!
'Cause Ol' Tippecanoe'll never surrender — he don't
know *how*. He's jest like ol' Mad Anthony —
they say he trained under that ol' war hoss — an'
he'll fight as long as he's got an ounce of lead left,
an' a flintlock to shoot it in. Look at him now,
Bright Wing. He's ev'ry inch a soldier, ain't he?"

"Ugh!" the imperturbable Wyandot assented.
"Tippecanoe him heap sight brave. Him kill many
bad Shawnees, Winnebagoes, Pottawatomies. Him
fight till me, you — all dead."

"Well," Farley groaned resignedly, "I s'pose we
can stand it, if the rest of 'em can. But the good
Lord knows we've stood 'bout enough! Dodrot
it! Sometimes I think the Lord has sent all my
latter trials an' tribulations upon me, fer growlin'
'bout whackin' them bulls from Fort Harrison
to the Prophet's Town — I do, by flapjacks! An'
then ag'in I git to thinkin' my punishment is jest
the natur'l result o' the heartless way I've used the
women folks. W'y, Injin, I used to be a reg'lar
heart-breaker. I didn't have no mercy on the

unfortunates that bowed down an' worshiped my
beautiful face an' form. I was a reg'lar Apoller in
them days, I was — purty as a pictur'. But look
at me now! Whackin' bulls an' sufferin' Injin torment has jest 'bout ruined me. Where's my purty
hair, eh? An' look at this nose, an' these ears, an'
this face! Injin, my beauty's suffered a blightin'
frost — it has, by my gran'mother's petticoat!
W'y, ding-it-all-to-dangnation! A few more hard
knocks, an' I won't look no better'n the average
man — I won't, by ginger! An' to think that an
Injin squaw — the oldest an' ugliest one in the
whole Winnebago tribe — follered an' tagged me
from Dan to Barsheber! Follered an' tagged me
till I couldn't eat n'r sleep — an' the frogs inside o'
me jest natur'ly got disgusted an' quit business. It
was awful — awful! Injin, clap y'r eyes upon me
an' tell me what I've done to deserve such a fate."

And Joe solemnly lifted his well-worn coonskin
cap and faced his companion.

Bright Wing looked upon his loquacious and
whimsical friend and smiled, while his beady eyes
twinkled; but he said nothing.

Farley was indeed a comical object. His clothing hung in tatters upon his angular form; his toes
peeped from his cowhide shoes. During his captivity,
the Winnebagoes had essayed the hapless task of
making an Indian of him. They had plucked out
his scant hair, leaving his scalp bare and shiny —
excepting a straw-colored tuft at the crown. They
had pierced his nose and ears, and ornamented those

necessary appendages with large shell rings. And, to complete the fantastic whole, had tattooed the totem of the clan, whose prisoner he was, in blue ink upon his forehead. He was a sight to excite mirth and commiseration at the same time.

"Well, what do you think o' my looks, any-how?" he asked, when Bright Wing had finished his silent inspection and was looking toward a distant part of the inclosure.

"Joe him very much pretty — heap nice sight," the Wyandot chuckled gutturally. "Him Winne-bago now — big chief."

"That's it — that's it!" Farley moaned lugu-briously. "I knowed it — my beauty's gone fer-ever! I'll never dare to peep in a lookin'-glass ag'in — the shock 'ld be too much fer my delicate constertution to bear. By King David's cross-eyed wives! But my punishment's too great fer mortal man to stand! Drivin' oxen an' bein' the human habitation of a colony o' frogs wan't enough; the Winnebagoes had to have a whack at me. An' they've finished the job——"

Then, with sudden animation:

"But what 're you lookin' at, Injin?"

Bright Wing silently pointed toward the command-er's quarters on the southern side of the inclosure. General Harrison was just entering the door of his tent, and, hurrying toward it, were an officer and a number of soldiers.

"That's Cap'n Hamilton an' his squad," Joe cried excitedly. "They've jest got back from the'r scoutin' trip down the river. Now we'll know what's comin'. Le's mosey out that way.''

Captain Hamilton, leaving his men outside, entered the commander's tent and stood at attention.

"Well, Captain," Harrison remarked calmly, "you're back soon. What's your report?"

The inferior officer saluted and replied :

"Three miles down the river we came upon the main body of the enemy, rapidly advancing in this direction.''

"Who's in command?"

"General Proctor."

"And Tecumseh commands the savages?"

"He does, General."

"Is their force as large as reported?"

"I judge from what I saw that they have a force of fully three thousand men — British regulars, Canadian militia, and Indians."

"Are they well supplied with heavy artillery?"

"I think they are, General. At any rate, they have some heavy pieces.''

"Is that all you were able to learn?"

"It is, General.''

"The enemy will be here in a few hours at the most," Harrison remarked. "They mean to invest us — to storm us, if necessary. Their force is six times that of ours. But we must repulse them. To surrender means to lose all for which we have planned and fought — and to court death at the hands of the savages. If General Clay and his Kentuckians were only here ——''

Then with fiery energy:

"But we must bestir ourselves. Captain, go and give the order that the gates be tightly closed at once — after a supply of water, sufficient to last several days, has been brought from the river."

The captain saluted and withdrew. Turning to an orderly standing near the door, the commander said briskly:

"Find the field commissary, Captain William Oliver, and send him here."

A few minutes later Captain Oliver put in an appearance. He was young and beardless, but strong, active, and courageous.

By this time, a number of officers had gathered at the commander's quarters and were holding animated conference with him. All looked up at the young Captain's entrance. Harrison broke off in the middle of a sentence and, advancing, took the newcomer's hand.

"Captain Oliver," he said solemnly, "you know the strait in which we're placed. If re-enforcements don't arrive within a few days this place, with all its stores, will inevitably fall into the hands of the British. Such an event would be an incalculable disaster. It mustn't happen. But we must have help. General Green Clay is on his way hither, with a regiment of Kentucky militia. I have received word that he's coming by way of the Auglaize. At the present time he must be near Fort Winchester. I've decided to send a dispatch to him, apprising him of the condition of affairs and urging him to hasten to our aid; and I've chosen you to perform the perilous mission. Your brother officers approve my plan — and my choice of messenger. Are you willing to venture upon the hazardous undertaking, Captain Oliver?"

The assembled officers craned their necks, and listened breathlessly for the young commissary's reply. It was not long in coming. Firm and clear his voice rang out:

"I'll go, General — willingly and gladly. I'll deliver your dispatch into General Clay's hands — or die on the way.

"Thank you, Captain," Harrison murmured, his voice soft with emotion.

Then quickly:

"How soon can you start?"

"At once, General."

"Very well — the sooner the better. You should be beyond reach of our enemies before they invest the fort. Make your preparations and return in a half hour. I'll have the dispatch ready for you. By the way, how many men do you want?"

"One, General — a guide."

"Hadn't you better take a score?"

"They'd be of no use to me, General — and you need them here," was the firm reply.

"True," the commander returned reflectively. "Well, come back in half an hour. I'll have everything in readiness."

Captain Oliver bowed and withdrew. Just outside of the tent he encountered Farley, Bright Wing, and a number of soldiers. Awkwardly lifting his cap, the whimsical Joe stepped forward and asked:

"Are we goin' to have a brush with the Britishers an' redskins, Cap'n?"

"More than a brush, I imagine," answered the commissary, edging his way through the crowd.

"An' what 're we goin' to do?" Farley inquired.

"Fight," was the curt response.

Joe was nettled.

"Any fool'd know that," he muttered; "'specially if he'd been in the fight o' Tippecanoe with the ol' Gener'l——"

Captain Oliver stopped suddenly and, wheeling around, interrupted:

"You were with General Harrison at Tippecanoe, my friend?"

"I was," Farley answered proudly. "Me an' Bright Wing, here, was both there."

"From your dress and general appearance, I judge you are a woodman—a hunter."

"I am—what ther' is left o' me, which ain't very much sence the danged Winnebagoes sp'iled my beauty."

"You've been a prisoner among the Indians?"

"Yes— both of us, ever sence the battle o' Tippecanoe. We jest escaped — jest got in here yisterday."

"Does the commander know you?"

"He used to—but I don't s'pose he would now. The danged Winnebagoes——"

Captain Oliver impatiently interrupted:

"I'm going on a journey. Would you and your red friend like to accompany me?"

"That d'pends," was the cautious reply. "If it's toward the Winnebago country——"

"Please step this way," said the Captain, plucking Joe's ragged sleeve.

When they were beyond earshot of the others, the officer explained:

"I'm going on a perilous mission. I want some-one to accompany me as guide—someone ac-quainted with the woods——"

"Well, where 're you goin'?" Joe persisted.

"I'm going to meet General Clay, who is com-ing by way of the Auglaize."

"An' you want me an' the Injin to go with you, as guides?"

"That's it. You're an American?"

"Did you take me fer a Britisher?"—indig-nantly.

"And you're acquainted with the country up and down the valley?"

"I know it as well as I know the road to my own mouth; so does the Injin—he's a Wyandot, an' true as steel. When do you want to start?"

"Immediately. Will you go with me?"

"Yes."

"And the Indian?"

"Of course."

" How soon can you be ready ? "

"We're ready now—if we only had guns an' ammynition. You see, when we got away from the Winnebagoes we hadn't nothin' but the clo'es on our backs—which ain't much to speak of."—And Joe glanced ruefully at his tattered garments.—"We lived on roots an' barks, on the road here. Give us guns an' ammynition, an' we're with you."

"You shall have what you want," was the decided reply. "Call your friend and come with me."

A half hour later, Captain Oliver and his chosen guides passed out at the western gate of the fort, and disappeared in the dense woods upon the southern bank of the river.

An hour after the departure of the brave dispatch-bearer and his two comrades, the enemy put in an appearance upon the opposite shore of the stream. General Harrison pushed the work upon the grand traverse. This was a wall of earth and timbers, running through the center of the inclosure, the full length of the fortification. It was nine hundred feet long, twenty feet wide at the base, and twelve feet high ; and was intended to serve as a protection against the shells of the British. Anticipating the fact that the enemy would erect powerful batteries on the opposite shore, the American commander ordered that numerous excavations be made in the south side of the grand traverse, to which his men could retreat in time of danger from exploding missiles.

All the afternoon, the Indians annoyed the soldiers of the garrison with a desultory rifle-fire; but as they fired at long range, their shots did little except to cause the Americans to reply in like manner. Late in the evening, two or three boat-loads of savages landed upon the south bank of the river, and, taking up positions among the neighboring trees, poured a more effective fire upon the fort. The soldiers answered briskly; and the fusillade was kept up until nightfall.

In the meantime, the Americans had trained two eighteen-pounders upon their enemies across the river, causing them to retire to cover; and the British had succeeded in crossing the stream and throwing up earthworks for the protection of their fieldpieces, a short distance from the southeastern angle of the fort. The place was completely invested. Preparations were active, on the one side, to storm the garrison; on the other, to repel the most vigorous assault.

On the morning of the twenty-ninth, General Harrison issued a general order, appealing to the patriotism of his men.

All day the rifle-fire was continued by both sides. Several of the Americans received serious wounds, and a number of the enemy were killed.

On the morning of the thirtieth, the condition of affairs was much the same. Within the fort, the grand traverse was nearing completion; and the British were placing their heavy siege guns in position on the opposite shore.

The Americans were well supplied with food, but they suffered much from want of water. They were digging a well within the inclosure; but, in the meantime, they had to procure their supply from the river at night — a hazardous proceeding.

On the following day, the British had a number of their cannon in position, and began a bombardment. The Americans returned shot for shot; and a number of men were killed upon each side.

For the next four days there was little change in the situation. Both armies were on the alert to take an advantage of the other, but none offered. General Harrison had removed all his tents and paraphernalia behind the traverses; and the enemy had nothing to shoot at but the bare earthen walls. The soldiers within the fort and the savages without kept up an incessant rifle-fire; and the great guns on both sides thundered. But the American commander's supply of shot and shell was running short.

Apparently, the enemy had abandoned all idea of storming the fort and had settled down to take it by siege.

CHAPTER XV.

Aʙᴏᴜᴛ sixty miles above Fort Meigs, near the junction of the Auglaize and the Maumee, lay Fort Winchester — formerly Fort Defiance. Within its walls, General Green Clay and his Kentucky militiamen were encamped — resting after their long and arduous march, and knowing nothing of the urgent need of their presence at Fort Meigs.

In the early morning of the thirtieth of April, three men entered the gateway of the fortification. They were Captain Oliver and his two guides. The former immediately made inquiries for the commander, and was directed to the officers' quarters. Farley and Bright Wing stopped with a squad of men near the gate, and the loquacious Joe entered into conversation with them. While the white men were talking, the Wyandot leaned upon his gun and swept his eyes about the place. Suddenly he gave a grunt of astonishment and laid his hand upon his comrade's arm.

"What is it, Injin?" Farley inquired, as he whirled about upon his heel.

"Dog — dog Duke!" muttered Bright Wing in awe-struck tones, his gaze fixed upon a distant part of the inclosure.

(303)

"Duke?" exclaimed Joe. "What do you mean? Where?"

"Dog Duke him over there — now gone," came the soft guttural reply.

"Say, Injin, you're gittin' loony," Farley asserted solemnly. "Ther' ain't no dog over there —n'r hain't been."

"Me see dog," the Wyandot insisted. "Look heap much like Duke."

"Yes, he saw a dog — 'r a bloodhoun', to be more exact," affirmed a raw-boned Kentuckian, pointing toward one of the corner blockhouses. "I saw it, too. The animal was jest passin' into the block-house. He's an unsociable brute, an' belongs to one o' the guides."

"Well, it ain't the dog we used to know, though it may look some like him," Joe asserted positively. "'Cause the redskins has made a meal o' him, long 'fore this. Come on, Injin. Le's see if we can't find somethin' to fill up on. I'm as empty as a frog pon' durin' a dry spell."

The two comrades left the group at the gate and went to another part of the inclosure. At one of the mess-fires they were proffered food, which they gladly accepted. After eating heartily, they leisurely sauntered about the place, Joe whimsically commenting upon all they observed.

They had finished a tour of the inclosure, and were irresolutely pondering what to do next, when Farley suddenly threw up his head and stood rigid as a ramrod, his eyes fixed upon a large bloodhound

that came from behind a tent and trotted toward
them.

"Duke 'r his ghost!" he whispered with trembling lips. "Injin, do you see him, too?"

"Ugh!" Bright Wing managed to ejaculate.

"Then it's Duke an' not his ghost," Joe said in a
relieved tone. "'Cause I've alluz heerd it said
that two folks don't see a ghost at the same time.
Injin, he's comin' right toward us—it *is* Duke, by
Katy Melissy! Here, Duke—here, purp!"

The bloodhound was trotting toward them, his
nose close to the ground. Evidently he was trail-
ing them. At the sound of Farley's voice, he threw
up his muzzle and set his eyes upon the two men.
Then with a short, hoarse yelp of joy, he sprang
toward them.

"Dang-it-all-to-dingnation!" shouted Joe. "It's
ol' Duke—an' he knows us! Injin, he had smelt
out our tracks an' was trailin' us. I know you, ol'
feller—of course, I do! An' I'm as glad to see you,
as you are to see me. But git down, purp; you'll
spile my nice clo'es, with y'r dirty paws—you will,
by cracky!"

Farley's voice was tremulous, and the tears were
running down his furrowed cheeks. He was laughing and weeping at the same time.

The hound crouched at the feet of his old companions and whined; he fawned upon them; he
circled about them, barking madly.

"Duke him heap sight glad see me, you—all of
us," Bright Wing muttered sagely. "Me, you, all

20

of us very much glad see dog Duke.   Him no dead
—him here.   Maybe master no dead—*him* here.''

"Shut up, Injin—shut up!" Farley cried
sternly.   "Don't go to raisin' no false hopes like
that, in a feller's gizzard.   Ross Douglas is dead—
me an' you saw him dyin'.   The redskins—led by
that dang Bradford—found him an' the dog together.   No doubt they scalped an' stripped the
master an' drug away the dog.   But somebody got
the houn' away from the thievin', murderin' red
devils—an' here he is.   I can read it all like
readin' a book.   A heap better, in fact, fer I ain't
much on book learnin'.   But ther's one thing we
want to do—find this scout that claims to own the
dog, an' make him tell where he got him."

"Ugh!"   And bright Wing nodded assent.

"Come on, then," Joe began excitedly, but
stopped and stared stupidly around.

"Wher's the purp?" he muttered.

"Duke him clean gone," muttered the Wyandot.
"Him gone that way"—pointing with his rifle.
"Gone hunt new master."

"Well, we'll foller him," Farley said decidedly.
"An' I'll mighty soon tell this new master he
hain't got no right to the houn', an' that we're
goin' to take the brute with us.   Eh, Injin?"

"Ugh!   All right—me, too."

And again Bright Wing nodded vigorously.

"An' if he gives me any of his sass," Farley
went on savagely, "I'll whip the scoundrel within
an inch of his worthless life—I will, by Lucindy!

Nobody but you an' me has any right to Duke now. An' we'll have him 'r know the reason why. Golfer-socks! How I wish Ross Douglas was alive an' here. I'd be willin' to let the danged Winnebagoes punch my nose an' pierce my ears an' pull out my hair an' whiskers, to the'r heart's content. Yes, I'd be willin' to let 'em destroy the last remnants o' my beauty, an pull out my lairipin' tongue by the roots — I would, 'r my name ain't Joseph Peregoy Farley!"

The two comrades were walking in the direction whence the bloodhound had gone. Just as they reached the spot where the Wyandot had seen the dog disappear among a cluster of tents, a militiaman crossed their path.

"Say, friend," Farley said hurriedly, "do you happen to know the man that owns the big bloodhoun' that's runnin' 'round the camp?"

"Yes," the soldier answered promptly.

"Well, we're huntin' him. What kind of a looking critter is he?"

"He's one o' the scouts — a youngish-like man, big an' stout; a kind of a surly feller, like his dog — don't have much to say to nobody. But he knows his business — an' 'tends to it. Anything more you'd like to know?"

"I'd like to know where to find him," Joe replied coolly, unheeding the sarcasm of the other's tone and words.

"You'll find him right in that big tent. He's in there holdin' a conflab with the Gener'l an' his staff. You act as if you had important business with him."

"I have," answered Joe, shutting his teeth with a snap. "What's his name?"

"I — don't — know —— " the soldier began slowly. "Yes, I do. I heard our Captain call him by name the other day. Le's see. It was somethin' like Ruggles 'r Duggles. No, that wasn't it. I guess I can't think of it."

Bright Wing's black eyes opened very wide, and he uttered a surprised "Ugh!" Farley's cheek paled under its coat of tan. He tried to speak; but the words would not come. At last he managed to stammer:

"It — It wasn't — Douglas, was it?"

"That's it — Douglas," exclaimed the militiaman, slapping his thigh. "Douglas — yes, that's the name."

"Ross Douglas?"

Joe's face was ashen as he put the question.

"Now you've hit it!" the man shouted triumphantly. "That's the very name I heard the Captain call him — Ross Douglas."

Farley and Bright Wing stared at each other, in speechless amazement. Their chests were heaving; their lips, apart. The militiaman looked from one to the other in silent wonder. The Wyandot regained the power of speech and grunted:

"Duke him not dead — him here. Master not dead, too — him here. Ross here — Fleet Foot — ugh!"

"Injin, you're a 'tarnal fool!" Farley cried

angrily, his face suddenly flushing — then paling.
"Fer God's sake, don't make no more remarks like
that! You know — an' I know — that Ross
Douglas's dead. You're a fool!"

"*Joe* big fool!" Bright Wing returned sullenly.

"No, I ain't!" Farley vociferated wildly. "I
can see the length of my nose — an' you can't.
Don't you understand, Injin. W'y the dang skunk
that's got Ross Douglas's houn' has got Ross Douglas's name — stol'd both of 'em, of course. Jest
wait till he steps out o' that tent, an' I'll give him
the infernalest lambastin' a man ever got in his life
— I will, by — by ——"

But Joe, in his excitement, could think of no suitable object by which to swear, so ended with a
gasping sputter.

"You seem to be terribly worked-up 'bout somethin', stranger," the soldier remarked coolly. "An'
you threaten to trounce the guide that calls hisself
Ross Douglas. Well, maybe you're like a singed
cat — better'n you look — but if I was you I'd hire
the job out. I seen the feller you talk o' whippin'
lick two men bigger'n you — an' not half try —
jest 'cause they spit tobacker juice in his dog's eye."

"It don't make no differ'nce who he's licked, n'r
who he hain't,' Joe answered obstinately. "A
man that's mean enough to palm hisself off fer Ross
Douglas — who's dead an' gone — has got to take a
trouncin' from me. Ross Douglas was my best
friend; an' I won't have his name stol'd an' disgraced by no two-legged critter that ever tramped

on new ground — I won't, by Queen Elizabeth ! It 'pears the rascal thinks a sight o' the dog — bein' ready to fight fer him ; but my mind's made up — the cuss has got to be licked."

By this time a knot of soldiers had gathered at the spot. Now they nudged one another and exchanged facetious winks and remarks. They were expecting to see no end of fun, when the guide should put in an appearance.

Farley muttered impatiently :

"I wish the critter'd come — right while I'm in a good notion. When he does, one o' you fellers p'int him out to me."

A number of the assembled militiamen offered to perform the service. Suddenly one of them remarked in a stage whisper :

"The council's broke up. Here comes the officers now."

"P'int him out to me!" Farley hissed between his set teeth.

And giving his gun into Bright Wing's hands, he rolled up his ragged sleeves, revealing his knotted and sinewy arms.

The officers emerged from General Clay's tent. Captain Oliver was among them. He caught sight of Farley and, noting the woodman's attitude and expression, walked up to him, saying :

"You appear excited, my friend. What's the matter?"

The assembled militiamen grinned broadly ; and the officers paused momentarily. But Joe kept his pale, watery eyes fixed upon the opening in the canvas wall and did not reply to the question. The Captain turned to Bright Wing with :

"What ails your comrade ?"

"Ugh !" was the guttural response. "Joe him heap mad man. Him want fight much bad."

At that moment a tall, broad-shouldered young man appeared in the doorway. At his side trotted a magnificent bloodhound.

"There he is — go fer him !" a mischievous militiaman whispered in Farley's ear.

Joe clapped his eyes upon the figure emerging from the tent, and, with a hoarse, inarticulate cry, staggered back a few steps and covered his face with his hands.

Officers and men were astounded, and could only stand and stare. Bright Wing gave a grunt of surprise and satisfaction, and became a bronze statue. The hound ran forward and fawned at the feet of the two woodmen. Then the young man in the doorway shouted joyously :

"Joe Farley and Bright Wing !"

Joe dropped his hands to his side, and for a brief moment stood with mouth agape. Then with the cry — "It's Ross Douglas hisself, alive an' a-livin'" — he sprang forward and threw his long, bony arms around his friend's neck.

Bright Wing grinned broadly and muttered :

"Dog Duke alive and here ; Fleet Foot alive and here. Joe heap sight big fool. Ugh !"

Duke capered about in mad delight, baying and

whining by turns.   Ross and Joe held each other
at arm's length and looked long and earnestly into
each other's eyes.   Tears were raining down their
cheeks, and their lips were trembling.

An oppressive silence rested upon the little knot of
soldiers who were watching the drama enacting before them.   Of a sudden a militiaman broke the
spell by shouting :

"Well, if that don't beat all the ways to lick a
man, I'm a numbskull !"

With shouts of laughter, the crowd gradually
dispersed.   Douglas tore himself from Farley's
grasp and, flying to Bright Wing, warmly embraced
him.   In return the Wyandot gave his friend a
bear-like hug.   Joe stood blubbering and wiping his
weak eyes.   For once in his life the power of speech
had deserted him.   Drawing the two together,
Douglas said with deep emotion :

"God knows how glad I am to meet you again
— to find you alive and well !   I've mourned you
as dead."

Farley suddenly found his voice and replied :

"An' maybe we ain't glad to see you, Ross ! We
not only thought you was dead — we *knowed* you
was.   We seen you dyin' — we left you fer dead.
An' dang-it-all-to-dingnation ! Hang-it-up-an'-take-
it-down-an'-cook-it !   I can't hardly believe my
senses.   Where've you been — how did you come
to life?   Tell me all about it right now — don't
wait a minute.   By King Solerman's six hundred
wives !   I never was as happy in my born days !"

"Come, my friends," Ross said softly, sadly, "let's find a quiet place, and sit down and talk."

He led them to a distant corner of the fortification. There, seated upon a log, they entered into explanations. Douglas told the two of his miraculous escape from death in the woods, of his multifarious adventures and experiences among the Indians at the village upon the Mississinewa, and of the bitter disappointment he had met on his return to Franklinton. Last of all, he showed them the Prophet's ring. Farley gingerly examined the talisman, but said nothing. Bright Wing would not touch the uncanny thing, but shudderingly remarked :

"Tenskwatawa big medicine man — bad Shawnee. Ring very much strong — make redmen sleep. Ugh !"

And he drew away from it.

When Douglas had finished, Farley began his narrative. In conclusion he said :

"Yes, Ross Douglas, me an' the Injin's been pris'ners 'mong the Winnebagoes, ever sence we left you — up to a few days ago. A dozen times they was goin' to kill us, but somethin' alluz happened jest in the nick o' time to save us. But look at me ! Where's the beauty that once was mine ? Gone — sacrificed by the dang redskins ! It's a sin an' a shame — it is, by my gran'mother's shoestrings ! An' we'd 'ave been in the clutches o' the red devils yit, but the most of 'em took it into the'r heads to jine Tecumseh on his rampage 'g'inst Fort Meigs.

That give us a chance to git away. But holy incense! Talk 'bout sufferin'! Hain't I 'xperienced it? Yit you've had a right smart taste y'rself, Ross. Yes, things has come out jest as I told you they would. I said if you left ol' Sam Larkin's gal an' went off to war, she'd marry that scalawag of a Hilliard. An' she's done it. But — gol-fer-socks! That's the way o' the whole feminine gender. Don't I know 'em — say? Still I don't fancy you're so much disap'inted over the turn things has took, Ross. Eh?"

And Farley smiled quizzically.

"What do you mean, Joe?" Douglas asked quickly.

"Oh! you know well enough what I mean," the other chuckled. "I think if you could find the little red-haired gal that set you free, you wouldn't hunt overmuch fer Amy Larkin. That's my 'pinion, at least."

"You're wrong, my old friend," Douglas hastened to say. "I have been true to Amy Larkin; I trust and believe she has been true to me. I shall continue my search for her — and never rest till I find her; although I have no knowledge of her whereabouts. But I must leave you now, to assist in the preparations for departure."

"Go ahead! — don't let us keep you," Farley assented. "Ol' Tippecanoe's in a bad box down there at Fort Meigs, an' the sooner we all git there, the better. How soon do you think the army'll be ready to move?"

" By to-morrow morning, at the latest. I'll see you again this evening. Then we can talk to our heart's content."

Douglas hurried from the spot, and Farley and Bright Wing, arising, again sauntered aimlessly about the place, followed by the bloodhound.

In the meantime, preparations for the hurried trip down the river were rapidly going on. Officers were stalking hither and thither, giving sharp commands. Hundreds of men were busily engaged in loading the camp equipage, arms, ammunition, and provisions upon flat, open boats that lay moored at the water's edge.

All day the work proceeded without intermission. When one set of men became weary, others took their places. By sunset the boats were loaded — everything on board but the men themselves. That night they slept in their dismantled camp, upon the bare ground. At daylight they manned their clumsy vessels and commenced their venturesome voyage down the Maumee.

General Clay had twelve hundred men in his command, and his fleet consisted of eighteen flats of various size. For four days the primitive flotilla moved slowly onward between walls of unbroken forest. The only motive power was the sluggish current, and poles and sweeps in the hands of the sturdy Kentuckians.

The weather was warm and sunshiny. Mating birds twittered and chirped in the budding boughs of the trees along the shore, and reviewed their nesting-places of the year before. The clear water lapped musically against the sides of the moving craft; and the militiamen, lolling in the genial sunshine, smoked their pipes and chatted cheerily, unaware of the black fate that awaited them.

CHAPTER XVI.

LATE on the night of the fourth of May, General Clay and his relief expedition arrived at the head of the rapids, a few miles above Fort Meigs. Captain Oliver and a squad of men — among whom were Farley and Bright Wing — slipped ashore and started afoot for the fort. Then — the pilot flatly refusing to proceed farther in the darkness — the commander was compelled to tie up his boats and wait for daylight.

Captain Oliver and his men succeeded in eluding the vigilant Indians, and entered the fortification at two o'clock in the morning. The youthful commissary immediately repaired to General Harrison's quarters, and apprised him of the near approach of the re-enforcements.

An hour later, after a hasty consultation with his officers, the commander sent Captain Hamilton and a subaltern up the river, to meet General Clay. They bore orders to the effect that Clay was to land eight hundred men upon the left bank of the stream, to carry the British batteries and spike the cannon ; also, that the residue of the militia were to disembark upon the south shore and fight their way to the fort. It was the design of Harrison to make sorties against the enemy upon the same side of the

river — whenever the Kentuckians should attack the
English artillerists upon the north bank.

In the gray of the early morning, General Clay
cut loose his boats and drifted into the rapids.
Scarcely were the unwieldy vessels under way, when
a hail came from the southern shore ; and Captain
Hamilton and his companion appeared at the water's
edge, frantically waving their arms. They were
taken aboard the craft upon which was the commander of the expedition ; and there the Captain
delivered his message.

Word was rapidly passed from one boat to another.
Soon all was animation and excitement. The
soldiers — who had had nothing to eat since the
evening before, and who still lay upon the decks,
wrapped in their mist-dampened blankets — hastily
threw off their coverings, sprang to their feet, and
prepared for battle. In low tones they conversed
and left messages with one another for the dear
ones at home. But there was no panic — no sign
of cowardice. Fixed purpose, not fear, was in each
rugged face.

Slowly the flats drifted into the middle of the rapids. Soon they gained in impetus and floated more
and more rapidly. The water chuckled and gurgled at the bows, and danced in creamy wakes behind. Except for a crisp command, now and then,
all was silence on board — the silence of determined
men ready to battle to the death.

Colonel Dudley was to lead the detachment
against the English batteries upon the northern

shore. His boat was in advance of the others. Suddenly a number of savages appeared upon the left bank, and, with hoots and yells, discharged their pieces at the advancing flotilla. One officer was wounded slightly. Then the militiamen returned the fire and the Indians fled to shelter.

Silence again reigned; and the flotilla drifted onward.

In a few minutes, it had reached the foot of the rapids. Colonel Dudley, detaching twelve boats and eight hundred men, steered for the northern shore, intending to land about a mile above the British batteries. General Clay, with the six remaining boats and about four hundred men, made an effort to disembark upon the southern bank, a short distance above the beleaguered fort. But wind and current were against him. Only fifty of the militiamen had got ashore, when the vessels were swept from their moorings. This little squad of Kentuckians valiantly fought their way through the horde of whooping savages that hemmed them in, and reached the fort without the loss of a man.

The remaining three hundred and fifty — under command of Colonel Boswell — after repeated trials and failures, finally effected a landing upon the right bank, at a point near the western end of the fortification. General Harrison sent a sortie to their aid; and the combined force repulsed the Indians and Canadian militia, and marched in triumph to the fort.

A short time afterward the commander sent another sortie against the batteries southeast of the garrison. A stubborn engagement took place. The sturdy Americans, though greatly outnumbered, drove the British from their position, spiked several of their cannon, and, taking a number of prisoners, made a safe retreat.

Fighting had commenced on all sides of the beleaguered fortification. A ring of flame had encircled the place ; the Stars and Stripes had received a fresh baptism of blood. Now the smoke of battle lifted ; and the brave men within the walls turned their attention to their brethren on the opposite side of the river. General Harrison, glass in hand, was anxiously scanning the distant shore. Suddenly, he dropped his hand to his side and groaned :

" My God ! They are lost — lost ! They've captured the batteries, but are allowing themselves to be lured into an ambuscade. Their impetuosity will be their undoing ! "

Let us follow Colonel Dudley. Without difficulty, he landed upon the northern bank of the river, a mile above the British batteries. Gallantly his men charged the English artillerists and drove them from their guns. Had they been content with spiking the cannon and returning to their boats, all would have been well. But the Indians in the adjacent woods were pouring a galling fire into the American ranks.

This the dare-devil Kentuckians could not stand. With lusty cheers, they charged the savages and drove them pell-mell into the depths of the forest. Colonel Dudley feared an ambuscade, and sought to restrain the ardor of his troops, but in vain. The reckless militiamen continued the chase, pushing farther and farther into the tangled woodland.

Presently the wily redmen rallied and essayed to outflank their pursuers. A pitched battle took place. The rattle of firearms became a deafening roar; the dense smoke obscured friend and foe. Colonel Dudley ordered a charge along the whole line. It availed nothing; the Indians could not be dislodged. Next came the order to retreat to the boats. This the Kentuckians were ready to do. They had suffered severely — they realized their mistake. Foot by foot, they began a retreat toward the shore, fighting every step of the way.

In the meanwhile, the English artillerymen fled to old Fort Miami, a short distance down the river — where General Proctor had his headquarters — and reported the loss of the batteries. The British commander, thinking a general attack upon his encampment was imminent, immediately recalled a large part of his troops from the south side of the stream, and dispatched them to the scene of conflict. They arrived in time to fall upon the American rear, completely cut off their retreat, and kill or capture almost the entire force. Only one hundred and fifty of the gallant but rash eight hundred regained their boats and reached Fort Meigs.

At the beginning of this engagement, Tecumseh, with a part of his savage band, was in the immediate vicinity of the American fortification. On receiving word from Proctor, the great chief swam the river

21

and, mounting a horse, galloped to the scene of conflict. Well he knew what would happen were his warriors successful in the fight. But he arrived too late. The battle was ended ; the butchery had begun.

With the wailing cry — " What will become of my red brothers — what will become of my red brothers ! '' he wheeled his steed and dashed along the path leading from the battle-ground to the British encampment. The way was strewn with the mutilated corpses of murdered Americans. At the sight he clinched his white teeth — and spurred on. Reaching the gateway of the encampment, he galloped through and leaped to the ground.

The butchery was still going on. General Proctor was allowing the Indians to select their victims and kill them as they saw fit. The savages were satiating their thirst for blood, to the fullest extent.

" Hold ! '' Tecumseh thundered, drawing his tomahawk and facing his half-mad followers. '' The brave who kills another defenseless prisoner dies by my hand ! ''

And drawing himself defiantly erect, he fixed his piercing gaze upon the assembled redmen.

Cowed by the commanding presence of the chief they loved and feared, the Indians relinquished their victims and sullenly returned their bloodstained weapons to their belts. But one stubborn Winnebago, unheeding the command, sprang upon a prisoner standing near him. The next instant

Tecumseh's hatchet descended — and the red fiend was a corpse.

Grunts of approval greeted the summary act.

"Listen, warriors!" the great Shawnee shouted. "I said no more helpless captives should die. They shall *not*. I told you I would kill any who disobeyed my commands. I have kept my word. Had I been here this slaughter never would have occurred. For shame! Are you warriors or wolves? Dare to disobey me — and *die!*"

He turned sadly away. Seeing General Proctor standing near, he boldly strode up to the Englishman and demanded:

"Why have you permitted this massacre — you, a paleface?"

"Sir," replied the general haughtily, "your Indians cannot be commanded — controlled. They refused to obey my orders."

"Begone!" the great chief sneered. "You are unfit to command! You are a squaw; go and put on petticoats!"

General Proctor's face flushed hotly, but he did not utter the sharp retort that trembled upon his tongue. And it was well for him that he did not.

Tecumseh folded his arms and, stalking up and down among his warriors, kept them from further acts of violence.

The garrison of Fort Meigs, realizing the fate that threatened their brethren upon the opposite side of the river, went wild with excitement and anxiety. The commander and his officers repeatedly

signalled the venturesome militiamen to return
to their boats and cross over to the fort. Privates mounted the parapets and traverses — unmindful of Indian bullets — and shouted themselves
hoarse in futile endeavor to attract the attention of
the impetuous Kentuckians.

As has been shown, all this was vain. Then the
soldiers within the walls demanded that they be led to
the rescue of their friends. This General Harrison
wisely refused to permit. But he asked for volunteers to cross the stream and recall Dudley and his
men from the pursuit of the savages. Lieutenant
Campbell offered his services. But when he reached
the British batteries on the other side, Colonel Dudley and his men had disappeared in the thick woods.
The Lieutenant immediately recrossed to the fort
and reported the fact to his commander.

General Harrison was almost beside himself with
rage and grief. Striding up and down in front of
his tent, he wrung his hands and groaned :

"When *will* my countrymen learn to obey commands ! Foolhardiness is as bad as cowardice —
and leads to as grave results. Colonel Dudley and
his command will be cut to pieces ; every man will
be killed or captured. And I dare not send troops
to his aid. My hands are tied !"

A light breeze, sweeping in from the lake, rippled
the surface of the river and brought to the ears of
those within the garrison, the rattling crash of firearms in the distance and the cheers and whoops of
the combatants. The smoke of the conflict rose

above the tree-tops and drifted lazily toward the fort. With the smell of burning powder in their nostrils, the soldiers were hard to restrain. They ran from one part of the inclosure to another, brandishing their arms, and grumbling and cursing angrily.

"Ding-it-all-to-dingnation!" Joe Farley bellowed, gripping the stock of his rifle and panting hard with excitement. "Injin, we'd ort to be over there — we had, by Jerushy! Dang the hard-headed Kaintuckians, anyhow! The idee of 'em pokin' the'r noses into a hornets' nest, like that! They hain't got a bit o' gumption. But sombody's got to go to the'r help, 'r ther' won't be a man of 'em left to tell the story. An' what's worryin' me — Ross Douglas is among 'em. That youngster don't more 'n git out o' one diffikilty, till he's plump into another one. He'll be in the thick o' the rumpus, too, you can jest *bet*. An' he'll git his everlastin' this time — 'r I miss my guess. Dodrot the luck, anyhow! What 're we goin' to do? Jest listen to that, now! They're havin' it hot an' heavy — an' no mistake. We've had fightin' all 'round us an' all over us this mornin'. Me an' you's been in two purty little brushes ourselves. But, dang it, this is worse an' more of it! Say — I can't stand it no longer! Ross is over there in danger. I'm goin' to him, if I have to swim the river to git there. What do you say, Injin?"

"Ugh! Me go, too," the Wyandot replied calmly.

"Come on, then!" Joe cried recklessly. "It don't make no differ'nce who says we can't go — Gener'l Harrison 'r anybody else — we'll go any——"

He ended abruptly and fixed his gaze upon the opposite shore. The Wyandot followed his example. A body of men had emerged from the woods, and were running toward the boats on the shore. Others quickly followed them — and still others. From the fort, it could be seen that many of them were without hats or guns. Pell-mell they rushed to the boats, and hastily pushed off.

"A rout and a slaughter!" General Harrison moaned as he entered his tent.

"Here comes a part of 'em, anyhow," Farley muttered grimly; "but it 'pears to be a mighty *small* part of 'em. Gol-fer-socks! I only hope Douglas is amongst 'em. If he ain't, he's knocked under fer sure *this* time. Well, it seems ther' ain't nothin' to do but wait, an' watch, an' pray — it does, by ginger!"

And, folding his arms, the lank and sorrowful-looking woodman sullenly watched the fugitives frantically poling their craft across the river.

Now all was bustle and confusion within the garrison. One of the gates was thrown open; and soldiers hurried down to the shore, to receive and protect the terrorized fugitives. Soon all were safe within the walls; but still the hubbub continued. Hundreds crowded around the survivors, to hear the story of their dreadful experience. General Harrison called one of the surviving officers into his tent, and there learned the particulars of the ambuscade and awful slaughter.

Colonel Dudley had been tomahawked ; many of the officers were dead. And of the gallant eight hundred less than one-fourth had escaped. It was not war ; it was butchery — annihilation!

Joe Farley and Bright Wing moved among the survivors, and eagerly scanned each face. But the man they sought was not there. Suddenly the Wyandot uttered a grunt of surprise and exclaimed :

" Dog Duke ! "

" Where ? " Farley demanded sharply.

Ere the redman could make reply, the hound saw them and bounded toward them. Dropping upon the ground at their feet, he tragically rolled his blood-rimmed eyes and whined beseechingly. His coat was soiled and roughened, and his muzzle was smeared with blood.

" He's been in the scrimmage, as sure's you live!" was Joe's muttered comment. " You can see that, Injin. Look at his nose—all stained with blood. He's give some 'tarnal Shawnee 'r other red devil his final sickness—he has, by Caroline ! But if he's here, his master *must* be here. I never knowed 'em to be far apart, if they could help it. Le's look ag'in."

They renewed their search, the dog following them, panting and whining. But they did not find their friend. Joe made numerous inquiries. All the answer he received from anyone was a sad shake of the head.   Discouraged at last, he murmured sadly :

"'Tain't no use, Injin.   Ross Douglas is among the missin'.   An' in this case, that means he's dead ; 'cause the whole thing's been a reg'lar butcher's job. I wish the dang Winnebagoes had killed me when they had the notion — I do, by Kizzier !   I'm sorry I ever lived to see this day.   Jest found him to lose him ag'in — an' ferever.   We made an awful mistake, Injin ; we ort to 'ave stayed with him, 'stid o' comin' back here with Cap'n Oliver."

Bright Wing nodded sadly.

" Duke, you're a pow'rful smart animal, in more ways 'n one.   I wish to glory I could make you understand what I want to know.   Wher's y'r master, purp?   Wher's Ross Douglas ? "

The hound lifted his nose and howled dolefully.

" Jest as I thought — jest as I 'xpected !" Farley said chokingly.   " He's dead.   That's what you mean, ain't it, purp ? "

Duke, as if in reply to the question, started toward the gate he had entered, casting backward glances over his shoulder as he went.

" Le's foller him an' see what he wants," Joe whispered.   " The poor brute's 'bout as near crazy as we are."

On reaching the gate, the dog scratched upon it, telling as well as he could that he desired them to follow him without the walls.

" Poor critter !" Farley said feelingly.   " You

want us to go with you an' hunt y'r master, don't you, purp?"

Duke bayed loudly, and scratched the earth in a frenzy of delight at being understood.

"Ugh! Duke him want find master," Bright Wing observed sagely.

Again the dumb brute manifested his joy.

"'Tain't no use, purp!" Joe sobbed softly, stooping and patting the dog's head. "If y'r master's over in them woods, he's dead — 'r a pris'ner, which is a dang sight worse. If he's dead, we can't do him no good; an' if he's a pris'ner, we hain't no chance o' rescuin' him this time. The redskins is buzzin' 'round over there thicker'n flies 'round a dead carcass. 'Tain't no use, purp! We'll keep you — me an' the Injin will — an' treat you well, fer y'r own sake an' y'r master's. But he's gone — an' we can't bring him back. Dodrot war, anyhow! It's an awful — awful thing!"

The homely face underwent a spasm, and the pale eyes were wet.

Regaining control of himself, he continued musingly:

"Yit I may be wrong; I was wrong once before, when I saw him dyin' with my own eyes. He was jest wounded that time — an' that may be the trouble now. He may be layin' over there in the woods, lollin' his parched tongue an' moanin' fer a drink o' water. Dogs knows a heap; an' this purp is tryin' hard to tell us somethin'. Dang-it-all-to-dingnation! Why *can't* a dog talk?"

Then to the Wyandot:

"Injin, I say we'd better take the dog an' go over there an' look fer Ross Douglas."

"Ugh!" assented Bright Wing, explosively.

At the same time he shouldered his gun, thus intimating that he was ready to start.

"Well," Farley continued, "we'll have to git a permit from somebody, I s'pose; that's 'cordin' to army rules. If we don't, they may take a notion to shoot us fer deserters, 'r fer disobeyin' orders 'r somethin'. I don't know much 'bout such things — an' I don't want to. Howsomever, we'll jest go to Ol' Tippecanoe, like we done before, an' git his p'rmission. Come on, le's not waste a minute. It's noon now."

A few quick steps brought them to the entrance of the commander's tent. The place was swarming with officers. Around the door was a noisy throng of excited subalterns and privates. Joe and Bright Wing elbowed their way through the mass and gained the doorway, Duke closely following them.

Just within, were two orderlies on guard. Without so much as a nod, Farley crowded between them.

"Stop! You can't come in here," one of the orderlies cried sternly, seizing the woodman by the arm.

"But I *am* in," Farley replied, a broad grin puckering his cheeks.

"Go out instantly!" blustered the orderly, as he whirled the intruder around and shoved him toward the door.

Farley's ire rose rapidly — reached fever heat in an instant.

"Take y'r hands off o' me, an' git out o' my road, 'r I'll break ev'ry bone in y'r slim, little body ! " he growled savagely.

The other orderly came to his comrade's assistance. The two threw themselves upon the angular giant and sought to eject him from the place. Bright Wing's hand flew to the heavy hatchet in his belt — a weapon he had picked up since his arrival at the fort. Duke crouched for a spring and growled sullenly. But Farley needed no help. His heavy fist shot out ; and one of the soldiers dropped to the ground. Quickly turning upon the other and catching him by the collar, Joe threw him half-way across the tent. Then the enraged woodman bellowed hoarsely :

"Take that, you cowardly, little whippersnappers ! Jump onto a feller, two at a time, will you? I'll learn you better manners — I will, by the Queen o' Sheby ! Come on ag'in, if you want to — I can trounce a *dozen* like you! I come in here to see Ol' Tippecanoe ; an' I'm a-goin' to see him, 'r die a-tryin'. If you two whinin' babies gits in my road ag'in, I'll pin back y'r ears an' swaller you — I will, by Mary Magdalene ! "

"What's the matter there?" rang out in clear, even tones.

And General Harrison, rising to his feet, looked toward the scene of disturbance.

"These men have forced their way in here, and

we are trying to put them out," explained one of
the orderlies, who stood brushing his soiled uniform and feelingly rubbing his bruised face.

"Who are they?" the commander impatiently
inquired.

"I don't know, General——"

Farley strode forward and interrupted:

"Gener'l Harrison, you ort to know us, whether
you do 'r not. Me an' the Injin was with you at
Tippecanoe— the dog was, too, fer that matter."

"Ah! You were with me at Tippecanoe?"

"Yes, Gener'l, we was there— an' right in the
hottest o' the scrimmage."

"Your names?"

"Joseph Peregoy Farley an' Bright Wing, the
Wyandot. I whacked bulls fer you, clean from
Fort Harrison to the Prophet's Town; an' the Injin
an' the houn' scouted with Ross Douglas. Ding-it-
all-to—— "

Joe's voice was drowned by an explosive roar of
laughter from the assembled officers. Even the
dignified commander smiled; and the two orderlies
grinned in a sickly manner. When quiet was restored, Harrison said quickly:

"Your names sound familiar. Who was it with
whom your red comrade scouted?"

"Ross Douglas."

"Ah!"— With animation.— "I remember you
well now. You are the two men who went to his
rescue, after he was captured by the Prophet's
band."

"We are, Gener'l; an' we've come to ask y'r p'r-mission to go to his help ag'in."

"Explain."

Farley did so — in his loquacious, rambling way. Deep silence reigned in the tent, as the simple-minded fellow told his moving tale and begged to be allowed to go to the aid of his friend. When he had finished, tears were in many eyes.

"To whose command do you belong?" Harrison inquired in tremulous tones.

"We don't belong to nobody's command," was the prompt reply. "We jest got away from the dang Winnebagoes — after bein' pris'ners a year an' a half — an' come here. We hain't 'nlisted yit. All the duty we've done was to go with Cap'n Oliver, to meet Gener'l Clay."

"You were Captain Oliver's guides?"

"We were, Gener'l."

"You're brave and true men," the commander said kindly. "You've not hesitated to risk your liberty and your lives in the service of your coun-try — not once, but many times. I appreciate your patriotism and your devotion to your friend. I'm very sorry to know he was in that — that dreadful fight across the river. But I can't grant you per-mission to throw away your lives to no purpose. If your friend be dead, you can be of no service to him; if he be wounded or a prisoner, he has been removed to the British encampment, ere this. You can't aid him. If he be alive, he will be exchanged in due time. Now I must bid you good-morning

— I'm very busy. But, believe me, I sympathize with you more than you know. I remember your friend, and grieve to know that such misfortune has befallen him. Good morning."

Farley and Bright Wing shook hands with the commander and quietly withdrew, followed by the pitying glances of the officers.

On reaching the open air, Joe heaved a deep sigh and remarked :

"Well, that settles it, Injin ; we can't go. An' I wouldn't wonder Ol' Tippecanoe's right, after all. We'd only lose our scalps by goin'— an' do no good. The Gener'l used us mighty kind, anyhow."

"Ugh !" rumbled up from the Wyandot's deep chest. "Tippecanoe him all much good heart — no bad."

"Well," Farley sighed in return, "as I said before, all we can do is to wait an' watch, an' hope an' pray. Le's go an' hunt somethin' to eat. I'm pow'rful hungry ; an' the purp must be 'bout starved. This life's a kind o' tangled snarl anyhow — it is, 'r my name ain't Joe Farley !"

On all sides the battle was ended. The heavy guns had ceased to belch flame ; the querulous voices of the rifles were silent. The powder smoke had lifted and disappeared ; the groans of the wounded and dying no longer fell upon the ear. The sun shone brightly ; and the birds in the adjacent forest sang gleefully.

Shortly after noon, a small boat was seen crossing the river. In the stern sat a British officer bearing

a flag of truce.   One of General Harrison's aides met
him at the landing, and inquired :

"Who are you, and why do you come?"

"I'm Major Chambers of his Majesty's service,"
was the reply ; "and I'm sent by General Proctor,
to demand the surrender of this fort."

"You'll have your labor for your pains," answered the aide.   "However, I'll blindfold you
and conduct you to General Harrison."

Ushered into the American commander's presence,
Major Chambers said :

"General Proctor has directed me to demand the
surrender of this post.   He wishes to spare the ef-
fusion of blood."

General Harrison smiled blandly, as he replied :

"The demand under present circumstances is
most extraordinary.   As General Proctor didn't
send me a summons to surrender, on his first arrival, I had supposed that he believed me determined
to do my duty.   His present message indicates an
opinion of me that I'm at a loss to account for."

Major Chambers' face flushed as he hastened to
say :

"General Proctor could never think of saying
anything to wound your feelings, sir.   The character of General Harrison, as an officer, is well
known.   General Proctor's force is very respect-
able, and there is with him a larger body of Indians
than has ever before been embodied."

General Harrison drew himself stiffly erect.   His
keen eyes flashed as he answered :

"I believe I have a very correct idea of General Proctor's force; and it is not such as to create the least apprehension for the result of the contest, whatever shape he may be pleased hereafter to give to it. Assure the General, however, that he will never have this post surrendered to him, upon *any* terms. Should it fall into his hands, it will be in a manner calculated to do him more honor, and give him larger claims upon the gratitude of his government, than any capitulation could possibly do."

Major Chambers did not push the matter further, but, after an arrangement for an exchange of prisoners had been made, bowed and withdrew.

The afternoon passed quietly; hostilities were not renewed. No further communication was held between the opposing forces; and at nightfall Bright Wing and Farley had heard nothing of their absent friend.

CHAPTER XVII.

WHEN Colonel Dudley disembarked his men upon the northern bank of the Maumee, Ross Douglas was among them. It was he who led the way toward the British batteries — his faithful four-footed friend at his side.

When the charge was ordered, he was among the officers who headed the attacking columns, and his gun was among the first discharged. With a cheer, he clubbed his empty rifle and helped to put the English gunners to rout. It was an easy victory ; the startled and terrorized artillerymen did not wait to fire a gun, but precipitately retreated toward their encampment down the river.

As soon as he saw the British in full flight and the Americans possessed of the batteries, Ross called Duke to him and seated himself upon a gun-carriage. He felt that the fight was over ; and he was ready — as soon as the cannon should be spiked — to return to the boats and cross over to the fort.

At that moment, victory was with Colonel Dudley and his men. But — as has been explained — the savages concealed in the woods commenced to pour a withering fusillade into the ranks of the militia occupying the open ground surrounding the batter-

22

ies. Dudley should have effected the purpose for which he had come and immediately re-embarked ; but he hesitated — and was lost. The impulsive Kentuckians grew restless under the hot fire, and, without waiting for orders, began an impetuous and disorderly advance upon their hidden foes. Their officers sought to restrain them, but in vain. They had tasted victory, and were intoxicated. With cheers of exultation and yells of defiance, they broke the leash of discipline and madly charged the enemy.

Knowing well what the inevitable outcome of the rash attack would be, Douglas leaped to his feet, hastened to Colonel Dudley's side, and shouted vehemently :

"For heaven's sake, call a retreat, Colonel ! Your men will fall into an ambush and be cut to pieces. It's an old trick — as old as Indian warfare. Act — act at once ! "

Ross's face was flushed ; his eyes were shining. The commanding officer smiled pityingly, as he said :

"You're exciting yourself over nothing, young man. It is a mere skirmish with the savages ; there will be no general engagement. As soon as my men have driven the enemy into the depths of the forest, they will return of their own accord."

Douglas turned pale with suppressed fury.

"I tell you it's an ambush, Colonel Dudley!" he exclaimed. "Recall your men, if you would not see them annihilated! "

Dudley returned coldly :

"My youthful guide, I don't need your advice. *I* am in command —— ''

He broke off suddenly and, fixing his eyes upon the edge of the forest where the militiamen were fast disappearing, he muttered :

"They are making a concerted charge. I fear myself they may venture too far and be drawn into a trap. I'll order a retreat immediately.''

He hurried away to put his tardy resolve into execution. But it was too late ; the mischief was done. Elated with the success of their first encounter, the Kentuckians refused to obey the command to retire to the boats. Colonel Dudley stormed and fumed ; inferior officers threatened and swore. It availed nothing. The regiment had lost all discipline — had become an enraged mob. Like a mad steed, it took the bit and dashed forward to destruction.

Douglas hurried from one place to another, warning the men of the ambuscade into which they were pushing, and beseeching them to return to the boats while there was yet time. His words fell upon deaf ears. Seeing at last that his countrymen had lost all reason — were drunk on the wine of success — he forced his way to the front, and fought like a demon. Duke kept at his master's side. Man and dog were in the thick of the fray. The hound's hoarse growl of rage sent terror to the heart of more than one dusky brave, and his gleaming fangs cut short more than one exultant war-whoop. Ross loaded and fired his gun with a speed and accuracy

born of years of practice. The smoke of battle
was in his nostrils ; the lust of slaughter was in
his brain. The savages slowly retreated until they
reached a place suited to their tactics. There they
promptly rallied and sought to outflank the Americans. The battle raged furiously on all sides.
British re-enforcements arrived upon the scene. Retreat became an impossibility.

Douglas became separated from his comrades —
but he fought on. His ammunition exhausted, he
clubbed his rifle and dealt blow after blow at the
heads of his red assailants. He felt his strength
gradually failing, but he set his teeth and grimly
resolved to die fighting. His faithful dog was no
longer at his side ; he was alone with his enemies.
And death was leering at him — face to face.

"Fleet Foot ! Fleet Foot ! Kill him ! Kill
him !"

The words reached the young man's ears. Instantly he understood why he had been singled
out from his companions, why so many red
fiends beset him. Among his foes, were the warriors who had tried to take his life at the Miami
village upon the Mississinewa. The knowledge
maddened him — renewed his energies. He resolved they should not have the pleasure of taking
him captive — of torturing him. Dropping his gun,
he drew his knife, meaning to resist as long as
breath and blood were his. But at that moment
the tide of battle surged toward him — around him ;
and his assailants were swept aside.

He drew a deep breath and looked around. The American columns were broken — scattered. The attacking army had become a fleeing rabble, in which each man was seeking his own safety. Realizing that the battle was lost, that there was no hope of rallying the flying militiamen, Ross groaned aloud :

"My God ! What a defeat — what a disgrace ! "

Then he picked up his rifle and set out after the fugitives. Scarcely had he taken ten steps, however, when clamorous yells assailed his ears and he saw that his escape toward the river was cut off by his old enemies. Quickly he whirled about and ran at full speed in the opposite direction, not heeding nor caring whither his course would take him. For a time he heard the heavy breathing and panted ejaculations of his pursuers. But gradually those sounds died out. Then all was silence — he was alone in the deep woods.

He dropped upon the ground and gasped for breath. His brain swam ; his throat was on fire. Red and green lights flashed before his eyes; and rills of sweat trickled down his powder-stained face. He had received a knife thrust in the right arm and a tomahawk cut in the left shoulder. These superficial wounds had bled freely and saturated his hunting-shirt. He was completely exhausted.

For several minutes, he lay breathing hard and listening for the footfalls of his pursuers. But the stillness was broken only by his own labored respiration and the querulous twitter of birds among the

boughs above him. He began to recover his wind.
His limbs ceased to tremble ; he felt his strength
returning. But his thirst was tormenting ; he
must have water. With some difficulty he got
upon his feet and looked about him. The dense,
leafless wood stretched away on all sides as far as
he could see. Near him was a pool of dark-colored
water — stained with the ooze of the forest. It
was warm and mawkish ; but he drank of it with
avidity.

"There !" he panted, "I feel much better. Now
I must find a hiding-place ; the woods is swarming with my foes. When night comes I'll make
my way to the shore, swim the river, and attempt
to gain the fort. What an awful day's work this
has been — hundreds dead, hundreds captured !"

Then, after a pause :

"But I must get my bearings. Let me see.
Where's the sun? I'm far back of the battle-
ground, and farther down the river. Fort Miami
lies between me and Fort Meigs. I'll bear to
the right of it, and strike the stream at a point between the scene of to-day's battle and the British
encampment. But I must hide until nightfall — it
wouldn't be safe to make the attempt sooner.
Well, I'm more fortunate than most of my rash
comrades ; I'm yet alive and free. My wounds
pain me some, but they're not of a serious character. If I had something to eat, I should be all
right. I wonder what has become of Duke.
Faithful old fellow ! No doubt he has been killed ;

else he would be at my side. No,——''—Reflectively,—'' he may have escaped and made his way to
Fort Meigs, with the few survivors. With the smell
of blood in his nostrils, he wouldn't be able to follow my trail. Well, I'll hide myself and rest until
dark. Then for Fort Meigs and safety!''

Concealing his trail as well as he could, he
pushed farther into the woods, leaving the river behind him. At last he lay down by a log and, hugging his empty rifle to his breast, fell asleep.
When he awoke, the sun was setting and the forest
was aflame with rosy light. Arising, he stretched
his stiffened limbs and carefully examined his
wounds.

'' Mere scratches,'' he muttered. '' But I'm
weak from fasting and loss of blood. Then, too,
I have no arms but an empty gun and a knife. I
shouldn't like to encounter a score of savages just
now.''—And he smiled grimly.—'' But it'll soon
be dark. I'll move toward the river.''

Shouldering his rifle, he set out, walking briskly
in spite of pain and weakness. The sun went
down ; the rosy light began to pale and fade. At
last he stopped suddenly.

'' I'm nearing the river. Perhaps I'd better
wait until it's darker. But then I'm afraid I
should run into danger without seeing it. What's
best ? Ah !''

He uttered the exclamation with vexation and
disappointment, and sprang behind a tree. In the
dusky twilight he perceived a cloaked figure mov-

ing toward him. Loosening the knife in his belt, he softly placed his gun against the tree trunk and peeped from his place of concealment. The obscure figure was coming on, slowly, hesitatingly. Its cautious footfalls fell upon his ear. He drew his knife and panted with suppressed excitement. Nearer and nearer to his hiding-place, the figure drew, its head bent low over a bundle it carried in its arms.

Douglas breathed hard and, gripping his knife firmly, held it ready for instant use. Then he made the discovery that the approaching personage was a woman — an Indian squaw, probably. For a moment he debated what he should do. Could he kill a defenseless female, even to assure his own safety? His soul sickened at the thought. Quickly he determined on a more humane course of action. He would confront the squaw. Should she seek to give an alarm, he would seize and overpower her. Then he would choke her into silence and carry her from the spot.

Acting upon this resolve, he boldly stepped from his place of concealment and coughed to attract the woman's attention. Flinging up her head, she uttered a half-suppressed scream and turned to flee. Ross sprang forward and threw his arms around her. She struggled to escape, but did not cry out.

The cloak fell from her shoulders. In the dim twilight he saw that she was a white woman, and that she held a small child in her arms. Instantly releasing her, he stammered:

"My good woman, I beg a thousand pardons. In the gloom I mistook you for a squaw, and, fearing that you might raise an alarm——"

He broke off and recoiled a step, a sharp exclamation upon his lips. The woman had lifted a wan face to his; and by the tremulous light of the dying twilight, he had recognized her.

"Amy!" he gasped.

"Ross!" she whispered hoarsely, leaning against a tree for support and closely hugging the child to her breast.

A short time they stood there without uttering another word, each staring wildly at the other's shadowy form and features—each hearing the other's labored breathing. Ross was the first to regain the power of speech.

"What are you doing here?" he asked in a strange, altered voice.

"Trying to escape from a bondage worse than death!" she replied in hard, bitter tones in which there was no hint of tears.

"You—you've been a prisoner among the Indians?" he inquired in kinder accents.

"Yes; but that isn't what I mean," she answered in a hopeless voice.

Again both were silent. The baby in her arms commenced to fret. She soothed and patted it to sleep—softly, sadly crooning to it. By this time, the lingering twilight had faded out; it was quite dark in the forest. Advancing to her side, Douglas laid his hand upon her arm and began:

"Amy Larkin——"

"Amy Hilliard!" she interrupted shrilly.

He drew back as though a venomous insect had stung him. Her voice grated harshly upon his nerves. To his overwrought imagination, she seemed a lost soul mocking at its own misery. Taking her by the arm, he remarked quietly:

"You're tired. There's no use in your standing. Seat yourself upon this log."

Silently she obeyed, trembling in every limb. Picking up her cloak, he placed it around her shoulders. His act of kindness softened her feelings; and her voice was tremulous as she said simply:

"Thank you!"

He stood looking down upon her, conflicting thoughts and emotions rioting in his brain. At last he murmured huskily:

"And you are Amy Larkin no longer — you are Amy Hilliard."

"Yes, I'm Amy Hilliard." — Her voice again hard and bitter. — "I must bear the hated name to my grave."

"You are George Hilliard's wife."

"I am."

Her words were scarcely audible.

"And the child?"

"Is mine."

"And his?"

"Yes. I — am — his — wife; this — is — our — child!"

Each word fell separately, like a ringing brazen coin. Then she screamed excitedly:

"But my innocent child shall never blush for its father—it shall never know him! I hate him—I loathe him! The brute—the coward—the murderer! Oh! that I had never seen him——"

"Sh!" he cautioned. "You're talking too loud. Remember we are surrounded by sharp-eared, lynx-eyed enemies. Where were you going—what were you trying to do, when I met you?"

"Trying to escape," she panted in a strident whisper.

"Softly!" he again cautioned. "From whom were you trying to escape?"

"From my captors, the Indians at Fort Miami—and from George Hilliard."

"I can't understand," he replied wonderingly. "Is your—your husband among the British, at their encampment just below here?"

"Yes."

"Then you and the child must return to him," Ross answered firmly, decidedly.

"Never!" she hissed through her set teeth. "We'll find a grave in the river first. I hate him, I tell you—I despise and loathe him!"— Then pleadingly: "Oh, Ross Douglas! If one spark of the old love for me yet burns in your bosom, save me—save me!"

"But what can I do?" he asked in perplexity. "You are *his* wife—the child is his——"

"Save me!" she interrupted. "I'm trying to reach the fort across the river. You belong there —I know you do. Take me and my baby with you—*please* do!"

"But I cannot, Amy," he replied chokingly. "You are another man's wife; I must not steal you away from him. Then, the fort is closely invested; I don't know that I shall be able to reach it myself—alone and unhampered. My gun is empty—I am practically unarmed. I'm weak from loss of blood, fasting, and excessive exertion. No, I can't take you with me; the risk is too great. You must return to Fort Miami——"

"That I will never do!" she answered determinedly. "If you leave me here, I'll drown myself and my babe in the river. Better a thousand miserable deaths than again to fall into that man's power!"

Douglas strode up and down in front of her.

"What am I to do?" he asked himself. "How perverse is fate! I have found her at last—but lost her forever. Poor girl! She is innocent; she was forced into the hateful marriage, no doubt. But I cannot love another's wife. If I abandon her, she will destroy herself and her child. She means what she says. If I take them with me, I shall risk their lives and my own. And Fort Meigs is no place for her. It may fall into the hands of the British. In that case, the savages will massacre every person within the walls. I must do one of two things—take her with me or——"

Stopping suddenly, he faced his companion and said in earnest tones:

"I've decided to take you and your child with me — to attempt to conduct you to Fort Meigs, in safety. I must leave you for a short time, however, to try to find some way of crossing the river. Remain here quietly until I return for you. I'll be gone but a few minutes."

"Ross," she faltered, "you — you will not desert me ——"

"Amy," he cried in a sharp whisper, "did I ever desert you — ever deceive you?"

Bursting into tears, she buried her face in the folds of the shawl that enveloped her child, and moaned brokenly:

"No — no! You were always true — always ——"

He left her softly sobbing, and made his way toward the river. Every few yards he stopped, peered into the surrounding darkness, and listened intently. But he saw or heard nothing of an alarming nature. Presently he emerged from the gloomy woods and stood upon the sloping bank of the stream. Above him, the black vault was studded with stars; beneath him, the dark water was softly lapping upon the sandy beach. Down the stream, he discovered the flaring fires of the British encampment; and up the river — and on the opposite side — the twinkling lights of Fort Meigs. The confused, indistinct murmur of voices in the distance was borne upon the evening breeze.

Then a dog's deep, mournful bay fell upon the listener's ear.

"Duke!" he muttered. "He has escaped the general carnage — he's at the fort. Farley and Bright Wing will care for him, if I lose my life."

Cautiously he began a search along the shore, for some means of crossing the stream. The soft dip of a paddle came to his ear. Silently retreating to some overhanging bushes, he waited, watched, and listened. The sound of the paddle became more and more distinct. Out of the shadows, emerged a small craft containing a single occupant. It rapidly approached the place where Douglas stood. The young man drew his knife and, gently parting the bushes, peered forth. The canoeman was a stalwart Indian. The next moment, the light vessel grated upon the sands and the unwary paddler sprang ashore. Hardly had his feet touched the earth, ere he sank in his tracks, a corpse, with Douglas's keen knife buried in his heart.

"It's little short of murder," muttered the young scout; "but there was no alternative. One of us had to die."

Quickly stooping, he rolled the body of his fallen foe into the river. Drawing the canoe ashore and secreting it among the bushes, he rapidly retraced his steps to Amy Hilliard and her child. He found her still seated upon the log, her face buried in the folds of the baby's shawl. Touching her upon the shoulder, he said simply:

"I've found a boat. Come."

Without a word, she arose. Picking up his empty gun, he led the way toward the river. She kept close at his heels, panting with fear and excitement. Like two silent specters, they threaded the intricate maze of the forest. On reaching the edge of the wood, he remarked in a cautious whisper :

"Now comes the most dangerous part of our journey. Whatever happens, you must preserve perfect silence. Step carefully — a breaking twig may bring a dozen warriors upon us. Keep close to me — and be ready to obey my orders. If you see me drop to the ground, do likewise."

She touched his arm, in token that she understood and would obey, but said nothing. Down the bank, and through the tangled bushes along the shore, they slowly made their way. Skillfully dragging the canoe from its hiding-place and launching it, he breathed in her ear :

"Let me hold the child while you get in."

"But it may cry," she whispered in reply.

"True," he answered. "Here — let me assist you. Seat yourself in the bottom. That's right." — Then placing his rifle in the bow of the craft.— "Now lay the baby in your lap, and take this paddle."

"What do you mean?" she asked, alarm in her whispered tone.

"The vessel is too light to carry all of us," he answered quietly, but firmly. "You must paddle to the opposite shore. I'll turn you around and

start you.   Don't lose your head — and you'll
land safely."

"But you?" she inquired, almost inaudibly.

"I'll swim after you.   Off you go."

Watching her until she disappeared in the darkness, he stealthily dropped into the water and
struck out in the wake of the frail boat.   A few
minutes later he stood upon the other shore.   His
garments were dripping and his teeth were chatter-
ing from the chill of the water.   He looked about
him but saw nothing of the canoe or its occupants.

"Amy," he called softly.

But he received no reply.

"Amy," he repeated, a little louder than before.
Still no answer.

"What can have become of her?" he muttered in
deep vexation and alarm.   "She should have landed
near this point.   Is it possible that the canoe has
capsized, or that other harm has befallen her? Ah!
she may have lost her paddle — she may be drifting
with the current."

He ran down the stream, peering into the gloom
that overhung the water as he went.   But he saw
nothing of her or of the boat.   Many times he
called her name, as loudly as he dared.   No answer-
ing voice came to him.   At last he turned and
swiftly retraced his steps.   He had just reached
the point where he had come ashore, when he discovered a dark object drifting a few yards from the
beach.   It was an empty canoe.   In it was his own
gun, but no sign of the woman or child.

"Lost — lost!" he groaned, wringing his hands. "Poor Amy!"— And the tears trickled down his cheeks.— "She's drowned — she and her baby are sleeping at the bottom of the treacherous river.— No! There is no water in the canoe, and my gun is where I placed it. The frail craft did *not* capsize. Some harm must have befallen her, just as she reached land — ere she could secure the vessel."

Snatching up his gun, he set off at full speed. He had gone but a short distance, when he stopped and sharply caught his breath. A cloaked figure was hurrying toward him. It was the woman he sought.

"Amy, it's you — thank God!" he ejaculated fervently, as she reached his side. "I've been searching for you. I discovered the drifting canoe and, for a moment, thought you were drowned. Where have you been?"

She was greatly excited. Abject terror was in her voice, as she whispered in reply:

"I have been hiding. I heard you calling me, but didn't dare to answer. Just as I stepped from the canoe, a number of Indians and a white man came down the bank toward me. I quickly cast the boat adrift and hid myself among some brush. There I lay quaking with fear, for — oh, God! the white man was George Hilliard. They stood near me and talked of my escape. They were searching for me. I could hear his hateful voice — could hear every word he said. I almost smothered my baby; I was so afraid it would cry and betray my presence. At last they left and went farther up the stream.

23

Then I heard you calling me, but was afraid to answer. Oh, Ross — Ross! *Do* save me from that man! If you find you cannot, kill me and my baby — in God's name, *do!* "

"There — there!" he said soothingly. "I'll save you — I'll get you to the fort. Let me support you. You can hardly stand. Come."

They scrambled up the bank and made a narrow detour to the left, to avoid the party she had seen. A half hour later, Douglas had skillfully piloted his companion through the savages encircling the fort, and was thundering at one of the gates for admission.

CHAPTER XVIII.

ON GAINING entrance to the fort, Ross placed Amy and her child in care of some refugees, who occupied a large tent at the eastern end of the inclosure, immediately behind the grand traverse, and went to hunt his comrades. He found them at a camp-fire, around which a number of lolling soldiers were talking and smoking.

Duke was the first to note the presence of his master; and, with a yelp of joy, sprang to meet him. Bright Wing uttered a guttural exclamation, which was smothered by Farley's lusty shout:

"Ross Douglas—'r my name ain't Joe Farley! Alive an' a-livin'—but wetter'n a drownded mus'-rat an' lookin' paler 'n a piller-case! Youngster, you've been in the dangedest scrimmage that ever was—anybody can see that. How in the name o' all the purty women in the universe, did you ever git out o' that yaller-jackets' nest, an' make y'r way here? Set down an' tell us all 'bout it."

Douglas dropped upon the ground and, affectionately patting Duke's head, replied wearily:

"I'm thoroughly exhausted, Joe. Get me something to eat."

"That's it!" cried one of the soldiers. "Git y'r comrade somethin' to eat, Limber Tongue. He's 'bout played out."

"Dang-it-all-to-dingnation !" grumbled Joe. "I never did have no sense! The idee o' askin' a man, who hain't had a bite to eat sence last night at this time, to set down an' spin yarns. I've a notion to pull my larripin' tongue out by the roots—I have, by Molly! An' you've got some scratches, too, Ross Douglas ; an' wher' you ain't pale, you're blacker'n a nigger with powder smoke, an' redder'n an Injin with blood. Set there an' rest an' dry y'r duds. I'll have you somethin', in a jiffy, that'll make you feel better—I will, by ginger !"

Still muttering to himself, of his own shortcomings, Farley left the group around the fire. When he returned a few minutes later, he cried exultingly:

"A long an' limber tongue may be a nuisance most o' the time, but once in a while it comes mighty handy. Jest now mine helped me to p'r-suade Ol' Tippecanoe to divide his supper with you, Ross Douglas——"

"What !" Douglas interrupted sternly. "Surely, Joe, you didn't go to the commander and ask him for food for me."

"Surely I did," Farley replied coolly.

The soldiers burst into roars of laughter. Ross's face flushed angrily. But Farley continued naïvely:

"You see, it was jest like this. You had to have somethin' to eat—an' you needed it quick. Well, our suppers was over—no chance fer you there. I could 'ave gone to the commissary an' got some *raw* grub, but it would 'ave took time to cook it. In the meantime you was starvin'. So thinks I, 'I'll

jest go to Ol' Tippecanoe — I'm purty well acquainted with him by this time, an' he's probably
at supper — an' ask him to divide his supper with
Ross Douglas.' So that's what I done. An' here's
y'r grub — steamin' hot an' calkerlated to make
you feel like a fightin' cock."

And with the words, Farley triumphantly spread
the food upon the ground before his exhausted
friend.

"There's hot coffee," he said, " an' hot pone, an'
hot meat. They'll warm up y'r in'ards an' limber
up y'r tongue. Fall to now — 'fore the things gits
cold."

Douglas required no urging. He was trembling
with hunger and fatigue; he felt as though he
should faint, if he fasted much longer. With
evident satisfaction, Farley and Bright Wing
silently watched him as he ate. Duke rested his
nose upon his master's knee and, heaving a sigh of
content, drowsily closed his great eyes. The soldiers knocked the ashes from their pipes and, one
by one, curled up in their blankets and fell asleep.
When Ross had finished, he stretched his feet to the
fire and, turning to Farley, asked smilingly :

" What did General Harrison say when you made
a demand upon him, for a share of his supper for
me?"

"Said it 'forded him great pleasure to do so — a
pleasure 'xceeded only by the pleasure he felt in
knowin' you was still alive an' *able* to eat. Then
he told me to say to you to call at his quarters, in

the mornin'; that he wanted to meet you ag'in, an' that ther' was a subject demandin' your attention — 'r words to that effect."

A pleased expression rested upon Douglas's powder-stained face, as he said :

"And I shall be delighted to meet my old commander again. He's one of nature's gentlemen."

Then he dreamily stared into the red embers, and was silent.

"Look here !" Joe cried in a testy tone. "Don't be goin' back into the past an' dreamin' 'bout things that can never be, Ross Douglas. Me an' Bright Wing wants to hear 'bout how you sarcumvented the redskins an' got here to the fort. Don't we, Injin ?"

The Wyandot lifted his head from between his knees and answered :

"Ugh ! Want know 'bout fight — heap much, all, everything."

Douglas smiled wearily and began his narrative. As he proceeded with his graphic description of the battle and the incidents and adventures following it, his interested comrades drew closer to him and listened with eager attention, to every word that fell from his lips. The camp-fires died down ; the garrison was wrapped in silence and darkness. Nothing broke the stillness but Douglas's whispered tones, the heavy breathing of the sleeping soldiers, and the muffled footfalls of the sentries pacing their beats about the walls. At last Ross closed his recital, and yawningly remarked :

"I've told you all. Now let's lie down to
rest; my eyes are so heavy that I can hardly keep
them open."

"An' no wonder," Farley murmured. "Ross,
you've been through a heap to-day — a dang sight!
But jest let me ask you one question. Now you've
found ol' Sam Larkin's gal — an' she's a wife an' a
mother — what're you goin' to do?"

"Save her from the brute who has ruined her
life," Douglas replied fiercely.

"That's all right," Joe persisted. "But how're
you goin' to do it?"

"I don't know yet," Douglas answered. "I've
not learned what she desires."

"Well, you can't marry her, of course."

"What nonsense you're talking, Joe!" Ross
cried sharply. "She's the wife of another. Let's
drop the subject."

"Ugh! No Fleet Foot's squaw — fat paleface's
squaw," grunted Bright Wing sagely.

"An' Fleet Foot takes it mighty cool, too," Farley
muttered to himself. "'Pears to me he's thinkin' a
heap more 'bout the little red-headed gal he *hain't*
found, than he is 'bout this gal he *has* found. But
I don't blame him. Amy Larkin's played him false
— she wan't forced into no marriage. You can't
fool me on women folks. Hain't I had the 'xperience, I'd like to know? Oh, gosh, yes!"

The three rolled over upon the ground, and two of
them were soon snoring loudly. But Ross did not
fall asleep so readily. For an hour or more, he lay

with closed lids thinking—thinking. At last, however, outraged nature asserted itself.

Early the next morning, the young scout managed to procure enough water to remove the stains of battle from his person. After he had washed himself, dressed his slight wounds, and eaten his breakfast, he went to call upon General Harrison.

The commander's seamed visage was alight with genuine pleasure, as he took Ross by the hand and led him to a seat. Closely scanning his caller's face, the old warrior remarked:

"Douglas, I'm delighted to see you—to again grasp your hand. I didn't know you were with General Clay's command; that you were in yesterday's terrible battle"—the commander's careworn features twitched—"until your two old comrades came to me and asked permission to go to your aid."

"Did they do that?" Ross quickly inquired.

"Yes, indeed. Didn't they tell you?"

Douglas shook his head; tears were in his eyes.

"They're loyal fellows," Harrison continued feelingly; "they would give their lives for you, at any time."

"I know," Douglas answered chokingly. "I've four good friends, at least, General Harrison—yourself, my two old comrades, and my dog. I've had a varied experience in the last eighteen months. I've endured much——"

"And all for your country's sake," the general interrupted. "You have suffered mentally and physically."

Douglas remained silent and Harrison continued :

"And the worst is not come. But we'll go on to the glorious end."

"Yes," was the firm reply.

"Yes," the commander went on, "all of us have made sacrifices for home and country. But opposition will not appal us ; defeat will not discourage us. We are *Americans*. This exacting service, with its suspense — its disappointments, is calculated to discourage and unnerve. But, pshaw !" — with a light laugh — "of what am I talking? We're American patriots — we can stand *anything*."

Then with animation :

" But I didn't bring you here to talk of such things. During yesterday's sorties we took a number of prisoners — British regulars, Canadian militiamen, and Indians. At present they're confined in the blockhouses ; and among those in the blockhouse at the southeastern angle of the fortification, is an old acquaintance of yours."

" An acquaintance of mine?" Douglas remarked wonderingly.

" Yes — a man both of us have good reason to remember."

" Ah ! Who is it, General ? "

" Hiram Bradford."

Like one electrified, Douglas sprang erect — his lips apart, his cheeks flushed.

"Hiram Bradford !" he ejaculated.

General Harrison nodded.

"And you have seen him, General?"

"I have."

"Did he send for you?"

"No; I knew nothing of his capture, till I went among the prisoners, yesterday evening. I recognized him instantly, although he has changed much since the Tippecanoe campaign. Evidently he is not in good health. He's emaciated, and his hair is white as snow. But he's the same cool, self-reliant villian."

Harrison uttered this last sentence, in a tone of intense and bitter hatred. Ross Douglas winced. Instantly he realized what Bradford's fate was likely to be. But hiding his feelings as well as he could, the young man inquired :

"Did you talk with him, General Harrison?"

"A little. I called him by name. He didn't attempt to conceal his identity. He asked about you; and when I informed him you were with Colonel Dudley, in the battle across the river, and hadn't returned to the fort with the survivors, he groaned aloud. When he had recovered his equanimity, he exacted from me a promise that, should you return, I would send you to him. For some reason, Douglas, that scoundrel is interested in your welfare — for some reason he likes you very much. His actions toward you in the past, his agitation about your welfare yesterday, prove it."

For a moment Ross stood with downcast eyes and said nothing. Then suddenly looking up, he inquired with a show of emotion ;

"He didn't ask for mercy at your hands, General?"

The general slowly shook his head, all the while keenly eyeing his companion.

"Nor inquired as to his fate?"

"Not a word."

"But he asked that I be sent to him, upon my return?"

General Harrison again nodded, and remarked:

"Here's a pass that will admit you to his presence. When you have talked with him, return to me."

Douglas silently took the bit of paper extended to him, and turned to leave the tent. At the door he paused and, looking back, said:

"General Harrison."

"Well?"

"Will Hiram Bradford be exchanged?"

"He — will — not!"—slowly and distinctly.

"And his fate?"

"An ignominious death — probably! It all depends upon what a court-martial may do."

And General Harrison's thin lips were firmly drawn; his brows, lowering.

Douglas again bowed, and quickly withdrew. On reaching the open air, he took a deep breath and, lifting his eyes to the clouded heavens, moved his lips as though in prayer. Then, at a brisk pace, he set out toward the blockhouse where Bradford was confined. As he passed along, he observed a number of children playing in front of a large tent.

"I must call upon Amy, first," he thought; "she may be needing something."

Gently pushing aside the children who crowded the doorway, he entered the tent. Several families were quartered within. Bedding and cooking utensils were scattered about promiscuously. Near the entrance sat a plethoric matron industriously knitting. She looked up at Douglas's unannounced entrance and, chuckling asthmatically, remarked by way of greeting:

"Come in. But I don't see how you got through the swarm o' young'uns. As the Britishers has quit the'r shootin', we thought it 'ld be no harm to let the little things go out an' play. They was pinin' fer fresh air, you know. Say!—how long do you think it'll be 'fore we can go back to our cabins?"

"I have no idea," Ross replied, pausing momentarily.

"You hain't?"—in evident surprise.—"Hain't you got somethin' to do with managin' the war?"

Douglas shook his head.

"Well—well!" she continued. "I knowed you wasn't an officer, 'xactly, fer you don't wear no uniform; but I thought you surely was a soldier o' some kind—such a trim young feller as *you* be. Then you hain't got nothin' to do with runnin' the war?"

Ross smilingly disclaimed the honor.

"Oh!" the woman exclaimed suddenly, laughing until her fat sides shook and she threatened to

suffocate. " I know you *now*. You're the feller
that fetched the poor young woman here, last night.
You've got y'r face washed — an' I didn't know
you. They say you was in the fight 'cross the
river. Had a hard time of it, didn't you? The
young woman? She's over there on that pile o'
beddin'. She ain't feelin' re'l peart, this mornin'.''

Douglas hurriedly passed on to the spot indicated.
Amy lay upon an improvised bed near the center of
the tent. At his approach, she arose to a sitting
posture and smiled feebly. In the semi-twilight of
the interior, she looked wan and haggard. Her
clothing was threadbare and shabby ; her brown
hair, falling about her shoulders, was a tangled mass.
The corners of her mouth were sagged. Truly she
was a wreck. Little of her girlish beauty remained.
Douglas looked upon her, and shuddered at the awful change in her appearance.

Near the bedside sat a middle-aged woman, striving vainly to soothe Amy's fretful child. The
emaciated, peevish baby was a miniature of its
mother. Its cry was weak and querulous. Apparently it was about six months old ; but it had the
claw-like hands and mummified features of an old
woman. Yet Ross noted its resemblance to its
mother.

Taking the thin, calloused hand extended toward
him, he seated himself and asked kindly :

" How are you feeling this morning, Amy ? "

" Not very well. Baby's cross — and my head

aches." — Then, after a slight pause, she added gloomily :

"But I'm feeling as well as I ever expect to feel."

"Don't say that," he remonstrated. "You'll regain your health and strength — and again be happy."

Sadly shaking her head, she replied :

"I'll regain my health and strength, I hope. I must do so for baby's sake ; she needs my care and protection. But, for me, happiness is a thing of the past."

"Why do you say that ? " he asked.

She turned away her face and made no reply. The woman holding the babe arose and sauntered to another part of the tent.

"Why do you say that for you happiness is a thing of the past ? " Douglas pursued. "You are young, Amy — life is all before you ——"

"Listen!" she interrupted. "I say there is no further happiness for me, because my heart is broken — is dead within me."

For some seconds both were silent, neither looking at the other. At last he inquired :

"Where will you go when you leave here ? "

"I don't know — yet."

There was a world of meaning in the last word. And as she uttered it, she turned her hollow eyes full upon her questioner. Ross saw the soul-hunger reflected in her face — and he started. Their eyes met. She dropped her white lids, and the hot blood mantled her pale cheeks. An embarrassing silence fell upon them. He was the first to speak.

"Amy," he murmured softly, "I want to help you — I want to be kind to you ——"

Passionately she caught his hand in both of hers, and whispered — all her soul in her voice and manner :

"Ross — Ross ! Listen to me ! Say that you'll take me away from here — to a place where George Hilliard can never find us — where we can begin life over and ——"

The look in his eyes repelled her advances ; and breaking off in the middle of the sentence, she trembled and was silent.

Gently but firmly withdrawing his hand from her clinging clasp, he said — almost sternly :

"Amy, what you have in mind can never be. I loved Amy Larkin tenderly and truly. Amy Hilliard I have no *right* to love!"

For a moment she stared at him, as though she did not comprehend. Then, with a groan, she fell back upon the bed and, hiding her face, burst into tears.

Ross was greatly moved. He pitied her sincerely ; yet he felt that he had done right in telling her the truth. Now he bent over her and whispered soothingly :

"Do not weep. The past is forever past. For months, I was a wounded prisoner among the savages. As soon as I could, I made my escape and went back to Franklinton. But you were gone.

No one knew of your whereabouts — you had left no trail behind you. I went to your old home in Pennsylvania. I was disappointed. At last I have found you. But you are the wife of another. Of course you were forced into the hateful marriage ——"

She had been convulsively sobbing. Suddenly she snatched her hands from her face and, springing erect, cried excitedly :

" Ross Douglas, I've been deceiving you. I hoped that you still loved me — that I could win you back — that I still might be happy with you. That hope is dead. I'll deceive you with my silence, no longer. I'll tell you the truth — all — everything!"

For one fleeting second, she paused and hungrily searched his face, still hoping to detect there some faint glimmer of the passion he had borne her. His features were pale, but calm — impassive ; his manner was keenly expectant. Stifling a sob, she dashed the hot tears from her eyes and proceeded hurriedly :

" When you left me at Franklinton and went to join General Harrison's army, I was piqued. I argued with my better self that you didn't love me, as you had professed, or you wouldn't have left me. I felt angry — spiteful. I wanted to do something to make you suffer. My father and George Hilliard taunted me with your desertion. They said you had been too ready to leave me — that you didn't love me — that you wouldn't return. I listened to them — I half believed them. A month from the day of your departure, I had convinced myself of your perfidy and had consented to marry George Hilliard."

She paused momentarily, to moisten her dry lips. Ross Douglas's eyes were shining with a strange, indefinable light. But he said nothing. Hastily she resumed :

"Let me hurry over the events of my brief married life — I cannot bear to recall them. I promised to marry George Hilliard, on condition that my father should sell off everything and remove to a place where you would never find me. For, in spite of all my reasoning, I felt guilty. We disposed of our property and removed to Frenchtown, between here and Detroit. On our arrival there, George Hilliard and I were married. Before our marriage he had been very kind to me ; humored me — spoiled me. But scarcely was he my husband, ere his whole nature seemed to change. He began to drink heavily, to curse me, to abuse me. Then I realized the sad truth that I had married a drunken brute !"

For half a minute she could not proceed. When she had regained control of herself, she said huskily :

"He was jealous. He accused me of still loving you. And — God help me ! — I couldn't deny the accusation. He tormented me — he beat me. My father remonstrated ; and the two had many fierce quarrels. At last my child was born — six months ago. A few days after, my husband demanded that

24

my father give him money with which to buy land. My father refused — and again they quarreled. In a whirlwind of drunken rage, George Hilliard caught up an axe and struck my father a blow that laid him dead upon the floor. I — I saw it all, while lying helpless upon my bed ! ''

Once more she stopped in her recital. No sound broke the stillness of the place, but the fretful cry of her child in another part of the tent. Douglas's jaws were set ; his hands, clenched. With a fluttering sigh, Amy continued :

"After he had murdered my father, George Hilliard took all the money he could find and fled. For weeks I lay between life and death, hardly realizing where I was or what had happened. The good people of the settlement provided for my wants, and took care of me. Slowly I regained something of my wonted strength. But I had no means of support ; so, with a number of others who were returning to the East, I set out for western Pennsylvania, hoping to find a shelter among my father's people. But a short distance up the lake from here, our company was set upon by a band of Indians, and we were taken prisoners and brought to the British encampment. Among the savages who attacked our party was George Hilliard, disguised as an Indian. He recognized me — of course. He mocked at my misery, cuffed and kicked me, and threatened to kill my baby ——''

Here her voice almost failed her. But she went on resolutely :

"I believe he would have done so, had it not been for an angel at the encampment — I can't call her anything else — a beautiful girl who shielded me from his violence, and helped me to escape. Oh, how beautiful her face was — but how sad! She had red-gold hair, and eyes of heaven's own blue —— "

Ross Douglas had arisen to his feet. Eagerly he asked:

"And her name — her name?"

Amy Hilliard keenly eyed her questioner, before replying. Presently she said slowly:

"I heard my captors call her La Violette."

Douglas, in spite of a strong effort to control himself, uttered an exclamation of joyful surprise. His countenance was alight, his eyes were shining.

"You know her?" Amy said, with lifted brows.

"Yes — I know her," he replied cautiously. "Go on with your story."

But she did not. Instead she inquired:

"How long have you known her?"

"Ever since I was a captive among the Indians," he answered candidly. "She nursed me when I was wounded; she helped me to escape."

Her woman's intuition enabled her to arrive at the truth at a bound. Calmly she said:

"Ross, you love this beautiful girl — you love La Violette."

He made no reply in words. But the hot blood crimsoned his tanned cheeks and mounted to his white forehead. Then the tell-tale tide receded as quickly as it had arisen; and again he was outwardly calm.

At that moment, the woman who had been caring for the baby approached the mother and remarked:

"The little thing's gone to sleep, at last. I see you're feelin' better,"—in a slightly sarcastic tone—"so I'll let you take care of her now, while I look after my own affairs."

"I thank you for your kindness," Amy murmured confusedly.

"You're welcome," the woman replied, with a slight toss of the head, and turned and left.

"You love La Violette," the young woman repeated, again fixing her gaze upon Ross's face.

"Yes, I love her, Amy," he answered deliberately. "But I didn't fully realize the fact until this hour. She was very kind to me during my captivity. She loved me—and I knew it. But I thought of you; and blinded myself to her charms. I was true to you through it all—in deed and in thought. As soon as I escaped, I returned to your home, intending—desiring to make you my wife. You were gone. But still I thought you true. I had no idea that you would marry George Hilliard, of your own choice. I searched for you—longed for you. I loved you still—I believed in your love for me. Yesterday I found you. I said to myself: 'She has been forced into this marriage—she isn't to blame. But she is lost to me forever; I have no right to love her now.' Then La Violette's face arose before me. And I knew that I loved her — that my love for you was a thing of the past. Last night was the first time that I acknowledged to myself that I loved La Violette. But I argued with myself that you hadn't been at fault, and that it would be cruel — heartless for me to think of marrying La Violette, should I ever find her. In the silent watches of the night — alone with my God — I resolved to give up all quest for her, to remain faithful to my plighted troth. But this morning ——"

He broke off abruptly and looked her full in the eyes.

"Go on," she whispered, with pale lips.

"But this morning you have told me your story; and ——"

Again he stopped.

"Well?" she breathed faintly.

"*I — am — free!*"

Spasmodically hugging her baby to her breast, she sank back upon the bed and turned her face from him. He saw that she was pale and trembling; and he sincerely pitied her. Bending over her, he whispered gently:

"I'll be your friend, Amy, as in the past. I'll do all in my power to find you a home, to make your future life comfortable and happy."

She made no reply, by word or sign.

"I believe you said you had started to return to your relatives in Pennsylvania?" he remarked.

She slightly inclined her head.

"Very well. When we can leave here, I'll find you company and send you thither. Now I must be going. Don't think me cruel. I'm trying to be just and merciful."

A few moments later, he was without the tent. The heavens were thickly clouded; the rain was falling drearily. A short time he stood with bared head, unmindful of the buzz of human life around him. Then, sighing, he took his way toward the place where Hiram Bradford was confined.

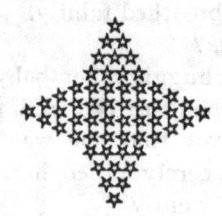

CHAPTER XIX.

DOUGLAS presented his pass to the guard at the corner blockhouse. The soldier glanced at it and silently stepped aside. Ross entered the large unfloored room and looked about him. The place was damp and gloomy ; the pent air was musty and offensive. A number of whites and Indians were sprawling upon the bare ground. In one of the farther corners was a solitary individual. Ross made his way toward him. By the murky light that struggled in at the loopholes and crevices, the young man recognized Hiram Bradford. At the same instant, the older man recognized the newcomer and, arising to his feet, held out his hand, saying :

"Ross Douglas, I'm glad to see you. I'm overjoyed to know you escaped death in yesterday's battle."

"I'm glad to meet you, Bradford," Ross replied ; "but I'm sorry to meet you here."

"I understand," Bradford returned coolly. "Sit down. I've something of importance to tell you."

They seated themselves upon a puncheon bench that stood against the log wall. Douglas noted the marked change in his companion's appearance. The older man's hair was white as snow ; his face, lean and cadaverous ; his figure, emaciated and bent.

(375)

Noticing Ross's commiserating look, Bradford remarked :

"Yes, I'm changed, Douglas — greatly changed. An incurable malady is rapidly sapping my vitality. I've but a short time to live — even if I escape death at the hands of your commander, which I don't expect. You saw General Harrison before you came here?"

"I did."

"Did he say what disposition would be made of me?"

"He — he said you wouldn't be exchanged," Ross stammered.

"It's unnecessary to say more," Bradford returned calmly. "He intends to court-maitial me — to have me shot as a spy and deserter. Well, according to the usages of war, I deserve the fate. It's best that I should die so. It's a fitting climax to a misspent life. I have but a short time to live at best — a few days can make no difference. And a sudden, painless death is to be preferred to one of lingering torture from a slow disease."

Then, seeing the pained look upon Douglas's face :

"Tut-tut, my boy ! Don't grieve over my fate. I tell you it is best that I should die so. But I don't care to talk of it ; it's just a little *unwelcome* to contemplate."

Here he paused and smiled feebly. A lump rose in Ross's throat ; he could say nothing in reply. Bradford asked quickly :

"Where have you been since you escaped from the village upon the Mississinewa?"

Douglas found his voice, and told his companion of his wanderings and adventures. When the younger man had finally finished, the older remarked:

"It was well that La Violette helped you to escape; otherwise, the treacherous Indians would have killed you. When I returned to the village and found you gone, I was furious; but La Violette explained the situation to me — and I was satisfied. Immediately, I took the dear girl with me and went to Canada. Then I instituted search for you. I sent a messenger to your old home at Franklinton——"

"Why were you so anxious to find me, Bradford?" Ross could not refrain from asking.

"Don't interrupt me," the other cried irritably. "I have much to tell you. I mean to explain all, but I must do it in my own way. As I said, I hunted for you far and near; but I couldn't locate you. My health was failing. I realized that I was affected with a fatal malady, and I worried night and day — I feared I was to die without again seeing you. Finally my business led me to this vicinity. I came not as a spy" — the color mantled his pale cheeks, and the puckered scar flamed scarlet — "but as a British commissary to look after the needs of Tecumseh's warriors. Yesterday I was captured; and here I am — doomed to an ignominious death. But it doesn't matter; I've found you — I can carry out my plans ere I die."

The husky voice was hardly audible.

For a few moments neither spoke.   Mastering his emotion, Bradford asked abruptly:

"Douglas, would you like to see La Violette?"

"Very much," Ross replied promptly.

"Do you know where she is?"

"At the British encampment across the river."

"Ah!   You *do* know.   Did you see her there— did you meet her?"

"No; but I heard of her presence there, through another."

"Ross Douglas, do you love La Violette?"

Anger blazed in the young man's handsome countenance, and he replied hotly:

"What is it to you, Hiram Bradford, whom I love?"

"Much more than you suspect, my boy," was the cool rejoinder.   "Answer my question, please.   Do you love La Violette?"

Douglas shut his fists and set his teeth.   For a full minute, he sat and glared at his audacious questioner.   But Bradford did not quail.   On the contrary, he smiled and said with provoking coolness:

"I must have a positive answer from you.   Do you, or do you not, love La Violette?"

"Yes, I—love—her," replied Ross through his shut teeth.

"You don't know how happy I am to hear you say that!" the older man exclaimed joyfully.   "She loves you, my lad—you know that, as well as I. Will you marry her?"

"You are carrying this thing too far, Bradford,"
Douglas cried. "Why do you meddle in my affairs
— why have you done so in the past?"

"You want to know?" Bradford replied,
his scarred countenance suddenly losing its expression of mocking carelessness, and becoming grave.

"I want to know," was the decided answer.

"Then prepare yourself for a disagreeable surprise," Bradford said in a husky whisper.

"I'm ready for anything," Ross replied. "Go
on."

"Ross Douglas, *I — am — your — father!*"

With a hoarse cry — half-groan — the young man
arose and staggered against the rough wall. His
face was colorless; his limbs were shaking; and
he threatened to sink to the ground.

Bradford quickly got upon his feet and, grasping
his companion by the shoulders, forced him to
resume his seat, saying in bitter accents:

"Don't let the disagreeable truth unman you.
Sit down. I shall not disgrace you long with my
presence on earth."

Ross sank upon the rude bench, murmuring
brokenly:

"*You, my father!* Hiram Bradford, the *spy* —
the *deserter* — the British *tool*, my *father! Oh,
God!*"

Then both were silent. Douglas bowed his head
upon his hands. Bradford leaned back against the
wall and panted. His face was deathlike. The
red scar upon his cheek was purplish. But he kept

his keen eyes immovably fixed upon the bowed form at his side.

At last Ross slowly lifted his head; and, extending his hand toward his companion, whispered hoarsely:

"Forgive my hasty words. The — the surprise — the shock was almost more than I could bear! For the moment I was dumbfounded — crazed."

The older man eagerly grasped the proffered hand and replied in agitated tones:

"I have nothing to forgive, my son. Would to God you could say as much!"

"You — are — my — father!" Ross muttered mechanically.

"I am John Douglas, your father," was the convincing reply.

Each had partially regained control of his feelings. Now the son said softly:

"Tell me all — *all!*"

There was intense bitterness in the father's voice, as he answered:

"Yes, my boy, now I'll tell you everything. The whole truth can't make you despise me more than you do already — than I despise myself. Are you ready to listen patiently?"

Ross nodded; and his father proceeded:

"My real name is John Douglas; though for years I have borne the *alias* — Hiram Bradford. I cruelly deserted your mother when you were an infant. We loved each other, but we couldn't agree. The fault was all my own. Your mother

was a sweet-tempered angel; I was a hot-headed
brute. In those days I drank heavily. I was un-
reasonable — abusive; but she meekly bore with
me. Her meekness only angered me. It maddened me to meet her reproachful looks. At last I
could stand it no longer. Like the base knave that
I was, I deserted her and you. I must have been
possessed of a devil — I can't explain my actions
otherwise. And the same devil has dogged my
footsteps through all the years."

He paused and drew a sighing respiration, ere he
continued :

"But let me hasten. What use to dwell upon
my past mistakes and misdeeds? I went to Canada and entered the service of the English government, as an Indian agent. I partially reformed —
I made money in abundance. But I was unhappy;
I wanted to return to your mother — to see you.
At last I could endure the torture no longer. I set
out upon my return journey. All the weary way, I
pictured to myself how I should take your mother
and yourself in my arms and beg your forgiveness;
but fate cheated me. I was doomed to such black
and bitter disappointment — to such poignant sorrow as" — his voice faltered — "a remorseful
conscience alone can know. I reached the old
home. Your mother was dead; you were gone.
The neighbors informed me that your uncle had
taken you away — they knew not whither."

Again he paused, as though expecting his listener
to make some remark. But Ross's countenance

remained stern and impassive. The father cleared his throat and went on:

" I returned to Canada and resumed work for the British government. The demon of perversity still followed me. I deserted the flag of my native land, as I had deserted my wife and child. I became the Englishman's spy — his tool — his dog. But I didn't forget you, my son. My business led me among the Indians. From one end of the Northwest Territory to the other, I searched for you; but I could gain no tidings of you. I thought you dead, and gave up the fruitless quest. You know how I met you at last and learned your name. It's unnecessary to say more."

" And La Violette ?" Ross suggested.

"You wish to know her history ? "

The son inclined his head.

" About seventeen years ago," John Douglas resumed, " I was stationed at Quebec. While there I made the acquaintance of a wealthy Englishman, Charles Brownlee, in this manner : He had a beautiful wife, and a little daughter one year old. One day the family was out driving, and their horses became frightened and got beyond their driver's control. I caught the maddened animals, and, at the risk of my own life, brought them to a stop, receiving this wound for my temerity " — pointing to the puckered scar upon his cheek. — " Charles Brownlee became my fast friend. I visited at his house. I learned to love and respect the parents and to worship the angelic child. Also,

I learned much of their family history. Charles Brownlee had inherited his wealth from his grandfather. A cousin, who felt that he had been wronged out of his rightful share of the estate, came to Quebec to demand restitution. My friend refused to listen to the claimant's demands; and the disappointed and angry man left the house, vowing vengeance. A week later, Charles Brownlee and his beautiful wife died very suddenly. The murderous cousin had hired an unscrupulous domestic to poison them. This was never proven, but I know whereof I speak — for I have some knowledge of drugs, and I was in the house at the time."

The speaker stopped and wearily shifted his position.

"Go on — father," Ross whispered, his face alight with interest.

The son hesitated at the paternal term, but resolutely used it. The father's drawn features relaxed into a happy smile, as he took up the thread of his narrative.

"After the death of her parents," he continued, "I stole away Charles Brownlee's little daughter, and hid her among the Shawnees. Her life alone stood between the unprincipled relative and the estate he coveted; and I felt that it was necessary to hide her from him. Tenskwatawa adopted her. The tribe believed — and yet believes — her a gift from the Great Spirit. The Prophet has loved her — has been kind to her. But when I sought to take her from him, to send her to school, he was exceedingly angry and threatened to have me killed. However, my will was the stronger. I had my way, and sent her to a mission school in Quebec. There she remained — securely hidden from the prying eyes of her relative's agents — for five or six years. At the end of the time, I restored her to the care of the Shawnees. There you met her. She learned to love you ; you fell in love with her —— "

" Have you told La Violette her life's history?" Ross interrupted.

" Call her Violet Brownlee — that's her English name," the father answered. " Yes, I have told her all."

" Why — why do you wish me to marry her ? " the son inquired hesitatingly.

" For this reason: You are my son ; and I love you. I love her as a daughter. Ever since I met you at the Prophet's Town, I have felt you should marry her. She loves you — she needs your protection. The murderer of her parents still lives. He is in undisputed ownership of the property. But he knows that she isn't dead ; and is anxiously awaiting for her to put in an appearance and lay claim to the estate — that he may dispose of her forever. I have in my possession documents that establish her identity and her title to her father's wealth —— "

" Isn't it for the sake of this same wealth that you wish me to marry Violet Brownlee, Hiram Brad — father?" Ross asked haltingly, his face flushing.

"Not at all," John Douglas replied in a tone of deep sincerity. "I have property and money — I'm wealthy. All I have is yours. I've never enjoyed my riches — now it's too late. In giving all to you, let me fondly imagine that I'm making some slight atonement for what I've made you and your mother suffer. You'll find my deeds, mortgages, and other private papers — including those pertaining to Violet and her inheritance — in this leathern packet. I've carried it with me for months, hoping to meet you and give it to you."

With these words, the father drew from a pocket within his hunting-shirt a large leather wallet, and extended it toward his son.

Silently Ross took the pocketbook and thrust it into his bosom.

"You'll carry out my wishes," the older man remarked quietly.

"If you don't live to carry them out yourself, father," Ross replied with feeling, "I will see that Miss Brownlee gains possession of her own ——"

"Please say that you'll marry Violet, my son," the father said pleadingly.

For a few minutes the younger man was silent — wrapped in deep thought. Then he answered slowly and solemnly:

"If I find everything as you have stated — and she'll consent to become my wife — I'll marry her."

25

"Thank you — thank you!" John Douglas murmured huskily.

Then after a momentary pause:

"Now, let me tell you what you must do first. Under the protection of a flag of truce, you must go to the British camp and bring Violet here. Tell her I'm a prisoner and wish to see her — but don't let her know that I'm to die an ignominious death ——"

His voice failed him. And covering his face, he wept silently.

"Don't despair — don't give way to grief," Ross said kindly, at the same time arising and laying his hand upon his father's shoulder. "I'll intercede for you — I'll do all in my power to save you."

John Douglas, lifting his tear-wet face, whispered tremulously:

"You — you say you'll try to save me?"

"I will," Ross answered firmly.

"Then — then you don't hate me — despise me?"

The son's voice was thick with emotion, as he replied:

"No, father, I don't hate you; neither do I love you. But I pity you — and will use what little influence I have, in your behalf. I freely forgive you all the wrong you have done me; but I can't forget that you were cruel to my mother — that you have been a traitor to your country. Still you've been kind to me in many ways — you've had my welfare at heart. And I've learned to like you. In time, perhaps —— "

"Say no more!" the father cried, dashing the tears from his eyes. "I'm more than satisfied. You don't know how you have sweetened the bitter draught that I must drink. Oh, Ross — my son! If only I could live my life over —— "

Again he broke down. Ross felt the hot tears upon his own cheeks. Presently the father regained control of his emotions, and, rising, said calmly:

"You spoke of interceding in my behalf. To whom will you go?"

"To General Harrison."

"Don't go. It will avail nothing."

"I'll make the trial," was the decided reply. "This evening I'll see you again. Keep in good heart until I return. Good-by — father."

Silently they shook hands and parted.

CHAPTER XX.

THE rain still fell; the wind still blew in fitful gusts. The canvas walls of the officers' tents swelled in and out, and cracked and popped boisterously. In the shelter of the traverses, soldiers huddled together and smoked in silence. The parade ground was deserted; and the sodden and trampled earth, the dripping flags clinging closely to their staffs, and the cloaked figures of the sentries stubbornly pacing their beats, gave to the interior of the American fortification a gloomy and depressing aspect.

Ross Douglas left the blockhouse, where he had found the father he had never known, and at a rapid pace walked toward General Harrison's quarters. The young man's countenance reflected his contending emotions — the varied and exciting experiences through which he had gone. He was glad he had learned La Violette's history — but sorry he had heard of his father's misspent life; he rejoiced at the thought that the sweet girl loved him, that he loved her, that she was to be his wife — yet he grieved over his father's impending fate. Then, also, he sincerely pitied Amy Hilliard, and worried that La Violette was still among the British and Indians. Indeed, his heart was torn and bleeding!

On reaching the commander's tent, he pushed

past the orderlies at the door and stood in the General's presence. He was preoccupied and did not stop for ceremony, but said abruptly :

"General, I have seen Hiram Bradford, and have returned, as you ordered."

Harrison was closely studying a map that lay spread out upon a rough table before him. Without looking up, he made reply :

"And you found him much changed?"

"In many ways, General."

The commander lifted his head and answered sharply :

"I noted no change in the scoundrel, except in his appearance. His health is broken ; but he is the same cool, unscrupulous, defiant knave."

Ross winced, but sturdily returned :

"We didn't observe alike, General Harrison. I found him in ill-health, weak, repentant —— "

The hero of Tippecanoe whirled about upon his stool. His rugged face darkened ominously. A storm was brewing.

"My young friend," he interrupted in hard, cold tones, "you talk as if you came to plead his case."

"I came to intercede in his behalf," Ross replied calmly.

General Harrison sprang to his feet, his face black with rage.

"By heavens !" he cried. "You are —— "

Then the grizzled warrior stopped suddenly. He bit his thin lips — and was silent. At last he said quietly, but firmly :

"What I would say, young man, is this: It's useless to ask me to show clemency to Hiram Bradford—the spy, the deserter. I can't blame you —I *don't* blame you—for feeling sorry for him. He has befriended you—in a way, perhaps. But you're an *American*—you love your country. And you mustn't forget that this man is your *country's* bitter and avowed enemy. That's not all. During the Tippecanoe campaign, he entered my service as a scout—he enlisted regularly. At that time, he was in the employ of the English—was their spy. He plotted against my life—he deserted. I needn't tell you all this; you know it only too well. *You* were the first to arouse my suspicions. *You* put me on my guard—and saved my life. After your escape from the savages—at Franklinton, you remember—you told me that Hiram Bradford had confessed all to you. As a spy, I should let him go; for his scheme failed—and his attempt upon my life was in another war. But a deserter once is a deserter forever; "—fiercely—"and the penalty is *death!* To-morrow a preliminary court-martial will be held; and you will appear as a witness against Hiram Bradford."

Douglas dropped upon a stool, moaning:

"I can't! Oh, God!—I *can't!*"

His keen, mental agony was shown in his face. General Harrison was surprised. Advancing, he laid a hand upon the young man's shoulder and said kindly:

"You mustn't take the matter so to heart, my

boy. Hiram Bradford deserves to die. He shall have full justice; but no mercy will be shown him, if proven guilty. I cannot fathom why you — a pure-minded patriot — are so anxious to have a traitorous deserter escape merited punishment."

"Let me tell you, General Harrison," Ross cried, springing to his feet. "Then do as you will. Hiram Bradford, the English spy — the American deserter, is John Douglas — my *father!*"

Had a British shell exploded within the tent, General Harrison could not have been more dumbfounded. He tried to speak, but failed. After staring blankly at his companion for some time, he commenced to pace rapidly up and down the room, clasping and unclasping his brown hands, in an agitated manner. At last he stopped in front of Ross, and said calmly:

"Sit down and tell me all about it."

A number of officers entered the tent, before the tale was concluded. The commander paused long enough to say: — "Be seated, gentlemen; I shall be through presently." — And again he gave Douglas his attention. At last the two arose. Taking Ross's hand, the commander murmured:

"Circumstances change the aspect of many plain cases. Your father shall not be tried for his crime; he shall go free. But the matter must forever remain a secret between ourselves — even your trusty comrades mustn't know. This afternoon an officer and escort will bear a flag of truce to the British camp, to complete arrangements for an exchange of prisoners. You will take your father and accompany them. Bring the young woman back with you ; but leave your father there, with the injunction that he is to make his way to Canada and never set foot upon American soil again. Wait a moment— I'll give you an order for his release."

A quarter of an hour after, father and son issued from the blockhouse together—and John Douglas was a free man. In the full light of the murky day, he looked bent, worn, and feeble ; and he kept close to his stalwart son's side, as though looking to him for guidance and protection.

Shortly after noon, the two joined the officer and escort, who were setting out for the British encampment. On their way toward the eastern gate of the fortification, they were joined by Farley, Bright Wing, and the hound.

"Where've you been all the forenoon, Ross?" the old woodman demanded in an injured tone. "Me an' the Injin an' dog's been huntin' you all over the place. Duke nosed 'round, an' said you was down at that blockhouse "—pointing with the barrel of his gun.— "But me an' the Injin knowed that couldn't be, 'cause ther's pris'ners in there— an' you wouldn't have no business with them. Then the houn' took up a 'maginary trail, and tracked you to Ol' Tippecanoe's tent. We knowed that was a lie, too ; 'cause we peeked in, an' you wasn't there. So we've kind o' lost faith in the purp. The smell o' blood, yisterday, must 'ave spiled his scent. But where've you been ?"

Scarcely slacking his pace, Douglas replied briefly:
" I was at the blockhouse and at General Harrison's quarters. Duke told you the truth."

" You was ! " Joe ejaculated.   " Well, dang my
skin if the dog didn't know more'n a couple o' human critters — he did, by Tabithy ! Purp, I beg
y'r pardon. But where 're you goin' now, Ross ? "

" To the English camp."

" I've heerd it said." Farley grumbled, " that
the burnt child dreaded the fire ; but you seem to
be an 'xception to the rule. Ross Douglas, what in
the name o' goodness 're you goin' over there fer ?
Oh, I'm an ol' fool ! I might 'ave knowed. You're
goin' over to git that little red-headed gal, of course
—— "

He suddenly stopped speaking. His watery eyes
bulged ; his jaw dropped. He had caught a square
look at Ross's companion.

" W'y, dang—it—all—to—dingnation ! "he mumbled. " If that ain't the scar-faced scout that was
with Gener'l Harrison, at Tippecanoe, it's his ghost.
An' he looks more like a ghost 'n a mortal man —
he does, by cracky ! "

" Ugh ! Scar Face — much sick, sight lean,"
Bright Wing grunted.

Ross made no reply ; John Douglas did not glance
around, even. By this time, the squad of soldiers
had reached the gate and were passing through.
Father and son hastened to overtake them. Farley
and his companion kept close upon the heels of those
in advance : and with them left the fortification.

Ross thought his comrades had stopped within the walls — and felt relieved.   He did not notice their presence, until he stood at the water's edge.

" What are you doing here, Joe ? " he demanded sharply.

" We're goin' with you," Farley returned coolly.

" You cannot," Ross said firmly. " Take the dog and return to the fort."

But Joe and the Wyandot stubbornly shook their heads ; and Duke, dropping upon his haunches, looked appealingly into his master's face.

"Take Duke and go back to the fortification," Ross repeated, with difficulty repressing a smile at the childlike pertinacity of his friends.

" We ain't a-goin' back," Farley answered sullenly.

" Ugh ! No go back — go with Fleet Foot," the Indian muttered.

" Why ? " the young man asked impatiently.

" You may need us," Farley explained. " We don't over an' above like the company you're keepin'." — With a jerk of his thumb toward John Douglas.

Ross dropped his eyes to the ground. His face flushed hotly. He was in a quandary ; he did not know what to do or say.

The soldiers had launched a boat, and were scrambling into it.

" Come on — don't delay us," the officer called.

" Here are two of my comrades who desire to accompany me," Ross hastened to explain.

The officer cut him short with :

"Bring them along — but be quick about it. The boat will accommodate us all."

A few minutes later, the entire party had landed on the opposite shore and were making their way toward the British encampment. There the American officer engaged in a consultation with General Proctor and his staff, while Ross Douglas and his companions went to the quarters of Tensk-watawa and La Violette, at Fort Miami.

John Douglas led the way into the stockade of the old fort. The place was filled with Indians and white prisoners. Some of the latter were ill-fated settlers ; others were the luckless Kentuckians of General Clay's command. Several of the militia-men knew Ross Douglas and, calling to him, asked what were the prospects of a speedy exchange. He answered their questions briefly as he hurried along. Occasionally a guttural voice exclaimed — " Fleet Foot ! "; and the young man became aware that many of the savages recognized him and were scowling at him. But they did not offer to impede the progress of the small party. Scar Face, whom they hated and feared, was leading it.

On reaching the farther side of the inclosure, John Douglas stopped and whispered to his son :

"Here's the cabin Violet occupies. You'll enter with me ; your friends will remain outside — on guard. The Indians are dissatisfied — restless — and ready for any desperate venture. I don't think they'll dare to interfere with us in any way

— but they may.   Caution your comrades to be discreet — to give no heed to threatening words and gestures, unless the savages offer to attack them."

Ross, turning to Farley, said in a low tone :

"You and Bright Wing will keep Duke with you and guard the door.   Do nothing rash — you understand ?"

Joe nodded gravely ; and Ross continued :

"We'll transact our business and get out of here, as soon as possible ; the place is unsafe.   Be careful of your words and actions, and restrain the hound."

Again Joe nodded.   For a wonder, he did not utter a word in reply.

Just as father and son were about to enter the low door of the hut, the latter caught sight of a burly, thick-set Indian swaggering up to the spot. His fat and flabby features were grotesquely and hideously painted.   He wore a complete suit of coarse cloth, and carried an English rifle.   Nearing the group at the door, he stuck his tongue into his cheek and leered impudently.

Ross started.   There was something about the obese brave that seemed familiar ; yet the young man could not recall that he had ever seen the bloated wretch.

"Who is the greasy knave ?" Ross murmured to himself.

Farley caught the words and muttered in reply :

"I don't know — but I've seen him somewheres. He's as sassy as a pet fox — he is, by Jerushy !"

"Ugh!" Bright Wing ejaculated explosively — and was silent as a graven image.

"Come," John Douglas said, plucking his son by the arm. "Things are not to my liking. You must take Violet and be off."

Together the two passed into the cabin. The place was in semi-darkness. Ross heard a startled exclamation in the far corner of the room. Then he became aware that someone had arisen and was moving toward him. His eyes grew accustomed to the gloom; and he dimly perceived a sylphlike figure advancing toward the center of the floor. There it stopped. The murky light streaming in at the hole in the roof fell upon it.

Ross Douglas distinctly saw a halo of red-gold hair, the outlines of a fair, sweet face — and murmured tenderly:

"La Violette!"

"Fleet Foot!" was the joyful exclamation.

She stood leaning far forward, her hands clasped in front of her; but she did not offer to move nearer to him. Ross swept a hurried glance about the interior. He was alone with her; his father had left the cabin. The young man heard her quick respirations — saw her attitude of indecision — and opening his arms, he called softly:

"I love you, darling! Come to me!"

With a glad cry, she flew to him and nestled in his arms. He strained her to his breast — too happy to speak. At last he breathed into her ear the needless question:

" Do you love me, La Violette? "

Lifting her golden head and reproachfully fastening her violet eyes upon his face, she answered :

" Can you ask me such a question, Ross Douglas? You *know* I love you — have loved you ever since you saved my life. But do you really love *me ?* "

In answer he kissed her ripe lips and murmured :

" I worship you, dear — love you better than I love anyone else on earth. I've loved you ever since I first met you. But I was betrothed to another; and I wouldn't admit to myself, even, that I loved you. But to-day I am free. I have come to take you from this place — from this life. Will you go with me, La Violette? "

" To the ends of the earth, " she whispered.

Holding her from him at arm's length, he asked playfully :

" Violet Brownlee, will you be my wife? "

" Ah ! you know all," she returned smilingly.

" I know all," he returned sober'y. " My father has told me."

" Your father? " she remarked wonderingly.

" Yes, my father — Scar Face, Hiram Bradford, John Douglas."

Again she nestled in his arms, and for a moment was silent. Presently she murmured musingly :

" I used often to wonder why Hiram Bradford took so great an interest in me. A few months ago he told me my history. Then I fell to wondering why he had kept you a prisoner against your will, yet was anxious for your welfare. Nor could I un-

derstand why he was so worried over your escape
and the fact that he could not find you. Now all
is plain."

He stroked her red-gold hair, but made no reply.
He would have been content to hold her thus for
hours. Suddenly she lifted her head from his
shoulder, and whispered :

" Ross."

" Well, darling?"

" Let me see your hand. No, the other. Ah !
you still wear Tenskwatawa's ring. You carried
off the Sign of the Prophet ; now you come to carry
off his daughter."

He bent his head and breathed in reply :

"I valued the Sign of the Prophet ; it assured
my safety. I value his daughter much more ; she
assures my happiness."

Standing upon tiptoe and pulling him down, she
fondly kissed him and answered :

" This is a fit reward for your pretty speech. But
Tenskwatawa will be here presently ; your father
has gone for him. Do not let him see the ring. He
has lost much of his power ; and it is better so. He
and Tecumseh have deceived their people and led
them astray. I see it all now. The wisest of them
are but ignorant savages. And the English — my
own people — have made tools of them ——"

She stopped speaking and hastily withdrew from
her lover's embrace. He turned to discover the
cause of her action, and observed Tenskwatawa entering the door.

Not deigning to notice the young man, the Prophet walked up to La Violette and, laying his hands upon her shoulders, murmured gutturally :

"My daughter, Scar Face has told me that you mean to leave the tribe—your father, forever. Is it so?"

"Tenskwatawa, my father, it is true."

"Has Fleet Foot stolen your heart, my daughter?"

"He has, my father," she replied in a voice hardly audible.

"And La Violette will accompany him to his lodge and dwell there?"

The girl looked her interrogator in the face and nodded. Tenskwatawa remained silent. The stillness of the room was oppressive. At last the Prophet removed his hands from her shoulders and, bowing his head, muttered brokenly :

"It is well. Where her heart is, La Violette should be. She is a paleface maiden ; she loves a paleface brave. She shall be the light of his lodge —as she has been the light of Tenskwatawa's life."

Then, extending his hand to her :

"My daughter, farewell. The Great Spirit gave you to me—he takes you from me. Great is my sorrow; but I will bear it as becomes a Shawnee. My sign is lost; my power has departed. My children spurn my words of advice ; the English laugh at my undoing. My sorrow is great. I can bear it—I am a Shawnee. My daughter, farewell —farewell, *forever !*"

Impulsively she threw her arms around his neck and sobbed upon his breast.

"Tenskwatawa, my father, you have been kind to me. I have tried to be a daughter to you. Now I am about to leave you forever — to return to my own people. The Great Spirit wills it so. My father, I would exact one promise from you at parting."

Gently he disengaged himself from her embrace, and answered :

" What my daughter desires, I will do."

" Then," she cried, " use all your influence — all your power — to dissuade your children from fighting longer under the English banner. The Seventeen Fires will conquer in the end. The Great Spirit wills it. The redmen will lose their lives and their lands to no purpose. Promise me you will do what I ask."

" It is too late," he replied dejectedly. " My children are mad with the taste of blood. No longer will they listen to my voice. I helped to lead them into this; now I cannot drag them out. They are dogs for the English ; they bay along the trail — they obey the lash. Tecumseh, my brother, has their ears ; they will not hear my words. I have sinned ; and thus the Great Spirit punishes me. My daughter, I shall see you no more. Farewell ! "

Drawing his blanket over his head, to hide his emotion, the Prophet quitted the cabin. His thin lips were set ; and his horrid, painted face was

26

drawn and ashen. A moment afterward, John Douglas entered and remarked briskly :

"You must be off. Make haste! I'll accompany you to the river."

La Violette made a compact bundle of her few effects, and announced herself as ready. John Douglas led the way from the cabin. Farley and Bright Wing still stood without ; and Duke was smelling around the door. As La Violette stepped into the open air, the dog fawned upon her, evincing his pleasure at again meeting her. Tears sprang to her eyes ; and, patting the animal's head, she murmured :

"Ah! You remember me, good fellow."

"Duke forgets neither his friends nor his enemies," Ross said smilingly.

Farley stepped forward and, doffing his cap and extending a grimy hand, remarked :

"So you're La Violette, young woman. I've heerd somethin' of you in the last day 'r so."—He grinned maliciously at Ross.—"This youngster here couldn't do nothin' but talk 'bout you—he couldn't, by ginger! I'm glad to meet you, I am. Thought I'd intr'duce myself—seein' Ross Douglas wasn't goin' to do the job fer me. He's 'fraid o' my beauty, little gal—'fraid you might shine up to *me*. An' this is Bright Wing, a Wyandot. He's a purty good feller, if he *has* got a red skin. Me an' the Injin's Ross's ol' comrades. Lordy! Hain't we been in many a scrimmage? Gol-fer-socks! I guess so."

La Violette laughed musically at Joe's absurdities; and, grasping the extended hands of each, said: "I trust we shall become better acquainted in the future—and be fast friends."

"Ugh!" was the monosyllabic response of the Wyandot, as he stepped aside and, leaning upon his gun, fixed his black eyes upon a distant part of the stockade.

Farley had not yet had his say, however; and there was sincere admiration in his voice and manner, as he resumed:

"You're a dang sight purtier 'n I 'xpected you to be, little gal—you are, by Katherine! As near's I could git it from Ross Douglas's ravin's, you was a kind of red-headed Injin squaw—somethin' like the Winnebago jade that wanted to marry *me*. You see, miss, the women's alluz been after *me*——"

"Joe—Joe!" Ross cried, smiling in spite of himself.

"It's a fact, as sure's my name is Joseph Peregoy——" the woodman began.

But John Douglas impatiently interrupted him with:

"This is no time to recount your love affairs, my friend. After you have reached the other side of the river, you may boast to your heart's content. Let's be off."

With the words, he started toward the gate of the dilapidated palisade, the others of the party closely following him. Farley grumbled as he went along:

"Ol' Pucker Face is as imperdent as a squawkin' catbird—but he's *right*. Ding-it-all-to-dangnation! When *will* I learn not to let my limber tongue git the best o' me?"

Then aloud to Ross:

"That fat an' greasy redskin, that come sidelin' up to us jest as you was goin' into the hut, has been slippin' 'round 'mong the other Injins an' doin' a heap o' talkin'. I'll bet a new ramrod he's up to some devilment. I wish I could place him — I've seen him somewheres."

Ross merely nodded; and, taking La Violette's arm, hurried her onward. Just outside the walls, John Douglas turned and whispered in his son's ear:

"We'll proceed to the landing-place at once. If the officer who came over with us isn't there with his soldiers, you must hail your friends on the other side and have a boat brought to you immediately. The Indians know and hate you and your comrades. There's mischief brewing. Let's hasten."

The little party moved rapidly. John Douglas's whispered words and anxious demeanor had warned his companions, of the gravity of the situation; and they realized that no time was to be lost, if they would escape. At last they came in sight of the place and, to their great relief, beheld the American officer and his escorts just ready to embark. An English officer and two subalterns were among the group upon the shore.

Ross frantically waved his hand and hallooed at the top of his voice. The American soldiers gave him a ringing cheer in reply, thus signifying they would await his arrival.

At that moment, a score or more of savages, quickly emerging from the shelter of the trees, confronted Ross and his companions.

Bright Wing uttered a sharp grunt and cocked his rifle. Farley did the same, muttering as he did so:

"Jest as I 'xpected! Ther's that dang fat brave leadin' 'em."

Ross placed himself in front of La Violette, and looked to the priming of his weapon. John Douglas carried his own gun, which had been restored to him on leaving the blockhouse at Fort Meigs. Now he boldly stepped forward—his hollow eyes blazing—and shouted authoritatively, in the Shawnee tongue:

"Out of the way, you hellhounds! Do you not know me?"

From force of habit, the Indians retreated a few steps. But the thick-set warrior, who acted as leader of the band, scowled fiercely as he replied in blunt backwoods English:

"You needn't fire any Injin lingo at me, Mr. Scar Face—as the redskins call you. I don't understand it. But I know you—I've seen you 'round the camp. An' I know what y'r little game is now—an' I'm goin' to block it."

"George Hilliard!" Ross exclaimed.

"The low-lived critter!" Farley hissed, nervously fingering the trigger of his rifle.

The fat warrior overheard Ross's exclamation, and returned savagely :

"Yes, I'm George Hilliard; an' I've come to have a final settlement with you, Ross Douglas ——"

"Out of the way, you infernal renegade!" John Douglas cried menacingly.

"Not till I'm through with my business, Mr. Scar Face," Hilliard answered coolly. "An' you'd better not be callin' hard names, 'r you'll git a dose o' the same medicine we mean to give that young dandy at y'r side. I'm commandin' this squad o' redskins; an' they don't like *you* much better'n they do *him*. You jest keep quiet till I git through with my business."

Then turning his attention from father to son :

"Ross Douglas, you an' me's goin' to have a final settlement right here. You toted off my wife last night — me an' my gang trailed you 'cross the river. An' now you've come to carry off the Prophet's gal. You ain't content with one woman — you want two. But then I happen to want this young miss myself — an' I'm goin' to have her. Fair 'xchange is no robbery. You can have my wife; I'll take your plump little sweetheart. Hand her over peaceably, an' you an' y'r crowd can go on to the fort; refuse, an' my warriors 'll kill an' scalp the last one o' you. Do you understand?"

"I understand you — you devil incarnate!"

Ross answered in a voice hoarse with rage. " Do
your worst! You shall not lay your vile hands
upon this pure being, as long as the breath of life is
spared me!"

" Which won't be very long!" Hilliard muttered
with an oath.

Farley and Bright Wing set their teeth and
calmly awaited the attack. Ross turned to his
father and asked :

" What can we do?"

" Fight to the death !" was the cool and determined reply.

Slipping an arm around La Violette's waist, Ross
whispered :

" Good-by, darling! Lie down behind that
mound, out of the way of flying bullets. As soon
as the first discharge of firearms is over, run toward the boat at the top of your speed. If I
escape death, I'll rejoin you there."

She was very pale ; and her limbs were trembling. But she replied firmly :

" I will not leave your side, Ross. If you must
die, I die with you!"

The soldiers on the shore had been witnesses of
the whole proceeding. At the distance, they could
not tell what was going on ; but knowing that
something was amiss, and fearing the worst, a
number of them had left the boat and started
toward the scene of disturbance. Now they came
running at full speed along the bank. The Wyandot's quick eyes caught sight of them and he
grunted :

"Palefaces come — heap many. Ugh!"

"That's a fact, Injin!" Farley muttered in reply.
"If we can only hold the red devils off till —— "

Ross Douglas was anxiously watching the actions
of the savages. Suddenly he saw them quit talking and make a move to encircle their victims. An
inspiration came to him. Taking a step forward,
he raised his right hand and cried in ringing tones:

"Children of Tenskwatawa!"

The attention of the Indians was arrested. They
stopped and stared hard at the speaker.

"Behold the Sign of the Prophet!" Ross
shouted.

At the same time, he slowly waved his hand to
and fro, and, imitating the sinuous movements of
the red hypnotist, advanced upon the semicircle of
warriors. The effect was marvelous.

"The Sign of the Prophet! The Sign of the
Prophet!" they wailed in terrified accents, shrink-
ing away from him — their eyes immovably fixed
upon the talisman.

For a moment George Hilliard was dumbfounded.
He could not understand what was happening.
Realizing that Ross, in some way, was sending terror to the hearts of the red fiends, the thick-set
villain's face grew purple with rage. He stormed
and raved. But all to no purpose; the savages
were spellbound — they could not hear his voice.

Slowly advancing — and continuing his serpentine movements — Ross continued:

"Children of the Prophet, I wear his sign — I
have his power! I am doing the will of the Great

Spirit. Away — away ! Go — ere I strike you blind——"

"Curse you, Ross Douglas! *I'll* strike you blind ! " Hilliard howled frantically.

Quick as a flash, he threw his gun to his shoulder and fired. But quick as his movements were, John Douglas's were quicker. Just before the roar of the firearm rang out upon the air, the father sprang in front of his son. The next moment he sank to earth, mortally wounded. With a lionlike roar of rage, Duke leaped upon the murderer and dragged him to the ground. Three rifles cracked in rapid succession ; and three painted braves met death.

The spell was broken. The savages gazed about in stupefaction. Then, dimly realizing what had happened, they broke and fled toward the cover of the woods, just as the soldiers, cheering lustily, dashed up.

La Violette dropped upon the ground and pillowed John Douglas's head upon her lap. Ross bent over the dying man, and in a voice full of anguish asked :

" Father, can you see me — can you speak to me ? "

The fast-glazing eyes looked steadily into those of the questioner, and the white lips whispered faintly :

"I see both of you, my — my children ; but very — very dimly. Do not — move out of my sight. I'm dying! It is best so. I have given my life for you, my son ; and I — I die happy. I am going — give me your hands! Good-by — I — I —— ''

With a deep, tremulous sigh, he closed his eyes. Twice the deep chest heaved spasmodically. And he was dead.

"My father — oh, my father!" Ross moaned, still clinging to the dead man's hand.

Joe Farley overheard the words and muttered to himself :

"Ross Douglas's father! Scar Face — Hiram Bradford — John Douglas — all one an' the same. Dang-it-all-to-dingnation! Hang-it-up-an'-take-it-down-an'-cook-it! Won't wonders an' mysteries *never* come to an end?"

Then, in a low tone, he said to the Wyandot :

"Injin, we'd better call Duke away from that painted lump o' taller out there. I s'pect the dog's worried the cuss a good 'eal by this time."

"Ugh!" Bright Wing snorted contemptuously. "Duke no worry fat paleface-redman now ; fat paleface-redman heap much dead. Me stick knife in him."

"Huh!" Farley ejaculated. Then to the dog :

"Here, Duke, come away from that carcass. You'll git p'izened nosin' 'round such a varmint — you will, by Molly! Come away, I say!"

The hound obeyed.

Ross, had arisen, and stood silently gazing into the face upturned to the clouded heavens. La Violette was weeping bitterly. The English officer advanced to Ross's side and said with much feeling :

"I can't tell you, young man, how sorry I am that this thing has happened. But the savages are unruly ; they can't be controlled ——"

Then he abruptly stopped speaking and peered into the upturned countenance. Starting back, he exclaimed excitedly :

"Why, this is Hiram Bradford — one of our own men !"

Ross nodded stiffly.

"Curse the savage brutes !" the officer muttered as he turned and strode away. "Whom will they turn upon next?"

Taking with them the body of John Douglas — but leaving George Hilliard and his red associates where they fell — the company made their way to the boat, and embarked for Fort Meigs.

CHAPTER XXI.

L A VIOLETTE, during her short stay at Fort Meigs, lived in the tent of the refugees. By many gracious acts, she endeared herself to her simple-minded companions. She spent much of her time in caring for Amy's sick and fretful child ; and the heart-broken young mother learned to love and respect the gentle, sweet-faced nurse. The two women exchanged confidences ; and each shed tears over the trials that had fallen to the lot of the other.

One evening, Ross and his sweetheart were walking up and down in front of the refugees' tent. The air was balmy ; the sky was studded with stars. From the camp-fires, twinkling like fireflies in the sweet dusk, came the sounds of merriment ; from the interior of the tent, came the cry of the peevish baby.

"I pity her so!" La Violette said softly. "She has very honestly told me all, Ross. She never loved you as I do ; but she loved you in her way— I am sure. And she lost you. Yet I am selfish enough to be glad, while I pity her ; for had she not done what she did, you would not be mine to-night."

"I don't know," he replied, carefully weighing each word. "Perhaps I wouldn't have married her. I'm beginning to doubt that we ever really loved each other. At any rate, I love *you* now, darling — you alone! Now let us talk of our future."

They sauntered from the spot; while the stars smiled down upon them, as they have smiled down upon lovers since the race began.

John Douglas found a grave just without the wall of the fortification. In an obscure corner by himself, he was laid to rest. An erring son, he had spent the best years of his life in the service of an alien power; but he came home to sleep his last long sleep.

In after-years, Ross Douglas returned to Fort Meigs, with the intention of erecting a monument to his father's memory; but the surroundings had changed so much he could not locate the grave.

When General Harrison was informed of the manner of John Douglas's death, he immediately sent for Ross. Taking the son by the hand, the old soldier said with emotion :

"I'm sincerely glad I freed your father — sincerely sorry he's dead. Yet it is best. His death atones for his life. He died for you. It was a noble self-sacrifice. Your father had in him the elements of a great and noble nature; but his whole life was a failure, because his talents and energies were misdirected. Whatever comes, my young friend, be true to yourself, your country, and your God!"

For several days after the return of Ross and his friends to Fort Meigs, the weather continued foul.

Then it grew warm and bright with sunshine. With the change in the weather, came a change in the aspect of affairs. Hostilities were not renewed ; an exchange of prisoners was effected. The savages, discouraged by Proctor's want of success in reducing the American garrison, began to desert his standard in large numbers. Realizing the uselessness of prolonging the siege, the British commander prepared to abandon the enterprise ; and on the ninth of the month he took his departure.

The investment of the post had lasted thirteen days. During that time the enemy had fired eighteen hundred shells and cannon balls into the fort, and had kept up an annoying discharge of small arms ; yet the American loss in killed and wounded was only two hundred and seventy.

Offensive operations were for a time suspended. The American troops remained at Fort Meigs and Sandusky. A few days after the British had withdrawn, General Harrison left General Clay in command of the post, and set out for Franklinton, to forward re-enforcements. With the commander and his escort, went Ross Douglas and his friends. Without mishap or adventure, the whole company reached their destination in the latter part of May.

At Franklinton, Amy Hilliard bade farewell to Ross and La Violette and, joining a party of returning settlers, went to her father's people in western Pennsylvania.

Upon their arrival at Franklinton, Ross Douglas and Violet Brownlee were married. In the early

part of July the young husband returned to Fort
Meigs. He served throughout the war, as scout
and guide, with credit to himself and advantage to
his country's cause.

Bright Wing went with his white friend, and
was his companion in many a perilous enterprise.
Farley and Duke remained at Franklinton, with La
Violette.

"I am loth to have you go, Ross," she said when
he informed her of his purpose. "You may never
come back to me. Still, do whatever you feel is
your duty — I would not hold you back. *Your*
country is *my* country now. God bless and keep
you!"

Fondly kissing her, he bade her farewell. At the
door of the cabin that was his temporary abode, he
met Farley. The eccentric Joe held out his hands,
saying:

"Good-by, Ross Douglas. I hope this trip'll be
as lucky to you as y'r last one — I do, by ginger!
I'll take good keer o' y'r purp an' the little woman.
An' if you git killed, I'll marry La Violette myself
— I will, by King Solerman's six hundred wives!
I think she's kind o' struck with my good looks an'
beauty a'ready — I do, by—— "

"Good-by, Joe — good-by!" Ross interrupted,
smiling. "Let no harm befall her, old friend.
Good-by!"

And he was gone, leaving Farley staring after
him.

At the close of the war, the young couple went to Quebec, to obtain possession of their property. La Violette's relative was dead; and she had no difficulty in proving her title to the estate. Ross, with some trouble, obtained the bulk of his father's fortune. Turning their real estate into money, they returned to the land they loved — to the shelter of the Stars and Stripes. To the day of his death, Ross Douglas wore the ring that had finally brought him such good fortune — the gift of La Violette — *the Sign of the Prophet.*